Dark Thane

Other books by Miller Lau

Talisker
Book One of The Last Clansman

Dark Thane

Book Two of The Last Clansman

MILLER LAU

EARTHLIGHT

SIMON & SCHUSTER

London • New York • Sydney • Tokyo • Singapore • Toronto • Dublin

A VIACOM COMPANY

First published in Great Britain by Earthlight, 2002
An imprint of Simon & Schuster UK Ltd
A Viacom Company

1 3 5 7 9 10 8 6 4 2

Simon & Schuster UK Ltd
Africa House
64–78 Kingsway
London WC2B 6AH

Simon & Schuster Australia
Sydney

A CIP catalogue record for this book is available from the British Library

ISBN 0 7434 0401 7

Typeset by Palimpsest Book Production Limited,
Polmont, Stirlingshire
Printed and bound in Great Britain by
Omnia Books Limited, Glasgow

DARK THANE is my first commissioned work – a whole different ball game and a fast and furious learning curve! My heartfelt thanks to the team at Earthlight: John Jarrold (editor and Keeper of the Faith) Darren Nash and his better half Michelle, Nigel Stoneman, Jane Ellis and all those other hardworking folks who I *don't* actually get to harass by any electonic means possible! Mark Salwowski, thanks so much for the beautiful realisation of my characters. Love and thanks to Stella Wilkins and my 'bezzie mate' Jessica Rydill (even if she does bat for the other team) for the occasional gentle prod when I was flagging. The As & Js – still luv ya – even if I haven't been around much lately! Finally, thanks a million to David Gemmell – some things in publishing may be par for the course David, but your kindness and wise counsel are a rarity and truly valued.

For the generations: My grandmother, 'Nana Peggy' – Margaret Wrightson – whose story I would dearly love to write; my mother, Elizabeth Ibister Spence (the true warrior Thane!) and, my daughter, Tiffany Lau, in this her eighteenth year – with love always . . .

PROLOGUE

All around is darkness. Above, the night sky blazes with the glorious silver heat of the stars but their light does little to illuminate the black rocks of the mountainside and cannot penetrate to the reaches of the valley floor far below. On the plateau of the mountain an old man and a young girl are sitting near the flames of a meagre fire. An unlikely couple at first sight . . . the wind sweeps around them, causing the old man's words to drift out into the darkness, across the open spaces of the valley, to be lost, to dissipate into the nothingness of the stars . . .

'It is true, I am very, very old, yes. But I am not immortal, my bones ache and my eyes tire, just as any ancient creature's. If I am special at all, it is because the gods thought me useful at one time but then neglected to destroy their plaything when they tired of it. I am a Seanachaidh *first, as you will be one day . . . Are you cold? Here, take an extra blanket. You must learn how to still the voices of your flesh, little one, but then, that will come with time . . . If you have much to learn it is only because I have much to teach you, so there is little fault to be found there. I might tell you to enjoy the coldness on some other night, but tonight, well . . . it is pretty chilly, isn't it . . .?*

'Where was I? Oh yes . . . I have brought you here

so I may teach you the simple truths of scrying. It is a lowly form, a magical equivalent of say . . . my mule over there. But like a mule, it does good service and unlike other, more complex, pretentious magics, scrying has no repercussions. It is passive only. You might well wonder as you sit there shivering, can't the stupid old man do this in his own front room where there is a proper fire? Well, yes, yes I could. But, as you will see Nimah, there is something inspirational about the calm reflection of the stars . . . Shall we begin?'

The water is like a silver mirror, just as Morias has said. He is chanting quietly to himself, his eyes half closed, gazing into the taut reflection. Nimah sits quietly, hardly daring to breathe. Soon, she will have to move, she can feel pins and needles in her foot – she hopes he won't be angry with her. It is her first lesson and she really does want to become a Seanachaidh *. . .*

He stops his chanting and bends forward again trying to look more closely into the pool without casting his shadow across it. 'C'mon boy. Where are you?' he mutters. As if in response to his impatience, the reflection of the water changes. The silver track of a shooting star glows briefly across the heavens and the pool holds onto its brilliance. Then, an image forms in the pool, sharp and clean lined in its detail; Nimah can scarcely hold back a gasp of excitement. It is a boy or a young man, riding a huge stallion which is far too large for someone of his stature. The boy is riding fast, clinging on for dear life. Every few seconds he tries to look behind him but cannot manage to turn as he rattles and bumps about on his steed. It is just as well he cannot see his pursuers.

Behind the boy is a pack of huge hounds. They are . . . unnatural; as tall as the fetlocks of the stallion, their steel-grey fur is rugged and mane-like about their deep chests, their long legs covering a large distance in a single stride. They snap and snarl at the terrified horse and rider, great foaming streams of saliva trailing from their maws. Occasionally a flash of sliver starlight reflecting from the beasts' heads and necks confirms what Morias suspects; the pack of hounds can belong only to one patron. Only one would breed such monsters and gird them so, with steel greaves and spikes. The hounds grow ever closer and the stallion more panicked, its eyes large and bulging with fright.

'Ride, boy, ride!' the old man urges. Nimah has clapped her hand over her mouth, afraid to cry out least she disrupt Morias's concentration.

Then, the image shifts as though something has deflected Morias's view. He frowns and crouches down beside the pool, muttering the arcane words necessary to keep his scrying open. He stops speaking abruptly and groans aloud.

The vision has shifted to allow him to see ahead of the rider's reckless flight. Ahead, obscured from vision by the darkness, is a deep chasm. There is nothing to mark the rim, no trees, no break in the features of the moorland. Rider, stallion and hounds are destined to fall to the rocks below. It is inevitable.

Nimah cries out in despair and without thought, she plunges her hand into the cold water disrupting the spell. Tears spill from her blue eyes as she watches fragmented starlight ripple out across the bowl. 'I – I'm sorry, Seanachaidh. *I couldn't bear to see. Is this what I must learn? To watch men's deaths and not to be able to help anyone . . .' Her voice trails off as she looks at her teacher's face – it is difficult to know if the old man is angry with her, his shaggy white brows are pulled together, but his expression is one of patience.*

'Nimah. Do you know who that was?'

'No, Sir.'

'It was Tristan Talisker – Thane of Soulis Mor.'

'But I thought they had a lady Thane there?' She sniffs and wipes her nose on the sleeve of her robe, embarrassed by her outburst.

'Twins. Regan and Tristan.'

'Oh yes.' She thinks he will say more but his gaze becomes distracted, unfocused again. After a long pause she prompts him. 'Is he going to die?'

'Perhaps. But what you have seen in the water is not happening now, Nimah – the water can show the past and the future. I think the vision was of tomorrow.'

'We can help him then,' she beams, her girlish delight is infectious and Morias smiles in return, caught up in her relief.

'Possibly,' he nods.

'But we've got to help him. He's in trouble.'

'Is that what you imagine Seanachaidhs *do, Nimah? We cannot rush around curing the ills of the world. Why, we would never be finished. Where would it end? Perhaps we would become like gods eh?'*

'Please, Morias. He looks so young . . .'

'Ah well, that is why when receiving such a vision from the scrying one should always look to the past . . .'

'I don't understand.'

'Tristan is not a boy. He is a young man twice your age – twenty-six I believe – but he has been crippled from birth . . .' Morias shrugs, 'he looks younger than he is.'

'Still too young to die though,' she persists.

'It's all right, Nimah. You are right. I was going to help Tristan anyway – his father, Duncan Talisker, is a special friend of mine . . . but perhaps we should learn this lesson together and find the circumstances which brought our friend Tristan to this awful situation . . .'

'Can we do that?'

'Oh yes child. But first, bank up the fire . . .'

'. . . Now, remember Nimah, what you will see in the water this time is in the past . . . some flashes may seem strange, disconnected from our friend's plight, but trust me, the destiny of everyone you see will, eventually, be intertwined. Sit still and quiet . . .'

CHAPTER ONE

It's in the High Street, the Heart. It's made from red cobbles with a double border of grey. It has been there for a long, long time. Officially, it's known as the 'Heart of Midlothian' and people say that it marks the very centre of that district which is home to the capital city of Scotland. There is a local football team of the same name but, beyond that, the local inhabitants don't pay much attention to it; it's not very spectacular and is often covered by thick snow.

There is a custom attached to the Heart however, although people have long forgotten the meaning of that custom. Passers-by spit on it, and it is said that if you can spit in the very centre you will have good luck for a year. Spitting was once said to ward off evil and the sign which was simultaneously made with one's index and little fingers when crossing those stones has fallen into disuse in modern times.

No one remembers. The Heart of Midlothian, which marks the site of the entrance to the Old Tollbooth is also a seal, a capstone set there hundreds of years earlier by a man possessed of magic. Few such men and few magics still survived even in those times. Now there are none, except perhaps in the memory of the stones and the ghosts who linger in the darkness of the Old Town . . .

* * *

It was getting dark already and it was only four o'clock in the afternoon. Nathan leaned back against the cold stone of the cathedral wall and watched the crowds of people moving purposefully up and down the length of the High Street. Hugging his heavy winter coat more tightly around his angular frame to shut out the chill, he tried to pick out a likely prospect from those coming towards him.

'Force eye contact from as far away as possible,' Daniel had instructed when he dumped a couple of hundred leaflets into his arms that morning. 'It makes them uncomfortable – they have to acknowledge you to make their excuses for not stopping. That's when you strike.'

He had grinned his wide disarming grin and winked towards Esther who had blushed and smiled. Nathan had scowled in response, telling himself that Daniel was a complete prat and that was why he disliked him so much, but deep down knowing the truth; that he was jealous of his friend's easy charm.

A woman was walking towards him. She was well-dressed in a business suit and carried a large soft-looking handbag. She had spotted Nathan and was now studiously avoiding his gaze, looking at her watch as she came closer.

'Excuse me, miss . . .' Nathan stepped forward his hand outstretched with one of the colourful leaflets. 'Miss, do you feel that God has forsaken you?' He blurted it out too fast, he sounded desperate. 'Desperation never sold anything.' Another of Daniel's gems of wisdom. To his surprise, the woman stopped and took the leaflet, her eyes flickered over it quickly then she looked up at him.

'No,' she said quietly. She looked inordinately angry at his approach, her pale features were tense and strained looking. 'I don't believe in God.' To emphasise this she screwed the leaflet into a tight angry ball in her leather-gloved hand and dropped it at his feet. 'Get a life, why don't you,' she snarled. Just before she turned her back on him she gave him a look which was mostly malicious but contained also a hint of humour. Then, unexpectedly, she knocked his arm sending his pile of leaflets flying into the air. Nathan scrambled to rescue them as they landed on the wet cobblestones.

'You cow,' he yelled. 'There was no need . . . I was doing you a favour. Your soul is . . .' but she was already over the other side of the street, no doubt congratulating herself on her idea of a joke. Nathan watched her go. 'Your soul is doomed,' he finished, his voice dropped almost to a whisper as he wondered if he could have said it with any less conviction.

'Don't worry, Nathan.' It was Esther. He hadn't seen her arrive but she was already beside him, helping to scoop up the sodden leaflets. She smiled encouragingly, the only warmth in the darkening street, 'Some people . . . they just don't understand about being saved. They feel threatened.'

'No,' he shook his head, his expression still angry. 'Some people are just stupid and shallow.'

'But Daniel says . . .' she began.

'Well he's wrong, Esther. God didn't save everyone before the flood did he? And he certainly didn't do it by handing out bloody leaflets. He knew when to cut his losses. This is a waste of time.' He tossed the last of the leaflets onto the pile in her arms. 'Daniel's a fool and I'm going to tell him.'

They began to walk back down the street towards the Bridges, a strong wind was blowing up from the bottom of the High Street, causing people to quicken their pace and bow their heads against the onslaught of the elements. Nathan's dark coat caught the edge of the gale and billowed out around him; he was frowning, his long legs moving fast, covering a lot of ground with each stride. Esther said nothing, walking a double-time step to keep up with her friend, but Nathan knew what she was thinking, what they were both thinking: he wouldn't have the nerve to say such a thing to Daniel.

'I'm sorry, Daniel. I'm really sorry . . . I just lost it.'

God, get up, Daniel. Get up . . .

But Daniel wouldn't get up. Nathan knew that really. His grip tightened on the warm iron of the poker in his hand and Nathan stared down at his handiwork, his features a curious mixture of shock and guile. The storm had not abated and the Old Town was being lashed by gale force winds and rain. Outside, the guttering of the old building was struggling to cope with the sudden torrent and the window frames rattled as though someone or something was demanding entrance. In the far corner, rain which was leaking through the roof, plinked into a rusty iron pail.

But what if he does wake up? What if he's not dead, just unconscious?

Nathan squatted beside the body in the cold darkness

of the room and prodded it with the end of the poker. 'Daniel,' he whispered urgently. There was no response but Daniel's blue saintly gaze seemed blankly accusing.

I am sorry, you know . . .

Nathan sank down on the floor beside his victim.

Daniel had changed his life, 'rocked his world', as he was so fond of saying. Now, the colours of that day seemed unbearably bright . . .

He had been in Princes Street Gardens, late spring and a clear crisp day, still edgy and cold but the locals were pretending it was summer. All around people lazed on the grass, couples ignoring their shrieking children; only telling them off when they really annoyed other sun seekers. Nathan sat observing as was his habit, his knees bent up to his chin, perching like a lank, black bird; a living shadow on the bright idyll. A small girl of about three years old came up and stared at him curiously and he returned her penetrating gaze without smiling. They considered one another for long moments before her mother called her back. Just before she turned away she wrinkled her nose, 'You smell, mister,' she said.

Nathan couldn't help but smile. It was true after all, and something about her confidence in uttering the flat statement was quite brilliant. He'd been sleeping rough for a few weeks and often the choice between a shower at the Waverley Station or a fix had gone the wrong way. He rubbed his eyes as he watched her walk back to her mother who promptly scolded her for talking to strangers. His eyes were quite sore and puffy now, and he thought he'd managed to get some kind of infection in them.

'Good morning. Is anyone sitting here?' It was a male voice, soft and melodic.

Nathan looked up frowning. There was no 'here' just the grass beside him. The figure looking down on Nathan was in shadow as the sun was behind him.

'Whatever you're selling, I've got no money,' he muttered coldly. 'And,' he added as an afterthought, 'I'm straight, so back off.'

The speaker laughed seemingly unoffended. 'I'm not selling anything. Actually, I suppose you could say I'm giving it away.' He moved to sit down, and as he did so, the sunlight was momentarily caught and diffused in his hair giving him a golden halo, an appropriate harbinger of what was to come.

No, don't think that way . . .

He sat close to Nathan, too close, invading his personal space which made Nathan uncomfortable, and yet, after the thought of edging away briefly flashed through his mind, he stayed where he was, next to the stranger.

'I'm Daniel,' the stranger announced. 'What's your name?'

Nathan narrowed his crusty eyelids and scrutinised this innocent abroad. 'What do you care?' he muttered.

'I'm just being friendly,' Daniel shrugged. 'It's such a nice day, don't you think?'

'Nice?' Nathan snorted. He hated the word 'nice' and, generally, people who said things were 'nice' instantly aroused his suspicion as tree-hugging hippies or upper-class toffs cocooned from the harsh extremes of reality.

'Well, just . . .' Daniel seemed to sense his disapproval; something Nathan later learned about Daniel was his innate intuitiveness, which bordered on . . . miraculous.

Stop it. He was never Holy. Never Divine.

'Just . . .' Daniel leaned back on his elbows on the grass and laughed unselfconsciously, '. . . nice.'

Nathan pursed his lips, unsure of whether he should laugh also.

'Look, I'll be honest,' Daniel confided. 'I wondered if you needed a meal and bath. No offence like. I know somewhere that doesn't cost anything.'

'What's the catch?'

'There's no catch. Well, we might ask you to peel the tatties or wash the dishes,' Daniel smiled . . .

Nathan stared down at the corpse, a stupid smile on his face.

You were so clever, Danny. Gathering up your lost souls.

If Daniel had sat down and told him the truth; that he had come to save his soul, ensuring he would be Raptured at the time of the Deluge with all the other Children, he would have laughed or called him a freak. Occasionally prone to violence, that day, a year ago now, Nathan had been close to the edge; it was possible he may have attacked his saviour. As it turned out he had only prolonged Daniel's life by a year. Daniel had found drugs, coke and a small amount of weed in Nathan's room and the confrontation which ensued had brought them here, to this . . .

Suddenly, without warning, Daniel moved, such a

tiny fluttering motion that Nathan almost missed it in the shadows of the room. Then, it came again, the fingers of his left hand spasmed slightly, twitching open.

Alive? For a moment Nathan considered the proposition. *You could say it was an accident. You could say that the Devil possessed you for a moment. Daniel would like that. He could exorcise you in front of everyone. More glory for him, the Golden Boy. More power. More love . . .*

'No,' he said aloud into the darkness. His voice was soft and low, his dark eyes round, 'Not this time, Danny. It's my turn.'

Raising the poker high above his head he struck three more times. By the third blow, Daniel, his golden friend, charismatic prophet, founder of the Children of the Deluge, was unrecognisable. Half of his head was a messy pulp and now it appeared as if that handsome, classical face had been dismantled. A calm blue eye stared lifelessly from the undamaged half and the mischievous curl of the mouth could still be seen. Blood was everywhere, but Nathan seemed unaware of the warm incrimination; he sank to the floor and lay beside his friend still cradling the poker in his arms. He stared at the still beautiful side of Daniel's face and he seemed to be listening.

'No, no, Daniel, don't you see?' he whispered. 'It was you. You made me do it.'

He laughed quietly. A cracked broken sound. Then, as the church bells of the Old Town chimed midnight, he slept.

* * *

'But I don't understand, Morias. Who are those people? Why are they wearing such funny clothes?'

'Shhh, little one. I do not know myself yet. But the water is never wrong. Let us watch together . . . Ah, look, people you might recognise – here they are . . .'

Bright sunlight washed the meadow in warmth. All around where he sat, evening moths whirred and danced and tiny motes of pollen hung in the still air. It was late summer and the Valley of Mirranon was at its most beautiful, carpeted with wildflowers and blessed by the sweet song of skylarks whose nests were hidden in the tall grasses. Tristan cared nothing for all this; he was crying. A few feet away, his pony, which had just bucked him off, was chewing the grass unconcernedly, as though it was completely innocent of his plight. He hated horses now he decided. Nasty, windy creatures. People who talked of their nobility were full of . . . horseshit. He carried on crying hard and loud, vaguely aware that it was as much fright as anything else. It was hard to catch his breath and he felt as though something was clamped around his ribs. Deep down, he knew it probably wasn't the horse's fault; it was part of what Father called his 'disability'. His legs were always going to be weak despite his constant exercises, and he was unable to grip as hard as he needed to control a pony, let alone a full sized horse. His parents had been against him riding at all, but Regan had persuaded them to buy him a small mount knowing how important his independence was to him . . . He stopped his crying and wiped his face on the back of his sleeve as the sound of an approaching horse reached him.

'Regan!' he stood up and waved, trying to appear nonchalant. She rode confidently and fast as always, her red dress and long black hair streaming out behind her; and there, there was the picture of nobility people intended when they spoke of horse and rider in such poetic terms.

'Tris. What happened?' She reined in her horse effortlessly and jumped lightly to the ground.

'I'm all right,' he shrugged as he struggled to his feet. 'Honest.'

'Liar,' she said flatly. She frowned as she waded through the long grass towards him, lifting her long riding skirt to stop it from snagging. 'I saw your fall from the top of the rise there. It looked nasty.' She stopped in front of him and took hold of his face, tilting the chin to get a better look at the cut on his temple which was bleeding quite badly. 'Sit down Tris,' she commanded slightly more gently, 'I can't do anything while you're wavering about.'

They both sat down and Regan cleaned the wound without much comment. It wasn't as deep as she had at first feared but Tristan would have the tiny white scar as a memory of this day for a long time.

'Father's right,' he volunteered eventually, 'I can't ride.' Hot tears of frustration welled up in his eyes which Regan chose to ignore, 'I can't do anything. I'm useless . . . a useless bloody cripple.'

Regan gripped his shoulders and shook him lightly. 'Father never said that, Tris. He would never say that.'

Tristan was faintly surprised at her defence of their

father; it seemed to him that both Regan and Talisker possessed a strong streak of something which at best could be strength of character, but at worst was sheer bloody-mindedness. Regan continued as she dabbed the hem of her skirt against his temple. It could not be denied that her next words were slightly grudging. 'He's a good man and he does love you even though he has trouble showing his feelings. But he can be wrong. Think how proud you'll make him when you show him you can ride Pip.'

Tris studied her face for a moment, his boyish mind trying to pinpoint what it was that bothered him about her tone. 'He loves you too, Ree,' he muttered. She smiled in response but didn't say anything so he changed the subject. 'Who chose such a babyish name for my pony anyway?' he complained. 'Would you respect anyone who named you Pip?'

Regan grinned. She had a beautiful smile which transformed her dark intense looking features; it was at its best when she had mischief afoot. 'Well, Ma named him, so we can't really change it.' They both glanced over to the rather tatty looking grey pony which was happily absorbed in cropping the lower branches off a nearby tree. 'We could . . . no,' Regan trailed off, 'never mind.'

'What? What is it?' Tris was ever ready to go along with any of his sister's ideas.

'Well, we could give it a secret name. One that only you and I – and the horse – know. Something more suitable.' She appeared deadly earnest and glowered over at the unfortunate beast. 'I think your pony is a big horse trapped in a small horse's body.'

'You mean like me?' Tristan remarked mildly.

Regan coloured and appeared slightly flustered, she hadn't meant to be so careless with her remark at all. 'Well, in a way, yes,' she rallied. 'He's strong-willed and demands respect, he's obviously of above average intelligence . . .'

'Oh yes,' Tristan enthused, carried along with the idea.

'. . . he'd also look much handsomer if he was groomed once in a while.'

Tris giggled, his pains forgotten. 'So, what should we call him?' he wondered.

Regan held out her hand and helped her brother to stand up. 'Let's go and ask him shall we?'

'Ask him?'

They walked over to Pip and Regan caught hold of him quite easily, the evening sun was making him docile. She reached her arm over his withers and held onto him.

'Now, Tris, look into his eyes . . .'

'What for?' Tris began to complain, feeling self-conscious.

'Just do it,' she commanded seriously. 'That's right. Now keep looking in his eyes and think to yourself – what does he want to be called?'

'Well . . .' Tris stared into the soft brown eyes of the horse. Regan was right, he was a big horse in a little body; when you really considered his face he was solemn and thoughtful looking. For a moment, Tris let his imagination wander; what would Pip have been like if he had been born a bigger breed?

'Well?' Regan was becoming impatient.

'Majesty,' he smiled.

'Are you sure?' For a moment she looked as though she was going to laugh at him and Tristan began to lose confidence.

'I – I . . .'

'No, it's good; really,' she nodded. 'You'd better tell him eh?'

Tristan reached out and stroked the velvety nose of the pony. He kept his gaze fixed on the eyes of the beast and spoke softly. 'Now then. You and me are going to start over, Pip. I know . . . I know it's hard being little and clumsy. People don't respect you like they do the big sleek horses . . .' his voice sank almost to a whisper as he felt unexpectedly emotional. 'But I know, Pip. I see your big heart. I see how clever you are. You're special to me because I know that you could be a king amongst horses. So, from today, when we are together, I'll only call you Majesty. Because we both know what's in here don't we?' He touched his chest lightly and then kissed the newly named Majesty on the nose. He never saw Regan hastily wipe away her tears he was so absorbed in the idea of the secret.

They rode home at a walking pace through the sunlit meadow and Tristan fancied that he sensed a change in his pony. Years later as an adult he would smile and shake his head at the memory, but at the time Regan had given her brother a gift to treasure. As they rode though, Tris glanced over at his sister, her face was solemn and tired looking.

'Ree, are you still dreaming about the birds?' She

nodded. 'You must tell someone, Ree. It can't be good for you to lose so much sleep.'

'I don't think there's anything to be done about it, Tris. Anyway, I've told you – that will have to do . . .'

Tris smiled and turned his attention back to Majesty. He felt pleased that his sister would only tell him her secret.

'Years later, in a fit of vicious rage, she had the elderly beast slaughtered to punish Tristan for defying her. They were ten years old then, Nimah – not much younger than you – when Tris made a new relationship with his pony. Six years later, around their coming of age, everything would change. But even as they rode homeward that very day, dark clouds were gathering in the north. Another child – an intelligent, wilful child – was yearning for adulthood . . . See, there he sits in our mirror; pensive is he not? Well may he be . . .'

Jahl loved the sounds of the sea; the crashing of the surf and the screaming of the seabirds made a constant chaotic music. He sat with his feet in a rock pool and gazed out at the line of the breakers as though hypnotised – something indefinable in that moment when the wave peaked and then died had captured his young soul. Feeling the cold spray on his face and the salt fingers of the wind tussle his hair almost made him forget that, once again, his mother was angry with him and he with her.

Unlike most ten-year-olds Jahl had the innate

perception to realise that his mother was not entirely omnipotent – and this was ironic really, because his mother, the Lady Phyrr, was in fact, a goddess. She had caught him practising a spell, a summoning, and she was *furious*. He had almost succeeded too, he was sure he had seen something flickering and moving in the darkness before she had crashed in and yelled some stupid words of banishment.

'Are you trying to get yourself killed?' she fumed. 'You are mortal, you stupid child . . .'

'How will I learn if you won't teach me, Phyrr?' he complained. 'How can I develop my skills?'

She had reached out and slapped him, a stinging blow around his head. 'You are not going to develop those skills, Jahl,' she stormed. 'We've been through this countless times. You are a normal little boy.'

'How can I be a normal little boy? That's the most stupid thing I've ever heard,' he shouted back defiantly before running from the room in tears of rage.

Now, by the seashore as the breeze cooled his still smarting cheek, he reflected with satisfaction that she could not deny he was right. Jahl had no friends, they lived in isolation from the world in the northernmost tip of Sutra bounded on the east and west by the cruel Northern Ocean; often beyond the breakers, ice floes and icebergs drifted by in the grey, storm-tossed waters. He knew Phyrr had been thinking about sending him away soon, in fact, she regretted not having done so when he was a baby . . . Jahl felt that if he could prove to her that he had magic ability like her own, she might reconsider this idea – she might concede that he had some god-like abilities and as such, should not be treated like or considered to be a normal little boy.

It began to rain, a serious lashing downpour sweeping in from the ocean. Jahl sighed and covered his head with the loose hood of the riding cloak he wore. He didn't want to go in, not yet, actually, what he most wanted was to try again. Casting his gaze around he noted a gaping hole in the nearby cliffside; at high tide this hole would fill with booming waves which would shoot up inside the cavern and vent out onto the cliff-top like the spume of some great whale – now though it would provide a dank shelter and perhaps enough darkness to continue with his work. Grabbing his shoes from the rocks nearby Jahl ran towards the cave mouth, his bare feet splashing through the pools and puddles, his haste more from salacious anticipation than a desire to escape the downpour. Like any ten-year-old, the consequences of his actions were far from his mind, only the thrill and desire to succeed at his task. He jumped from puddle to rock pool with a carelessness which belied his purpose. To any casual observer he might appear like a normal little boy – but Jahl was on his way to summon a demon.

It started well. In a calmer, darker corner of the cavern where the light and the waves seldom reached even at high tide, Jahl drew the symbols he had been learning in the sand with a stick. He had the naïve lettering of a young boy, still un-styled, unformed by the character of its creator. The sand was dry and he wiggled his toes in its cold grainy surface trying not to become distracted by the irritation of the grains sticking to his damp feet. He wondered briefly if it was perhaps too dark; what if he summoned a demon which was as black as darkness and it said nothing to him? He might never know he had succeeded . . . However, once all the symbols were complete, they began to glow from beneath the sand as if they were composed of a kind of solid fire. Their light illuminated the rock walls of the cavern with a soft orange glow. Some other boy might have felt nervous about this, might pause and question himself; not so Jahl. With a single-mindedness which he had inherited from his mother, he continued. Standing with his legs wide apart, his feet burrowed into the sand, he began the incantation which he estimated would take twenty minutes.

He was wrong. His earlier attempt – thwarted by his mother – had not been entirely unsuccessful. A demon had indeed been awoken, pulled through from the deepest pits of darkness; this summoning, indeed any summoning, meant pain for such a creature although it was always bound to come. Worse still, in this earlier instance, the demon was not dealt with and then allowed to return to oblivion, Phyrr's intervention had caused it to be left in limbo for many pain-wracked hours. In short, the demon, when it came, was very, very angry . . .

Phyrr was already running across the storm-swept beach when the first thin, boyish scream issued from the cave. Although the deluge obscured her range of vision, she could see the flickering lights escaping the cave mouth in a release of energy which she knew represented a challenge which would be extremely difficult even for her to contain. She cursed loudly but then resolved to save her breath for running. When she entered the cave, the sight which confronted her was beyond the wildest nightmare of most mothers.

The demon had materialised and struck out at its summoner in the instant it came to physical being. The self-congratulatory sound Jahl was about to make was cut short in his young throat as a black, taloned hand, the size of his scrawny torso, shot out and grabbed hold of him, pulling him close to a face which had bright yellow teeth and eyes, and breath which stank like the pits of hell from whence it came. That was the moment Jahl screamed, as he felt sure the creature was simply going to bite his head off. The reality was far worse – this creature killed by absorption. After a cursory glance at its young tormentor, it clasped him to the bulk of its shapeless, leathery body. Jahl screamed again and then passed out as he felt the burning of the contact between himself and the demon. As he lost consciousness he remembered the final word of binding, too late.

'Put him down now!' Phyrr's voice echoed around the cavern, its tone of maternal fury as elemental as the rocks. 'Put him down, you bastard creature,' she shrieked. She could not kill the beast for fear of injuring Jahl, but began to speak words which Jahl had not learned, containment and submission; they ripped from her throat as fast as she dare speak them without losing their form but her desperation was palpable. Jahl was being subsumed into the black mass of the demon – his head lolling back limply from his shoulders – and she feared him lost already. Finally, after what seemed like an eternity, the last words were spoken and the demon captured to her will. If her son was dead she thought, she would trap the beast here in the world, ensuring its eternal agony in vengeance.

'Stand still,' she commanded. The demon obeyed, although this did not stop its process of absorption which had become involuntary. All that could be seen of Jahl was his head and face, his eyes were closed. Phyrr walked up to the immobilised demon and touched Jahl's temple, feeling the tiny flutter of his obstinate heartbeat. But now, she had something of a dilemma – there was only one magic she knew which could separate the boy's body from that of the beast; she must mark his face with symbols of warding and protection, but, so marked, the magics of chaos would ever be drawn to Jahl, his whole life. If she did not teach him all she knew of chaos, the chances of his survival even to eleven, were negligible. Sighing, she drew her dagger from her waist and a vial of blue powder she had the foresight to bring. She began to cut and scar her boy's beautiful face, tapping the powder loose and muttering different words from before. Phyrr could not heal – her own damaged eye was proof of that – but at least her simple spell would ease his pain.

'And so, unwittingly, Jahl received his heart's desire; the knowledge he sought must now be learned quickly for his own protection. And as she cried and cut and

tipped the blue powder, the Lady Phyrr was well aware that people should be careful what they wish for . . .'

It was painful today. Sometimes Tristan's twisted limbs pained him as though they had a sudden prescience that they were in fact bent the wrong way. His neck especially hurt, dull pains throbbed down the length of his spine and there was nothing to be done except wrap himself in a blanket and keep warm. His father was outside in the barn and Regan, well, who knew where she was. Regan was a law unto herself sometimes disappearing for days on end and returning completely unrepentant. Talisker said little about this but Tristan could tell he worried about his wayward daughter. Regan could easily have put his worries to rest, she was usually only at her friend Morag's farm across the valley, but she chose not to tell him where she was, it was part of her game.

Perhaps due to his disability, Tristan had become a great observer of people. He knew that Regan and his father had played a hurtful game with one another since the death of Una, his mother. Neither of them were really aware of this, but they were distant and cold with each other, going through their daily lives as though just passing through the time. No one spoke of Una, and Tristan, living in the middle of this frozen grief and anger, missed her desperately.

He was watching the view through the window vaguely waiting for Regan's return when he saw a rider crest the hill. He knew straight away it wasn't his sister, the rider, obviously a man, sitting further back in the saddle than a woman, wore a black riding cloak over a dark green plaid. As the figure grew closer, riding fast, the hood of the cloak fell back caught by the wind and Tristan, although alone in the house, whooped with glee. Ignoring the pain in his legs he rushed to the door and began to run towards the stable.

'Father, Father, come quickly! It's Uncle Sandro! The *Seanachaidh*'s coming!'

Talisker came rushing from the barn, a rare smile on his face which made him look younger than Tristan had seen for some time. They stood together watching the rider approach, Tristan hopping up and down and waving at his uncle.

Sandro dismounted and embraced Talisker warmly before turning to Tris. 'Tristan . . . hey you've grown!' he ruffled Tris's hair affectionately. 'Have I brought a story for you!' he grinned. But Tris could tell he had serious business, behind his smile there was something worryingly sombre. 'Tris, I have to speak to your father. Would you stable and feed Jagger for me?' For some reason Talisker laughed when he heard the name of Sandro's horse, it seemed perfectly reasonable to Tristan. Jagger was a massive beast, at least eighteen hands and jet black.

'Oh, Tris has a special way with horses,' Talisker nodded, 'he can handle any beast.'

Tristan glowed with pride at his father's remark and began to lead Jagger into the stables talking quietly to him.

* * *

He didn't quite understand about the *Seanachaidh* and his father. When he was young his mother had told him they were special men who came from another world to fight at Ruannoch Were and Soulis Mor. Although she had seemed perfectly serious at the time, Tristan was sure this must have been a story worthy of the *Seanachaidh* to impress a son with his father's prowess in battle. He did know that both men were veterans of the battles although his father never spoke of it – he also knew he was born in Soulis Mor at the time and his parents moved to the valley when he was only months old. There was something about Uncle Sandro; his skin was quite a nice colour, kind of gold, but lighter than a Sidhe's . . . perhaps he really came from a far southern clan or perhaps even from over the sea. Whichever it was, there was something unusual about the *Seanachaidh* which meant that his rare visits were special and exciting. Tris began rubbing down Jagger and realised he could hear snippets of the men's conversation as they were still outside the barn.

'You can't be serious, Sandro,' his father's voice was incredulous, 'he's just a boy.'

'Come on, Duncan,' Sandro chided gently, 'things aren't like that here and you know it. Fourteen is considered adult – old enough to die in battle.' Tristan held his breath, afraid that any noise would give away his eavesdropping or drown out his father's response.

'Don't remind me,' Talisker responded grimly, 'I saw them die too. Just children. But Tristan . . . you know he's different . . . I planned on keeping him with me.'

'Let's go in,' Sandro said quietly. 'We should discuss this over a drink eh? I've brought letters from Isbister . . .'

'Yeah, I need a drink. Sorry Sandro, that's what living in the wilderness does for you, I've no manners left. Come on . . .'

Their voices faded as they walked back towards the house. Tristan, who would normally be thrilled at stabling such an amazing beast as Jagger, continued his task automatically, his mind racing. The *Seanachaidh* had come to discuss his future!

He didn't go into the house after he'd finished with Jagger, as much as he wanted to know, he sensed his Father would need time to talk things through with Sandro – perhaps the *Seanachaidh* wanted an apprentice . . . they did take an apprentice occasionally he had heard . . . but then, people would not want to see him at their feasts or celebrations. Those who knew him had come to accept and love him but Tristan was enough of a pragmatist to know wider acceptance was not probable for him. It began to rain softly and Tris took shelter within the doorway of the stable listening to the indignant chorus of the birds, deep in thought.

'What are you doing out in the rain? You know it gives you the aches, Trissy.' It was Regan, she had come up on the pathway behind the stable and he was so lost in thought he hadn't heard her. He told her about Sandro as she led her pony into the stalls and put his blanket on. When he told her what he'd overheard she stopped what she was doing.

'So they're in there deciding your future. And you're out here. Why?'

'I'm – I'm just waiting. Giving them time . . .' he explained.

She took his hand and looked him in the eye. 'You have every right to make your own decisions Tris,' she said sternly. 'Let's go in.'

As they walked into the warmth of the house, both Talisker and Sandro turned and looked at Tristan. Sandro did not even greet Regan immediately although he smiled a tight, slightly dismissive smile towards her. Regan – almost always centre of attention – bridled at this.

'What's going on, Father?' she squeezed Tristan's hand tightly.

'Come and sit down, you two,' Talisker sighed. 'There's some things you should have been told a long time ago. And now, circumstances have forced my hand. I'm sorry, some of this may come as a bit of a shock.' Tristan sat beside his father and Regan next to Sandro. Both looked expectantly at Talisker who groaned softly. 'I wish your mother was here . . . she was always good at this kind of thing . . .'

'What kind of thing?' Regan demanded.

Talisker seemed to gather his strength. 'It's about you, Tris. We . . . Una and I . . . we're not your real parents. We adopted you. Una was the midwife at your delivery and your mother died in childbirth. Your father . . .' he broke off, unable to say the hurtful truth to his son. Sandro took a deep swig of his beer and took over.

'Your father was not a good man, Tristan. He didn't

understand about your physical problems. He disowned you at birth. Una had promised your mother just before she died that she would look after you and so she did. She brought you to live with her and Duncan here.'

There was silence for long moments while Tristan digested this information. Only the quiet sparking of the fire and the light patter of rain on the roof of the house could be heard. Regan reached across the table and took hold of her brother's hand. 'It doesn't matter, Tris,' she said quietly, 'we're your family. Ma loved you, that's what matters.' Tris said nothing, but the light of the fire reflected unshed tears in his eyes. Regan rounded on her father. 'Why are you telling him this now?' she blazed. 'What difference does it make? You should have just left it alone.'

Talisker was notoriously slow to anger but as he looked at his daughter, Sandro blanched to see a flare in those blue eyes he hadn't seen for many years. 'Do you think I would just spring this on you both for no reason? You always think the worst, Ree, don't you? You never stop to think I—'

'There's more' she said flatly, seemingly unphased by Talisker's anger, 'isn't there?'

'Yes. Tristan's father confessed his disowning of Tris on his deathbed five years ago to Isbister, Thane of Soulis Mor.'

'But why should she . . .' Regan began.

'Because Tristan's mother was the Thane's younger sister and the Thane never married or had children. Tris is – by birth – successor to the throne of Soulis Mor.'

Both Regan and Tristan gasped and stared incredulously at one another. Regan was the first to break into a broad smile. 'My brother will be Thane of Soulis Mor,' she grinned.

'No,' Talisker shook his head. 'Your brother *is* Thane of Soulis Mor. Isbister died two weeks ago.'

There was another stunned silence and then Tristan spoke; his voice was shaking and he was working hard to keep calm. To Duncan and Sandro his voice within the confines of the silent cabin, sounded achingly young. 'What will happen now, Father?'

'Well, Sandro here rode out to tell us soon after Isbister passed away. She left instruction that you are to succeed her so they will be sending an escort to take you to Soulis Mor as soon as her funeral is over. The other Thanes are coming for the ceremonies so they'll stay for your coronation.' Talisker swallowed hard, emotion threatening to overwhelm him. 'You must go and be Thane, Tristan. It seems it is your birthright.'

'But you'll come with me, Father, won't you?' It was evident from Tristan's voice that he sensed Talisker's answer before he finished asking the question. Talisker stood up and walked over to the fire; leaning on the lintel he stared into the flames and said nothing.

'No, Tristan. Your father won't be coming.' Sandro intervened. 'Terrible things happened at Soulis Mor, to both of us and all the warriors that were in the final battle . . .'

'But you've been back there,' Regan frowned. 'Other warriors must have stayed on in the city—'

'I won't go back, Regan,' Talisker said.

Regan lost her temper immediately and sprang from her seat knocking it to the ground behind her. 'Anything could happen to Tristan there,' she fumed. 'People might not want him to be Thane. He could be killed. Will you just abandon him to his fate? What would mother say – your precious Una – if she knew you were a coward?' Without waiting for a reply she rushed to the door but just before she left, she turned, her face a picture of fury. Tears were rolling down her cheeks but she seemed oblivious to them. 'You coward!' she screamed. Slamming the door she ran out into the rain.

'Regan, wait!' Sandro stood up to follow her but Talisker motioned him to stop.

'Let her go, Sandro. She's right after all.'

'No. She's not right. It was worse for you – you could see the souls. You've got to make her understand that. And what was all that about her mother? When did she become so . . .'

'Hostile? It's been a while. Since before Una died. I'm sorry, Tristan,' Talisker came back to the table and patted his son on the shoulder. 'I've tried . . . really hard, but your sister . . . there's something eating away at that girl but she won't let me help her.'

Tristan nodded but said nothing at first. He took the pitcher of beer and refilled his father's flagon and then, taking another leather pint from the shelf, he poured a drink for himself. Talisker and Sandro watched in silence; Tristan had never drunk alcohol before but now seemed a good time to start. Finally, he smiled a wistful little smile at the two men.

'Tell me all about it, Father,' he said quietly. 'All

about the battle, why it was worse for you than the other warriors, about my mother and about Soulis Mor. If I'm leaving here to rule it . . . I just need to know everything.'

CHAPTER TWO

. . . so she was already crying when the black rain began to fall. Crying because her daddy had lost her and the rats would be coming. When the first soft threat brushed against her cheek, she thought she knew it was a rat on her shoulder, dancing through her hair, ready to scratch her tear-soaked face. But she knew wrong. When she opened her eyes and saw the rain she gasped aloud. It was falling from above the level of the sword-light rays of the evening, piercing in through the gaps in the ancient brickwork; flickering through the layer of brightness in a silent, iridescent storm. No rats. No rain either, not really; reaching out she caught one of the ebony droplets, but it wasn't wet just soft cold; a feather . . .

More feathers and then more, and a sound, a horrible, rasping squabbling. The sound that filled the grain store was pure evil chaos and although she had ceased her sobbing only moments before, Regan emitted a thin, young wail of terror. Standing up, she ran over to the door, hammering piteously on the unyielding oak.

'Help meeee,' she sobbed. 'There's something here . . .'

But then they came. Their wings sounded like an echo of her shrieking; high, thin sound. She looked back and saw their outstretched talons and the sharp cruelty of their great hooked beaks.

'Daddy . . . Daddy,' she screamed. Something raked across the back of her head pulling away a whole chunk of her hair. The birds screamed back, taunting her. She turned around, lashing out ineffectually with her arm and they gripped onto the thin cotton of her sleeves, ripping the fabric and scratching at the tender young flesh.

Regan fell to the ground, flailing her arms and kicking her legs. She was still screaming but the crows didn't seem to care, they were on her back now, she could feel the light strong touches of their claws and hear their sound – all of it – the rasping, whirring terror. 'They even hate each other,' she thought; in the midst of her fear she simply knew it to be true. 'Hateful, hateful creatures . . .' but still she screamed and thrashed.

'Regan! Oh gods, Regan . . .'

There was light then, and noises, a strange, rushing thumping sound as the birds were beaten away with something. Then she was wrapped in a blanket and someone held her in strong protecting arms. It was Daddy. He'd come at last . . .

'That's horrible, Seanachaidh *. . .'*

'I know, Nimah. But it is both a childhood memory and a dream which haunts Regan. Sometimes, our dreams can have the power to mark us, if we give them such power . . .'

It was four days later when they came to take Tristan away. Sandro had risen at dawn, watching for the riders and inside the house Regan, Tristan and Talisker breakfasted in sombre silence having already said their goodbyes in advance. Now, the waiting seemed the worst part. Sandro seemed sure it would be today and the omens did not seem good. Tristan had fallen the day before and his legs were hurting which caused him to limp along slowly like an old man. He had dressed in his best white jerkin, his specially shortened plaid which Una had made for him and his favourite soft leather boots. He looked smart and tidy but Talisker knew this would not mean acceptance for his son. Sandro had been unsure whether Isbister had warned the assembly of Thanes of Tristan's condition and he knew of old how superstitious the Fine could be.

'They're coming,' Sandro looked around the door. Without knowing why, Talisker moved to the fireplace and took down his sword which he strapped around his waist; it felt heavy and unnatural after so much time but he felt better for it being there.

'Stay inside until we call you out,' he instructed the children. Regan and Tristan looked concerned but they both nodded.

Outside, Sandro was equally apprehensive. He hadn't drawn his sword but like Talisker, his hands fidgeted near the hilt and his gaze was fixed on the horizon. Without a word, they took up position on either side of the doorway as though on guard.

There were about twenty riders and they were coming at speed. Although still quite far off, the sound of their horses' hooves could already be heard as they sent up a red dust cloud on the dry dirt of the track.

'I might know some of them, Duncan,' Sandro commented, his voice tense and low, 'let me do the talking.'

Talisker nodded, grimly watching the riders grow closer. He didn't think he recognised any of them but the rider at the front was certainly striking: he was an older man with a long, pale face and ashen blond hair – he wore a jerkin of silver mail and the winter sun caught a flash of silver around his head. It seemed he was a Thane, but from where, Talisker had no idea. Immediately behind this Thane – slightly separate from the remaining riders – rode two other men with the thin silver circlets; they seemed younger and less remarkable somehow although their robes and horses were as fine as their leader's. With a shock of recognition, Talisker realised that one of the second Thanes seemed familiar. He leaned over to Sandro, his gaze still fixed on the man.

'Is that . . . ?'

'Yes, it's Eion. He must be representing Ulla,' Sandro said.

The group of riders halted in front of the house, and for a moment no one spoke. The leader silently eyed Sandro and Talisker before addressing them, noting they both wore weapons.

'Greetings,' he said eventually, his tone somewhat curt. 'I am Thane Huw of the Southern Clans. This is Thane Lachlan and Eion, representative for the Lady Ulla. I recognise you, *Seanachaidh*, so I believe you must know our business. We have come for the boy Tristan to take him for coronation at Soulis Mor.'

Huw faltered and frowned slightly. 'He is here, is he not?'

'Yes,' Sandro assured him, 'he is here. This is Duncan Talisker, Tristan's adopted father . . .' at the mention of Talisker's name the warriors in the entourage began to mutter amongst themselves obviously impressed at actually seeing Talisker, whose name was legendary amongst the Fine. Huw held up his hand imperiously to silence them.

'We seek assurances of the boy's safety,' Sandro continued mildly.

'I don't understand,' Huw frowned. 'Why would you need such a thing? He is heir to Soulis Mor, why would he be harmed?'

'There are no other claimants then?'

'Well, one. A cousin of the Lady Isbister's – but Tristan is in direct line. Are you questioning the loyalties of this party?'

'No, no,' Sandro assured him, 'It's just that Tristan . . . is not strong . . . physically.'

Huw's eyes narrowed slightly giving his features an unfortunate sly appearance. 'What do you mean, *Seanachaidh*?'

Talisker stepped forward. 'He means what he says. Before I hand my son over to you, I need to know he is safe.'

'Talisker,' Eion moved his horse to stand beside Huw, 'you know me. You fought beside me at Ruannoch Were. I've never met your son but I will happily guarantee his protection in your honour. I give you my word that no harm will befall him. I will stay beside him until his coronation.'

'Very well, Eion,' Talisker reached up and shook Eion's hand warmly. 'My thanks.' He turned into the doorway, 'Tristan, come out now.'

There was a long moment of silence and the riders seemed to hold their breath as they watched the doorway. Talisker knew Tristan was coming but due to his limping, his progress seemed to take an eternity. Huw frowned and was about to speak when Tris appeared, blinking in the bright sunlight.

'Is this a joke?' Huw growled, his hand dropping to his sword.

Tris, now sixteen, was only around four and a half feet tall; his short legs were slightly bowed outwards as though to accommodate his seemingly top-heavy bulk. His chest was as broad as it would have been had he grown to his proper size, but worst, and most difficult of all for Tristan, he appeared to have no neck at all, his overlarge head sat askew atop his broad shoulders causing him to stand slightly to one side in order to even up his vision. Tristan spoke clearly and well, causing Talisker's aching heart to swell with pity and love. 'Do you see me laughing, Sir?'

Huw said nothing so Tristan continued. 'My name is Tristan Talisker. I am told my mother, who died in childbirth, was the younger sister of the late Thane. I will come to Soulis Mor as is my birthright.' There was a stunned silence broken only by someone suppressing a laugh by coughing. Huw's horse skitted uncomfortably and Tristan, who had walked forward as he spoke, reached out to calm it. 'You have overtired your mount, Thane Huw,' he remarked almost absently. 'You must rest him and give him plenty of water,' he stared into the beast's eyes as he spoke, frowning. 'He's in danger.'

'Danger of what?'

'His heart is labouring,' Tristan replied. 'Can you see how he takes a small double breath on each second lungful?' Huw said nothing, reluctant to admit Tristan was right, his horse had been giving him cause for concern for about an hour now.

Sandro stepped forward. 'Please feel free to water your horses all of you. The trough is just over there by the barn.'

'Yes, I must gather my things,' Tristan agreed. No one moved.

'Is there a problem?' Sandro asked, keeping his tone perfectly even.

'Surely you must see the problem,' Huw growled. 'I'm sorry. I have no wish to offend anyone but we cannot take this . . . this . . . boy back with us.'

Talisker's hand dropped to his sword. 'Mark your words, Huw,' he warned. 'Thane or no . . .'

'Are you threatening me?' Huw seemed unsure how to react although several of the riders also put their hands to their weapons.

'I would get off that horse if I were you,' a young female voice cut across the clearing from the barn. 'If my brother says it's going to go, it's a certainty.'

Regan rode out of the barn on Sandro's black stallion Jagger. She wore her red dress and a voluminous black riding cloak, which Talisker recognised as having been Una's. She had drawn her long black hair back from her face and cleverly held it in place with a silver band which echoed those worn by the Thanes. As she drew nearer to her father and the other riders, he also noted she was wearing a sword which he knew had been lying around his workshop rusting away for sometime. It was no longer rusty though, Regan or Tristan must have spent hours cleaning it and honing the blunt blade. Had they planned this last night, he wondered?

As she reached Tristan, Regan bent down and, taking his arm, lifted him up onto the saddle in front of her. Talisker and Sandro exchanged worried glances.

'My name is Regan,' she said, looking imperiously at the assembled riders. 'And I am Tristan's twin sister.'

'Twin?' Huw echoed incredulously. 'No one mentioned a twin. You . . . you don't look like a twin.'

'As I'm sure you're aware, Thane Huw, twins are not always identical. Also, I believe my natural father was not the kind of man to worry about girl children,' she said gravely. 'Una, my adopted mother, thought it best to keep us together.'

'But you knew a woman could equally inherit Soulis Mor,' Huw frowned towards Talisker and Sandro. 'Why weren't we told?'

'Is this true, Talisker?' Eion asked.

Talisker was aghast. He understood what Regan was doing and yet, his heart ached at her denial of her true parentage – at that moment, he had never seen her look so much like her mother. And yet, he was trapped by the situation; he could hardly call her a liar in front of these people. He hesitated for long moments before he replied, aware that Regan's assertion, if proven false, could be considered treason – she could be arrested or worse. 'Yes . . . yes, it's true,' he said finally. 'I would have told you immediately but Isbister's letter only mentioned Tris which stands to reason because their father, Alistaire, was never told about Regan.'

'That's my horse,' Sandro whispered urgently. 'She can't take my horse.'

'We must consider this,' Huw nodded. 'We will rest our horses if we still have your leave.'

'Of course,' Talisker agreed.

The riders moved across to the barn and dismounted, the leaders amongst them going into a huddle and shooting curious glances back towards Tris and Regan. Talisker looked up at his daughter; she seemed to be suppressing laughter as she watched the group; a small smile played across her lips giving her a mischievous expression so familiar to Talisker from when she was a child. It occurred to him that Regan was possibly not doing this for entirely altruistic reasons – her child-like desire to constantly be centre of attention had influenced her actions as much as concern for her brother. He quelled the thought as soon as it surfaced, ashamed of his harsh judgement of her.

'Ree,' he urged quietly. 'Do you know what you're doing? This is not a game.'

Her smile vanished. 'You saw them, Father. They weren't going to take Tris or they may have even hurt him. He might not have survived the journey . . .'

'But Eion promised me.'

'He seems like a good man, Father. But he's not family.'

He sighed, reluctantly realising that her reasoning made sense. It seemed he was to lose both of his children but at least they would have one another.

'Are you all right with this, Tris?'

'Oh yes,' Tris smiled. 'If Ree comes, it'll be even better fun.'

'Fun . . .' Talisker echoed darkly. 'Ruling Soulis Mor is not going to be . . . oh what's the point . . .' He gave up and went and sat glumly back in the doorway.

Sandro came over and patted him on the shoulder. 'It makes sense, Duncan. If the Thanes accept it, it seems the children have come up with the solution.'

'I know. It's just . . . I suppose I didn't expect them to go out into the world quite so suddenly and spectacularly,' he shrugged.

'I'll go with them,' Sandro smiled, glancing over to Regan and Tristan who were watching the group of riders closely. Regan sat bolt upright, her arms protectively around her brother's shoulders. 'I know image is important to Regan at this precise moment in time, but I'd kinda like my horse back.'

Eventually, they left, Huw deciding to take both of the children and defer the decision until the Council of Thanes could confer on the matter. Tristan was elated that Regan was to travel with them, but took the opportunity before he left of transferring to ride Pip/Majesty. As the riders rode back up the hillside, Talisker watched the way they grouped defensively around Regan, who seemed to have fallen into her role with little difficulty. Tristan straggled slightly behind with Eion on one side and Sandro on the other, chatting amiably to both of them. As they crested the hill, Tristan paused, turned back and waved to his father but Regan did not stop. Talisker waved and smiled until his son was out of sight.

A week after Tristan and Regan left for Soulis Mor, it seemed as though the rain would never stop. Talisker shifted listlessly in the saddle and stared at the shadowy bulk of the building which had been his home. His happiness and his love – for whom it seemed he had waited a lifetime – had both found expression in that small space only to be overwhelmed after a brief season by this grey cold. She had been the bringer of this winter – Regan, his own daughter. It seemed as though he heard her voice, a child's voice, trembling on the wind.

'There's been an accident, Father . . .'

He had looked into her eyes and seen the flare of something disquieting, something contemptuous there. And he knew then; a notion had crept unbidden into his mind and would not be denied even as he comforted his children. A thought which struggled to find form as though it had an independent worm-like life of its own. Eventually, in the bleak darkness of his first night in his widower's bed, the thought screamed through his mind, demanding that he acknowledge its existence: *. . . but you could have saved her, Regan. You could have saved your mother . . .*

Once there, the idea would not leave him. Una died in the springtime and yet there could be no summer without her.

Urging his horse forward, Talisker tossed the flaming torch he carried in through the doorway of the house.

Inside, the neatly stacked furniture and bedding caught fire at once, illuminating the interior with haunting orange warmth. His horse fidgeted uncomfortably, feeling the heat begin to build within the room and vent through the doorway, but for long minutes Talisker could not tear himself away and he watched the destruction in silence. Perhaps it was the reflections of the flames but the expression on his features was unreadable; there was grief there, and longing, but also, anger. Finally, he turned away from the house and spurred his mount towards the dark outline of the forest. Just as he crested the hill, where his view of the house would be gone for ever, he pulled the reins tight around, almost causing his horse to lose its footing. He paused to watch again as the main beams of the roof could be heard collapsing, sending showers of ash and sparks briefly into the night sky to be extinguished by the rain like some transient firework. For an instant, only grief was written on Talisker's face, he had no tears left and felt they were an irrelevance at best, but, his eyes were bright reflections of the fire. His lips were moving although the whispered sound of his words were carried away by the storm.

'Goodbye, Una . . . I . . .' There seemed no point in continuing. He was sure she knew.

First sight of Soulis Mor was something neither Regan nor Tristan would forget. The idea that anyone could rule over the huge fortress city was almost preposterous. So ancient was the vast dark structure, that no one, not even the *Seanachaidhs* who kept the oral history of the Fine, knew who had built it; it straddled five miles of the jagged valley between the Blue Mountains to the west, and the end of the Ruamorr ranges to the east. In the winter, its basalt rocks became blackened by the sleet and snow, giving it a grim, menacing aspect but now, in the early summer, its stones appeared softened by the warmth of the sunshine and the yellow and blue wildflowers which dotted the plain before it.

'Look!' Tristan cried out and pointed excitedly. 'I've never seen such big buzzards before.'

Eion smiled at his enthusiasm – it didn't take long to become fond of Tristan, his warm wit and easy manner had won over most of the escort riders in the last few days. He noted that even the taciturn Thane Huw had gradually lowered his guard in the face of Tristan's excitement and interest. Tristan had a way of making people feel as if they were the most important thing in the world when he was talking to them; his attention never wavered, he actually listened, really listened to what people were saying to him rather than wait for his moment to speak as so many people did.

The night before, Tris had asked Huw about his domains in the south – was it true, he asked, that the birds there were beautiful colours and the sun shone all day? Huw seemed to consider Tristan's questions seriously – realising that the young man had never been further than the foothills of the mountains – he appeared relaxed under Tristan's honest scrutiny.

'No, it's not entirely true, Tristan, but it is notably warmer there. Lachlan's kingdom is nearer to Ruannoch Were – around a hundred and fifty miles south-west. My own domain is much further south, and from my Fastness of Karmala Sev, I can see out onto the ocean where the world is eaten up by the mist. Few times before have I made the journey to these northern lands – for myself it is almost four hundred miles and takes a number of weeks depending on the weather. Oh yes, and we have the best horses in the world . . .'

'Really?' Tris looked fascinated. 'I must go to Karmala Sev one day.'

'No, don't waste your time, young man,' Lachlan had come over to the fire to listen to the conversation. 'Everyone knows the best horses in Sutra hail from Durghanti – *my* kingdom.' Both of the Thanes laughed good humouredly and rather than rise to the bait, Tris turned around and looked back to where the horses were tethered overnight. After a few seconds of appraisal, he turned back to the Thanes.

'Are you teasing me, Sirs?' he asked. 'It seems to me that both of your horses come from the same stock. In fact, if they are wild rather than captive bred, I would say they are from the same herd.'

Huw could not disguise his surprise at Tristan's astute reasoning. 'Indeed,' he nodded, 'You are right. Between our two kingdoms runs a massive divide – a split in the land,' he drew a line in the ground to illustrate his point. 'We call it Cerne's Gorge because it has many dark, hidden reaches. It's almost one hundred miles long and over a mile deep – that's where the wild horses live. We take only what we need one day in a year.'

Tristan nodded seriously, trying to imagine the scale of such a place. Sandro, Eion and Regan had come to sit beside them during the conversation and Sandro joined in. 'Also, that's where the bear clan Sidhe live, Tris. They are the biggest Sidhe clan of all and they share their allegiance between Huw's and Lachlan's people.'

'Hmm. Well, in theory,' Lachlan said. 'In fact, we seldom see them, but they are useful to us; they carry messages between our two cities – a bear can travel fast and tirelessly for many days – and they know the gorge better than any Fine. We cross rarely, in fact Huw and myself arranged to meet at Ruannoch Were when we received word of Isbister's passing. It is my first time this far north . . .' he shivered. 'Is it always this cold?'

Tristan laughed unselfconsciously. 'This is summer! It gets a lot colder at the ending of the year after Samhain. It will snow then.'

'Snow,' Lachlan repeated darkly. He shivered again in an exaggerated fashion causing Tristan to laugh once more. Even Huw smiled slightly but as his gaze rested on Tristan it was troubled. It would take great strength to rule Soulis Mor, the largest domain in Sutra . . .

Regan had said little during the journey and privately, Eion and Sandro were concerned that she made little effort to endear herself to the Thanes and appeared distant and cold. Eion, who was not party to the lie of the 'Twin Thanes' disliked her instinctively but Sandro knew that the enormity of what she had undertaken was slowly sinking in; Regan was frightened.

Sandro had woken in the early hours of the morning and most of the entourage were still asleep apart from the sentries. His bladder was uncomfortably full and he left the shelter of his tent to relieve himself. As he walked past the fire he saw Regan; she sat staring into the embers, a blanket around her shoulders, she clutched at a tin mug as if it were somehow reassuring, although its contents could at best be lukewarm. Picking up a blanket, Sandro walked over to where she sat – Regan didn't look up, didn't even acknowledge that she had heard him approach.

'Can't sleep, eh?' he muttered. She didn't respond. Sighing, he sat down beside her and also stared into the fire, his position mimicking hers. 'I think you're doing a very brave thing, Regan,' he said.

She looked over at him then; her features – stark white in the coldness of the moon – were drawn with tiredness and stress, her eyes were like deep, hollow pools. For a moment there was something haunted in her expression, something older than the sixteen-year-old should have to know. 'I can't sleep, Uncle Sandro,' she said. 'I keep dreaming . . .'

'Oh?' He sat forward. 'How long has this been going on?'

'A long time,' she said disconsolately. 'There was an incident when I was six – I got shut in a grain store – but actually, they've always been there.'

'"They?"'

'The birds.'

'Birds?' he echoed. His eyes narrowed, 'Ravens?'

'Or crows maybe . . .'

'Would you like to tell me about it? The details – sometimes it helps.'

She shook her head miserably. 'I can't . . . I . . . Uncle Sandro . . .' Regan seemed keen to change the subject, 'do you ever do something and you didn't know you were going to do it – or say it – before the words came out?'

'I think I used to – when I was younger maybe.'

'It was like that . . . there was the sword of course . . . I thought Tris might need that. But then . . . it was as if something woke up inside me. When I said . . .' she glanced around, 'you know . . .'

'Was it like another voice, Regan?' he frowned.

'No. Oh no.' she sounded sure.

'Then perhaps it is just your destiny. Perhaps you had some small recognition when you saw it unfolding – happening before you.'

Regan nodded and looked happy with Sandro's vague explanation. 'Yes . . .' she sipped her cold tisane, 'that could be it. I wanted to look after Tris – you do believe me don't you?'

'Why wouldn't I believe you?'

She shrugged. 'I think Father thought I was being selfish, demanding attention – but it wasn't like that . . .'

'He was just worried for you both, Regan. You should try to get some sleep, we're arriving tomorrow—'

'I . . . I'm afraid to sleep. The dream and . . .'

'What?'

'I don't know.' She looked bereft, the confident young woman who had ridden out and declared herself Tristan's twin was gone for the moment, hidden behind some dark, nameless cloud.

'Here.' Sandro reached into his pouch and withdrew a round object about the size of his palm. 'Take this, Regan – the Sidhe say it gives courage and strength.'

The object glinted silver in the moonlight.

'What is it?' she asked. 'Is it silver?'

'No. It's a special kind of stone called hematite – but the Sidhe call it moonstone – you can see why . . .'

She stared at the stone for a moment and then quirked her brows at him. 'You must think me a child still, *Seanachaidh*, if you think a stone will salve my fevered dreams. Are you going to check my bedroll for monsters also?' She sighed. 'You're right, I should get some sleep.'

Sandro was surprised by her cynical response but determined not to show it. 'I'll stay awake near your bed, Regan – it's got to be a charm to have a *Seanachaidh* nearby.' He smiled, trying to reassure her, 'I'll catch hold of your dreams and turn them into *Seanachaidh* tales . . . Don't worry – I'm sure you and Tris will love Soulis Mor. And it will love you.' She smiled tiredly towards him as she walked back to her small tent and, for a moment, it was there again; that *hauntedness*. He found himself wondering exactly what she might be dreaming. As promised, he stayed awake, wrapped in his blankets just inside her doorway – and he noted with some satisfaction that, as she slept, she kept the moonstone curled in her palm.

Now, the following morning, there was no sign of Regan's night fears, just dark lines beneath her eyes . . .

'They're not buzzards, Tris.' Eion explained. 'They're eagle Sidhe. Although the Sidhe tribe aligned with Soulis Mor are lynx, many others have come for the naming of the new Thane.'

Regan had also come to watch the birds, her hands shielding her eyes from the brightness of the sun. 'And what business is it of theirs who becomes Thane?' she frowned. 'Only the Fine may decide surely?'

Eion raised his brows but said nothing. Sandro on the other hand was not so wary of Regan. 'You'll have much to learn, Ree. It's different here than in the villages, the Fine and the Sidhe are proud of their affiliations. The eagles are flying to welcome Tristan to the city.'

Regan seemed to take this as a slight, although no one in the city could know that there were two potential Thanes travelling to Soulis Mor. Spurring her horse forward, she passed Sandro on the narrow pathway and spoke quietly to him. '*Seanachaidh*, I'd appreciate it if you didn't call me that from now on.'

'Wha . . .' Sandro was about to laugh but then he saw the serious expression on Regan's face. 'I understand, Regan,' he nodded. He turned back to Tris and rolled his eyes and Tris giggled. Regan said nothing but carried on until she was at the front of the group of riders, beside Huw.

'Shall we go?' she said pleasantly. 'It seems Soulis Mor is in for a bit of a shock.'

It took almost a week for the Thanes to make their decision; that Tristan and Regan were to rule jointly. During that time, Tristan and Regan were 'interviewed' by the Lairds of Isbister's clan and visited by dignitaries of the Fine. Before their coronation the two were not allowed to leave their apartments in the upper levels of the central castle building. It mattered little, the apartments were luxurious, hung with rich warming tapestries, the floors strewn with sweet smelling herbs; they were also much larger than the size of the tiny house they had so recently left, and both Regan and Tris revelled in their new found luxury, sleeping in the huge soft beds and eating whatever and whenever they wanted.

On the second day, Tris was lounging around in the main living room trying a new tune on his battered wooden harp when Regan walked in from her bedchamber.

'Look, Tris,' she giggled breathlessly, 'who am I?' She was walking slowly, balancing four cushions on her head which were wobbling precariously. Immediately grasping her meaning, Tris rose and made a mocking bow.

'Why, Milady, with such glorious posture, you can only be the Thane of Soulis Mor.' He cast his eyes around the room and settled on a bowl of apples and figs. 'Aha,' he mocked, 'but can Milady cope with the responsibilities of all the fruit in the kingdom?'

'Huh?'

Tris grabbed up a handful of the fruit which he juggled until Regan came near him. Then he stood on the chair and began balancing them on top of the cushions on her head. 'Tris, you idiot,' she laughed, 'They're all going to fa—'

'No no, wait,' Tris hurriedly finished arranging the strange little crown, and then topped it off with an armful of flowers which he scooped from the vase in the middle of the table.

'Tris, they're dripping on my dress!' Regan moaned,

but she was still laughing although trying to keep her head still.

'Go on,' he chuckled, 'let's see how a real Thane walks.'

Picking up her skirts without looking down, Regan began to promenade slowly towards the doorway of the apartment. She did her best to look solemn but giggled along with Tris as the flowers began to cascade down. Reaching the doorway, she turned around quite quickly but still managed to keep most of her crown in place.

'Bravo! Bravo!' Tris began to jump up and down on the chair, clapping in an exaggerated fashion. Without warning, the doors of the apartment opened making Regan jump. Everything toppled from her head, landing in a heap on the floor – for some reason, the look on Regan's face was priceless, as though she had forgotten her strange load. Both she and Tris howled with laughter, ignoring their visitor, a fairly senior servant who had been allocated to look after them. The old women stood looking completely unamused, staring at the two as if they were mad.

'The *Seanachaidh* Sandro Chaplin told me to tell you he's coming up in about half an hour, Miss,' she said to Regan, her voice clipped and annoyed sounding. 'I'll just clean this up.' She started towards the pile of wet flowers, fruit and cushions.

'Leave it,' Regan said sharply, her laughter instantly vanishing. 'Get out.' The old woman said nothing, simply bowed out of the room. 'Sour faced old bag.' Regan kicked one of the cushions across the room.

'You were a bit hard on her, Ree,' Tris smiled, still shaking off the last of his giggles.

'Hard? Hard? I'm going to fire her scrawny old arse when I'm Thane,' Regan fumed. 'See if she manages to find a sense of humour when she's scrubbing pots for the rest of her days.' She stamped her foot. 'I won't stand for it, Tris.'

Tris, still in the grip of good humour made a wry face, 'What? So everyone's gonna have to laugh at all your jokes now, eh? Better not tell them the one about the shepherd and the shepherdess then – you'll have to behead the whole city.' A cushion came flying across the room and hit him smack in the face but it was accompanied by her laughter. In those early days, Tris could laugh her out of most things.

'Regan was always going to have trouble with the Sidhe. She didn't like them and she made it obvious. It started with the memorial on the Northern plains – the badlands as most people still call them – which had been commissioned by Isbister just before her death. It was their first major duty as Thanes to approve the final design. The huge silver and granite slab would be erected a mile north of the city so that it would serve as a touchstone on the horizon marking the battlefield of the final conflict for Soulis Mor where thousands of warriors died. Tristan and Regan were aware of their "adoptive father's" hero status in that conflict and both were looking forward to the duty, so the day started happily enough . . .'

Regan had grand, new quarters in the central bailey of the fortress castle and Tristan, feeling alone and slightly self-conscious in the original rooms once his sister had relocated, moved into some rooms on the lower floors. Regan had objected to this, saying they did not reflect his new status, but Tris merely shrugged and moved in anyway. He didn't tell her that the long, sweeping flights of stairs up to the upper floors hurt his legs, sending shooting pains up to his hips whenever he climbed so many. In days past Regan would have realised this without Tris explicitly telling her, but then, she had so much on her mind now. In retrospect he knew it had been a mistake to distance himself in such a way, but it was a mistake made for purely practical reasons.

The morning they were due to approve the memorial, he was toiling to climb the stairs – some days it was worse than others – and he had stopped halfway up the second flight trying to regain control of his breathing. Hearing a noise behind him he turned around, probably to reassure some anxious servant he was all right. Tris let out a small exclamation of surprise and gripped the handrail of the stairs as though in the vain hope the iron rail would provide some protection. A huge brown bear – the first bear Sidhe Tris had seen close up – was ambling up the staircase behind him, almost filling the span of the stairs; unlike Tristan it seemed to find them no effort at all and moved in a steady rhythm, its large, square head moving from side to side. As the creature approached Tristan, its dark brown eyes fixed him in an appraising glance, then it stopped and bent down slightly, inviting Tris to climb on his back. Tris hardly dared move for a moment, unsure if he had misunderstood. The bear looked sideways at him and grunted impatiently so Tris climbed onto the broad shoulders of the beast and held gingerly onto the scruff of its neck as it continued its effortless climb. He noted that the creature must be quite old; the honey brown pelt which smelt pleasantly musky, was streaked with silver-grey and also the bear wore little adornment, only a silver earring with a large feather attached to its right ear. He and Regan had not met any of the Sidhe tribal Elders yet and it struck him as a strange introduction to be riding up the stairs on the back of the great beast.

When they crested the top landing, Regan was standing by the door watching them. Tris dismounted and the bear stood upright on its hind legs – it stood at least seven feet tall – and bowed its head. Tristan returned the bow ceremoniously and Regan walked forward and gave a slightly uncertain, brief curtsey.

'Welcome, Sir,' she nodded.

Sandro emerged from the antechamber of the room, curious as to what was happening in the stairwell. 'Markomete! You old . . . bear you!' he beamed. 'I didn't expect you to come this time!'

The bear stood back down on all fours and grunted something towards Sandro, then a green glow enveloped the creature, so bright that the onlookers had to avert their gaze. Within moments the figure of the bear could not be seen within the brightness and then, as the light diminished and shrank away, the figure of a tall, stately looking man could be seen. He wore a cloak made of colourful feathers and soft, leather clothes; a jerkin and loose trousers. His long grey hair was decorated with tiny thin plaits and more feathers and – most interesting of all to Tristan – he had bare feet with silver rings on his toes.

'*Seanachaidh*,' he smiled towards Sandro, his teeth startlingly white against the warm golden colour of his skin. 'It's been a while since you graced our halls. Are you saving up your tales for the winter?' He bowed again towards Tristan and Regan, 'I am Markomete, Elder of the bear Sidhe who are Sidhe to the Southern Clans. You must be young Thane Tristan and the Lady Regan. Forgive my arriving unannounced but I am also an advocate to the Council of Tema and they requested I come.'

Regan frowned. 'Forgive me, Sir, but why exactly have you come?'

'Why, to see the final version of the monument, Lady.'

'I see,' she responded haughtily. 'Could you excuse us for a moment please, Markomete? Sandro, I need to speak with you.'

As soon as she and Sandro were in her living room and the door closed, she rounded on the bemused *Seanachaidh*. 'I know I'm new to this *Seanachaidh*, but have I missed something here?'

'I don't understand, Regan? Did he say something wrong?'

'What has the monument got to do with the Sidhe? Do they always meddle in the affairs of the Fine as a matter of course?'

'Ah, I see,' Sandro nodded. 'Perhaps all will become clear when we see the monument, Lady Regan.' Regan's frown became deeper, her mouth a tight line which Sandro absently thought was not very becoming.

'Don't patronise me, Uncle Sandro. Tell me now.'

'Regan . . . Lady Regan . . .' Sandro was perplexed. 'There's really nothing to worry about. There are representations of each of the Sidhe tribes also on the monument. The Council of Tema probably wants to ensure that each is represented fairly.'

'But why?' she demanded. 'Why are they on it in the first place?'

Sandro sighed. 'Because without the Sidhe, *Braznnair* would never have come north in time for the final conflict. Also, they fought beside us in both of the major battles – many died beside us.'

Regan paced back and forward in front of him seemingly deep in thought. 'Who authorised the design with the Sidhe included *Seanachaidh*?

'Isbister,' Sandro shifted uncomfortably sensing trouble brewing.

'Regan,' Tristan came in, 'What's going on? We can't just keep Markomete waiting, it's very rude. We're supposed to be there already.' Sandro shot Tris a warning glance. 'What's up?' he frowned.

'Lady Regan thinks there may be a problem with the design of the monument,' Sandro said as tactfully as he could.

'How does she know? We haven't even seen it yet,' Tris replied slightly impatiently. 'Sandro, we've got to meet someone on the roof for some reason?'

Sandro nodded. 'It will be Druvien and his entourage, they had to go and notify the Council of Tema of the date of your coronation. Shall we go, Regan?' Regan nodded but said nothing.

* * *

She should have known if she had thought it through – why else would they be meeting on the battlements? Since their arrival at the city Regan and Tristan had not been introduced to any of the Sidhe eagles and now, three of them were flying towards her . . .

'Oh no! But she's afraid, isn't she, Seanachaidh*?'*

'Stop interrupting, Nimah . . . Just watch . . .'

There was quite a gathering on the battlements; Thane Lachlan – who had stayed on for the coronation – a couple of Soulis Mor Lairds whose names she didn't know yet, Markomete and two other Sidhe who looked to be of the same clan. Regan stood to the fore of the gathering with Markomete and Tristan just behind her. A freshening wind was getting up from the south and it found its echo in a tightening anxiety which began to grip Regan's stomach as she saw the three Sidhe eagles. As they came closer, Tristan, entranced by their majestic flight, suddenly remembered Regan's fear of birds and stepped forward to say something to reassure her. She held up her hand in a dismissive gesture. 'I'm fine, Tris,' she murmured.

But she wasn't fine, far from it; cold, nauseating fear was gripping her body, her chest grew tight, her breathing shallower: despite the freshness of the breeze, Regan began to sweat. The birds came ever closer, their leader, a huge eagle whose plumage was almost black, fixed Regan with its sulphurous yellow eyes. As they came to land on the crenellations of the battlements the updraft from their wings sent a wind whirling across the battlements causing the welcoming party to hold onto their cloaks and plaids. The two flanking eagles transformed immediately into their Sidhe form much to Regan's relief; but the leader – Druvien – was watching Regan closely. Did he sense her fear she wondered? She felt she had managed to appear calm although she was shaking inwardly. Her hair, ruffled by the breeze the Sidhe had created, was trailing onto her face, but she made no attempt to push the strands back – she and Druvien had locked their gaze and, for what seemed to Regan to be the longest time, neither one moved.

'Welcome,' she managed finally, 'Prince Druvien.' She bowed her head. From where he stood Tris could see that his sister's features had drained of all colour. He nudged Sandro's arm, '*Seanachaidh*,' he whispered urgently, 'Regan doesn't . . .'

Before he could finish however, Regan's and Druvien's stalemate was ended. The great eagle opened his massive yellow beak and uttered a harsh cry – unintentionally causing Regan to lose control. The new Thane of Soulis Mor let out a smaller sound, an involuntary cry of fear, and then fainted. There was consternation on the battlements as everyone rushed to Regan's aid, however she lost consciousness for only a few seconds and, as she came round, her fear was transmuted to embarrassment and then anger.

'Get off me,' she snapped as Sandro and Markomete tried to help her. 'I'm all right. Stop fussing . . .' She was tight-lipped with fury – it seemed to Tris that, for some reason, she imagined Druvien had deliberately frightened her. During the time everyone clustered around her, Druvien had transformed to his human shape and rushed over to Regan with a look of utter confusion on his face.

'I'm – I'm so sorry, Lady Regan. I didn't mean to startle you . . .' He bent down and offered her his hand to help her up but she ignored his gesture and pushed away from Sandro who she had fallen back on as she passed out. As she glared up at Druvien, for the smallest instant there was a twinkle of merriment in his gaze which he immediately stifled.

'I am fine,' she flustered. 'I forgot to eat breakfast and I became a little light-headed, that's all.'

Druvien nodded and offered her his arm. 'Allow me to escort you down to the stables by way of an apology, Lady Regan,' he said. She stared at his extended arm with an expression of alarm and revulsion on her face for a second. Then, as had Druvien, she masked her feelings and lightly touched his forearm to allow him to walk back down the tower with her. The look did not pass unnoticed and Regan's reaction to the Sidhe eagles – so beloved by the late Thane Isbister – was seen to be the worst of omens.

'Let us go and see this monument, then, shall we?' she smiled. Only Tristan recognised the chilled upturn of her mouth as anything other than a smile.

It was beautiful. In the morning sunlight the monument sparkled and shone, its silver designs were inlaid into the red granite which had taken eight months to transport to the city. It stood almost twenty feet tall and it was only this morning that the masons and silversmiths had raised it upright from its prone position which took a large amount of manpower. Consequently, the masons' yards were full of people anxious to see the monument or to catch a glimpse of Tristan and Regan for the first time.

Amidst the melee a small area had been roped off for the visiting party of dignitaries and women were still hurriedly sweeping away as much dust and mess as they could. In the middle of it all the obelisk stood like a silent sentinel radiating a somehow calming presence. Tristan and Regan arrived on horseback accompanied by the group who had witnessed the incident on the battlements. No one else could have foreseen Regan's reaction. In all, examination of the pristine, inspired object took Regan just two minutes. Without waiting to be introduced to the craftsmen and women she dismounted her horse and walked up to the obelisk; Tris remained on his pony, trying his hardest to look calm although he was still unused to the public attention. He rode up to the base of the monument and admired the beauty of the carving.

The silversmiths had depicted the battle for Soulis Mor in a glorious and stylised manner. Anyone who had been there – and there were many present – could have told the crowds that real battles were just not like that; that more usually, men did not die so decorously but rather cursing in horrible pain. However, the craft of the young silversmiths shone through and the idealism which the new generations of Fine felt about their forefathers was evident to see. Above the depiction of the battle, Sidhe eagles flew in a sky where a double image of the sun shone and amongst the warriors were the Sidhe bears and lynxes.

* * *

Sandro and Markomete had walked forward to see the carvings also; they stood quietly, each deep in thoughts of sorrow and remembrance. Druvien stood slightly back watching Regan thoughtfully. Tristan thought it must have been a fine thing to know such men and women as those who had died on that day. He wished his father was here to see the monument; it was for him after all. It was beau—

'No, it won't do,' Regan snapped. She turned towards the chief silversmith who was puffed out with pride. 'You there, you'll have to amend the design. I'll send instruction.' As she marched back to her horse and mounted in a fluid easy motion, a murmur began to build in the crowd as they realised she had rejected the piece, she jerked on the reins of her horse and left the courtyard.

'Regan?' Tris wasn't sure he understood what was going on and cast around wildly, his composure before the crowd threatened by the departure of his sister.

''S'all right, Tris,' Sandro leaned in close to his pony, realising Tristan's nerves might overwhelm him. He began to lead the pony back towards the enclosure so he could retrieve his own mount. His expression was one of quiet fury. 'I wish your father was here, Tris,' he muttered softly. 'That girl needs a good smack.' Privately Tris agreed entirely with Sandro but he bridled, his loyalty to his sister unquestioning.

'She's not just a girl, Sandro. She's a Thane now, your Thane.' They had reached the enclosure and Sandro mounted his own horse, raising his height much higher than Tristan. He smiled slightly, understanding the boy's dilemma.

'I'm sorry, Tristan. I know she's your sister but . . .' he shrugged, 'look around you. This is a bad start.' Tris looked around the courtyard; people were standing in small groups discussing the Thane's brief appearance. The craftspeople, their moment of glory after months of work snatched away, stood beside the obelisk, some apparently arguing about which part Regan didn't like and others just looking dazed. One young woman looked close to tears '. . . and anyway, I'm a free man.'

'What?'

'*Seanachaidhs* are free men.' Sandro looked tight-lipped as they left the courtyard. 'With respect, Tristan, neither you nor Regan will ever be my Thane. I'm here for your father.' Tristan looked immediately crestfallen and Sandro laughed lightly. 'And for you, of course. I said I'd see you settled in.'

Markomete spurred his horse and drew level with them. 'Salkit's teeth,' he cursed. 'What's going on, *Seanachaidh*? Your pardon, Thane Tristan. Everyone is just confused.'

'We'll find out soon enough, Markomete,' Tristan replied, his tone sombre. 'But I suspect you're not going to like it.'

'What the hell's going on, Ree? Are you trying to offend everybody in Soulis Mor?' Tristan was furious and his temper was all the worse for being such a rare event. Even Regan blanched slightly, so unused to her placid brother railing against her. 'Did you see those people – those poor craftsman? Sandro says they've worked on the monument for over a year . . . how could you . . . You've made us look insensitive, uncaring and . . . and bloody stupid.'

But Regan was unrepentant, she rounded on her brother and gave him a stinging slap across his cheek. Sandro, the only other person to have been allowed into the room, barely stifled a gasp of surprise. 'Listen to me,' Regan raged. 'If we are to be Thanes here we must show them immediately that we are not to be trifled with. The monument must be changed . . .'

'It's the animals, the Sidhe birds, isn't it?' Tris challenged. He held his hand to his cheek as if he were afraid she would slap it again. But he wanted the truth from her.

Regan at least had the grace to look uncomfortable, 'No, no . . . not exactly. I just don't trust the way the Sidhe are so much . . .'

'Part of the life of Sutra?' Sandro intervened but kept his voice low, unconfrontational. It was obvious to him that Regan was overwrought; her eyes had a glazed expression and he knew from experience that she was suffering some level of anxiety. There was little to be gained by baiting her now. 'That's because they are, Lady Regan. As I said on the way here, you have much to learn . . . Don't worry though, I'm sure the damage is not insurmountable . . .'

She glared at Sandro well aware he was attempting to placate her. 'I am going to bed,' she said firmly.

'But Ree, Lachlan is hosting a banquet in our honour tonight,' Tristan frowned. 'It would be rude to . . .'

She arched her brows. 'I am a Thane, Tristan. I can be rude if I like. Tell Lachlan I have a headache. Now, get out. Both of you.'

For a moment, Tristan stared at her as if he couldn't quite believe what he was hearing – it was worse than the slap. Sandro shook his head sadly, 'C'mon, Tris,' he said quietly putting his arm around Tris's shoulders. 'Regan is tired . . .' He steered Tristan from the room and they shut they door carefully as if an invalid lay within. Once outside, Sandro crouched down in front of Tris and looked him in the eye. 'Listen to me, Tristan,' he said. 'You can't let her push you around like that. Do you understand? You must speak to her in the morning when she's calmed down . . .'

'She's just tired, *Seanachaidh*. The birds frightened her but she won't admit it. She'll be fine.' But Tristan's expression said that he was convincing no one – least of all himself.

CHAPTER THREE

'Look, the image is fading . . . quickly girl, you must stir the waters again . . . gently, gently, ah, very good, Nimah. I can see now why the land chose you . . . There, there it is . . .

'Yes, Regan and Tristan fought often, but actually for the first five or so years of the reign of the Twin Thanes, things were fairly harmonious in Soulis Mor. That is not to say Regan courted the Sidhes' favour but rather, that she left any such matters to Tristan. In their way the brother and sister complemented each other, but although Regan was perceived to be strong and Tristan weak, none would say they loved her as their Thane. Isbister had held the heart of her people but Regan was ever imperious and aloof. Tristan, on the other hand, was held in great affection, although this grieved him slightly as – ever perceptive – he realised that this affection was like that given to children; that is to say, he felt that no one respected him . . .

'Perhaps that is ever the way with rulers, they are never satisfied by the perception of their subjects . . . anyway, I digress. Look back in the water little one . . . I will try and direct you to where history changes its course. Look, there . . .'

Regan was out riding. She wanted to be on her own but that wasn't allowed. Some irritating rule stated that the Thane must be accompanied – she supposed it was in case she had an accident, but it was irritating nonetheless. Something of a game had sprung up between Regan and the entourage whereby she would give them the slip; she could outride any of them. Often she would hide in a copse of trees and watch them pass her by, laughing to herself but at the same time, noting the names of those who cursed her in their bad humour. After the first couple of times the entourage had changed their strategy, taking with them an expert rider – usually a stable-hand or a huntsman – whose job it was to keep up with the Thane but report back to the lagging party when any sizable gap developed. Of course, Regan pretended to be oblivious to this but she knew it had become a matter of pride amongst the stable lads – on only two occasions had the riders managed to keep up with her and, although she feigned nonchalance, she made it her business to find out who those riders were and had them promoted. She told herself this was purely pragmatism on her part but really, the game satisfied her vanity.

Today, however, the novelty of the game had palled. The rider the entourage had chosen was too good, she couldn't lose him. And it was raining, a fine drizzle washed over the foothills of Ruamorr turning the rocks black and slippery, and raising the loamy smell of the earth from the ground. She couldn't go faster than a canter in these conditions and even then only on a straight. She had come higher than she had intended and the path had petered out, slowing her gelding to a walking pace as the terrain became too rough. Regan was considering looping around if possible so that her pursuer would even then fail to see her and might continue wandering around while she was back in Soulis Mor drinking honeyed mead. Grinning slightly maliciously, she turned her horse around and was about to leave the trail when a sudden thought occurred to her – she hadn't seen or heard from the rider for almost an hour now. She frowned, that was unusual, she must have lost him a while ago and not realised . . . Lost in thought her attention strayed from directing her horse; the hapless creature lost its footing and stumbled, throwing Regan from its back.

It was a bad landing – an outcropping rock caught her just below her ribcage knocking the breath from her lungs; having thrown her hands out instinctively to brace her landing, she yelped as pain shot up through her right arm. She was dazed and breathless as she turned over, cursing aloud and looking for her horse – that was when she first saw the puma. There were many such creatures in Ruamorr although Soulis Mor was the extent of the creature's westerly range – this one was big and hungry looking, its tawny fur matted. Regan knew it was unlikely the beast would normally attack a human, but it looked hungry enough to try if it sensed her injury made her easy prey.

'Get!' she yelled. 'Go on, scram . . .' she picked up a fist sized rock from the ground and threw it at the puma which backed away but did not turn and flee as she had hoped. Instead, the puma settled into a short pacing rhythm – back and forth, back and forth, its gaze intent on Regan.

She was worried now, she glanced to her left, her horse was about forty feet away but she knew there was no chance of it turning back to her as long as the puma was there. Bracing herself, she tried to stand up; the pain seared up her right arm once more as she had to put her body weight onto it briefly. She tried to push herself upright but slipped on the slick surface of the rocks. Cursing and sweating, she was about to try again when she heard a rider approaching.

At first she assumed it was the entourage rider but then realised the sound was coming from further up the vague trail. The horse was in little hurry but its pace quickened before it appeared in her view – probably because its own rider had seen Regan's loose horse.

'Hello,' she called, 'I'm over here . . .'

The rider came into view. It was a man, dressed in deep crimson tunic and trousers which were of a fashion unusual in Sutra; he had black hair which was swept back from his sharp, clean features. Heavy-lidded brown eyes flickered as his gaze swept across the path, assessing the situation – most notably, across his right cheek was a line of blue symbols which accentuated the ridge of his high cheekbones. The stranger did not immediately speak to Regan, however; he stared directly at the puma which had sunk into a springing posture and was snarling up at him. As if in response to something the creature had actually said, the man quirked his fine eyebrows and spoke quietly to the beast, so quietly that Regan was unsure what he said. The puma made a sound in its throat – which sounded curiously like a complaint – and then stood up and left without looking back.

'Thank-you,' Regan smiled. 'Really, there was no

need . . . I mean, there is a rider behind me but . . .'

The man glanced pointedly back down the path – there was still no rider in view – and then dismounted his horse and walked towards Regan. As he did so, Regan felt some anxiety; perhaps her saviour was no saviour at all. At his side she noticed he carried a long dagger with a curved blade. Still he said nothing to her but his demeanour was not overtly threatening, on reaching her he crouched down and took hold of her arm.

'Oww,' she yelped. He only nodded in response and this irritated her. 'Look, whoever you are . . . aaargh!' As she spoke, the stranger had pulled and twisted her arm in a sudden movement. As the flare of pain died away, Regan was momentarily furious: 'You stupid . . . oh.' She moved the arm again, flexing her fingers and rubbing at her forearm, the pain was gone.

'It was dislocated,' he said quietly. He had the richest, most melodic voice Regan had ever heard. He gave a quick, reassuring smile, 'let me see the other one.' Reluctantly she did so and braced herself in readiness for his sudden cure – but her left arm had suffered only a sprained wrist. 'It's fine,' he said after some feeling of the bone. 'We should get you home. Do you live around here?'

'Soulis Mor,' she replied, quietly amused that he had no idea who she was. 'I am . . .'

'Thane Regan . . . Milady . . .' The missing rider came up the path at last and Regan felt a small pang of regret that she and her strange rescuer would not be able to spend more time alone. 'Get back!' Misinterpreting the situation the rider drew his sword.

'No,' Regan commanded. 'Put that away. This man is a friend. My horse threw me and then I was almost attacked by a wildcat. He will ride with us to Soulis Mor and have supper with me. Go and find my horse,' she scowled. 'He went that way.'

The rider did as he was bid.

'So, are you asking me to supper or commanding me?' the stranger asked. He helped her to her feet but held onto her hand for seconds longer than was strictly necessary before letting her go.

'Well, I . . .' Regan was flustered. 'Which would you prefer?'

'I am no bound subject, lady,' he replied gravely. 'But I would be honoured if you would ask me.'

'Very well. Will you take supper with me?'

He paused. For a moment, Regan had the sinking feeling he was about to say 'no' – but then he smiled and bowed his head. 'Delighted,' he said.

The rider returned with Regan's horse and they began the long ride back towards the city. 'What is your name, sir?' she asked.

'Jahl.'

The puma watched them go, its tail twitching in agitation. She didn't know why the man had told her to threaten the woman – there wasn't much eating on her bones anyway – but she hoped he had been as good as his word and released her three-month-old cub unharmed, further up the mountain.

'And so, that is how they met. Innocuous was it not? The beginning of Jahl's four-year climb to power. In

the first year, he appeared to do little and his presence went unremarked in the city; perhaps, with hindsight it can be seen that this was the most important time in terms of building his bond with Regan. Jahl was playing the long game, although in truth, I doubt he knew himself what he hoped to achieve – perhaps he felt that power over Regan and thereby Soulis Mor, was to be its own reward – but it was never going to satisfy him . . .

'Regan was fascinated by her new companion whose status she changed almost to suit her mood – he was at times her private physician, her secretary, her aide, her confidant . . . None could dissuade her – not even Tristan, who instinctively disliked Jahl. Some have considered that Jahl's increasing hold over Regan's affections was achieved by drugs, herbs and potions. I doubt this is true myself, he is a powerful magician in his own right, but like many powerful men, his allure is quite intrinsic to his nature. His influence was something more basic . . . don't misunderstand me, Nimah, I am not talking about sex; curiously, to my knowledge and that of my sources, Jahl and Regan have never slept together . . . no, he is wise enough to know that such a level of intimacy would destroy Regan's idealised view of him. There are other ways of gaining influence over people . . . some of them, extremely unpleasant . . .'

It was a trick he had. If she knew how often he played it, she would have been furious. Jahl could picture Regan's face, her heavy dark brows drawn together, her voluptuous spoilt mouth setting in that firm little line.

He chuckled slightly and continued walking through the frozen rooms towards her bedchamber. All around him the fortress of Soulis Mor was achingly silent, frost limed the walls and a faint white mist rolled across the stone floors. Jahl had 'stolen' the castle, suspended it in time. He walked past clansmen and servants alike, their bodies petrified as their time stood still. As he passed through the Great Hall where a few drunken revellers remained, he plucked a coloured ball away from a young man who was juggling to impress a girl, and threw it on the floor. When time reasserted itself, the youth would drop all the balls, his hands missing the beat, clutching at air where the ball should have been.

No one knew of Jahl's frequent escapades but rumours had begun in the city of a ghost that moved amongst them. People spoke of a passing sensation of cold or an unexpected wind moving their hair or clothes. Jahl always contrived to look sceptical if he heard such 'nonsense' but it quietly amused him. Climbing the stairs to Regan's rooms, he self-consciously preened himself, pushing his hair back from his face; it wasn't as if she would see him, she should be frozen also and would have been asleep by now. Jahl had chosen the moment with typical care. Pushing back the heavy door, he walked in, feeling the usual tense excitement.

She was not alone. Jahl could not contain his sense of shock and cursed aloud. Regan lay curled in the warm embrace of a handsome young man – her lover had apparently not been asleep at the moment of suspension, but lay watching her, a rapt expression on his features. Jahl moved closer to the shadows of the four-poster bed and stared at the young man, for a few moments, he didn't recognise him but then he realised who it was. He was Fraser, son of Regan's Chief Minister. Regan herself had described Fraser as 'brainless' but, obviously, that description bore little relevance to her love life. It was ill-advised of her to allow the youth into her bed. Jahl sat for a few minutes, his gaze also on Regan's face, unconsciously mirroring Fraser's expression. Then he reached down and touched her, running his fingers down the smooth curve of her cheek, to her neck, down past the slightly colder ridge of her collarbone. He stopped as his finger lightly brushed her breast, revelling in her vulnerability; Regan, his Thane, his Queen . . . just his.

Jahl's gaze returned to Fraser for a moment as a sudden thought occurred to him; his mouth twitched as a mischievous, lethal smile slid across his features. Then he cast about the room until he found what he was looking for; Regan's own eating knife was still on the table, the juices of her meal still dulling the gem-encrusted handle. Moving swiftly, Jahl grabbed the knife and plunged it into Fraser's neck without pause. Of course the youth could not die, could not even bleed, in his suspended state, but it would be an interesting death, truly instantaneous. And when Regan awoke, she would need help, his help.

Jahl bent down and kissed her cold lips. Soon, she would be his. It would have been a simple matter to take her by force, enslave her and control Soulis Mor by breaking her spirit, but for the moment, this game was far, far greater sport. His fingers toyed with the curl of the ribbon on her bodice, but then he flicked it away.

'Later, Lady,' he muttered. He turned and walked back to his rooms.

'Jahl. Jahl. Wake up. Please wake up.'

'Wha . . . ? I'm coming. Just a moment.' Jahl sat in his chair staring at the door, not moving. Taking a deliberately slow swallow of his drink, he stood up sighing quietly and ruffled his hair to make it appear he had been sleeping.

'Jahl . . .'

'Thane Regan? Is that you?' He walked silently over to the door and stood with his face pressed against the wood, listening to the soft panic of her breathing, the faint catch in her throat. Finally he pulled the door open and stood blinking in the light of the sconce outside. He bowed slightly, pulling his robe around him. 'Majesty,' he smiled smoothly. 'I am at your command, day or night.' There was no mistaking the innuendo but Regan simply stared at him, her eyes wild with fear.

'He's dead, Jahl. Fraser's dead.'

'Fraser?'

'Laird of Brodeen. Son of my First Minister.'

'But I don't understand . . .'

'In my bed,' she snapped. 'We are – were – lovers. He's in my bed, Jahl, with my knife through his throat.' She began to shake, reaction setting in. 'L – look,' she opened her cloak to show him the spattering of blood which stained her nightgown. Jahl did not react immediately, his eyes registering no sign of shock.

'We must act quickly.' He said. 'We must . . .' he paused, seeming to consider something, then he sighed. 'We must dispose of the body.'

Even in her troubled state, Regan noted the calm of his reaction. 'Aren't you going to ask me if I killed him?' she whispered.

'It is no concern of mine, Regan,' he held her gaze steadily as though seeking to calm her but the casual use he made of her name was not lost on either of them.

'I – I can't go back there, Jahl,' Regan sat down heavily in his chair and covered her eyes with trembling fingers.

'Regan. Regan, look at me.' He took her hand away from her face, slowly and gently. 'You do not have to go back to your rooms until I have dealt with the situation.' He crouched in front of her, still holding her hand and reached to push hair from her cheek where it was stuck with drying spatters of blood. She flinched involuntarily and although Jahl pretended not to notice, he felt a vague sensation somewhere between anger and sorrow. He ignored this, however, and smiled reassuringly, wondering why she couldn't see the truth in his eyes. 'Just wait here. I'll deal with it. Wasn't he due to leave for home soon anyway?'

She nodded dully, 'Tomorrow.'

He stood up to leave the room but then paused to look back at her dejected figure. It would ruin everything if she gathered her wits and raised an alarm . . . 'Highness?'

She raised her pale, bloodied face; when she spoke her voice was leaden. Was it possible, Jahl wondered, that he had been wrong and she had loved the unfortunate Fraser?

'What is it?'

'Look.' He reached his hands out towards her from where he stood in the doorway and as he uncurled his fingers, a bright mote of light appeared from nothingness and began to drift across the chamber towards her. As it reached the space just before her gaze, it stopped and began to grow and change into a shape, drawn in silver whiteness.

'Jahl,' she breathed. Slowly the light became a rose and she reached out as though to touch it, her expression one of wonderment like a delighted child. The light moved slightly to be just beyond her reach and began to change once more, turning and transforming in a way similar to the Sidhe. This time, the light became a tiny dragon, its minuscule reptilian wings beating the still air of the chamber.

Jahl watched for long moments as Regan's features relaxed, the signs of shock which had marked her moments before easing out of her brows and shoulders. And with that relaxation, the next stage of reaction, sleep; she rubbed her eyes.

'I had no idea you could conjure such things,' she murmured.

'Just a little trick I learned somewhere . . . it will keep you entertained until I return . . .' Jahl turned to go.

'Jahl. Can you do other magics?'

He smiled back at her, his expression and demeanour completely self-effacing. 'Alas, I have little talent. It took me a year to learn this one.'

'Oh.' Regan leaned back in the plush cushions of

the chair, fighting exhaustion. 'I don't know how to thank you, Jahl.'

He stepped outside into the stairwell of the fortress city which he had plucked from time once more with a slight motion of his fingers while they spoke. 'I'll think of something,' he muttered.

'Indeed he would. For that is how the seeds of obligation were sown. And it seemed the fates were with Jahl: Fraser was not missed for a long time – perhaps six months – because it was assumed by those in Soulis Mor he had departed from his family's province of Brodeen as planned, whilst those at home imagined he was detained at court . . .

'At first, Tristan stilled his dislike of Regan's companion as much as he could. He thought he was doing so for the right reasons and assumed Regan strong enough to make her own choices, but gradually, over the next couple of years, Jahl's influence could not go unnoticed. You see, the ironic thing was that, unlike most manipulators, Jahl did not strive to rise through Regan's weakness of character but rather by her strength. He recognised the strong spark of independence and stubbornness within her – qualities which can be admirable if applied wisely – and he directed her hand as law-giver to Soulis Mor, talked eloquently to her about politics, border treaties, trade, but most of all, the Sidhe. Only in regard to Regan's dealings with the Sidhe did Jahl exploit any weakness; he sensed Regan's fear . . . and he used it to bitter and mischievous ends . . .'

* * *

The monument had stood on the northern horizon for almost eight years now. It was beautiful still; the craftsman had consulted with *Seanachaidhs* and the Sidhe shamans on how to position the monolith and it caught the sun at midday, flaring bright shafts of sunlight from the silvered surface. In the end, still in the early days of her reign and with a lack of confidence which would never have happened now, Regan had relented, and the monument had been erected as Isbister had planned: it was the only landmark on the northern plains for miles . . .

. . . Except, Tristan had discovered that morning, around two miles further north from the monument, its shape undistinguishable from the highest towers of the city, was a huge crater in the ground. Tristan was out riding alone – something he was allowed to do, unlike his sister. Depending on his mood this fact, a tacit indicator of his perceived lesser status, either irritated him greatly or not at all. Today, an unseasonably warm autumn day just before Samhain, was a not-at-all day; Tristan knew his lack of an escort could be deemed a sign of little respect by the court, but then at least he had some privacy, time to think alone. He had been thinking, or rather, worrying about Regan and Jahl when he discovered the crater. His horse came to a sudden halt at the crater rim, jerking him to attention. He had been deep in thought, his gaze slightly unfocused, the gentle rhythm of the horse's walk and the warmth of the sun almost lulling him into sleep. Tristan guessed the history of the crater immediately, he had made it his business to learn about the battles in which his father and Sandro had played such a pivotal role – it was the crater caused by Corvus being released from the spell which bound him and landing here, amongst his assembled army of Corannyeid. Delighted to find such an important battleground, Tristan heeled his reluctant horse forward and started down the rim towards the crater floor.

The air was still and silent as he slowly picked his way downwards; sound seemed to be truncated by the rim of the crater, glancing across the top where there should have been earth. The sunlight also disdained to penetrate further than the first few feet and Tris was plunged into cold shadow. As he neared the bottom where a wild tangle of brush and trees had grown, he heard the first sound, the harsh rasping sound of a bird – not a raven – but a crow. The sound was answered by several others and soon, an indignant chorus rang out from the bushes towards the intruder.

Unlike Regan, Tristan was not afraid of birds, but something about the defensive cry of the crows against the otherwise silent backdrop was unnerving. His neck began to sweat and anxiety gripped his stomach. Calming himself, he guided his mount around the outside of the copse hoping the crows were not protecting any late clutches of eggs which might cause them to mob him. The copse was too dense to enter anyway and he moved slowly around the outside, peering in to see if there were any remains of a building; there was nothing as far as he could tell. Stilling his disappointment he was about to turn back, deciding that the sooner he left the crows behind him the better, when he thought he saw a movement in the copse, still black, moving in the same fragmented shadow-style of the crows, but larger . . .

Tristan dismounted his horse and crept into the copse, his nerves jangling, ready to run if the crows made any sudden attack. Just within the fringes of the scrub he could see something glinting on the baked earth – from this distance it looked like gold! Dropping to his hands and knees he scrabbled forward, cursing quietly as brambles and honeysuckle creepers snared his clothes. As soon as he was near enough he reached out and closed his fingers around his prize.

As he did so, the copse erupted into sound. The crows screamed and railed, black wings beating furiously amongst the trees which began to bend and bow with the movement. Tristan didn't wait to see if they were descending on him; without looking at the object clasped in his hand he ran back to his horse. The beast was snorting and beginning to panic as the crows were making such a din – Tris knew it would be useless to try and ride the horse back up the slope so he grabbed the reins and started to run – the horse however had other ideas and dug its heels in. Tris glanced back to the copse; the crows were coming, wheeling down towards them in their lazy liquid flight.

'C'mon, dammit!' he tugged at the reluctant horse's reins again and this time the beast sprang into motion. Tristan laboured up the slope, his short legs carrying him too slowly. The lead crows dipped down and grabbed at his hair, making him yell angrily and try to bat them away with his free hand. There was no real damage done but his head stung where he'd lost a chunk of hair. Coming into the sunlight at the top of the crater was a relief and as they crested the rim he glanced back; the crows had fallen behind, probably reluctant to leave their nest site, and it appeared as if they had been reclaimed by the shadow. As his breathing slowed down and returned to normal, Tristan gave a happy grin and opened his fist to look at his prize for the first time.

It was a bone; covered in gold and studded with what seemed to be precious gems, a gold chain ran through the hollow in the middle turning the strange item into a horizontal bar necklace but it was unmistakably a bone. Ivory white could be seen at one end where the thin layer of gold had been worn away or perhaps damaged by the crows. Who could have lost such a thing or perhaps left it there was a mystery but Tris decided what to do with the necklace almost immediately – he would give it to Regan.

They had been arguing about Jahl again the night before, Tristan urging his sister to question her confidant's motives more closely. Tris had heard rumours that worried him deeply concerning orders Regan had given for a lynx Sidhe settlement to be resettled further to the east. The lynx Sidhe were the affiliates of Soulis Mor and this move – supposedly for their benefit – would mean that the nearest Sidhe settlement was now over fifty miles away, effectively preventing their Elders from being present at any functions within the city . . . this didn't bother Regan who made little attempt to disguise her dislike of any Sidhe, but the common people of Soulis Mor would miss their Sidhe who they regarded with superstition and pride, like some lucky charm. Tristan was no statesman but had sense enough to know that Regan was courting disaster if she ignored the feelings of her people.

He was almost back at the city walls now, riding for the gates at the west end when he noted something he had apparently missed on his outwards ride. There were scrubby bushes dotted around the plain giving it a desert-like appearance and perhaps that was why the natural brown colouring of the eagle had failed to catch his eye. Amongst a low tangle of scrub was the corpse of an eagle Sidhe. Tristan rode closer to have a look, the bird had obviously been dead for a while, its form had a dry, deflated appearance. The reason for its death was obvious, a throwing spear was through its neck.

Tris noted the colour of the feathers tied around the creature's huge talons, it appeared he had been one of Druvien's warriors – who could have done such a thing, he wondered? He glanced at the spear but there was no clue as to the identity of the murderer. Making a mental note to send word to Druvien, he carried on into the city, the silent gnawing of true realisation eating at his gut which he swallowed down like so much bile.

'Did he give her the necklace, teacher?'

'Oh yes. Tristan is a master of denial. He cannot help himself, he sees goodness in everyone. But only a week later, he saw Jahl wearing the cursed thing. He was angry of course and challenged Regan as to why she had given his gift away. She gave a curious reply: "Because he said he needed it," she said. When Tristan pressed her to explain she laughed the matter off –

"He liked it so much Tris, he seemed hypnotised by it. I'm sorry to say, I didn't find it very charming at all, so I gave it to him . . ."

'And there the matter might have ended; Jahl's and Regan's oppression may have unfurled at a slower more considered pace but for the final piece of the puzzle – the evidence which Tristan could not ignore . . .'

It was going to snow soon, Tristan could feel it in his bones more keenly than most. He climbed the stairs to Regan's tower apartment slowly, like an old man. He didn't curse his wasted legs any more but there was no denying the familiar pang of bitterness which overtook him sometimes – as well as the occasional servant. They held back respectfully behind him until he ushered them past – then they did their funny bowing-walking thing which made him want to laugh despite himself.

As he reached the door to the antechamber of Regan's apartment, he stopped for breath and cast a glance around before he started doing any stretches. His maid, Grace, had taught him how to stretch out the aching tendons and muscles but it wasn't something he would do if anyone was watching; done by Grace of course, they looked like some elegant slow dance but not so on him. As he glanced towards the doorway, something which he first took to be a bundle of grey rags slumped at the base of the door, moved.

It was a young woman of around eighteen to twenty summers. She had unusual grey eyes and the features of the bear clan Sidhe.

'Hello,' he smiled and nodded. She scowled fiercely

in return. He tried again. 'What are you doing there? That's Thane Regan's apartments – housekeeping will move you . . .'

'They cannot,' she said. Tristan expected some kind of explanation but nothing was forthcoming.

'Well, why not?' He tried not to sound angry or anything, perhaps the girl didn't know who he was. She fixed him with a hard dignified stare which reminded him of his sister.

'It's ancient law,' she explained. 'I am fasting against the Thane – both Thanes actually,' she ended rather pointedly.

'Oh.' Tristan had never heard of such a thing. He walked over to the doorway and sat down beside the girl who looked somewhat surprised. 'So how does that work then?'

'Are you making fun of me?' The frown had become thunderous.

'No, no really . . .'

She narrowed her eyes coldly. 'I fast at the Thane's doorway until she hears my point or I die.'

'You d-die!'

'Yes.'

'But you're only young. What political point could be worth dying for?'

'Political? It's not political – your . . .' she glanced around as if afraid someone might be listening at the door and then lowered her voice. 'Your sister and her . . . advisor are murdering the Sidhe.'

'What! No, really . . . you must be misinformed.'

The girl stared at him coldly, something somewhere between scorn and pity in her gaze. 'Do you think I would be here if I had any doubt?' she said.

'No. But your information could be wrong.' Even as he spoke, an unbidden image of the murdered eagle Sidhe came into his mind.

'Many are missing,' she said. 'Disappeared. My brother has been gone for three moons.'

He sighed, unsure if he had any answers for her. 'Look . . .'

'Marila.'

'. . . Marila. I am also a Thane. I have heard your complaint and I will speak to my sister – I'm sure there must be a misunderstanding – you don't have to continue with your fast. How long have you been up here? I don't come up here to see Regan very often because of my legs and . . .'

'Sir, I can see you are a kind, considerate man, but . . . I do not wish to offend you but . . . I must speak to Thane Regan. She knows the truth of my complaint. I have been here for almost a week.'

'A week? But she must have passed you in that time!'

'Yes, Sir, she has. And I will wait until she acknowledges me.'

Tristan stood up. 'This is outrageous,' he blustered. 'I am going to speak to her now. Do not go away, Marila.'

'I have no intention, Sir.'

Tristan crashed open the door to Regan's room. 'What's going on, Regan?' he demanded. Regan, who was having her hair brushed by her maid jumped as the door banged back against the wall. 'Leave us,' she said quietly to the maid. 'What are you talking about, Tristan?'

'The Sidhe,' he frowned. 'What's going on with the Sidhe?'

She continued patting at her hair for a moment although there was something distracted in her movement. 'Well, I have banned them from the city if that's what you mean . . .'

'What? No . . . I . . .' Tristan was confused. 'Why would you do such a thing, Ree?'

'Because I wanted to,' she replied evenly. 'Tris, don't pretend you know what's going on in the city – you have no idea – the Sidhe have been too involved with the running of Soulis Mor for too long.' She waved her hand in a vague motion. 'I'll let them come back eventually,' she said. 'It's more of a gesture than anything.'

'Are you killing them, Regan?'

'What?' She appeared genuinely shocked. 'No . . . who said that? Was it that girl? The one outside?'

'You have spoken to her then?'

'No, but I imagine she has some grievance. I will speak to her, soon. There's no point in making it easy for her, is there? If she wants to make some stupid dramatic gesture, the least I can do is oblige . . .' She smiled, her wicked humour coming to the fore. 'I won't let her starve herself to death, I promise.'

And she didn't.

'Tristan, Tristan, wake up.' Grace was shaking him urgently. He reached out to pull her towards him. 'No, no, stop it. There's something I have to tell you . . .' The urgent tone of her voice cut through his befuddled brain – Tris had never been a morning person.

'What's wrong?' He sat up rubbing his eyes.

'It's Regan, she's done something awful.' Grace looked upset, in fact, she had been crying. 'I went down to the kitchens to get your breakfast tray and one of the kitchen boys told me . . . Regan has had people hanged for treason.'

'No!'

Grace nodded miserably, 'I'm not sure how many, possibly ten . . .'

Tristan was already up and pulling his clothes on, his normally mild expression was dark and grim. 'When?' he demanded.

'At dawn. Over in the eastern market square.'

'Sidhe or Fine?' He was pulling his boots on now.

'I don't know.'

'Stay here, Grace. There may be some trouble . . .' he gripped her shoulders and looked into her frightened face.

'No, wait, Tristan. Listen to me. You can't deal with this alone. You must get help. Take some warriors with you at least . . .' He appeared to be ignoring her, his face set into grim lines. 'Please Tristan, listen, listen to me,' she begged.

'I hear you, Grace,' he nodded.

'Just promise you won't do anything rash.' She stood up from where she sat on the side of the bed. Grace was not a tall girl but she still had to look down at Tristan – normally this didn't bother him, it was just a fact of life – but this morning, it was like a slap in the face. He was powerless in the city; Regan had successfully isolated him, there was really little he could practically do. He was crippled and powerless.

'This can't go on, Grace,' he muttered.

'I know.'

It was raining hard and there were ten corpses in the market square. A pall of almost tangible sorrow and disbelief tainted the air – the marketplace was deserted as people had fled either the weather or the sight of men and women being murdered. Tristan was soaked to the skin, his clothes stuck to his freezing flesh and he clenched his jaw to stop his teeth from chattering, but he rode his horse at a walk along the gallows making himself look directly at the blue engorged faces of Regan's and Jahl's first public victims. The eastern marketplace was the furthest away Regan could have had the gallows built without attracting too much attention in the central bailey – but she couldn't possibly have hoped to keep the executions a secret. They were mostly Fine but, at the end of the row, three young Sidhe. An exclamation of shock and sorrow escaped him as he recognised Marila at the very end, her beautiful grey eyes mercifully covered by the veil of her long hair. *'Sir, I can see you are a kind, considerate man,'* she had said. Tristan almost laughed aloud now at the bitter irony of her remark. What she had really meant was – *'You are useless.'* And she had been right . . .

A cold wind drove the rain harder through the empty square making a sound like a hissing sigh and still Tristan sat on his horse staring at the corpses, his tears unnoticeable and irrelevant. Eventually, he took out his dagger and, riding close to Marila's body, he cut her down. It was hard work, his hands were numbing with the cold, the knife and the rope were slippery, but eventually the body crumpled to the ground landing gracelessly in the mud. Tristan didn't stop but moved onto the next corpse, a young Sidhe warrior, and then, an old man. By the time he reached the fourth, he was insensible with cold, shock and anger. Hearing a sound behind him, he turned around and saw a small group of people had entered the square to watch the strange behaviour of their useless Thane.

'H-help me,' he stammered through his tears. For long moments no one moved; they stared at him curiously as if he was speaking some strange language. 'Help me,' he repeated. Still no one moved. They huddled together, their eyes round with shock and sorrow.

'You heard the Thane, help him.' Grace's sharp tone broke the strange paralysis of the scene. She had ridden into the marketplace with three warriors behind her and they moved to assist Tristan. As they cut the victims down, the onlookers drifted towards the gallows and clustered in sorrowful groups around the released corpses. It had not occurred to Tristan that they might be relatives of the deceased. A woman's low sobbing carried across the market square. Tristan slumped forward across the pommel of his saddle, his mind almost blank. He felt someone wrap a blanket around his shoulders but he shrugged it away – why should he be comforted? he thought.

'C'mon, Tristan,' he heard Grace's voice and someone began to lead his horse from the square. He jerked upright.

'No, wait,' he turned back, twisting in his saddle to

see the grieving people. 'I . . . I'm . . .'

'Let's go, Sir.' It was a man's voice this time and Tris turned back to look at the face of the warrior who was trying to direct him. 'I think we should go,' the man said firmly. Tristan wearily nodded assent and allowed himself to be led from the square.

He said nothing to Regan that day. It was not unusual for them not to see one another over the course of the day and Tristan could not bring himself to seek her out. By late afternoon when the initial shock had worn off he had forced himself to face some hard truths about his sister. He still chose to believe that things would have been different without Jahl's influence but there was no denying the fact that Regan was unfit to rule. It wasn't as if she was the first Thane in history to execute prisoners but, from the information he managed to gather, these people had been killed for merely complaining about Regan in public or remembering Isbister fondly. None of them had any importance within the court – they were just ordinary people. And Tristan was forced to admit that Regan had killed four Sidhe that he now knew of – the eagle Sidhe and the hanged victims – and Marila had probably been right about the rest of it.

Something else had been brought home to him that morning, something he had seen in the eyes of the victims' families: he was weak in every sense. His people didn't know him or he them. He had no existing allies in Soulis Mor and, while he had always thought he had people's affection, that was not the same thing as their respect. In short, he needed help.

At dusk a rider left the city heading for Ruannoch Were, Thane Ulla's city, home to Druvien and his warriors and the Sidhe Princes Tecumseh and Tenskwa. The rider was carrying a letter; a plea for help from Tristan to both the Sidhe and Fine rulers – Ulla would relay word further south to Durghanti and Karmala Sev if she agreed to help. Regan was to be arrested on the authority of the Thanes and the Council of Tema and Jahl was to be considered dangerous and killed if necessary . . .

It took almost a week for his answer to come from Thane Ulla and during that time Tristan lay low, hardly leaving his quarters. Regan sent a servant to enquire after his health and he told her he was suffering from the chills and breathing problems which often affected him in the late autumn. She must have heard of what had happened at the gallows but she seemed as reluctant as he to effect their inevitable confrontation and she stayed away.

'And so, Nimah, we have almost arrived at now. See, the light of dawn is creeping across the valley floor. Tomorrow has become today and Tristan will need my help all too soon. I must go . . .'

'But teacher, I don't understand. If they are coming to arrest Regan, why is Tristan running away? Why is he being pursued?'

'You must keep watching little one . . . keep watching . . . oh, perhaps you should be aware of something the waters have not shown us. Tristan has stolen back the necklace.'

'But why? It's just a necklace isn't it?'

'That is exactly what Tristan thinks, Nimah. And as such, it was a rather petty act brought about by anger and jealousy – but we must forgive poor Tristan, he is struggling to cope. When the answer came from Thane Ulla, the plan was set . . . And I must go and play my part. Take care, little one. You can continue to scry in the house if you wish – keep watching for me and wish us all the luck we will need. I promise I will return when I can . . .'

CHAPTER FOUR

'Regan, wake up.'

Regan awoke with a start – she had been dreaming of the feathers again, the black feathers and . . . She blinked, 'Jahl? What are you doing here? What's going . . .'

'There's no time to explain.' He threw a dress and riding cloak onto her bed. His expression was one of quiet fury and he paced back and forth impatiently across the space at the bottom of her bed. 'Get dressed.'

'What?' Regan was shocked at his lapse in manners; usually such a self-contained person, he seemed on the verge of an explosion of anger. 'No. Not till you tell me what's going on.'

He stopped and frowned at her as if she was a stupid or obstinate child. 'All right,' he said slowly. 'People are coming to kill you. Will that do?'

'What? No, there must be some mistake.'

'There's no mistake. Look, just put your clothes on. We've got to go.'

'Go? Go where?' She clambered out of bed and began to put the dress on, the urgency in his voice beginning to cut through the last vestiges of her sleep. 'I'm not running away from the city if that's what you mean. This is *my* city . . .'

'Yours and your brother's,' he spat the words out like so many curses.

'Tris – what's Tris got to do with this?' A sudden chill of alarm spread through the pit of Regan's stomach. 'Is he all right?'

'Oh yes, he's fine, I'm sure,' Jahl sneered, 'given that he's betrayed you to the other Thanes. A delegation is riding towards Soulis Mor now to depose you.'

'Tris did that?' she was appalled. 'No, he wouldn't . . . I haven't done anything. Is he upset about the hangings?'

'Can we discuss this on the way please?' Jahl put his arm around her waist the instant she had wrapped the cloak around herself and began to steer her towards the door.

'But where are we going?' she insisted.

Jahl picked up a lantern he had placed on the shelf by the door when he had slipped into her bedchamber. 'We cannot allow them to reach the city, Regan. And the safest place for you until this is over is with me.' He was about to reach for the door but he stopped suddenly and turned back to face her. 'You do trust me, don't you?' he frowned.

'Of course.'

'Good. Then we can . . . talk to Tristan later.'

They rode across the plains towards Or Coille at a full gallop. It was pitch dark. Regan's world became a dizzying frenzy of cold and the steam which both she and her mount exhaled into the night air. She sat forward and low, level with her horse's neck; the exhilaration of the chase coursing through her, her heart pounding, aware her horse might collapse beneath her, but she could only think: 'Tristan has betrayed me . . . Tristan has betrayed me . . .' She was aware of Jahl beside her, riding his own tall white mare and she dimly wondered why they had brought no escort.

As they approached the fringes of Or Coille she reined her horse back, taking her lead from Jahl. He had slowed and seemed to be choosing a more deliberate route, he pointed towards a low escarpment ahead of them which was less thickly populated by trees. 'We can wait there,' he said. 'We should be able to see them coming.'

'But Jahl, how many will there be? How can we stop them from reaching the city?' Either he didn't hear or he chose to ignore her. He rode ahead in silence.

They didn't have long to wait.

'Look,' Regan breathed. A party of around fifteen people were riding fast down the forest track which dipped in towards the escarpment. She recognised only a few of the riders; Druvien, four other eagle Sidhes, Eion, Lady Ulla's delegate – he was a good age now, around the same as her father she thought. Also, rather worryingly, two Lairds who she last saw at the coronation, from Thane Lachlan's southern domains. This conspiracy to oust her had carried far . . . 'Jahl, what are we going to do?' she whispered.

Again, he did not answer her directly. 'Stay here,' he replied. 'Whatever happens you must stand behind me. Do you understand?'

'Yes, but . . .'

'Regan.'

'Yes.'

* * *

Jahl walked out into the road ahead of the riders, the gap between them closing fast. Regan could not see clearly in the grainy night darkness but after a few moments a sudden white light flared up illuminating the scene, then another. The riders reined in fast, their horses whinnying in fright. Jahl stepped from between the two lights to stand before the party. All the time, up until the next few seconds, Regan seriously thought Jahl would simply talk to them. Stupid. So stupid . . .

'Gentlemen,' he said.

'That's him!' Druvien shouted, 'That's him – Jahl!' Because of the bright flaring lights he was struggling to control his horse and he suffered a delay in drawing his sword. The other riders behaved in the same manner, brandishing weapons and preparing to charge on Jahl with little in the way of explanation.

Jahl clicked his fingers.

They came from within the white light. That was the only explanation Regan's confused brain would allow. Demons. Creatures. Black looming shapes. They moved outwards from the lights towards the riders and they were as tall as the mounted men. The riders cursed in fear and fury at the supernatural beasts and began to hack panic-stricken with their swords. Their weapons were plucked uselessly from their grips and there was the cold clatter of metal falling to the ground.

Druvien was the first to die. He was pulled from his horse and then the demon twisted and pulled him apart, massive talons gripping around his waist and snapping his spine like a sapling. Druvien continued to scream in agony until the demon-beast dropped his broken body to the ground and trampled him in its haste to reach out for another victim. The creatures were mindless killers. The other riders were also screaming now, the sounds and curses that filled the air were horrible and horrifying.

She could not believe it. Why didn't he warn her? But then, what would she have said? Regan watched in hysterical disbelief as the demon-beasts literally tore the party to shreds, a cry of revulsion stuck in her throat. She saw Eion, the only man still on his horse, desperately hacking around himself as he was beset on either side – fleetingly she remembered his kindness to herself and Tristan.

'No!' she screamed and, before she had given it conscious thought, she charged from her hiding place drawing the short-sword she was wearing and raced behind the creature to Eion's left, impaling it before it even sensed she was there.

'Regan?' Eion was stunned and confused but had no time to assess the situation before the other beast was upon him, pulling at his terrified mount to try and unseat the rider.

'Regan!' Jahl yelled in fury but he could not reach her without passing through the creatures.

She was as defenceless as the others although she still gripped her blade determinedly and slashed out at their attackers. They were like shadows made flesh, except for their eyes which glinted viciously in the light and, although her sword appeared to cause them pain, it passed through their shadow-flesh without inflicting actual damage. She was so preoccupied by the beast in front of her that she didn't see another to her left which had finished slaying one of the Sidhe. It grabbed her by the throat lifting her high in the air – she could feel her lungs burning with exertion but she screamed again. 'Flee, Eion! Get out of here . . .'

For a moment there was blackness and confusion. The beast had dropped her with a strange abruptness. She realised they were gone – all of the demon-beasts were gone. She sat up and stared around her. The delegation had been murdered. Brutally slain by those abominations. Hot blood and entrails were everywhere. *Food for crows,* she thought. At least there was no sign of Eion. Pulling her knees up to her chin she began to cry.

But she was not to be allowed such luxury. Someone grabbed her unceremoniously by the hair and yanked her to her feet.

'You stupid woman!' It was Jahl and he was furious. 'You stupid, stupid . . .'

She would not stand for it. '*Me* stupid?' she screamed into his face uncaring of her tears and sweat. 'What in Cerne's hell was *that*? You murdered them . . . you bastard – *you bastard*!' She ran the few steps towards where he had backed off and shoved him hard in the chest. Flung backwards, Jahl almost lost his balance – his face contorted with rage.

'What did you think I was going to do? *Talk to them*? They were coming to kill you . . . They were coming to kill you, Regan . . .' his breathing slowed slightly and he moved towards her. 'I couldn't let that happen,' he lowered his voice as if confiding in her. 'I couldn't let them kill you, Ree.'

She remained inconsolable. 'Don't you call me that – don't you *ever* call me that,' she screamed. 'No, stay away from me. Don't you touch me . . .' She began to walk from the clearing with no true idea of her intention. Then she stopped. 'Look at them, Jahl. Look at what you did to them . . .' Her voice cracked with emotion and a deep sob welled up from within her chest. She covered her mouth as if seeking to hold the emotion inside. Jahl walked slowly and cautiously towards her, his expression one of concern now he had calmed himself. He stopped a few feet away – out of reach of her sword – and dropped to his knees on the edges of the blood-soaked ground.

For long moments there was no sound from either of them as if Regan's shock exerted some physical force. Then, there was the low hiss of a blade being drawn. Jahl did not have time to react, when Regan turned she held a short-sword in her right hand and a leather scabbard in her left – she had taken the weapon from a corpse. Flinging the scabbard aside, she strode over to Jahl and pointed the tip to his throat, her hand completely steady despite her fright. 'Give me one good reason not to kill you, Jahl,' she snarled.

'Lady,' he said. 'I am your servant. I did what I had to do to protect you. I am sorry.' His voice was quiet but steady. 'And I'm sorry I lost my temper . . .' Regan pushed the blade, a tiny motion, which drew a dark blossom of blood at Jahl's throat.

'It's clear to me now that you have always had your own plans, Jahl. I am just a way to power for you am

I not? Answer carefully!' she snapped without waiting for his answer.

'It is true I am ambitious, Thane Regan, but never at your expense.' The pressure of the blade did not ease and despite the chill of the night air, Jahl was sweating profusely – a glistening bead of sweat leached down his cheek from his forehead and Regan thought distantly that it was the nearest thing to a tear her confidant might ever shed.

'When we get back to Soulis Mor, pack your things and get out. If I see you after today I will have you executed.' She dropped the tip of the blade and then flung the weapon aside in a gesture that was a mixture of exhaustion and self-disgust. 'You have taught me well how easy that is to arrange.' She stalked off without further comment to find the nearest horse which had not panicked and stayed near the clearing. Jahl stood up slowly, his expression a bleak mask. Regan rode over leading a horse and dropped the reins before him. She didn't wait for him to mount but turned away to begin the ride back to the city. As an afterthought she stopped and turned back. 'And Jahl . . .' she said.

'Yes?'

'If anything has happened to my brother, I'll kill you myself.'

Tristan was still awake at three bells. He stared at the necklace; there was definitely something strange about it. Twice now as he had glanced towards it on his bedside table, he imagined he had seen a green tendril of light wrapped around it like some errant vine – but, once he blinked, the light was gone. It wasn't the reason he couldn't sleep though. Tomorrow, the riders would be here from Ruannoch Were and, with such support, he would confront Regan and perhaps put a stop to her obsessive rule. He sighed heavily, his heart was sore with worry but he knew there had been no other recourse open to him but to involve the other Thanes . . .

The door to his bedchamber burst open. A man stood there gasping for breath. Tristan blinked, the light from the hallway was behind the figure and at first he couldn't make out the features of the man's face.

'Tristan?' the stranger gasped.

'Eion?'

'You must escape, Tristan.' Eion gasped. 'We were ambushed . . . Jahl takes no prisoners.'

'What about Ree?'

'She's fine. Alive. I don't know what to think – but Tristan, Jahl is deadly. Go. Now . . . I have friends in the city and can hide for a while. I will get back to Ruannoch Were and warn the Southern Clans.'

Tristan lost no time. Within the hour he was riding east towards the furthest edge of Or Coille. He was completely alone and no one in Soulis Mor knew he had gone. Not even Grace – although it grieved him, he couldn't endanger her by saying farewell. After the initial flight across the open plain he slowed his horse to a walk thinking there would be no pursuit. However, after another hour, as the first tinges of the dawn lit the eastern skies, he heard an echoing call in the distance which sent a shiver down his spine. Jahl had returned to Soulis Mor and released his hounds.

* * *

'*We work in the dark – we do what we can – we give what we have. Our doubt is our passion and our passion is our task. The rest is the madness of art.*' Henry James.

Beatrice stared at the quotation in the little inspirational book, unable to say initially what it was about it that spoke to her. Quite unseasonably, it felt like spring in the garden and Beatrice sat underneath the twisted ivy of the arbour trying to ignore the touches of winter cold and the traffic sounds which constantly gave the lie to her idyll. Perhaps it was the part about doubt being a passion, the quotation could have been written especially for forensic scientists. The purest form of doubt was something which scientists acknowledged as a constant companion and friend; but recently, that friend had turned on Beatrice and become a viper in the nest.

She had been thinking, as she often did at this time of year, about the death of her friends. Two years earlier, in a burned out basement she had tried to convince herself that they were gone. She had been so sure, especially after speaking to the fire investigators who had pointed out that the fire in the centre of the room had actually been hotter, more intense than that used in a crematorium. So that was what Bea had written into her report, just the facts because she was good at her job; the best even. But then, as her grief for Sandro and Duncan had taken hold, she had returned, in her mind, to the scene in the basement many times. She had examined the photographs again and again, staring at the scorched black outlines on the floor, looking for anything which might suggest they had actually been there. There were not even traces of the grey, slightly greasy ash produced by a burnt corpse; not one bone had survived the conflagration. Then, doubt, the unscientific sly version, assailed her. What if – and she hardly dared think this, even to herself – what if Sandro and Duncan had escaped the fire? Where the hell were they? Why didn't they come forward? She sighed and idly flicked through the pages of the book. From inside the house, loud opera music was playing, some depressing aria. Since she broke off her engagement with Miles as she had slumped further and further into a depression which he could not understand, she had tried her hardest to hang onto her love of opera, but if she was honest with herself, that love had exited her life at the same time as the little baritone. Now, all the idiosyncrasies of the form irritated and depressed her; large, huge bosomed women pretending to be dying of consumption, the nonrecognition of the actors dressing up as their own servants. It was all so false, and whereas once she had found that falsehood acceptable, even endearing, now she could not turn a willing blind eye. It was part of the doubt in some subtle way.

There was something else. Something which fed the doubt. As she walked across her cluttered living room to change the CD for a more upbeat tune, her eyes strayed almost reluctantly to a drawer in her dresser; it was in there. A clue, she supposed, but one which opened possibly the biggest, most unbelievable can of worms ever. Switching off the music, she approached the dresser and opened the drawer with almost reverential quietness. Inside was a small wooden jewellery box which she took out and placed on her dining table. She held her breath as she opened it, as she did each time. A dull green glow was emanating from inside the box and the cedar lining was slightly warmed by the glow, releasing a woody smell. Gingerly, she removed a small plastic bag, a sample bag from her laboratory, and held it up to the light of the window. Inside, were three long strands of something which was very much like coarse hair. Except, Bea knew that there was no hair like it from any animal or human being in the world. She should know; she had checked every possible resource. And, when the hair-like strands were removed from the bag and placed under a microscope, they vanished slowly in a discharge of green light.

Originally, there had been around twenty strands, removed from a murder scene in which Duncan Talisker had been implicated. It seemed Duncan was the link and the reason for the mental itch which Bea just could not scratch. He and Sandro had disappeared all right, disappeared, not died. And what Bea held in her hand was the evidence of that. Because Beatrice believed they had left behind evidence which was not from this world but was somehow, magical.

Shit, she thought to herself grimly, *I've thought the word now. It's official, I'm losing my marbles. I need a drink.*

In the early evening, the traffic noise from the High Street was unbearable as commuters hurried home.

Inside the cramped meeting house of the Children of the Deluge, in Upper Bow Street, Nathan paced back and forward staring down at a crumpled sheet of paper covered in his spidery handwriting. Occasionally, he checked the time on the large fob watch he carried and then went back to pacing and reading his notes once more. Absently, he waved a hand in the air as though he was rehearsing the lines of a play, then he sighed and ran his hand through his hair in a habitual nervous motion.

'What are you doing, Nathan?' A blast of fresh air from the courtyard outside announced Esther's arrival and she stood in the doorway looking breathless and fragile in that way of hers which Nathan so secretly cherished. She wore the drab, tattered grey dress which the women of the Children wore but this only seemed to accentuate the taut underlying curves of her young body. He felt his mouth go dry as soon as he looked at her; he was always slightly nervous when speaking to Esther, but today, if he wasn't careful, she would condemn him as would all the other Children. He forced a smile – not just a normal casual smile, or even a very happy smile – a radiant smile; one which could, in the context of their meeting be described as rapturous. Nathan had been practising both the smile and his subsequent manner in his mind and in front of the yellow tainted mirror in Daniel's room for the last day or so.

'Esther,' he walked forward, still smiling the smile and took her hands in his, 'Esther, I have something wonderful to tell. Truly wonderful. But I must wait until you are all here. It wouldn't be fair to tell you alone, much as I'd like to.'

Esther's brown gaze met his and, for a fleeting second, she seemed uncertain. 'Are you all right, Nathan? You seem . . . different.'

'Really?' he whispered the word, gazing into her face. 'I'm fine. Really. Better than fine. Look, sit here at the front.' He pulled her into the meeting room where he had carefully laid out the old wooden chairs in a semicircle facing the unadorned box of the pulpit. In his state of nerves, Nathan was reminded of a giant twiggy nest in which he would become either a glorious, phoenix-like bird, or a cuckoo.

'Where's Daniel?' Esther frowned.

'D-Daniel?' It was the first time anyone had asked him directly and Nathan steeled himself. 'He won't be coming. My news . . .' he busied himself by moving one of the chairs slightly inwards. '. . . my news is about Daniel.'

'Oh, do you know where he is? It's just that no one has seen him for a couple of days.' She looked distracted and her obvious concern irked Nathan. He patted her lightly on the shoulder.

'No one need worry about Daniel,' he tried the smile again but found it to be unconvincing, even to himself.

As the remaining thirty-five Children of the Deluge arrived, it was raining outside, and a faint, musty smell emanated from their damp clothes as they chatted amiably amongst themselves. Nathan was relieved that there was no obvious air of tension, they were assuming this was a normal prayer meeting. Finally, when all were gathered, the last arrivals closed the doors and the cold oak-brown stillness of the old room asserted itself. Nathan stood up in the pulpit, his heart racing.

'Children . . .' he began.

'Where's Daniel?' Someone immediately called out. Nathan quailed inwardly but simply smiled and held up his hand.

'I have great news, about Daniel . . .'

'Where is he?' someone else called. 'He's all right, isn't he? Only I haven't seen him since the weekend . . .' A murmur began as people began comparing notes as to when they had last seen their leader. Nathan felt his command of the situation slipping away before he even began.

'Please listen . . .' he called out, biting down panic and anger.

'Listen. Listen all of you.' Esther's clear honeyed voice rang out. 'Nathan has something important to say. About Daniel.' Gradually, the voices subsided after a few 'shhhhs' and all eyes were fixed again on Nathan who smiled nervously at Esther.

'Thank-you Sister,' he nodded. 'I have come to bear witness to the most exciting event in our lives. We, the Children, must now prepare for the End of Days. I know this because Daniel told me . . .' he paused, and cast his gaze around his audience. '. . . moments before he was Raptured.'

There was a stunned silence for long moments and then complete chaos broke out. Nathan watched and waited. He knew once all exclamations of wonder were over, hard questions would be asked. The Children of the Deluge believed in The Rapture as did many other Christian groups; that only those who had dedicated their lives to Christ would be Raptured at the time of the Tribulation.

The Rapture entailed one's physical being simply vanishing, and the spirit of the person ascending through the sky to meet with God. It didn't matter where you were when The Rapture happened; driving a car, at the supermarket, flying a plane, you would simply vanish. The resultant chaos of thousands of people vanishing was something much discussed by those who believed. Nathan believed none of this, but, as he saw it, the essential power of The Rapture was that those who believed tried hard to recruit others to their view, because even their loved ones would not be spared unless they too dedicated their lives to Christ. However, at this moment in time, his concern was that it was supposed to happen to everyone at once and he knew the questions would be coming . . .

'That's not p-possible,' someone stood up at the back of the gathering. It was Gordon, known as LearnToFly – some of the Children chose such names when accepted into the group – he was one of Daniel's most ardent admirers. A tall gangly youth, LearnToFly blinked rapidly behind bottle-glass thick spectacles when agitated, as he was now. 'We all go t-together, at the same t-time. No one has ever said . . .'

'LearnToFly,' Nathan smiled encouragingly towards his prey. He knew the youth disliked him because he had spent so much time with Daniel and, he also knew, to underestimate LearnToFly would be folly. Beneath the clumsy stammering exterior lurked a mind as sharp as a blade. 'I know. That's exactly what I thought.

In fact, when Daniel told me – he knew it was coming – I didn't believe him either. But then, I saw it. I was there.' He put his hands before his eyes as though in danger of being overwhelmed with emotion. 'God called to Daniel and Daniel went willingly as Elijah did. Taken up in a golden light. It – it was beautiful.' He paused, and tears welled up in his eyes. 'We all know, don't we, that Daniel was special? Beloved.' Some of the Children began to nod agreement, it was true after all; Daniel had been exceptional. They could see why God might choose to favour him in this way.

'But—' LearnToFly began to object but was shouted down.

'Let Nathan speak . . .'

'He must bear witness . . .'

'Let him speak . . .'

Nathan fought to control a smile of satisfaction which threatened to sneak across his face. They were all so . . . malleable.

'Did he say anything, Nathan? Did he leave us a message?' It was Esther's voice from the front of the crowd. He looked down to where she sat; she was staring up at him, her brown eyes sparkling with fervour, her lips slightly parted. For a moment he was entranced, suffused with his power, and he knew in that moment that Esther would be his.

'Well, yes . . .'

'Tell us, Nathan,' someone called out.

'He said he loves you all and . . .'

'What?'

'I – I . . . you may think I am unworthy . . .' he put

his hands before his eyes again, counting the seconds for sheer dramatic pause.

'What did he say?'

'He said that I must help to lead you all until the End of Days. I must join the Elders and change my name in order to recognise the new time we are living through. I will be called Knox, because I am descended from the great John Knox and I must preach and carry the Word forward as he did . . . until the time of Revelations, which will be soon.'

LearnToFly objected once more. 'But Nathan, you have only b-been with us for a year. Surely there m-must be stronger c-candidates. There must b-be only four Elders.'

Nathan smiled beneficently, 'Does time make us more worthy then, LearnToFly? Daniel knew my strength, should we question his wisdom when he was chosen by God in such a way?'

'Nathan . . . Knox is right,' Joshua, InGodsGrace, one of the Elders in question, stood up. At the age of thirty-two he was actually one of the older members of the Children and his intellect and strong grasp of issues when in debate had earned him great respect. 'If Daniel is gone from us we must continue as he wished. Knox must be counted as an Elder.'

'But how d-do we know?' LearnToFly almost wailed. 'Why d-didn't he tell us?' His voice was drowned out in the excited hubbub as the Children marvelled at the events. Nathan/Knox let them continue for several minutes, his expression a careful, guiless mask; he allowed himself a small smile towards Esther who was gazing up at him in unconcealed amazement. Then, he held up his hands – and to his delight – the Children stopped talking.

'Children. God's Chosen. We must pray for guidance on this. God . . . and Daniel will hear us.' Knox bowed his head, and thirty-six followers bowed theirs also, in a sea of brown and blonde submission. 'Let us pray.'

As most of the Children filed out of the meeting hall, Knox pretended to busy himself gathering together prayer sheets and moving chairs. From under lowered lashes he glanced over to where LearnToFly was discussing something with a few friends.

'LearnToFly,' he called over, 'Can I have a word with you?' LearnToFly came over, scowling slightly. His slightly hunched appearance did nothing to lessen the impression of a large, ugly bird such as a vulture. The newly-named Knox smiled brightly. 'I need your help LearnToFly. You're right, I haven't been in the Children as long as some and I don't want to do anything unintentionally that might go against the basic doctrine of our beliefs. Perhaps you'd be so kind as to become my advisor?' He leaned in conspiratorially, 'I especially don't wish to offend the Sisters. I know their role is so important.'

LearnToFly seemed uncertain for a moment and fixed Knox with an appraising glance, then he nodded sombrely. 'All right then, N-Nath . . . I mean, Knox. I think that's a good idea . . . v-very insightful of you t-to think of it.'

Knox nodded earnestly. 'God loves our humility does he not, LearnToFly? I'll have to attend the Elders meeting in a couple of days – once I've had the chance to pray and meditate – to talk about the future of the Children – our responsibility as we go into the time of Revelations. Perhaps you could meet with me in The Ark before the meeting so we can discuss my ideas privately before I present them.'

'Oh yes,' LearnToFly positively glowed with delight and self-satisfaction, 'I'm sure that would be most helpful. You know I don't live at The Ark, don't you? But I'll come specially . . .'

'LearnToFly, I think you should consider moving in. After all, you wouldn't want to miss anything at this time would you? When The Rapture happens, it will be a double blessing to be amongst friends and fellow worshippers.'

Behind the thick glass of his lenses, LearnToFly's grey eyes looked grave. 'Yes, I'm sure you're right, but . . . there's Mother, and—'

'Just think about it then.' Knox patted him on the shoulder before turning away towards Esther.

'Yeah, yeah, I will.' LearnToFly nodded and smiled warmly for the first time towards his supposed competitor. Knox watched him back away, almost tripping over a chair as he did so. He waved absently. 'I'll call you. We'll set it up . . .'

'That was so nice of you, Nathan,' Esther stood beside him smiling, partly at LearnToFly's clumsiness but also directly at Knox. She was standing so near, Knox could smell the warm apple scent of her hair. He lowered his lashes and smiled back, connecting their gazes in a warm fusion.

'Knox,' he corrected gently.

'Sorry, Knox,' she flushed a delicious pink above the severity of her grey dress.

''S'all right,' he murmured. 'And I wasn't being nice. LearnToFly, I'm sure, will prove most useful.' It was one of the few things his bastard of a father had taught him: '*Keep your friends close, but your enemies closer.*'

That night, cosseted in the warmth of Daniel's old room, Knox dreamt of his friend.

'Nathan, Nathan? Where are you?' Daniel walks towards him from a shifting background of gold and green. He's wearing his grey robes which he wore when leading the prayers of the Children but his face is disfigured and bloody, one blue eye out of its socket, resting obscenely on the ridge of his cheekbone. Daniel does not seem in pain however, he's smiling his beneficent smile.

'I'm here, Daniel.' Knox hears his own voice drifting across the space between them and distantly wonders if he is speaking aloud into the emptiness of the room. 'I'm here . . . but you shouldn't call me that now. I've chosen another name . . .'

Daniel stops walking, apparently only a few feet away. 'I know – Knox. After John Knox I presume. He was a great, learned man. I can't imagine you will honour his memory particularly well.' He pauses and seems to become aware of his injury for the first time. Reaching up to his face with questing fingers, he grasps the eyeball and puts it back into the empty socket – Knox feels his stomach turn over – as he does so, all the other marks of the assault which killed Daniel disappear until he appears as he did in life: beautiful.

'Is that why you killed me, Knox?'

'Huh?' The question catches Knox off guard. It seems Daniel can read his thoughts even as they form.

'Because you desired me? Do you always destroy what you admire?' Behind Daniel, the colours of the background ripple as though a wind has blown across the colours; they darken, intensify. Is this because Daniel is angry?

'Desire . . . ? No, don't be ridicu—'

Daniel's voice cuts across his own, louder, stronger. 'Why then? Why did you do it, Knox?' The wind which is moving across the space behind Daniel suddenly changes direction and Knox is assaulted by an icy blast which chills the blood in his veins. Rather than intimidate him however, the wind only steels his resolve. He raises his face to meet Daniel's accusation, is sure that he can feel crystals of ice forming on his cheeks, beneath his eyes like unrepentant, unshed tears.

'Look, I just lost it. I didn't mean to kill you . . . I never believed it all, but it was good here, food, warm bed . . . the people are okay really as well – a bit sanctimonious at times but . . .' he shrugs. 'They all loved you though, you smug bastard. All of them, Esther . . . even me . . .'

The wind stops. Daniel looks troubled. He sits down and from behind him, the homogenous mass of the colours moves to catch him.

Knox feels warmer and the ice begins to slough off his face as though he really is crying. He wipes the water away hastily, aware of his fingers – of his physical, dreaming body – touching his face. He doesn't want Daniel to think he's sorry, that he wants him back. 'It was all just an ego trip to you anyway,' he begins angrily.

'That's not true!' Daniel looks shocked. He shifts slightly in his strange chair. 'But Knox, look at all the good things we achieved . . .'

'It's a lie!' he blazes. 'How can you seriously believe all of us are going to just vanish as you say? And you didn't have to pretend to be some kind of Messiah to achieve the good things . . .'

'And you actually don't believe but your motives are better are they?' There is a short silence as Knox considers this. 'Nathan . . . Knox. You are an Elder now. A position of power within the Children.' Daniel almost laughs at the irony of it but then looks serious once more. 'What will you do next?'

'This isn't really a dream, is it? Not a proper dream . . .' Knox is confused suddenly; he stares around wildly feeling the first freezing tug of the wind once more.

'Answer me. What will you do next?' He can't see Daniel anymore. The colours have engulfed him; there's just his voice.

'I – I don't . . . Why should I justify myself to you, Saint Fucking Liar! You used me and the rest of them just to feed your ego. You used me and I . . .

. . . loved you.'

He woke as the words left his lips, the transition between his dream and the cold darkness of the room instant. The window had been left open and a light drizzle was blowing in, the soft droplets flashing silver, touched briefly by the light of the full moon.

'No.' Knox spoke firmly, emphatically into the shadows. 'Not like that, Daniel. It wasn't like that.' He felt nauseous, all day he had been fighting with the sensation, the growing emptiness between his ribs made it feel as though someone had kicked him there.

He walked over to the window and stared out briefly at the dark shapes of the garden. 'The Ark' – as Daniel had so grandly christened it – was in a derelict state when Daniel and his first few followers had moved in, over two years ago now. Technically the Children were squatters here except that no one seemed to care. No one knew and no one asked what had happened to the original owner possibly because – from what Knox had heard – he had been a recluse. The house was well set back from the road and the gardens were large; huge yew trees were planted around the lawn and in the past they had been clipped into shapes, animals and birds mostly. The outlines of the neglected tree-shapes could still be seen and under the bright silver of the moon they appeared surreal and dream-like, perhaps also, they had an air of sadness about them. Knox rubbed his stomach and groaned softly, watching the rain and the trees, his mind reaching for the sense of the dream.

'It was a dream, wasn't it?' he thought. Despite what he had said to Daniel, the images of the dream were now slipping away, less real than the black solidity of the yews. But more than his confused confession of love for Daniel, something else about the dream bothered him. Daniel had articulated, made real even from . . . wherever he was, something which Knox was just coming to terms with.

'*What will you do next?*'

Exactly. He almost had the Children now. He was in a position of potential power. Esther was just a matter of time and tantalising delay. But, what now? He supposed the first thing would be to dispose of Daniel's body.

A week later, it stank. He had known that it would, but that didn't make it any easier. The body, wrapped in as many sheets as he could find and finally, a shower curtain – the horrible thought of seepage had drifted across his mind – was bundled into the large walk-in wardrobe of Daniel's rooms in The Ark. Fortunately, Knox had had enough foresight to lay the body down flat as it was now completely stiff and heavy. He'd avoided looking at the bundle for the first few days still unsure of his plans but, now he had officially moved into Daniel's old rooms on the top floor with the other Elders, he knew he had to deal with the problem. Perhaps if he disposed of the body, the dreams would stop. And if the dreams stopped perhaps he'd find enough self-possession to finally think about Esther.

But now, Knox had a plan. There was no way he could dispose of the corpse in the grounds of The Ark without being seen, most of the Children did live in the old house and with Knox's new status he could not just walk amongst them unremarked. He had decided to move the body to the old meeting house in the West Bow, the air in the basement there was remarkably dry and he had a vague idea that the body might dehydrate or even mummify in the chill air.

There was an ancient furnace there also which hadn't been used for years, maybe if he could steel himself enough, he might light the thing and burn the body. He had no idea how hot the furnace would have to be – pretty hot he guessed – but then he'd cross that bridge when he came to it. Knox eyed the large carpet in the centre of the room; it was heavy pile with a thick hessian backing and he was sure once it had been rolled up, a body concealed within would be undetectable. His lips curled into a thin smile, 'The Lord will provide,' he thought with just the merest hint of irony. Frantically, he began to move the furniture back off the rug, knocking over a couple of chairs and scattering clothes in the process. When there was a knock at the door he froze.

'Who is it?'

'Knox, it – it's LearnToFly.'

'Just a minute, LearnToFly.' He cast his gaze around wildly, the furniture was randomly scattered around the room but worse, Daniel's shrouded corpse was on the floor just outside the wardrobe. 'Shit-shit-shit,' he bundled the body back into the wardrobe, slamming the doors then he flung open the windows, ignoring the fact it was pouring with rain outside. 'Just coming . . .' he called. He made a brief half-hearted attempt at moving the furniture back, lifting one of the heavy easy chairs and setting it back in its position, before giving up. Feeling rather too flustered for comfort he opened the door to LearnToFly. 'LearnToFly, it's good to see you,' he lied. 'I'd invite you in but as you can see, I'm in a bit of a mess.' He held open the door to display the fruits of his labours.

'Oh,' LearnToFly's eyes widened; this had been Daniel's room, how could Knox decimate it for no reason? Seeing his expression, Knox smiled reassuringly.

'Don't worry, I'm going to put it all back. It's just the rug . . . the rug . . . the rug was where Daniel was standing when it happened. You know, when he was Raptured, or Ascended – there seems to be differing opinions. Anyway, I thought it would be inspirational for us all to have it in the meeting rooms. What do you think?'

'That's a lovely idea, Knox,' LearnToFly beamed. 'It looks heavy though, why don't I give you a hand to roll it up.' LearnToFly walked into the room, 'G-good heavens, what's that smell?'

'I know, horrible isn't it? I think the old drains have backed up,' Knox shrugged. 'I'll tell you what'd be a great help LearnToFly. Could you go and ask Matt for the mini-van? If you could just drive it round to the front, it'll be easier to get the rug in.'

'Yeah, okay,' LearnToFly nodded, eager to escape the smell. 'I'll be b-back in a minute.'

Once LearnToFly had gone, Knox whizzed around the room like a man possessed. First he wedged a chair under the door handle as there was no lock on any of the doors in The Ark and then he dragged the body back out of the wardrobe and began to roll it into the rug. 'Sorry, Danny boy,' he muttered, 'I guess you should've been a Buddhist.'

LearnToFly came back just as Knox was finishing the wrapping; fortunately he had been right, there was no way anyone could tell there was anything inside the heavy folds of the carpet.

'Here, let me t-take the end.'

'Erm . . . okay. Listen, once we've got this into the van, could you do me another favour, LearnToFly? I need to look at the household accounts for The Ark – I have to be up to speed before the meeting – could you get everything together while I'm gone and I'll meet with you once I get back?'

They were on the stairs now, Knox eyed the carpet fearfully, almost expecting Daniel to defy him even now, expecting to see an arm flop out of the side of the carpet; rationally, he knew this wasn't possible, Daniel's shroud was wrapped tight and sealed around with almost a whole roll of brown sticky tape. Still, his sweat was due to more than simply his labour.

'But you'll need a hand with this at The West B-Bow,' LearnToFly objected.

'No, no, I'll be fine. I can get the van right up to the double doors and then just drag it in. No problem,' Knox smiled brightly. 'I'll be back by about four yeah?'

He drove off into the rain darkened streets of the city with as little apparent haste as he could stand, watching the receding image of LearnToFly in the rear view mirror. Listening to the rhythmic hiss of the windscreen wipers, his gaze steadied to a blank calm. He'd reward himself when this was over, he decided. Once Daniel was settled in his new resting place maybe he'd go and score, or maybe, maybe he'd go for a natural high – Esther. Maybe Esther would be tonight.

Strange though, he didn't have to go that way and yet, he ended up driving along Princes Street past the Gardens where he and Daniel had met. As he stopped at the fourth set of traffic lights his listless gaze rested on the exact spot of their meeting and a small smile crept across his face. 'Miss you Danny,' he whispered.

The lights changed and the driver in front of him didn't move fast enough, Knox blared his horn. 'C'mon you old bastard,' he yelled, 'wake up!' He glanced back once as he moved away and then laughed quietly at himself. 'Yeah, miss you, Danny boy. But I'll get over it.'

CHAPTER FIVE

'Run Tristan! Run!' The dogs were almost upon them. Morias stopped beside a tree, his breath coming in ragged gasps, his aged features alarmingly pale, framed by locks of his white hair plastered to his face by the rain. Tristan was worried about the old man.

'I can't go without you, Morias,' he protested.

'You must, boy. I will come when I can. Be careful. Just wait for me. The world on the other side is a dangerous place.' Tristan shot a dubious glance down the slope at the clearing ahead; what had once been a ring of standing stones encircled the edges where the tree line abruptly stopped but now only three of the stones were still upright, the others lay toppled amongst the encroaching brambles as though some giant child had used them for toy bricks. Some of the stones were broken, one reduced entirely to rubble. But Morias had assured him when they met that morning there was enough magic in the ancient circle to send Tristan out of reach; far from the dogs and Regan, and Jahl's spite.

'What if it doesn't—'

'Just go!' Morias snapped impatiently. 'I'll hold them back as long as I can.'

Tristan ran, his short legs meant his stride was small but he had never run for his life before and he moved as fast as he was able, crashing through the green with all thought of stealth gone. His feet caught on a bramble creeper and he fell, headlong down the slope which was made slippery and muddy by the incessant rain. Bushes and trees flashed by in a whirl of green and Tristan hid his face as best he could from lashing creepers which sought to scratch and cut him. The second his momentum slowed, he scrambled to his feet without looking back and ran the rest of the way into the stone circle, breathing hard, his breath almost coming in small sobs. As he reached the ring of stones he expected something to happen instantaneously, but nothing did. Frantically, he ran into the middle of the clearing and looked back to where he had left Morias but there was no sign of the old man. 'Morias?' he yelled, panic churning his gut, 'Where are you?'

A dog crashed down the slope, growling and slavering as it came, covering the ground in massive strides only slightly impeded by the undergrowth. Another broke cover at the crest of the bank, then another. There was still no sign of Morias.

'Morias! Nothing's happening!' Tris screamed. He drew his sword and widened his stance in readiness for the assault, he had been cut and stung by a thousand nettles and somewhere on his face the heat of a trickle of blood itched and warmed its way across the cold wetness of his skin. Tris could hear his own heartbeat hammering in his ears. He knew he had little chance of survival against the hounds.

As the lead dog reached halfway down the slope a sudden white flare erupted, apparently from the branches of a nearby alder tree. The dog fell to the ground, letting out a sound somewhere between a shriek and a howl. Tris looked into the branches, but if Morias was there he was somehow invisible. The second dog also fell victim to the white flare but a third and fourth were now halfway down the slope and there was no response from Morias for long moments. Perhaps his magic was limited and he had done everything he could. The dogs were nearer now, almost upon him; Tristan let out a useless yell of despair and watched them come on, his legs heavy and leaden, rooted to the spot. Both dogs leapt at the same moment, their maws wide, strands of saliva trailing behind them, their huge paws outstretched – their claws were sharpened and cased in silver – in a manner more cat-like than canine. Tristan was screaming insensibly, when suddenly, they froze. In mid-leap, in mid-air.

There was little time to marvel at this however. Tristan's world had grown darker; that is, the space between the stones grew darker, blacker. Tris could see nothing beyond the furthest stone, he was enveloped by the quiet black; although, he thought he heard from a great distance a whining noise as the hounds lost their quarry. It looked as though he could walk through the dark space if he chose, but there seemed little reason, no landmarks of any kind. 'Morias,' he heard himself whisper, 'Is this it? Is this the other world?'

There was no response and the sound of his voice crept away into the distance without rebounding from anywhere. Tris became aware that he was still brandishing his sword as he looked around; he sheathed the weapon and tried to dab the blood off his face with the sleeve of his jerkin, groaning quietly to himself. It seemed he had injured his shoulder, probably bashing off a tree trunk, he moved his arm experimentally back and forth a few times. Not naturally a daring or adventurous person, Tris decided to conserve his strength and sat down on the ground; Morias had told him to wait after all. He burned with the cuts and stings he had gained during his fall but now that the adrenalin was leaving him he felt tired and extremely lonely and it was as he realised he was in danger of falling asleep on the ground, a movement in the corner of his vision, attracted his attention.

At first it seemed like a strange worm was tunnelling its way in through some hole in the fabric of the dark. The 'worm' itself was made up of grainy dark shadow, dark on dark, and only the movement of the thing caused Tris to notice it. As the apparition grew, it fanned outwards, rather like the peel of an apple, making the shape of a rose. This continued to grow; the darker blackness shedding away around its edges. Tris could see something forming within the grainy scene but his eyes were so strained he couldn't bring any definition to the image. He stood up and walked towards the area where the thing hung in the air. As he approached, he noted two things: one, that there was something red and shiny in the image and, two, that cold fresh air was blowing towards him. Instinctively stretching his hand out before him, he pushed on into the image and all of a sudden, was sure he was inside it. There was no feeling accompanying the transition, just a certainty that he was now somewhere rather than, well, between anywhere. As if to confirm this, although he was still in darkness, when he turned around to look back the way he had come, he saw a natural, grainy dark which his eyes could adjust to.

He looked around, sure now that he had arrived. For another world, it didn't initially seem all that exciting; he was in a small damp room, he could hear dripping noises from somewhere, and there were no windows. Perhaps he was in a dungeon. He bent down and picked up the red shiny thing and stared at it curiously. Originally, it had been a squat cylinder, but someone had squashed it, bending it across the middle. Tris sniffed it cautiously – it was beer! Inferior to his father's own brew but definitely beer. As his eyes fully adjusted, he realised there was another of the red metal things lying near what appeared to be a doorway. Without picking up the second can, he opened the door. Brighter light filtered in but still not daylight, Tris decided his assumption must be correct, this place must be a dungeon – but what kind of dungeon had no guards?

Walking slowly and cautiously up the corridor, he noted a random trail of the red metal objects which seemed as though it might lead somewhere. The corridor sloped upwards quite sharply and Tris's already tired legs began their dull ache which meant he would get little sleep that night, but Tris ignored the pain, he was used to it. As the corridor climbed uphill, the quality of the light began to change, Tris could make out the details of the walls on either side; they were houses, or rather, had been houses. Similar to some parts of Soulis Mor, made from dark stones, the houses seemed incredibly tall, the doorways huge – Tris briefly considered that the people of this world might be giants – also, the window spaces were wide but seemed to have no shutters, it was hard to see how they kept out the wind and rain. He glanced upwards and seemed to find his answer, there was some kind of roof over the houses . . .

'Hey you. Sonny. As if to confirm his fears, a huge man shambled out of a doorway recess to his right. He must be the guard, Tris decided, although it seemed the houses were all deserted and derelict, obviously they had left a guard. The man had the biggest, shaggiest, red beard Tris had ever seen and tiny brown eyes which appeared almost pin-like in his ruddy face; he was holding another of the red cans. 'What're ye doin' here on yer own, sonny? Whaur's yer maw?' The man staggered slightly as he said this and Tris realised he was drunk – 'as the proverbial' his father would have said, although he had no idea what that meant. He was about to respond to the man's query when his inquisitor bent down and peered at him more closely, blasting him with yeasty smelling breath.

'Here, you're no' a wee laddie at aw. You're one o' them, whaddyacallit? A gnome – naw, naw, a dwarf – aye that's it, a dwarf.' He seemed rather pleased with his own deductive reasoning even though the evidence was right before his eyes. 'Here, have ye got any cash wee man?'

Tris shot a furtive glance towards the end of the

corridor, he could clearly see now a brown doorway, all around the door frame, bright white light was visible: daylight. He tilted his chin and tried to copy the defiant look he had so often seen Regan give.

'My name is Tristan, Thane of Soulis Mor. You have no right to detain me in these dungeons.'

The man frowned, obviously worried Tris thought, then, quite suddenly he reached out and grabbed Tris by the neck and pinned him against the wall, lifting him off his feet as he did so. 'You taking the piss, laddie?' he growled.

'Wha . . .' Tris was about to protest further and kicked his feet feebly when he noticed the man was staring at the necklace which was still on the chain around his neck. 'No, don't touch th—'

'Is that pure gold like?' His attacker reached out and simply snatched the prize away, pouring over it avariciously. He released his grip on Tris as he did so and Tris promptly kicked him in the shin.

'Give it back,' he demanded, 'give it back.' He tried to snatch it from the man's hand but of course the man was too tall and simply raised the necklace above his head.

'Away ye go. Me an' yer jewellery here are going for a few Carlys.'

Tris didn't know who or what Carlys were but he knew the situation was desperate. To have suffered so much and run so far . . . this . . . this . . . it was unbearable.

He stood back slightly and drew his sword. 'Give it back now,' he intoned as threateningly as he could. The man stared in disbelief at the three foot silver blade; tiny shards of daylight from the doorway danced along its edge.

'Whoa there wee man. I wiz only kiddin' with ye,' he gulped. 'Goan put that thing away eh? Here, here's yer necklace back aye? I didnae mean anything.'

Tris took the necklace back and put it in his shirt pocket. He began to back away towards the brown door and the jailor, gradually aware that the threat was receding, sat back down in the doorway and picked up his can again. 'Aye, and shut the bloody door behind ye,' he growled. 'It's freezing doon here.'

Tris pushed open the brown door and climbed the stairs outside. He paused at the top and gasped. It seemed this new world was complete bedlam.

Edinburgh was basking in the relative warmth of autumnal sunshine; the cobbles of the High Street glinted like the dull metal scales of some vast serpent which stretched for over a mile. The air had a stillness about it which was unusual for the city; sounds seemed almost muffled, trapped beneath a layer of haze. Tristan's mind reeled at the sight of the buildings and, more urgently, the traffic. Cars, buses and taxis cruised along the cobbles in their stop-start dance, the taxi drivers scootching right up behind the exhausts of any vehicle unfortunate enough to get in their way. Tristan crossed the space of the large courtyard he found himself in and stood at the foot of a statue, watching for a few moments. Across the road was a most impressive building, a temple he guessed, almost as tall as the walls of Soulis Mor and hewn from the same dark stone. As the light moved, Tristan was entranced to see the rich blue and red of the stained-glass windows. He began to walk forwards intending to cross the road to admire the building further, when a terrifying noise split the air; it was like nothing he had ever heard before, a roaring, banging noise as if some great beast had reared out from the ground. With a cry of fright, Tristan ran out into the road and was immediately hit head-on by a car.

Beatrice didn't work any more. She wasn't working now, she decided, she was simply doing Stirling a favour and then, she'd go home. Resources were stretched, they always were in pathology. However, at the present moment at least three of her ex-colleagues were off work with the flu and Stirling – bless his heart – was kind of desperate. And he'd have to be to phone Beatrice, she knew that. Word was out about her suspected drinking habits and a pathologist with the shakes was little good to anyone. However, as it turned out, all Stirling needed was someone to escort a couple of bodies from the hospital morgue to St Mary's Street, it wasn't exactly far, but like all such procedures it needed a signature and someone in attendance. To occupy herself as she waited for the paperwork to be completed she sucked polo mints and pretended to read a tattered copy of *Hello* magazine which was celebrating the marriage of Lord and Lady Something-hyphen-something; the magazine was so old, they were already divorced.

'Hi Beatrice, I thought it was you. What're you doing here?' She looked up, Cal Baxter was standing there, Sergeant Cal Baxter. She smiled, horribly aware that she was wearing no make-up and her hair was a complete mess.

'Oh you know me, Cal, I just like hanging around where the dead bodies are,' she joked weakly. 'Actually, Stirling asked me to escort a couple of corpses back to St Mary's Street. How about you?'

'Just routine.' He sat down next to her and Beatrice shifted slightly nervously, vaguely trying to remember if she'd brushed her hair that morning – she'd left in such a rush – luckily, she thought she had.

'Funny thing though,' Cal frowned, 'this wee guy, I mean really wee, almost a dwarf, I suppose you call them, although I'm not sure if that's politically correct . . . Anyway, he got hit by a car in the High Street, witnesses say he seemed to take fright at the sound of a pneumatic drill, just charged out into the traffic. Boy, you should see his personal effects . . .'

'What about them?

'Want a look?'

'Yeah, I don't think my paperwork's going to be ready any time soon.' Bea shot a look at the desk clerk who moved with the calm efficiency of someone with the urgency gene removed from their DNA.

'Grab a coffee. It's on ward three, upstairs.'

Bea was delighted to have a break from her vigil and followed the young policeman along the corridor trying not to break into a wide grin. Cal Baxter had been christened the 'thinking girl's crumpet' by the women officers and staff at Ladyfield on the last night out she'd attended. Cal would blush scarlet if he knew – that was part of his charm. They climbed the stairs idly chatting about station gossip, although ignoring the fact that Beatrice's extended leave of absence was the prime target, and then turned into a small side room. 'Here we go,' Cal pulled out a long cardboard box, 'What d'you make of this?'

'Wow.'

Inside the box was a silver sword; Bea guessed it was a scaled down model if the owner was as small as Cal said; its pommel contained a large purple gem, and silver filigree twisted around the basket-handle and ended at the shank of the blade.

'It's beautiful,' Bea marvelled. 'Do you think it's real?' she pressed the point of the sword as she asked this, half expecting the blade to collapse like a stage dagger. 'Ouch, well it's certainly sharp.' There were some rumpled up clothes in the bottom of the box also, a rough cotton shirt and some trousers. The boots were interesting, obviously handmade, soft leather stitched into heelless functional slip-ons. Something else caught her attention as she examined the boots, turning one over in her hand; something was glowing green in the very corner of the box. She took it out. It was a necklace, strung on a leather thong, the main, amulet part of the necklace was coated in gold and studded with what might have been precious gems, but Beatrice knew immediately what it was; a metacarpal, the upper bone of the finger joint, from the left hand of a man. A large, elegant fingered man if she was not mistaken. Although studded with the gems, there was no reason why the object should have glowed green, the gems may have been diamonds and rubies; no emeralds anywhere.

'It's a shame this stuff will have to go to storage to

wait to be claimed,' she muttered, 'I'd like to have examined this.'

'Oh no, it won't be going into storage,' Cal frowned, 'the owner can have it back when he leaves – although I dunno about the sword . . .'

'He's alive?'

'Yeah, unconscious at the moment, but alive.'

She didn't stop to question what she said next, the words were out of her mouth before she knew why. 'Can I see him?'

Tristan was still unconscious when Beatrice and Cal entered the side ward. He looked childlike and defenceless at first glance and it was not until Bea noted the width of his chest that he seemed in any way different. On the left side of his face there was severe bruising from the accident and his right arm had also been splinted. 'Poor kid,' Cal muttered.

A nurse was just finishing tidying Tris's bed and she looked up at them both. 'He's not a kid,' she pointed out, 'We estimate he's about twenty-five.'

'Really.' Bea stared down at Tristan's features relaxed in sleep, his face still had the look of a young boy.

'Are you not family, then?' the nurse frowned.

Cal pulled out his ID, 'Police, miss. We'd like to talk to him when he comes round.'

'That may be some time, I'm afraid.'

'He's not comatose, is he?' Bea asked.

'No, no, just unconscious. It's often the body's way of dealing with shock.'

Bea smiled and nodded, she could tell the nurse that she was a pathologist and probably knew more about the body's chemical reaction to shock than the nurse might ever know, but she didn't. 'We could wait a while, it might not be long,' she said to Cal. 'My clients aren't going anywhere.'

Cal shrugged, 'Okay, I'll get another coffee.'

'Thanks, sweetie.'

Cal and the nurse left together leaving Bea watching over the sleeping Tristan. Once they had gone she took the necklace out of her coat pocket and pressed it into his hand. She couldn't say why she did it, it just seemed the right thing to do. Already, in the back of Bea's mind, a link between Tris, the necklace and the strange 'evidence' back at her house was forming. But she couldn't articulate it yet, for now it was just a nagging feeling, a recognition that here was something out of the ordinary.

'Here we go,' Cal came in and handed her another cup of coffee, as she took it her hands trembled violently and she wrapped them both around the polystyrene cup in order to keep it still. Cal looked away, embarrassed, fighting to keep a judgemental, slightly angry look from flashing across his features.

'Cal, it's not what you think,' Bea said quietly.

'It's all right, Bea. You don't have to justify yourself to me.'

'I know that. But maybe you can set a few people straight on my behalf.' *People I thought were my friends,* she thought angrily. 'I'm not a drunk, Cal.' She glared at her hands as though they had betrayed her. 'That's not why I'm shaking. I have a tremor.'

Cal paused for a moment as he digested this information.

'A tremor? It's not—'

'Parkinson's? They don't know yet. I'm due for more tests soon.'

Cal was sitting down now near the foot of the bed, he leaned forward and rubbed her knee in a 'there-there' type of gesture. 'I'm really sorry, Bea. Why didn't you say something at the station?'

She smiled thinly. 'You mean after they found me out of my skull in the wets room the day I had to go for the tests? People draw their own conclusions, Cal, but at the end of the day, it's none of their damn business. Stirling knows.' Cal stared fixedly at his feet, embarrassed for a whole new set of reasons.

There was a strangled scream from the bed. Lost in their workplace drama, they had been ignoring their charge and Tristan had woken up.

Tristan screamed and struggled. He had no idea where he was but they had taken his clothes and his weapon. Across his face was a strange shiny tube which fed into his nose; gods knew what torture they were about to use it for. His arm had been placed in a white cover and it was giving him great pain, sharper than his usual pain.

'Calm down. Calm down.' A woman sat down on the side of the bed just as he was about to lunge out of it. She put her face close to his and held him lightly at the top of his shoulders; she had a kind face, round features but beautiful green eyes, she looked wise and compassionate, and she smelt good. 'C'mon,' she said quietly, 'just calm down.' He could understand her more easily than he had the jailor – it was coming back to him now, the new world, the big dark building with the pretty windows . . .'My name is Beatrice,' Bea smiled as she felt some of the tension go out of his shoulders, 'What's your name?'

He scowled at this, he hated it when people treated him like a child and he mistook Bea's attempt to calm him as being patronising. 'Tristan,' he responded. 'I am a Thane. You can let me go now.'

Bea let him go, slowly, as though she feared she would have reason to grab him again. 'Okay, Tristan . . .'

'Well, look who's awake,' the nurse had returned, hearing some commotion from Tristan's room. 'I'll get the Consultant to look you over and you can go home. Nothing broken just a fracture to your arm. You're a lucky wee man.' She smiled brightly and Tristan intensified his scowl as she left the room seemingly oblivious to his wrath.

'What's a Consultant?' he asked Bea.

'It's just a doctor, Tristan. They have to check you over before they let you go home.'

'Home,' he echoed slightly despondently.

'Tristan. My name's Cal. I'm a police officer.' Cal stood up and offered Tris his hand to shake. This seemed entirely premature to Tris but he shook hands anyway as it was obviously the custom here.

'Don't you have anywhere to go? I can recommend a hostel. You see, we might need to talk to you about your accident and also, carrying your sword. It – it's not really allowed here.' He smiled slightly apologetically.

'Have you got my things? I want them back.' Tris was doing his best to cope but it was obvious he was on the verge of tears.

'Cal, can I have a word?' Bea motioned to the corridor.

'I want my things,' Tris stormed.

Bea and Cal stepped outside. 'Look Cal, let me take him back to my house. I've got the spare room, he's obviously exhausted. Don't send him to the hostel.'

'Bea, he's not some waif and stray,' Cal objected. 'I know he's disabled but we did find him carrying a lethal weapon. We don't know what his mental state is.'

'He needs help, Cal.'

Cal sighed, 'Yeah, I know.'

Three hours later Bea and Tristan arrived at her house in Colinton. It had taken Bea some persuasion to get Tristan into her car and once he was in there, he sat almost shaking with fear at both the new sensation of being driven, and the sights of the passing city. He hadn't said much the whole time but had ducked down on the back seat when they passed roadworks near Morningside. Bea glanced back in the rear-view mirror as he straightened up again slightly self-consciously.

'Is that what fri . . . gave you a shock before, Tristan? It won't hurt you.' They had drawn parallel to the works as they waited for the lights to change. 'It does make a horrible noise, doesn't it?' she smiled. 'But do you see the man holding it? He's in charge of it. He can switch it on or off when he wants.' They drove past and Tris kept his eyes fixed on the roadworks until they were out of sight as though he feared the thing would pursue him.

'I don't like this place,' he muttered.

'What, my car?' Bea replied evenly.

'This world. I don't like it.'

Bea said nothing in response but the hairs on the back of her neck stood up as if something had frightened her.

Tristan was quiet when they entered the house. Bea showed him into the spare room and then busied herself in the kitchen, leaving him alone for a while to settle in. Maybe he would come through and watch TV or something, she thought. She fed her cat Ziggy, with half an ear tuned to the living room.

'Well, Zig, seems we've got a house guest, eh?' She scooped the fishy pulp into Zig's bowl and he purred loudly in response as he bent to eat. It always amazed Bea that cats could purr and eat at the same time, she stroked his tiger-orange back as her gaze drifted to the gin bottle on the shelf – Bombay Sapphire – if she was a drunk as some seemed to think, at least she wasn't a cheap one. She poured herself the equivalent of a pub double measure but then topped up the tall glass with tonic, as she did so she heard movement in the living room. 'Would you like a drink, Tristan?' she called. There was no answer, so she poured him a lemonade and put it on a tray with her drink. 'So, what do you think of my humble . . .' she stopped.

Tris was standing in the middle of the living room, staring down at something he had lifted from her mantelpiece. His expression was a mixture of horror, bewilderment and awe and his knuckles were white where he gripped the filigree edges of the frame.

'What's wrong?' she whispered.

'Beatrice.' He looked up, all colour had drained from his face and he held the picture towards her accusingly. 'Why do you have a picture of my father?'

CHAPTER SIX

Jahl did not often experience self-doubt, in fact, only one woman in the whole world could cause such an emotion and he was looking at her now; or rather, an image of her.

'What do you mean, gone? Where could he have gone?' The image of a tall beautiful woman flickered slightly as the goddess Phyrr lost her focus. Conjured from far away in the Northlands using the blood of an unfortunate whore as a conduit, it was a quick and dirty sorcery. Jahl's glance flickered to the alabaster white corpse on the floor from which the image of his mother rose like the ghost of the girl's soul – except this girl could never have contained such grandeur or such intrinsic evil. He sighed, it wasn't that he felt remorse or sympathy for the girl, even though she had warmed his bed a couple of times while he was lying low in the top rooms of the brothel but he just hated the waste. Phyrr could easily have done this from her side without such aid – she was a goddess after all – but no, she always left the arrangements to him. She had said she really was coming soon, as soon as Jahl had secured his position at Soulis Mor, but now it seemed she was dragging her feet, perhaps she didn't really miss him, perhaps – Jahl felt his chest tighten at this next thought – perhaps she had a new lover.

Now there was the new complication of Regan. Jahl

was confident she would calm down and see reason and so he had simply moved to his rather tatty current address to avoid her for a couple of weeks. He pulled his cloak more tightly around him, shuddering slightly from the cold; the girl had come to light the fire, it had been a miscalculation on his part to kill her before she completed her task.

'Does it matter where he's gone? I'm glad to get rid of the little runt,' he shrugged. 'His sister, Regan, is much more amenable. There is something about that girl . . . she has such potential . . .'

Phyrr regarded him coldly and for a split second, Jahl imagined he saw something like fear on his mother's features. 'He may have gone to find his father,' she said simply.

'Talisker? So what? He must be an old man by now. What does it matter?' Jahl peered more closely at the shifting image. 'Is there something I'm missing?'

'No,' Phyrr bridled, 'no. Have you seen Alessandro Chaplin recently?'

'Who?'

'The *Seanachaidh*. Have him arrested and tortured if he's in Soulis Mor. He'll know where Tristan has gone. Is there anything else you want to tell me?'

Jahl briefly hesitated. He didn't want Phyrr to know about his pursuit of the necklace until he had decided how to proceed but he would be stupid not to realise she would be watching his every move. 'No, nothing important, Phyrr,' he smiled.

The room suddenly became much warmer and a blue fire sparked from nothing within the massive grate. Phyrr smiled in return, a feral smile. 'Then come here, my boy.' Opening her arms to him, Phyrr magically discarded her clothes, her naked form shifting in the blue light, her long dark hair swirling around her shoulders and breasts as though she was swimming in the ether. Jahl dropped his cloak to the floor, his own nakedness no longer cold, his arousal obvious. He walked forward to be enveloped by the fire, his breath coming quickly, his heartbeat pounding like the ocean in his ears. As soon as they were together Jahl lay down on the rug by the hearth, his eyes closed, pushing into her warmth, the sound of his blissful sighs punctuating the tiny noises of the fire. He had to be careful he knew; his lover must remain toe to toe with the corpse through which she had travelled or he would find himself alone. Reaching out with his left foot he touched against the cold ankle of the dead girl. Above him, Phyrr's face moved as though in a dream and her voice drifted across his consciousness like a breeze.

'You shouldn't lie to your mother, Jahl.' She reached down and kissed him long and hard, very hard, he cried out as a warm blossom of blood trickled from his lip across his cheek. He heard her laughter, her wicked musky humour; then, the world exploded . . .

Regan knew what people were saying – not to her face of course – but she knew the rumours were that she had had Tristan assassinated. She saw the accusation in the eyes of her staff and courtiers as they bowed, scraped and grovelled to their newly frightening Thane but none would openly question her and, despite the fact that this was in her best interests, this annoyed

Regan intensely. No one spoke of Tristan unless she did, within a very short time – a matter of days – it was almost as though he had never existed. Perversely, Regan would mention him to her staff and watch the blank shutters fall over their expressions; it was a kind of mental torture she used to punish herself.

It had been almost two weeks since the massacre of the delegation and no one could find Tristan; his disappearance weighed heavily on her mind; sleep eluded her until the first light of dawn tinged the skies and she ate little. She went riding each day for hours, returning white and cold with exhaustion. She told herself she was looking for him as if perhaps he was simply camping away from the city without having told anyone, but she knew the search parties she had sent out would have found him if that were the case.

There were other concerns of course; riders had arrived from Ruannoch Were demanding to know what had happened to the delegation they had sent and from which they had heard no word. Regan feigned ignorance and had sent word back reassuring Ulla that an investigation was underway – she confided in her letter that she was worried for Tristan's mental health given that he was crippled and prone to fevers which sometimes left him delirious – to her credit she shed a tear as she wrote this. In fact, she was aware she was only buying time – Ulla would send word to Huw and Lachlan and, if anything further happened to alarm her allies, perhaps they would try to depose her more openly next time. She was lying low, just like Jahl . . .

She had been dressing to go out riding again even though it was raining hard outside. Her maid, Alyss, could not hide her disapproval of this, her mouth set in a thin line although she said nothing, so Regan dismissed her and sat down to plait her own hair. When there was a slightly impatient knock on her door she assumed it was Alyss coming back to beg her not to go out.

'Yes, come in, Alyss.' She did not look up. 'I know what you're going to say but I need to get out, I . . . oh.'

It was Jahl. He stood in the doorway regarding her quite calmly. In her surprise, Regan caught the edge of the small dish which held her pins and it crashed to the floor.

'Get out!' The shout ripped from her throat before she even knew what she intended to say.

'Regan, I—'

'Get out!' she screamed it this time and threw her wooden brush hard as she did so. Fortunately for Jahl the missile hit the doorframe rather than his head. 'I told you to go. What are you doing here? Alyss, Alyss call the guar . . .' She sprinted across the room and was reaching for the dagger beside her bed when her calls were cut short. Jahl grabbed her and put his hand across her mouth.

'Listen to me, Regan. Listen!' His tone was at once beseeching and angry. 'You told me to go and I went. I went to look for Tristan.' This comment had the desired effect, Regan's eyes widened in surprise and Jahl took the gamble of removing his hand from her mouth. As he let her go Regan did not disguise the fact that she picked up the dagger.

'Speak,' she said coldly. 'You have one minute.'

Jahl refused to be flustered by this but rather sat down in her chair and stretched his legs out expansively. 'I felt guilty,' he began.

'Oh *please*. You never felt guilty in your—'

'Please, Regan. You have only given me a minute. Tristan ran away because of what happened on that night and I was partly responsible – so, I sent out my hounds.'

Regan's expression changed slightly as she thought of Jahl's beloved hounds. Tristan was sure they simply ripped their prey to shreds and she had to concede that they looked vicious enough. It might frighten Tris to be pursued by them, but then, he'd caused enough trouble. In the past Jahl had assured her they were trained to corner their quarry and not harm it. 'Did – did they find . . . anything?'

'At first no. Tristan is surprisingly clever, adept at hiding his scent – also, I suspect he had a Sidhe guide, possibly a bear Sidhe . . .'

Regan nodded. It made sense that a Sidhe would help Tris escape.

'Eventually I tracked him down.'

'Where is he?'

'At Ruannoch Were – at least he was for a few days . . .'

She frowned. 'That's odd, Thane Ulla didn't mention it in her letter . . .'

'Oh, he was travelling in disguise.' Regan's gaze hardened. If she was honest with herself she was almost glad to see Jahl but not glad enough to dismiss being lied to. 'Honestly, Regan. Look, he's given me a letter for you.' Jahl reached inside the folds of his cloak and produced a small, somewhat crumpled parchment. Regan snatched it from his hands as he smoothed it out.

Regan was half expecting to see a clever forgery but she was confident that she could detect any such thing; Tristan's handwriting did have some particular characteristics. In fact, Jahl was too clever to attempt such an easily detectable thing – written on the parchment was a spell which would be activated the second Regan started to read; she would see what she wanted to see. The parchment did appear to have been written in Tristan's rather erratic handwriting. Regan turned her back on Jahl as she read so that he could not see the emotion on her features.

Dear Ree,

I'm sorry to have run away – I know it's something you would never do, but I'm not like you – and that's the problem. Perhaps I overreacted in contacting Thane Ulla, maybe you are right to stop sedition in Soulis Mor – I don't know. I know you are easily capable of running Soulis Mor without me, gods know you've been doing it for years! Please don't try and look for me, I am travelling unofficially and Thane Ulla doesn't know I'm here in her city . . .

Regan glanced back towards Jahl as she read this confirmation and he smiled towards her.

Ree, remember I said once I wanted to travel to Karmala Sev to see the gathering of the wild horses? Well, I'll do that soon and then – who knows? Don't be angry with me Sis. I promise I will return to Soulis Mor soon, but only *as a visitor. You have always been Thane.*

All my love

Tris.

'Thank the gods he's safe,' she breathed.

'Indeed.'

'Thank-you, Jahl.'

He stood up as though preparing to leave. 'I just thought you should know,' he said. 'I rushed back from Ruannoch Were as quickly as I could but it was difficult to get to see you . . . 'Bye then . . .'

Regan almost laughed to herself, her anger dissipated by the relief of her news. She realised Jahl expected some token of forgiveness for his monstrous act two weeks earlier. In fact, during these last weeks she had done some hard, pragmatic thinking: Jahl it seemed was capable of strong magics – he had been holding out on her – and, however heinous his crime, he had done it for her benefit – *to protect her.* He was manipulative, strong, cunning and brave; the best possible ally and the worst possible enemy. She could not forget the screams of the dying men, the black demons which Jahl had conjured haunted her dreams still, and yet . . .

And yet, she thought she could control him. He was her servant.

'Jahl.' She had waited until he was at the door. 'You may stay. But understand, this is your last chance.'

* * *

'Your father? That's not possible, Tristan. Perhaps he just bears some resem—'

'Duncan Talisker.' Tris jabbed the picture towards her again, defying her to doubt him. 'He looks young here but it's him, isn't it? And the *Seanachaidh* Sandro Chaplin . . . and you.'

Beatrice sat down heavily and took a large swig of her drink, the inside of her mouth had dried up. 'Sit down, Tristan,' she said quietly. 'There are some things I need to know.' Tristan sat on the large yellow couch opposite her still frowning; Bea studied his face closely, it seemed she had been mistaken in thinking of Tristan as childlike. His expression and bearing as he sat awaiting her questions were that of a young man but he certainly didn't remind her of Talisker. Had Tristan been 'normal' he would have been a handsome man; his large brown eyes held the unmistakable spark of a great intellect, his features and his mouth were soft and kind which was what gave the impression of youth. She took another large swallow of the gin wondering where to start. 'Are they alive then?' She felt her throat tighten as she asked the question, the emotion catching her off guard.

'Alive? Of course they're alive. At least the *Seanachaidh* was there when I left Soulis Mor,' he shrugged, 'I haven't seen my father for years now, he doesn't like to come to the city . . . Sandro was the last person to see him. Me and my sister—'

'Sister? Talisker has two children? How can that be possible?'

'Well, I am adopted,' Tristan volunteered as though he thought it would be of help.

'Are you sure we're talking about the same person? Talisker's about well . . . he'd be about thirty-four or thirty-five now and he can't possibly have fathered children in the last . . . How old are you, Tristan?'

'Twenty-five. But my father is nearly sixty.'

There was a long silence as Bea digested this information. It just didn't add up. Even if Talisker had some strange *doppelgänger*, the ages were all wrong and Tristan knew Sandro as well. The gin was beginning to make her head swim but she knew this was never going to make any kind of sense even if she was stone-cold sober.

'Can you take me to them, Tristan? We're old friends,' she smiled sadly thinking of Sandro, but Tristan shook his head.

'I'm sorry, Beatrice but I think I may be trapped here until Morias comes and finds me.'

'Here?'

'This world. Whatever it is called. Sandro and my father are in my world, Sutra. I was brought here by magic and . . . what? Did I say something funny?'

Beatrice was laughing. 'No, no, Tristan. Not funny exactly,' she smiled. 'It's just that "magic" is a word I taunt myself with.'

'I don't understand.'

'Sometimes – lately – I think I'm going mad – I have – I've seen something magic and . . .'

Tristan looked confused. 'Why would that mean you are going mad?'

Beatrice gulped the rest of her drink, the sharp medicinal taste of the gin firing her synapses and making her eyes warm and stingy. She dumped the glass on the table and pulled a packet of cigarettes out of her shirt pocket. 'Because there's no magic in this world, sweetie. None at all.'

A world away, the question of magic was on someone else's mind. Sandro was quietly confident he was dying and for some reason this had prompted him to recall the only time he had channelled magic on his own. He had spoken the lineage of the Clans and survived, mainly thanks to the help of Ulla, now the Thane of Ruannoch Were. He sighed through bruised and bleeding lips, the rush of air stinging and tingling like needle points. At any other time, this pain alone would be enough to cause Sandro to cry out but now, in the grand scheme of things, in his tapestry of pain, it seemed almost irrelevant. He had bones broken which he didn't even know the names of, it was part of the art of the torturer he supposed, not the big bones, not first; first all the little fiddly connecting bones – fingers, toes, ankles, wrists – until every movement was like fire. Sandro hadn't moved much for the last two hours. It wasn't really the bones he was worried about, he glanced over the room at his assailant, an ox of a man with surgeon's fingers, bones healed given the chance didn't they? He was sure he must be bleeding internally, he'd coughed up a huge amount of stringy pulpy blood. How important was it to keep him alive, he wondered? Could the torturer afford a fatal mistake? He shifted slightly in his shackles trying to blank out the wave of purple nausea which slicked across his consciousness; at least he was lying down now since the ankles went . . . he almost laughed at the absurdity of thinking this might be a blessing, his mind was unfocused now . . . Yeah, he'd done magic once, all by himself, not like the other thing that had happened when he and Duncan and Malk became the One Big Thing . . . Malk. He hadn't thought about him for the longest time; Malk. Even now, as his broken body began to give up the fight, the thought of the wild, canny Highlander could swell his heart and bring the sad vestiges of a smile to his lips.

A noise near the door roused his attention, he peered over through the puffy crack of his eyelids. The torturer was coming over, smiling an incongruously white smile, he held something in front of himself, carefully keeping it away from his body: it was a glowing poker. Sandro wasn't sure if he groaned aloud or not, it was more a deep echo of despair that came from within his wracked frame. Then, as he watched the after-images of the poker waving across the gloom of the chamber it seemed surreal to him that the torturer was wearing large mittens to protect his own skin, his mind skitted away from the idea of prototype oven mitts but he felt his chest tighten as a hysterical laugh ripped through him. At the same time, his body, under its own instruction began to writhe in the shackles. He opened his mouth to demand 'who authorised this?' but instead, a burbling scream erupted forth accompanied by yet more blood.

The brand was in front of his face now. He could smell the heat, his own sweat and urine, he could feel the top layer of his skin fry although the brand had not yet made contact. His eye. He was coming for his eye. He couldn't stand to scream – it was agony – but he couldn't not scream. It was too late to pray for miracles and magic, too late. He screwed his eyes shut and continued screaming, his whole being possessed by the sound.

There was a dull thud, and then nothing. The heat from in front of his face vanished and cooler air played across his ravaged skin. Sandro refused to open his eyes though, unsure whether his torturer was clever enough to be mentally playing with him, waiting at a distance ready to jam the brand into his eye . . .

'Sandro, Sandro, can you hear me?' Someone slapped his face, a relative caress compared to what he'd experienced. He knew that voice, from somewhere. Still, he didn't open his eyes and thought distantly that he didn't really care. There was a bleak darkness growing within him, blossoming like a deadly flower; there was no pain in the grey retreat and he felt himself drifting towards peaceful surrender.

'I think we're too late, he's dead.' The voice was different to the first, warm but with slightly clipped tones. The speaker didn't really care. Sandro didn't either.

'No. Let me see.' The first voice again. He drifted slightly into the grey. He knew . . . he knew that voice . . . 'Sandro. I know you can hear me.' Someone stroked the hair back from his forehead. 'I know you don't want the pain. Where is your stone? Your stone makes you a *Seanachaidh*, remember?'

Remember?

Stone?

Stone Dreaming. That's what Talisker called it,

Talisker and . . . ? Something cold and hard was pressed into his palm. A simple stone, the stone which had awakened his latent *Seanachaidh*'s talent all those years ago. Given to him by . . .

Sandro opened his eyes to look up into the face of his old friend. He wasn't sure if he was crying, he wasn't sure of anything except the faded blue gaze and the reflection of sorrow and pain he saw there. 'Morias,' he whispered. 'Help me.'

For all he'd seen of battles, gods and magics, Sandro's dreams had never been troubled. But this time, his body dictated a tone of suffering and his dreams became a relentless backdrop to hours of healing. He saw Regan as a girl, he was dancing with her as he had when she was seven, her tiny feet were standing on his and he was waltzing around the room. She laughed and laughed, her eyes round with girlish pleasure. He could hear Una in the background laughing also . . . but then Regan began to change; blue-black feathers began to sprout forth from her body and her face, her long dark hair transformed into plumage also. But Regan danced on, seemingly oblivious to the change sweeping over her, until he was dancing with a great black bird, whose sharp beak pressed against his chest like a sword point. Except it wasn't dancing any more; Sandro couldn't escape the clutches of the creature and he struggled and writhed in his sleep. 'Let me go . . .'

'*Seanachaidh*, you can wake up now,' the voice was worried somehow. '*Seanachaidh*.'

Sandro opened his eyes. The first impression to deal

with was not visual; his body was merely aching. It was not wracked by searing pain any longer. As if to prove this to himself, he moved his feet around slightly, they felt tender and sore but that was all. Secondly, he was in a Sidhe lodge; he knew this because he had spent time amongst the Sidhe and although their round, low constructions lacked the permanence of the Fine's stone dwellings they were always warm, smelling of smoke and herbs from their fires. He was lying on a bed of soft animal skins which felt like heaven, sweet and soft. He sighed the contented sigh of a recovering invalid and closed his eyes again.

'*Seanachaidh*, you are awake?'

Unwillingly Sandro opened his eyes again and fixed his bleary gaze on the speaker. It was a Sidhe, as he had expected, except that he wore no totem of allegiance around his neck. He wore silver-grey robes and large eagle feathers in his hair . . . large enough to be Sidhe eagle feathers in fact. Although his face radiated a kind of concern, his features were sharp; an aquiline nose, thin lips and, most surprisingly for a Sidhe, pale blue eyes. Sandro had always imagined with the Sidhe that he could identify their tribe and animal attribution within moments of meeting them. With this Sidhe there could be little doubt and the realisation was worrying.

'Wolf clan?' he muttered. The clan of the Wolf had left the Sidhe Council at the time of the battles with Corvus. Having endangered the fate of both Sidhe and Fine by their selfish action they were outcast. But it mattered little to the wolves whose independence and pride had brought them to such circumstance, they had always been wanderers and had no hearth or home. They were never to be trusted, both Fine and Sidhe shunned them.

A flicker of amusement entered the watcher's gaze as he realised Sandro's thoughts. He nodded his head briefly and touched his hand to his heart. 'Eskarius Vermesh,' he said.

'Eskarius?' Sandro frowned. 'Eskarius is dead.'

'He was my father.'

'Ah,' Sandro couldn't think of anything to say. Eskarius senior had made an attempt on *Braznnair* – attempting to steal it for the wolf clan and killing Deme in the process – only to be killed by Makhpiyaluta. He was a traitor. 'Where's Morias?' he whispered finally. 'I did see him, didn't I?'

Eskarius nodded solemnly. 'Yes. He has healed you using potent magics. You were as good as dead when we found you. He is very tired now. Resting.'

'Yes, I . . . did you kill the torturer?'

'It was necessary. Yes.'

Sandro felt no remorse for this act either. 'Thank-you,' he said. He drifted back to sleep and dreamed of his torturer being torn apart by great grey wolves. It should have been a nightmare, but then, the scars of torture were far more than skin deep.

When he woke again, Sandro felt better than he would have dreamed possible. Even the dull ache of his healing bones had mostly died away. A thrill of energy ran through him at the mere idea he was still alive and he sat up, looking around the lodge with mild curiosity. He'd never been in a wolf lodge before;

as a *Seanachaidh*, he took less stories to the Sidhe who held to their own, more pragmatic myths concerning the creatures of Lysmair, their ancient homeland; although as a courtesy, Sandro would be invited to their campfires and was treated with great respect while there. He knew from these visits that, as of the battle for Soulis Mor twenty-five years ago, no fables were told concerning the Wolf clan, the wolves' reputation for wisdom, speed and tenacity was erased for ever. None had been in their lodges in all that time.

Initially, the building Sandro was in just seemed darker, more gloomy than others he had seen. For a few moments, Sandro couldn't fathom why, and then he realised the wolf lodge was dug into the earth so that from outside, only the smoke from the fire issuing out of the central hole would be seen. Now, a bar of misty daylight shone down through the hole and wisps of lazy smoke from the dying fire drifted up towards the sky. He could hear birdsong from outside and thought it was probably early morning, although it was difficult to decide how long he'd been unconscious. Wrapping one of the large animal skins around his shoulders to try and combat the chill he started towards the doorway to look for Morias when Eskarius entered carrying a bowl of steaming liquid.

'I need to talk to Morias,' Sandro began, 'I need to know what's going on, Eskarius.'

'First you must eat.' It seemed more a command than anything else and as Sandro was hungry and slightly shaky he took the bowl which was full of a thin oat gruel and began to sip the warm liquid.

'I can eat and walk,' he grunted ungraciously.

Eskarius said nothing but held aside the pelt which covered the doorway.

Outside the landscape was blanketed in thick snow and Sandro was momentarily dazzled by the stark whiteness. He still wore the tattered remains of his plaid and shirt under the borrowed animal skin and, as the fresh chill air washed over him, he became aware that these garments were stuck to his body by dried blood and sweat. Reaching down he picked up a handful of snow and rubbed it on his face, enjoying the tingling sensation this brought to his skin. The encampment was in a small forest glade where the trees, mostly birch and elder, were thin and leafless; the sun was high in the sky creating few shadows in the brown and white tapestry. Winter birds called intermittently giving an air of solitude to the scene.

About a hundred yards or so from Sandro and Eskarius, a skewbald horse and a dirty white mule stood, companionably eating a pile of hay which someone had laid down for them. Sandro grinned, recognising Morias's mode of transport immediately and wondering if the mule was in fact the same one his aged mentor had had years earlier.

'Where is . . .?'

Eskarius pointed dead ahead and with a thrill of recognition Sandro saw Morias. The old man was sitting on a log in the centre of the glade, perfectly still and perfectly at one with his surroundings. So much so, that Sandro had not registered he was there at all. As their gazes met, Morias smiled and began to stand up, using his staff which he leant on heavily. Sandro strode over and gripped his teacher in a tight bear hug, and was shocked by how light and frail he felt in his arms. 'Morias,' emotion threatened to overwhelm him. 'I owe you my life, it seems.'

'*Seanachaidh*,' the old man said gravely, 'the trouble you get into . . .' They sat down together and Sandro was aware that Morias was observing him closely. 'How are you feeling?' Morias asked.

'I feel . . . okay. Fine. A few mild pains but nothing worse.' He smiled, but Morias did not return the smile, merely nodded. 'What's wrong, Morias?'

'Sandro, I could not heal you properly. Your injuries were too severe . . .'

'But I feel—'

'It is an illusion only.'

Sandro frowned. 'I don't understand, Morias, what are you saying?'

In response, Morias raised his hand and opened his palm flat. Sitting in the middle of it was a small purple gem which was pulsing brightly, casting a purple light onto the snow. 'Magic is a great thing, Alessandro, as you know, but it cannot defy nature. This gem contains your agonies and injuries for the moment . . .'

'But?'

Morias sighed. 'You must take them back eventually. I have merely bought you time.'

'No!' Sandro was horrified. His mind would not even allow a memory of the pain he had experienced. He reached out to take the gem from Morias but Morias snapped his hand shut.

'Don't touch it,' he warned, 'the spell will be broken.'

'But why can't the spell remain for ever?' Sandro

frowned. 'Why can't you throw the gem away or something?'

'It would not work. The magic would simply escape at a random time and you would suddenly be beset by the agonies.' There was silence for a moment, broken by the plaintive sound of a curlew. When Sandro spoke next, his voice was thick with emotion and fear.

'You're telling me I'm a dead man, Morias. That I'm going to suffer a horrible painful death.'

'I'm sorry, Alessandro. It was the only choice.'

'No it wasn't. Why didn't you just let me go? It would have been kinder.'

'I know. But Sandro . . . you are needed. There is great danger coming and untold thousands might die . . .'

Sandro made a sour face. 'Aren't you asking the wrong guy? That's Talisker's thing.'

'Did you learn nothing from the last time?' Morias looked flushed, almost angry. 'You and Talisker are both necessary. You balance the forces within one another.'

'No we don't,' Sandro replied flatly 'We spent half of our lives hurting one another remember? Where is the balance in that? And we needed Malk to bring us together. He's gone now. I don't even know where Duncan is.'

'I know. That's why I've asked Eskarius to help guide you. I believe Talisker will be travelling south through the Blue Mountains, you could intercept him in ten days' time. At this time of year the passes are dangerous and sometimes impenetrable. It will take about ten days to reach him and another ten to return here . . .'

'Whoa, whoa, you're getting away ahead of me here. Why do I need to get Duncan? What makes you think he'll come anyway?'

Morias suddenly seemed to crumple; he rested his forehead against the wood of his staff and his pale features relaxed into an exhausted mask. 'Because I'm a stupid old man, Sandro, and I've done a stupid thing for all the best motives. I saved Tristan from Jahl – who is the threat to us all – and sent him beyond Jahl's reach to another world.'

Sandro's expression made clear he instantly understood the implications of Morias's problem. 'Edinburgh?' he whispered. 'You sent Tris to Edinburgh? He'll never survive there.'

Morias closed his eyes as though unable to deal with the idea of Tristan's situation. 'I know,' he muttered. 'It was only meant to be temporary. But now, he has wandered away from the gateway . . .' Sandro groaned aloud and Morias opened his eyes – his moment of weakness past – and fixed him with a strong unflinching gaze.

'I need you and Duncan to go and get him, Sandro. You must go back to your own world.'

Tristan was asleep when Cal called round that evening. Bea patted anxiously at her hair as she prepared to open the door, before catching herself and realising the effort was probably futile anyway. It seemed almost ridiculous that Cal might have any interest in her, he could have his choice of women at the station. Still, she couldn't ignore the faint thrill she felt when she looked through the spyhole on her front door and realised he was carrying a bottle of wine.

'Hi there,' he smiled as she opened the door, 'I just wondered how your patient was doing.'

Well, he thinks his father is Duncan Talisker who's now sixty and living in another world, she thought wryly. 'He's fine,' she said aloud. 'I think he's worn out with everything though.'

'Not surprising,' Cal strode into the living room. 'I hope you don't mind . . .' he said, showing her the bottle of wine.

'Not at all. In fact I should take it as something of a vote of confidence,' she smiled. 'I'll get some glasses and the corkscrew.' She returned with a tray of wine-glasses and a bowl of tortilla chips and they sat down to share the wine together.

'I take it he's in bed?' Cal nodded towards the spare room.

'Oh no, I let him go out on the town.' She watched his face changed and then giggled slightly. 'Of course he's in bed. What's the situation concerning his sword? Can he have it back?'

Cal shrugged, 'Stirling suggested that since you had taken such a personal interest in the case, you might like to go in and run some tests on it. If there are no traces of blood on it, I guess we could consider it purely decorative . . . the sort of thing some people put over their fireplaces . . .' he crunched his tortilla chip loudly and unselfconsciously, scooping up more into the flat of his palm. Bea warmed to him slightly more, enjoying the fact he could be so relaxed in her company.

'You mean a replica or something?'

'Yeah, that kind of thing. Some of the shops in the High Street sell that sort of stuff . . .'

'You don't believe that, do you?'

'You tell me. You're the expert.'

'Wait up. Is this Stirling's sneaky way of coaxing me back into work?' Bea was only mock indignant. She effected Stirling's deep sonorous tone. 'While you're here, Bea, would you mind just casting your expert eye over the corpse in exam three? Be a love and draw up the report will you?'

Cal grinned as he bit noisily into his next chip. 'So, calls you love does he?'

She snorted. 'Don't even think it. Me and Stirling go back a long way but . . .'

'I'm just kidding . . . most of the station always figured you and Alessandro were a perfect match.'

'S-Sandro? No. We dated for a while but nothing came of it. He never really recovered from losing his wife the way he did.'

'Yeah, Diane wasn't it? Awful. I was there at Ladyfield that day when he flipped out. Personally, I always liked him but some say—'

'He was a good man, Cal,' unexpected tears started in Bea's eyes. *Was a good man . . . that's what did it*, she told herself. They were discussing Sandro as if he were dead. 'Is a good man,' she corrected herself.

'I'm sorry, Bea. I didn't mean to upset you,' Cal put down his wineglass and patted her hand slightly awkwardly. 'But you can't believe he's still alive can you? It's been over two years since he and Duncan Talisker disappeared.'

'People disappear for all sorts of reasons,' she

sniffed, taking her hand away pointedly and topping up the wineglasses.

'Yeah, sure. And mass murder is a pretty good reason. But not for Sandro. Talisker was the one with the reason.'

Bea sighed heavily. 'Look, no offence, Cal, but you weren't involved in the case and so you're not fully acquainted with the facts. In the end there was enough evidence to put Thomas Willis in the frame . . . more convincingly than Talisker. At least enough to have had his previous conviction quashed.'

'If he'd stuck around,' Cal nodded. 'Who's Thomas Willis anyway?'

Suddenly weary, Bea shook her head. 'It doesn't matter now . . . it doesn't matter.'

There was a long silence; the evening had drawn to a close as they drank and the living room was illuminated only by the light of the wood-burner and the light coming in from the kitchen. Bea made a mental note to get up and put the lamp on, but somehow she didn't feel inclined to move; she stared moodily into the flames. From his chair, Cal was studying the pictures on the top of her grand piano, frowning in the gloom.

'Who's the little girl there?' he asked brightly.

Bea almost laughed bitterly at the irony of it. She realised Cal was politely, although rather obviously, trying to change the subject. 'That's Effie Morgan. Daughter of Shula Morgan? I'm her godmother. She comes to stay in the holidays sometimes . . .'

Recognition dawned slowly on Cal's face. 'Shula Morgan? Wasn't that . . .?'

'Yeah. The last victim. She was a schoolfriend of mine, also an ex-girlfriend of Duncan's.'

'But he—'

'No. He would never have hurt her.'

'Ah. Look, maybe I should go,' he stood up suddenly, dusting the chilli powder from his navy trousers. 'I, em . . . just seem to be em . . .'

'Putting your foot in it, is the phrase I believe,' Bea said mildly.

He looked at her face in the light from the fire; echoes of the tragedy which had enveloped the small band of friends seemed to him to be visible on her features. But also, the strange wisdom which such events often bring to people, an acceptance, a refusal to sweat the small stuff. She wasn't angry at his clumsiness, just deeply sad and perhaps now Cal understood how Bea had lost her focus at work, and how her much discussed relationship with a (now famous) opera tenor had simply fizzled out.

'God, I'm – I'm sorry, Bea.'

'For Chrissakes, stop apologising, Cal. Don't go. C'mon, pour me another glass of wine.' She smiled warmly and the confident, slightly brash woman she had been, which many of her colleagues admired, reasserted herself. 'Tell you what,' mischief twinkled in her eyes. 'Let's drink and talk till dawn. Maybe we can get some new goss going at the station.'

'Okay,' he laughed. 'Shall we check on Tris before we get too drunk?'

'Yeah.'

They walked quietly to the bedroom door and Bea's heart skipped a beat as she realised Tris wasn't in the bed. Just as she was about to say something, Cal tugged at her sleeve and pointed to the floor. Tris was curled up on the rug, sound asleep with his arms firmly wrapped around the uncomplaining cat.

'Seems the bed was too soft,' Cal grinned.

Bea sipped her wine, smiling slightly also. Perhaps, she thought, she'd run the tests on the sword the next day. She glanced at Cal wondering what he'd say if she told him she fully expected to find blood on the blade because Tristan had run for his life.

CHAPTER SEVEN

Over the years, Talisker had often dreamed of Una. In the darkest hours of the night he'd awaken from such dreams and the realisation of her death would creep over him within the first waking seconds like some dismal shroud. However, the pain of his loss had diminished gradually so that recently he would sometimes not think about her for days at a time, and then a vague strange guilt would come creeping over him as he would recognize he had almost let her go. In a world without photographs, memory, or loss of memory, was the silent assassin to grief, its gentle erosion over the years of her images, her face and her voice, easing the pain but replacing it with the bittersweet knowledge of a loss which was once in a lifetime.

Occasionally, a sense memory would conspire against such sweet denial. Talisker might be riding in the woods for example, and smell a certain herb or flower, or see a bird which she liked and he would hear her voice as clearly as if it were yesterday. He would pretend he did not hear her of course; he would steel his heart and ride on, distracting himself with the hunt or looking to the weather. It wasn't that he didn't want to remember his lost love, but rather that after her death he had buried his pain and thrown himself into looking after the children. But once in the isolation of the mountains there was nothing to stop his overwhelming grief and it hit him like a wall. He realised after about a week that in the other world they might have said he had suffered a breakdown; in Sutra, people would simply accept that he had lost his mind for a while.

But this was different from the dreams. This was as real as if she stood before him. If Morias had turned up and explained he had found a way to bring her back, Talisker would have believed him. He was sitting on the steps of the tiny one-roomed cabin he had built and was watching the night sky; there had been a meteor shower the night before and he was hoping for further displays – watching the stars had become a passion of his and he kept the details and sketches in a notebook written in a tiny spidery hand, trying to guard against the end of the pages. Beside him on the steps sat a small grey lynx; the lynx was not a Sidhe but a native creature to the forests, she came often and spent time with Talisker, sharing his food, occasionally donating a rabbit for the pot, and then she would leave for a while. Like all cats, the relationship was on her terms but that suited Talisker fine and he enjoyed the silent companionship when she did come back. He called her Princess (and he knew it was a bit lame) but it was more just a term of vague endearment than an actual title – he certainly never expected her to come when he called or anything like that.

Tonight the sky was an inky black; he stared

intently at the silver shimmer of the stars wondering whether the sense of anticipation he felt was really in the air, or whether it was something from himself. The heavens had no sense of time, did they? There was no 'last night' up there he reasoned, no night at all actually so . . .

'Duncan?'

It was her. Una. She stood just at the bottom of the steps on the narrow path. He couldn't make out her features in the darkness, but he just knew – like he knew she was wearing her green dress and had her family's dark green plaid wrapped around her shoulders even though the colours were flat shades of grey in the gloom.

'Una?' The word escaped his throat in a strangled noise. He realised in the instant of speaking it, that he hadn't said her name aloud for many years. 'What . . . ?' He began to stand up to go to her but she motioned him to stay.

'No, don't get up. You cannot touch me, my love. I am a mere shade and I am here on borrowed time. If you try to touch me, the spell will be broken.'

'At least come closer, Una,' he pleaded. 'so I can see you. Here, sit on the step. I promise I won't touch you.'

She came forward to sit on the step and he watched her every move, drinking in the details, each impossible moment seeming to stretch out into infinity. As she drew nearer, he smelt her familiar woody perfume and a feeling of deep tranquillity drifted over him like a warming blanket. She looked up to where he sat on the top step and he could see that she had been crying, her tears had left shimmering tracks on her pale skin. Despite his promise, before he knew what he was doing, he reached out to her and she shrank back.

'I'm sorry,' he groaned. 'Una, I'd sell my soul just to . . .'

'I know, Duncan. But listen to me, there is little time. Our children are in danger, grave danger.'

He frowned. He had hardly thought about Regan and Tris in recent weeks, assuming their safety in Soulis Mor as joint Thanes. And this moment, this meeting – why did it have to be about them? He shook his head.

'They're fine, Una. How can they be otherwise? They hold the highest office in Sutra. No one would dare endanger them – it would be treason even to talk of it.'

'No. How could you, Duncan? How could you turn your back on them like this? You have no idea what's happening in Soulis Mor, do you?'

He was stunned by her accusation. 'Well, if there was anything really wrong, the Sidhe know where I am, Sandro or Eion would have brought me word. I – I can't go to Soulis Mor, you know that.'

'Yes. And I understand your pain and unwillingness to revisit the place,' she nodded gravely. 'But much has changed, Duncan. Tsanuk, Elder of the lynx clan is dead, assassinated by an order which was signed by Regan. His son, Demukwa, has led his clan south to escape Regan's persecution.'

'No,' he stared at the apparition of his wife in horror. 'This is a trick, isn't it? You can't really be Una. Who sent you to taunt me?'

She stood up, her plaid wrap causing a faint warm breeze which carried her sweet scent to him once more. Her face became flushed and angry. 'And do you think this causes me any less pain than you?' she snapped. 'Do you think my soul rests easy? She is my blood and yours, husband, but that blood is surely tainted. She is under the influence of someone who professes to love her and that person has brought out her worst.' Una swallowed, trying to stop herself from crying once more. 'I fear her worst is evil.'

For some reason Una's anger and indignation reassured Talisker that it was indeed the spirit of Una. In life she had ever been quick to come to the defence of her children; it seemed the afterlife was no different. 'Who is this man?' Talisker frowned. 'It's not like Ree not to know her own mind.'

'His name is Jahl. He is Regan's confidant. That's all I know,' she shrugged helplessly and Talisker felt his heart would break she seemed so dejected.

'You're right, Una . . . even if it means I have to . . .' he stopped as though losing his train of thought for a moment and Una watched him closely, knowing that he was thinking something which to Talisker, was almost unthinkable: he must go to Soulis Mor. 'I must do something before it goes too far,' he muttered. His voice was low, almost as if he was loath to even say the words. He stood up, running his fingers through his hair as though wakening from a deep sleep, his features were ashen in the cold moonlight – almost as ghostly as Una herself.

'I would say it has already gone too far,' Una replied, unwilling to speak of Talisker's confrontation of his past. 'But Tristan is a far more pressing problem. I – I . . .' she began to sniff, fighting back sobs which shook her tiny frame. 'I fear he may be dead already, except that his soul is missing—'

'His soul, missing? What does that mean, Una?'

'I do not know. I only know I can not see him, either here in Sutra or in Lord Cernunnos' realm. I thought I must be mistaken at first, and I waited near the void to watch for him crossing through, but he didn't come. Duncan, I know they fought before he left Soulis Mor, I sensed their division, but surely . . . surely she would not have killed him?'

Talisker's expression hardened as the years of disquiet about his daughter came home to roost. And yet, in this moment, all he could remember was his joy when he held her for the first time. He sighed, 'I don't know, Una. I always felt . . . I always blamed her for your death.'

'Do not blame her, Duncan. She was just a girl and she was not responsible. She held onto my arm as long as she could.' Una did not meet his gaze.

'She could have done more though couldn't she? She could have done something else.'

'. . . perhaps . . . but she was panicking.'

'Gods bless you, Una, even now you love her still.'

Una smiled a tremulous smile. 'I am her mother.'

'So how can I look for Tris? If she's really hurt him I'll—'

'I do not have many answers, Duncan. But you must help them both. Perhaps Regan might know what has happened to her brother, although I'm not sure she will confide it. Jahl's influence grows stronger by the day. I wish I could help you all. Be sure I am watching . . . but I must go.'

'No. Please don't go.'

'This is very tiring for me.'

'Just sit there . . . you don't have to say any more . . . just . . . please, Una.'

She smiled warmly and new tears started in her eyes. Talisker knew that this time her tears were only for him and her, not for their children. 'I love you, Una . . . I miss you so much . . .' he said roughly, his throat closing around emotions which threatened to overwhelm him.

'I know, husband. We will be together again one day. For now, let's watch the stars together.'

They sat in silence; the meteor showers began again and the silver lynx snuck between them and curled up on the stair. Talisker watched first Una, and then following her gaze, the dazzling night sky. A tiny breeze stirred across his face, moving through his hair like a caress; a feeling of deep peace and contentment filled his being as though something inside which he had never known to be broken, was healed and made whole again.

'Una, I . . .'

But she was gone.

The falling stars reflected the silver tracks of his tears but Talisker was smiling.

Days later, Talisker approached the fortress city of Soulis Mor looking for answers; it had changed little in the years since Talisker had last seen it. The black stones endured the bitterness of the seasons in the north without detriment to the structure. As he paused on the plain before riding to the gates Talisker noted that if one looked carefully the damage from the battle for the city could still be seen; paler, less skilled brickwork patched the towers where fires had raged. The Fine maintained that no one remembered who built Soulis Mor, and certainly the gothic, almost surreal architecture was unlike anything else Talisker had seen in Sutra. The city fortress, squatting between the shoulders of two mountain ranges, had a presence all of its own and the Fine who inhabited it, Isbister's clan, now Tristan's and Regan's, treated the great city with respect and reverence.

To Talisker, Soulis Mor meant only one thing: fear. During the battle, Talisker's empathy had been unwillingly enhanced. He could see the souls of slain warriors still screaming their death agonies and in bleak despair for long after their corpses lay dead on the field. As the darkness of Corvus held Sutra in its thrall, no death was a release; the build up of tormented souls turned the already hellish scene of the battle into something which Talisker's mind would do anything to avoid confronting or remembering. Since the children had lived in the city he had never visited. Until now.

Finally he rode across the valley floor towards the great gates at a gallop least his nerve desert him. His horse – a tall roan mare unused to flatlands – sensed his anxiety and as they neared the city he had to fight to control what had become a headlong rush as she tossed her head and snorted, threatening to throw him. His heart was racing, everything in his mind was screaming for him to turn around, as he fought to calm the horse his voice shook slightly. But he stopped before the gates and forced himself to speak to the sentry.

'Tell Regan I would see her,' he demanded. His horse skitted and turned a full circle but he jerked her head around and fixed the man with a hard stare. The sentry looked unsure for a moment and then ducked back into the gatehouse. When he returned he had an older, probably senior guard with him.

'Who are you to demand audience with the Thane?' the man asked roughly. The younger sentry had obviously told him of Talisker's apparent lack of respect.

'Duncan Talisker. Tell her her father is here.'

She kept him waiting for over an hour. Talisker sat in an antechamber waiting to be summoned to see her. He realised after ten minutes that she was sending him a clear message: being her father lent him little or no respect in Soulis Mor. Few people passed by the doorway of the tiny room but Talisker imagined they noted that he was waiting. Word travelled fast in a city and word of how Regan decided to treat her father – contemptuously or otherwise – was bound to travel like wildfire. After half an hour he was furious and after stewing for a further half an hour he finally decided he'd had enough. He stood up suddenly and crashed through the double doors into Regan's chambers.

'Regan. What the hell's going on?'

She was sitting at a large desk with papers strewn across it apparently engrossed in something she was reading. For a moment she completely ignored his sudden entrance and when she looked up it was as if she had seen him only yesterday. It was the same Regan, the same sweet pale face, the same dark hair and intense gaze. He had expected changes perhaps but she still looked like Ree, his girl. Only when she next spoke did the differences in her character and demeanour become obvious; it was like a chill slap in the face.

'Father. Such a tender reunion after all these years.' She stood up and indicated to a seat on the other side of the desk. 'You must be weary from your journey. Have a seat and I'll get them to bring you some warmed wine.'

'No. I don't want a drink.'

'What do you want?'

'I want to know what's going on, Ree – Regan. I've heard things I don't like about your rule here.'

She arched her brows as though such an accusation could come as a complete surprise. 'From who? Who would say such things?'

'Well . . .' Talisker was uncertain of what to tell her. 'It doesn't matter who told me does it? I'm worried about you and Tris.'

At the mention of her brother's name Regan blanched and looked away. 'Do you know where Tristan is?' Talisker asked.

She shook her head, her expression bleak. 'He left,' she said. 'One night he just went. We'd had an argument.'

'About Jahl.' She stared at her father as though amazed by his blank statement.

'What do you know about Jahl?'

'Not much,' he said coolly, 'why don't you enlighten me?'

'We're just friends.' She looked distinctly uncomfortable now.

'I never said otherwise.' He sighed. 'Look, Regan, need I remind you why you came here? To look after Tris. We both know that Tristan is the Thane. We thought we were acting for the best but—'

'That statement could be considered treason around these parts.' The smooth voice came from someone standing in the doorway but Talisker stilled his first impulse to look over and didn't turn around.

'I was talking to my daughter,' he responded, still watching Regan. 'She knows what I'm talking about. As she is also Thane, she must decide whether I'm speaking treason.' Talisker fingered the hilt of his dagger; something about the speaker, even though he had not yet seen him, made the hair on the back of his neck stand up. He knew it was Jahl immediately and when Jahl walked into his line of vision, for some intangible reason, it seemed as if they had met many times before.

He was tall by Sutran standards, around six feet, and thin to the point of gauntness. Still, he had what Talisker knew would be considered a handsome face, ivory skinned and heavy-lidded dark eyes. High on one cheekbone he had a line of strange, arcane looking symbols tattooed into his skin. He wore jewellery and no weapons, not even a dagger to be seen; Talisker instinctively knew the little he had heard about the man was true, but how could Regan be so blind? He searched his daughter's face for the answer but where he half expected to find fear and signs of coercion, there were none. Her gaze was one of simple trust. Whatever their relationship was, it seemed Jahl had been clever enough not to underestimate Regan, he had taken his time and won her heart in a strictly conventional sense. Jahl was as smart as he was dangerous.

'You are quite correct, of course.' Jahl moved to stand behind Regan's high-backed chair, his arm resting possessively across the top. 'But from what I understand, Duncan, it has taken you nine – almost ten – years to summon this concern . . .'

Talisker didn't wait for him to continue. 'Do you often just walk in and interrupt the Thane's conversations? I want to talk to my daughter alone.' He looked pointedly at Regan; her whole demeanour had changed in the few seconds Jahl had been standing close to her. She leaned very slightly towards where he stood until her arm almost brushed against his and a faint flush had come to her cheeks. She reached up and touched Jahl's arm.

'Stay, Jahl,' she murmured. 'Father. There is little to say. I don't know where Tris is now, but I can assure you he has come to no harm through my doing. As for Soulis Mor, in his absence I must run it as I see fit. I am Thane here.' She fixed him with a cold gaze but, strangely enough, this only served to remind him of her as a girl – Regan was renowned in her teens for her smouldering glances when irritated.

'I never considered for one moment you'd hurt Tristan, Ree.' He stood up to go feeling saddened by her dismissal, having vaguely expected her to ask him to stay, to spend some time with her. 'If you need me, you can send word via Sandro . . .'

'Sandro?' She glanced at Jahl, 'Sandro has not been to Soulis Mor for a long time. No one has seen him, not even the Sidhe.' The implication of her statement was clear; if the Sidhe did not know of the *Seanachaidh*'s whereabouts, it was reasonable to assume he was dead.

'Oh. Just send word then . . . if you need me . . .' He scowled at Jahl. 'And you. If you hurt my daughter . . .'

Jahl's eyes narrowed but his tone remained deliberately light, 'Really, are you threatening me, Duncan?' he scoffed.

'You can call me Talisker. Yes, Jahl. If anything happens to my daughter, I'll kill you.'

Jahl didn't move or respond in any way, but for a second, the mask of smiling indulgence which he wore for Regan slipped away. He returned Talisker's angry scowl with an indefinable look of slow, brooding intelligence. Then, he smiled again and lightly kissed the top of Regan's head, his gaze still locked with Talisker's.

'Don't worry, I'll look after her,' he grinned.

'Goodbye, Ree,' Talisker growled roughly. He turned and walked away, feeling a hurt which had gripped him without warning. All this time he had imagined Tris and Regan to be . . . the same. It had almost never occurred to him that growing up would mean leaving him in every sense. He felt like crying and he wasn't sure what he would be crying for. Just as he began to descend the great staircase, he heard Regan's voice again.

'Father.' He ignored it. She was right, there was nothing to say.

'Father?' He was almost at the turn of the stairs now. He should never have come back to Soulis Mor.

'Father. Wait . . . wait . . . I – I command you.' Her voice was closer now. Was she following him? He quickened his pace.

'D – Daddy . . .' He stopped.

She stood near the top of the stairs. A beautiful young woman in a scarlet gown, all poise and fierce independence. Talisker felt a fierce swell of pride. He knew she would never fling her arms around him, that just wasn't Regan, but she wanted to say something, couldn't let him just walk away. For that tiny crumb of her, he felt inordinately grateful. He didn't move towards her, just waited for her to speak.

'Th – thank-you for coming. I know it cost you dear to enter Soulis Mor again.'

He nodded. 'Ree . . . he's poison. You must rid yourself of him.'

She shook her head, her obstinacy reasserting itself. 'You don't know him, Father. He . . . he cares about me, looks after me. It's hard to be Thane . . . lonely.'

'But Ree . . .' he stopped, knowing of old that his words were useless. 'Never mind . . .'

'Are you going to look for Tris?'

'Yes.'

She nodded, looking slightly tearful now. 'I hope you find him. Bring him home.'

'I will. Just promise me, you'll send word if you need me.'

She smiled, 'I'm fine, really, but if it makes you happy, I promise.'

''Bye then. Take care.'

'Goodbye.' She watched him go until the turn of the stair swallowed him up. Still she stood there, transfixed. Jahl came and stood behind her, tantalisingly close within her personal space, but not touching her.

'So that's your father,' he mused. 'I've heard he was a great hero.'

'Yes. What was your father like, Jahl?'

'I don't know. But my mother does not speak highly of him.'

Eskarius cursed the storm. As his wolf form, Vermesh, he could simply dig into any snow and wait out the blizzard, but his companion was far more vulnerable. The Fine were ever weak, he knew, depending on lowly animals for food and labour, cattle which had not even been allowed the dignity of the hunt before they died and lowly, stupid sheep which simply allowed the stripping of their coats and the killing of their offspring. What joy the Fine found in their existence was beyond Eskarius. There were few of the clansmen towards whom he felt any respect or affinity. And yet, this *Seanachaidh*, Alessandro Chaplin, was one of those few. He glanced back towards Sandro who was picking his way carefully across the snow-swept rocks like some aged clumsy bear. Eskarius knew him to be a good age – almost sixty summers – old enough to stay within one's lodge before the fire, old enough to be considered venerable. Sandro's long dark hair was streaked with silver and he wore a short beard which was grey but as they had talked and come to know one another over the last few days, Eskarius had noted the quickness in his eyes and the calm surety of his voice. Also, Morias had told Eskarius of the *Seanachaidh*'s plight concerning the nature of his 'cure'.

'Watch him well, Eskarius. I fear as the days pass, the burden of his own destiny may crush him,' the old man had cautioned. Eskarius knew that knowledge of one's death and the nature of that death, was something most men or Sidhe could not carry easily; Sidhe folklore told of such events and they were never happy tales, death could not be cheated or denied. As a *Seanachaidh*, Alessandro must know similarly discomforting stories. However, if Sandro was deeply troubled by the knowledge he carried, he didn't confide it to Eskarius, although his mood grew increasingly sombre as the weather closed in and made their journey hard, he hardly mentioned the subject. This seemed strange to Eskarius because he carried the gem of Sandro's death in his medicine pouch around his neck. Morias had decided they must take it in case anything should happen to him before they came back and so, each time Sandro looked at Eskarius, in a way, he saw death staring back. Usually, he smiled or joked, which in Eskarius's estimation made him a strong, wise man of great integrity.

On the fourth day of their journey, the *Seanachaidh* had been quiet, deep in thought it seemed for most of the day. As they settled down for the night, Eskarius Vermesh in his wolf form for warmth, Sandro began to talk quietly. So quietly at first, that Eskarius Vermesh almost thought he was talking to himself. The grey-brown wolf, who was at least the size of a man, regarded the *Seanachaidh* across the fire with solemn yellow eyes.

'I am telling you this story, Eskarius Vermesh of the clan of the wolf, so that when my death comes you may carry the story back to the Fine somehow. It is a tale of forgiveness.

'Once there were two friends, Arun and Dairmud. They were not alike as some friends are; it seemed to others of their clan that the two young men really had no common ground at all and they were friends despite this, as they grew up, both became tall and strong, much admired by the women of their clans. Arun became a soldier and Dairmud, a hunter.

'However, they grew in dark times and their paths took them apart. Years passed and Arun became the leader of a regiment of warriors, a respected lawgiver. One day, a prisoner was brought before him and Arun was shocked to see it was his friend Dairmud. Dairmud was accused of a terrible thing: murder. It was said he was possessed by a demon which would lash out and kill, turning Dairmud into a slavering beast. Arun spent many hours questioning his old friend. It seemed to him that his mind could see the facts, that Dairmud had done this thing, all the . . . evidence said so – but his heart told him it could not be true. As he looked into his friend's eyes, he knew this.

'But Arun ignored the voice of his heart and listened only to his mind – his intellect. A grave injustice was done and Arun was so sure of his cold logic that he did not stop it. Dairmud was sent away for many years to work in the mines of Assikla. The years passed and Arun thought of his friend often but never thought to see him again. But then, a small miracle happened; Dairmud, released from the mines, joined Arun's regiment. They went to war together and fought side by side although they could not overcome the bitterness between them. Then, one day, something came to light which made Arun know, with his mind and his heart, that Dairmud had been falsely accused. But here is the strange thing about forgiveness: Dairmud forgave his friend – he could see how Arun had followed what he thought to be true in his desire to uphold justice – but Arun, he could not forgive himself. Never. He did not seek to love again because he thought he was unworthy of love. He wandered the land like a lost spirit simply awaiting his destiny . . .

'And so it seems that forgiveness is not only to be given in order for a heart to heal. It must be gladly taken also . . .'

There was silence for a few moments as Eskarius Vermesh considered this; the gaze of the wolf rested on Sandro's face, watching the *Seanachaidh*'s reactions. Eskarius knew some of the forms of the Fine's tales and it seemed to him that this one was different; where was the glory and the magic? Transforming into his Sidhe form so that he could speak with Sandro,

Eskarius leaned forward across the fire and spoke quietly but earnestly.

'But your tale has no ending, *Seanachaidh.* What became of Arun?'

For some reason, Sandro looked mildly embarrassed. 'I suppose the tale is unfinished,' he said softly, 'you could say I'm trying it out on you.'

'Hmm. It needs work,' Eskarius replied frankly. He thought for a few moments, his head tilted to the side, almost as though he was listening. Sandro poked the fire trying to coax further life from the few spindly twigs they had found.

'Of course, you know the reasoning of your tale is flawed,' he said eventually. 'Forgiveness only has such power over one if that man or Sidhe should care about being forgiven.'

Sandro was about to respond when he realised that Eskarius was thinking about a whole different meaning for the story.

'Are you speaking of the wolf clan Sidhe?' he asked.

'Perhaps. We do not care for forgiveness,' Eskarius shrugged. 'Although it is just as well for there is none to be had from the Sidhe Nation. We walk alone. Always.'

Sandro nodded into the darkness, 'Then perhaps that should be the ending for Arun. Perhaps to walk alone with pride and dignity is no bad thing after all.'

Now, days later, in the freezing blizzard, just walking at all was a major triumph. The pass was a slipping, shifting landscape whose slick black slabs moved against one another for little or no reason. Sandro had already fallen three times and he was moving more slowly now, partly through caution, but also, Eskarius Vermesh suspected, nursing some injury to his only recently healed bones. The snow became heavier until it was difficult to see far in front of them.

'Eskarius Vermesh,' Sandro called ahead to the wolf. 'We should stop somewhere. This is impossible.'

Eskarius Vermesh agreed, he glanced back to where Sandro stood, his form shifting and indistinct in the snow. Ahead of their path he sensed something, a small pocket of stillness in the storm, if not warmth, at least cessation of the freezing onslaught. It was visible only through the mingling of his keen senses, a pale orange shape against the bleak backdrop.

'Yes . . .' he turned back towards Sandro to let him know of his find. But he realised with a shock that the *Seanachaidh* had disappeared without a sound. *'Sandro?'* More than anything, it was a rhetorical thought, he knew Sandro was unable to accept the mind-voices of the Sidhe but his calling out was instinctive. He began to scent back along the way he had just come, searching for the moment when his own distinctive scent mingled with the *Seanachaidh*'s lighter tone. When he reached such a place he stopped, frowning; there was no hole in the rock-face as he had almost expected there to be, but a wet outline where a rock had been until seconds earlier and then, tracks through the snow as if the rock had become a lethal sledge. Eskarius Vermesh groaned aloud which became a kind of whine in his throat, as his keen eyesight followed the trail down the slope towards the edge of a precipice; it would appear the *Seanachaidh* had slipped to his death but the wolf went to see if any faint hope might prevail. Walking very slowly, he picked his way across the deadly scree least he suffer the same fate as his companion; his gait more like that of a fox than the usual long strides of the wolf. The edge of the mountainside was almost indistinguishable against the bleached out colour of the sky and Eskarius approached cautiously, feeling the way with his front paws. On reaching the edge, he peered down into the crevasse, his head swimming giddily as his senses tracked the fall of the snow. It was impossible to make anything sensible of the view but there was warmth there, on a narrow shelf not far down on the wall of the crevasse – it might prove to be a buzzard's or eagle's nest with chicks inside, but Eskarius Vermesh allowed himself to think it may just as soon be Sandro. Without giving thought to why, Eskarius Vermesh sat down on the edge of the snow covered plateau and, throwing back his head he howled, a baneful howl. The sound echoed away across the Blue Mountains.

Such was the expanse of the wilderness they travelled, Eskarius Vermesh would have been most surprised to know that anyone might hear his cry. In fact, Talisker was only a mile away, heading for home after his failed search for answers in Soulis Mor. He stopped momentarily on hearing the howl of the creature, rightly guessing that travellers were in trouble. He hoped it was nothing they could not survive within the next ten minutes; although Talisker was fit and well adapted to the mountains the chill air was burning his nose and throat – his whole respiratory tract felt as though the ice and snow was packed directly in there. Glancing up at the darkening skies he cursed aloud before setting off again at a run.

'*Seanachaidh, Seanachaidh* . . . Are you there? Can you hear me?' Eskarius had transformed into his Sidhe form and was lying flat on the earth, peering over to the ledge. He was sure now that the indistinct heap of brown and grey on the ledge was Sandro, a few moments earlier he had heard a groan.

'Do not be afraid, *Seanachaidh*,' Eskarius called. 'Salkit watches over the mountain skies . . .' he cast around wildly trying to see some way of getting down to Sandro but he knew there was none, he knew that perhaps his only hope might be an Eagle Sidhe and it was doubtful indeed that one would answer the summons of a wolf. His voice dropped almost to a whisper as the hopelessness of the situation became unavoidable, 'If your death comes this day, Alessandro Chaplin, I will take your story of forgiveness back to the Fine as I promised.'

'Hopefully, that won't be necessary,' a voice behind him said. Eskarius sat up and looked around. A tall man was standing there, leaning on a thin stave of wood, he had long straight hair which was a faded red streaked with grey, a thin angular face unlike any Fine he had ever seen and blue eyes as intense as his own. The stranger wore clothes fitted for the mountains and carried a pack on his back.

'Duncan Talisker?' Eskarius frowned.

'Yes, wolf. Where is he?' Talisker asked abruptly.

Eskarius nodded towards the edge of tho crevasse and Talisker moved forward dropping to his hands and knees as Eskarius had done when nearing the edge. Using the staff he carried, he rubbed away the snow from the sill of the crevasse exposing the black rock beneath, then, opening his pack he removed a long coil of rope.

'Sandro,' he yelled down. 'Can you hear me? It's Duncan.' For a moment there was no answer and Talisker put his hand over his eyes as though to hide his emotion from Eskarius. 'C'mon, Sandro,' he muttered, 'Come on . . .'

'Duncan?' Sandro's voice was thin and weak, on the edges of fevered consciousness. He made a sound, somewhere between a laugh and a sob. 'Of all the gin joints in all the woild . . .'

'What did he say?' Eskarius frowned. For some reason Talisker was smiling now. Ignoring Eskarius's confusion, he leaned further towards the edge. 'Yeah Sandro . . . you played it for her, now play it for me . . .'

They were mad, Eskarius decided. Or this was some strange ritual of the Fine he was previously unaware of.

'Play it, Sam,' came the weak response from the cliffside. This remark was followed by feeble laughter. Talisker turned to Eskarius and handed him one end of the rope.

'Take this wolf. Tie it around that outcrop there – the one shaped like a bird.'

Eskarius eyed Talisker darkly. 'My name is Eskarius,' he said. Talisker did not respond so he snatched the rope and walked towards the rocks. 'What is wrong with this one?' he frowned as he came to the first outcrop.

'Trust me wolf, it's too soft,' Talisker called back.

Cursing under his breath, Eskarius tied the rope as he was bid.

'Sandro, there's a rope coming down. Can you tie it around yourself?'

'Yeah, I think so.'

With much apparent pain on Sandro's part, they hauled him up. Only when the *Seanachaidh* was lying in a crumpled heap in the snow did Talisker let go of the rope and, letting out a whoop of joy ran over to his friend, he knelt on the ground beside him and grabbed him in a strong bear hug. It was the first time they had seen one another in almost a decade – since Sandro had escorted the children to Soulis Mor – and the bond between them was undiminished by time. After their initial embrace they sat back, slightly embarrassed, still laughing. Eskarius looked on; he knew the Sutra component of their story as did all the young warriors of the Fine and many Sidhe and although his first meeting with Talisker was somewhat strained, he considered himself almost privileged to watch the reunion of two such remarkable men. The snow began to renew its assault on the mountainside and Talisker's and Sandro's energized voices were muffled by the elements and carried out across the solitude of the peaks.

'. . . lookit you. Look at your beard . . .'

'. . . how did you know . . .'

'. . . I didn't.'

'But we were looking for you. Morias . . .'

'Jeez, Morias. Is he still alive?'

Eskarius sighed and leaned against the rock outcrop. Snow or not, he guessed he could wait.

They sheltered in a shallow cave Talisker knew of at the end of the pass. Eskarius had said little but he helped the *Seanachaidh* to walk behind Talisker as he picked out a safe path between the shifting rocks. The cave was little more than an indentation in a rock-face but it gave fairly effective shelter from the blizzard. Talisker took kindling and candles from his pack and after a light meal of dried rabbit jerky and some herb tea, they settled down for the night.

'*Seanachaidh*, you didn't seem afraid as we lifted you from the cliff,' Eskarius remarked. It was something he'd been thinking about since the event – Talisker and Sandro had hardly dwelt on the subject and yet both must have known if Talisker had not arrived . . . Sandro smiled lightly, his face, reflecting the small light of the fire, was tired but relaxed. He tapped his throat to signify where Eskarius held his medicine bag; the temporary home of his death gem.

'Today, Eskarius, I discovered that knowing the manner of one's death can – very occasionally – have advantages.'

'What's this?' Talisker asked sipping his drink.

Sandro briefly explained about Morias's blundered attempt to save him, carefully choosing his words, mentioning only Jahl's name in relation to his recent torture. It seemed somehow inappropriate at that moment to burden Talisker with the knowledge that Regan must have signed the order. Talisker listened and nodded, only interjecting with, 'Christ, you've been through the mill, Sandro . . .' When Sandro finished telling about the gem, Eskarius opened his medicine bag, took the gem out and showed it to Talisker; the stone was warm in his palm and radiated the same soft purple light.

'I think you should take it, Duncan Talisker,' he said gravely.

'Oh no,' Talisker lifted his hands in the air in a gesture of denial. 'I couldn't. It's too much . . . responsibility.'

'But you don't understand. I cannot keep it in my bag. It is not mine.'

'Eskarius is right, Duncan. Only things sacred to him and the Wolf clan should be in there. It was good of him to carry it. Anyway, I'd be . . . honoured if you'd take it,' Sandro nodded.

Talisker took the stone from Eskarius and stared at it closely. 'Even when things were the worst between us, Sandro, I would never have wished this on you,' he said quietly.

'I know.'

'So tell me,' Talisker sighed as he wrapped the stone in a cloth and put it in his waist pouch, 'Why did Morias save your scrawny soul again? Has it got something to do with Tristan?'

'How did you . . .'

'I just know he's missing,' Talisker said. 'Or more exactly, his soul is missing, if that makes any sense. It cannot be seen either here, in the void or the . . .

afterlife.' He glanced at Sandro's and Eskarius's rapt expressions. 'You know where he is, don't you?'

Sandro nodded, 'Yeah. We know.'

CHAPTER EIGHT

Sometimes he felt this city was alive; he really did. Perhaps the city might endure the coming apocalypse, its silent streets rejoicing at the demise of the irritant which had infected it since the years it was built. Knox briefly imagined the empty spaces of the Old Town with only himself walking amongst the black stones and alleyways. He would walk into St Giles Cathedral – no, perhaps he would decide to live there – no one could stop him after all – maybe he would piss in the font and smash the sweetie-coloured, smug, glass saints – there'd be only him left – no one to stop him . . .

What was he thinking? It was a lie after all. He'd made it up. Or rather, he'd stolen Danny's lie and fashioned it into something altogether more spectacular. The End Of The World . . . yeah. The End Of The World Is Nigh . . . so repent, you poor sad bastards . . . except it wasn't – it wasn't nigh (whatever 'nigh' meant anyway) and sooner or later the Children would know it wasn't going to happen. Knox smiled briefly to himself; a spasm of twisted humour which reached his eyes for a mere second. In the meantime, there was fun to be had – fun in his efforts to manipulate the Children – influencing their new, and far more radical, agenda, and further fun in undermining the other Elders. Already they were down to three others from the original four. A small packet of cocaine planted under Joshua's pillow had ensured his fall from God's Grace. He had been the strongest and had to be the first to go. Leaving The Ark with his belongings he had glanced back to see Knox watching him from the leaded windows of the study where the Elders held their meetings. Knox had had the presence of mind to look serious and saddened before locking himself in his room to dispose of the drug.

Then there was Esther. She was still resisting him, playing a game which had a certain inevitability to it. He had been unable to catch her alone for a couple of days but he had seen her smiling towards him when she thought he wasn't looking. It wasn't as easy as he'd expected though, Esther was obviously waiting for him to make a move but Knox had precious little experience with women and wasn't sure what to do next. In order to get from A to D with her, he had to work through B and C, trouble was, he didn't know what that involved. He would speak to her soon; he'd already fixed the cleaning rota in The Ark so that she would be cleaning his room the following day. Soon, the apple scent of her hair would be on his pillow and he would bury his head in it and breathe her in like warm absolution.

Beatrice tucked the sword back into the large duffle bag she was carrying in order to conceal the weapon.

'Thanks, Paula,' she smiled, 'I just wanted to it check with you . . .'

'No problem, Bea,' Paula Wrightson nodded. 'It's certainly interesting as you say; the craftsmanship and styling are all consistent with early La Tene period. The maker did an amazingly good job – the markings on the handle and shaft are particularly fine of the period – but I'm pretty sure if we were to date it properly and test the metal, we'd find it's only about twenty years old. I'd say it's a fake. A dammed good one but . . .' she shrugged and sipped from a cold cup of coffee. Bea glanced around the tiny cluttered office, every inch of wall space was covered with sketches, maps and photos whose images were a lot less grim than those Bea had to deal with.

'Celtic's really your thing . . .' she muttered.

Paula looked pointedly over the rim of her glasses to where Bea sat, perched on the edge of the desk.

'What's up, Bea? Is there something else?'

'Nothing really, it's just . . . nothing . . .' Bea shifted slightly uncomfortably. She'd known Paula for years, they had met at university when their schedule coincided on the Archaeology front – for Paula, it was a passion which became her life and brought her to this tiny office in the museum and the grand sounding title of Senior Curator of Ancient Scottish History – for Bea the subject was something of a diversion which confirmed what she had already suspected; she preferred her corpses recently deceased so that the circumstances of their demise still mattered in the world. 'Well, there's this,' she sighed eventually. 'Tell me what you think.'

She put Tristan's necklace on the desk in front of Paula feeling a twinge of guilt – she had taken it while Tristan slept and she was hoping to get it back before he noticed it was missing.

'Wow. Where did you get this?' Paula lowered her head to stare closely at the object so that her dark hair touched the desk around it forming a little ring. She switched on the lamp without looking up and angled it down.

'Same place,' Bea shrugged, deliberately vague.

'I'm not sure it's meant to be the same period as the sword,' Paula mused. 'You know it's a finger bone, I imagine?'

'Yeah . . .'

'This gold-work is exquisite and I'm pretty sure the jewels are real. It reminds me more of something Abyssinian or even Egyptian. Can I hang onto it and confer with my colleagues?'

Bea felt a strange flutter of panic in the pit of her stomach. 'No, I'm afraid not,' she tried to sound casual, 'it's evidence.'

'Ah.' Paula frowned upwards. 'Well look, Bea, I want to see this again if I can. If this was found at a burial site or tumuli anywhere in Europe, it could be of major importance. Whoever this person was—'

'It was a man,' Bea interrupted.

'—he must have been really important. A king . . . possibly someone they believed had god-like powers . . .'

Keeping Paula's gaze Bea reached down and picked the necklace back up suddenly afraid that her friend would insist the artefact was treasure trove or somesuch. She couldn't fathom her own feelings of anxiety about Paula's investigation, she had invited the inquiry herself, but now it felt as though her friend was dancing around the edges of her secret.

'Okay, thanks again . . . gottogo pumpkin,' she smiled, slightly insincerely.

'Right. You okay, Bea?'

'Yeah. In fact I'm thinking of going back to work soon, within the next couple of weeks.' She began to edge towards the door.

'That's great,' Paula beamed, 'Really great. Listen, I'll call you – we must get together for a girlie evening soonish. My mum was asking after you by the way.'

'Yeah. Great. Give her my love. I'll call you . . .'

Paula stared after her departing back for a few moments. 'Hokay,' she muttered. 'Oh yeah, Bea,' she called, 'I'd use the side entrance if I were you . . .'

Bea didn't register what Paula had said. She walked through the airy white grandeur of the galleried main hall, her heels click-clacking on the hard marble floor. It was stupid, how she had reacted, she'd ring Paula later and apologise. High above her, rain whispered down onto the glass roof of the museum, the noise echoing around the space below like a cooling sigh; Bea sighed also letting the sound calm her thoughts as she walked to the main doors between the serene gaze of two huge bronze Buddhas. She hardly glanced to her right where the new Evolution gallery was sited and the realisation that it had been opened that very morning didn't touch her consciousness. Still thinking about Paula and the situation with Tristan, she pushed forward the heavy revolving door and walked out, into a riot.

At the bottom of the long flight of steps, police cars and vans were drawing up. Seemingly oblivious to the downpour, a large group of people were screaming slogans and waving placards. They were Creationists – the banners, now smearing in the rain, proclaimed things like '*Faith: the only missing link!*' and '*God created Darwin!*' It seemed as though the protest at the opening of the Evolution wing was descending into a pitched battle; the group had surrounded the Lord Provost who had opened the exhibition, along with a few notable SMPs. Someone had thrown bright red and yellow paint – probably at the Lord Provost – but the paint had spread further than intended and almost everyone involved in the inner circle of the tussle was covered in bright frenzied splashes. Bea watched the faces of the young protestors, their expressions were contorted with religious zeal, which had transmogrified into aggression. The dignitaries and journalists involved in the tussle seemed less inclined to talk or shout but simply struck out blindly at the protestors. A camera came flying through the air and smashed onto the steps where Bea stood; she thought she could pick out the photographers' curses from the general melee.

As she began to descend the stairs on the far right side trying to avoid the conflict, Bea noted a young man who had climbed up on the plinth of a statue of Robert the Bruce; he wore plain black clothes and his gaunt, rather angular build gave him the appearance of a great bird such as a crane. He had his right arm looped around the leg of Robert the Bruce's horse and was hanging off the side of this vantage point yelling at people in the crowd. It seemed to Bea that the youth was somehow in charge of the protestors but unlike his charges, his expression was one of sheer glee as he watched the proceedings. His boyish, mischievous smile was infectious and Bea found herself tempted to smile back in his direction. As he glanced over towards her, Bea snapped her gaze away and at the same moment, lost her footing on the steps, tripping down the last three or four. The colours of the absurd scene blurred about her as she fell and when the movement stopped and she looked up, he was there, crouching beside her.

'Are you all right?' he seemed genuinely concerned. He gazed down through a thin wet curtain of black hair, which he pushed back and stuck behind his ear, Bea noted the silver flash of an ear cuff.

'I'm – I'm fine. Really.' She began to push herself up and then hissed through her teeth as she realised she had grazed her hands quite badly.

'Here . . .' he fussed, 'let me help you . . .' He reached down and gathered her and her belongings almost in the same sweep. Without comment but suppressing a wry smile, he handed her her court shoe which had remained on the stair.

Bea stood up slightly shakily, knowing her face was burning with embarrassment. She had holed her tights and her knees were bleeding making her legs feel strangely hot and cold as the warm blood mingled with the rainwater. Trying to deflect attention from her pathetic situation she nodded towards the crowd. 'Are you in charge of this lot?' she demanded.

He grinned and stuck out his hand. 'Knox,' he said fixing her with an intense gaze. 'Only God can truly command them, but yeah, they listen to me occasionally.'

Bea shook his hand but didn't offer her name, maybe it was just the fall, but something about the youth unnerved her. 'I've got to go,' she said backing away. 'I'll get a cab . . . Thanks, Knox.'

He nodded, his smile fading as he watched her go. 'Come and see us, Bea,' he called. 'You too can know The Rapture . . . *Be patient and stand firm because the Lord's coming is near.*'

Although she still felt dazed she quickened her step moving swiftly towards the crossroads where she knew she could hail a cab. She stopped just before the corner; he had used her name! How did he . . . ? She turned back but he was no longer standing at the bottom of the steps.

She was almost home when she realised two things: one, her name was on her keychain and he'd probably read it as he picked up her bag and two, Tristan's necklace was gone.

Getting back to Morias was relatively easy after the initial 'falling-off-a-cliff incident'. However, by the time they found their old mentor again, Talisker felt he had aged a hundred years. On the third day, in the foothills of Cairn Dubh, the travellers came across an abandoned Sidhe settlement. There was little warning of what would confront them, Sidhe settlements always blended with their environment and this one was no exception, but Eskarius, travelling in his wolf form, halted suddenly, sniffing the air. Sandro, who was finding the pace difficult, also stopped immediately.

'What's wrong, Eskarius?' Talisker turned back

frowning, aware that the other two had stopped. The wolf Sidhe, knowing that Talisker could understand the Sidhe mind speech, sent his voice straight into Talisker's mind, the sensation like a clean cold echo. *'I can smell death, Duncan Talisker. Much blood . . .'*

'He says he can smell blood,' Duncan explained to Sandro. The two men paused and watched Eskarius as he moved towards the tree line, his posture low, his hackles up, slinking forward. It had been snowing for most of the day and the woodlands had an air of muffled stillness about them. Talisker drew a dagger from his hip and began to follow the wolf.

'C'mon . . .'

Nothing broke the silence once they stood within the confines of the settlement; the large wood and turf lodges and the smaller hide constructions were all burned away leaving only the supporting tree trunks and a few skeletal remains. A few belongings were scattered on the ground covered with a light dusting of snow. Talisker began to rummage around the buildings, lifting things with the vague idea that there may be people hiding.

'It happened over a week ago,' he turned to see Eskarius observing him. *'Do you see the weeds growing within the shell of the lodges?'* The wolf nodded towards the nearest building, *'This plant takes only one night to germinate where the ground is warm. See how tall they are.'*

'There are no bodies. These people fled for their lives,' Talisker muttered in response.

'They are lynx clan.'

'This was their home ground then . . .'

'Talisker! Eskarius! Over here . . .' Something about Sandro's tone made both wolf and man break into a run.

In a clearing behind the main area of the settlement were the bodies; warriors and lynxes. The freezing snow had preserved them where they fell, and then further snow had covered them over so that the clearing at first glance appeared full of gentle man and beast shaped mounds. Almost absurdly beautiful, the snow glowed a diffuse pink from the stains of the layer underneath. Silently Talisker and Sandro walked between the corpses stopping to clear the forgiving white shroud from their faces. All male faces except for one; the women and children had escaped, their menfolk making a stand against something which had apparently taken no casualties.

'What was it, Sandro?' Duncan whispered. 'Didn't they kill any of their attackers?'

Sandro cleared his throat and fought the impulse to whisper also. 'I don't know, Duncan, but some of them are badly burned.'

'Yeah,' Talisker's expression was bleak. He had found the young woman; she lay beside a young man and the soft white outline of her outstretched hand was unbearably poignant. At the edge of the clearing Eskarius Vermesh sat for long moments, his shaggy grey head hung in sorrow, then he raised his muzzle and howled into the encroaching darkness of the night.

It was after they had laid camp a short distance from the clearing that Sandro found the body of one of the aggressors. He had gone back to walk amongst them;

Eskarius frowned at this, not understanding the *Seanachaidh*'s desire to spend time with the dead but Talisker noted Sandro's fingers fidgeting and realised with a small shock of recognition that after all these years his old friend was still carrying his rosary. He was going to pray for their souls even though they were a world away from his concept of God. Once Sandro had gone Talisker and Eskarius – for the moment in his Sidhe form – said little to each other until the silence hung between them uneasily. Without Sandro around to mediate Talisker was useless at disguising his feelings towards wolf clan Sidhe. Finally, as he removed the rabbit meat from the fire, Eskarius spoke. His voice was so quiet, muffled sounding in the night air, Talisker almost thought he had imagined the Sidhe's words at first.

'He was a great man, a great Sidhe . . .'

'Huh?'

'My father. You cannot fail to think of him when you think about the wolf clan Sidhe – is it not so, Duncan Talisker?'

Talisker nodded his understanding into the firelight. 'The wolf clan never censured him or his memory, did they?'

'No. He is honoured among us.'

'He murdered my friend Deme and fatally injured Prince Makhpiyaluta.'

'Makhpiyaluta? Grey Ghost Stalker? He killed many women. Did he tell you of his dreamwalk? Of the women he killed?' Eskarius sounded scornful. 'He was a traitor to the Sidhe, not my father.'

Talisker's eyes narrowed and his gaze hardened in

the light of the fire. It was true he had heard some strange tales of Makhpiyaluta in the years since Soulis Mor but, although he and the Prince had been distant from one another, Talisker had been there at the time of his death and experienced through his mind the realisation that the Sidhe Nation 'home' could not be considered a legend. Makhpiyaluta had been instrumental in the last efforts to save the Fine from Corvus. He had brought the sacred gem which the Sidhe named *Braznnair* to the Fine.

'He believed he acted with honour. You know that.'

'So did my father.' Eskarius insisted stubbornly, 'And . . .' The wolf Sidhe was interrupted as Sandro crashed through the tangle of bushes between their campsite and the clearing. In his haste he slipped and stumbled through the snow.

'Come quick,' he rasped, 'come and look.'

Talisker stood up, drawing his dagger as he sensed his friend's panic. Sandro was having difficulty breathing, and was bent double, great gouts of warm breath issuing into the frozen night air like smoke. Talisker patted him on the back, 'Easy, Sandro, close your mouth and breathe through your nose,' he muttered. 'C'mon,' he glanced over to where Eskarius was transforming into his wolf form, 'Eskarius already thinks we're too damned old.'

Sandro groaned, 'I *know* I'm too damned old. Wait till you see this, Duncan . . .'

They grabbed a torch from the perimeter of the campsite and tracked back through the bushes, following Sandro's rather panicked trail with ease. Eventually they came upon Sandro's find lying at the very edges of the clearing, almost completely obscured by the undergrowth.

'What the hell is it?' Talisker breathed.

At first glance the creature appeared like a huge insect; its face, although formed from black chitin, had features like a man, it had long coarse hair and wore a gold circlet around its head. The rest of the body was more bizarre: the being had six insect-like legs and it appeared it would be capable of running on all six or rearing up like a scorpion, lifting its upper body. It had huge translucent wings which were badly damaged on this individual and, perversely, its upper body was encased in dark metal armour. One of the arms still held onto a long iron spear.

'Can you imagine the noise those wings must make when they fly?' Sandro shuddered. Talisker said nothing but removed the circlet from the creature's head and peered at it closely in the light of the torches.

'Gold,' he muttered. 'It's covered in inscriptions . . . look.'

As Sandro examined the circlet Eskarius suddenly stiffened.

'Wait. Be still. There is something there.'

Talisker touched his finger to his lips, gesturing Sandro to silence.

'To your left, Talisker. About five paces . . .'

Talisker darted forward without warning, there was a sudden shout and crashing noises from within the bushes and in the few moments it had taken for Sandro and Eskarius to follow his lunge into darkness they found him sitting astride his foe's chest ready to strike.

'Wait, Duncan!' Sandro yelled. 'It's only a boy . . .'

Talisker froze in mid-strike, realising his fear of the unnatural looking creature had partially caused his adrenaline-powered charge. He didn't lower his weapon though but pulled the boy closer by grabbing the neck of his jerkin. The boy said nothing, but Talisker knew he was afraid when he heard the tiny noise of a choked-back cry.

'Lynx clan.'

'I know.'

The boy was like Deme in his features; his skin and hair a soft burnished gold. He was dressed for battle and had a blue-black line of charcoal or paint across his nose and cheeks – he looked about fourteen. Talisker released his grip and dropped the boy gently back into the snow.

'He says he's looking for his father's body,' Eskarius thought to Talisker.

'Dammit, wolf,' Talisker snapped. 'Just wait . . . What's your name, boy?

'Zelzi,' the boy replied sullenly. He was scowling at Eskarius and the wolf was staring back unblinkingly.

'C'mon Zelzi, I'm sure you'd like a warm drink by the fire. Perhaps you can tell us what happened here,' Sandro said quietly. He held out his hand to help the boy up and Talisker stood up smiling slightly apologetically.

'I didn't hurt you did I, Zelzi?'

'No,' Zelzi tilted his chin defiantly even though a thin trickle of blood was sliding down past his upper lip. He wiped this away with the back of his hand. 'Why should I tell you anything when you travel in the company of wolves?' They began to walk back towards the fire, Sandro carefully positioning himself between Zelzi and his line of vision to the creature.

'You're right, you don't have to tell us anything,' Sandro nodded carefully as though considering this, 'but I am a *Seanachaidh* – Alessandro Chaplin – perhaps the spirits of the lynx warriors would want the world to know how bravely they died.' He put his arm around Zelzi's shoulders, partly to comfort him but also to propel him forward as the boy's footsteps became leaden as they crossed the clearing. 'Perhaps it would help their spirits to rest,' he suggested.

Once Zelzi was settled before the fire with a drink of warmed tea and honey, Sandro pressed him for more details of the massacre. Talisker and Eskarius said little, the boy obviously mistrusted them, giving them dark looks as he sipped his tea.

'It is kind of you, *Seanachaidh*, to offer to carry the tale of the lynx clan, but they would not thank you for it. There was nothing noble about the way they died . . .'

'We found one of the creatures, Zelzi. Do you know what they are?'

Zelzi shook his head wearily, 'They come in darkness. Skin burns when they touch it. Flames . . . flames come from the people. But that's not how they kill . . . their tail parts . . . whip up past their shoulder height, over their heads . . . and kill with a stinging blow.'

'Like a scorpion?' Talisker frowned.

'Yes.'

'But why would they attack a Sidhe settlement? Where did they come from?' Sandro mused.

'We are not the first settlement to be attacked by the

beasts – we have named them Naba Scoor – which means man-scorpion – although we don't know their given name. The Scoor have destroyed three settlements so far – two lynx and one eagle.' Zelzi looked tearful, his bravado slipping away as tiredness claimed his young frame. 'As for where they came from, everyone knows. She sent them.'

'She?' Talisker sat forward, his heart suddenly thumping in his chest, knowing what he was about to hear and unable to bear it.

'Thane Regan, curse her name.'

'No . . .' Talisker's horrified whisper carried into the freezing air like an agonised sigh. 'No, there must be some mistake.' He reeled backwards, landing heavily on his seat.

Sandro reached over and gripped his friend's shoulder in a mute expression of sympathy. 'How can you be sure, Zelzi? Why are the Sidhe saying this?'

'She hates us. And her cursed lover hates us,' he replied. His gaze travelled slowly between Talisker and Sandro sensing the tension; then he looked directly to Eskarius. Talisker was unsure whether the two Sidhe were shutting him out while conversing telepathically.

'Who are you people?' he said eventually. 'Did she send you to make sure the job was done?' He stood up, throwing back the blanket and grabbed a small dagger from his belt. No one moved but Talisker stared the youth directly in the eyes.

'She didn't send us, Zelzi. But I am Duncan Talisker – her father. Regan would never do such a thing.'

A slow hiss escaped Zelzi's lips. 'Her father?' He stepped around the fire to where Duncan sat – even sitting, Talisker was almost the height of the diminutive boy – for a moment, it seemed he would raise his blade and strike. Sandro's hand silently moved for his own blade although he was unsure whether he could bring himself to stab the youth. The decision was taken from him however when Zelzi spat forcibly in Talisker's face.

'Duncan Talisker. Gods curse you and forgive you. You have sired a monster.' Wrapping his blanket back around him Zelzi began to run from the scene.

'No, wait, Zelzi,' Sandro called. But it was useless, the boy disappeared into the shadows of the forest and no sound betrayed his passing. Eskarius transformed into his Sidhe form and walked to the edges of the clearing.

'Let him go, *Seanachaidh*. He will survive well enough,' he said. 'There is nothing left for him here.'

Talisker had not moved from his position by the fire; he stared almost blankly ahead. 'My God, Sandro,' he muttered, 'Can it be true . . . ? I only saw her a few days ago and she seemed just the same, just like . . .'

Sandro said nothing for a moment but passed Talisker a cloth to wipe his face. 'I don't know, Duncan,' he sighed. 'I had heard some things . . . just rumours . . .'

'It is true,' Eskarius had returned to the fire. 'She has been persecuting the Sidhe for almost two years now. Recently, she has become bolder, more cruel—'

'But these creatures,' Talisker protested, 'how could she conjure those things? She has no magic. She's just a girl . . .' His voice trailed away, his disbelief making him almost incoherent.

'She needs no magic, Duncan Talisker,' Eskarius's

tone carried no hint of censure and Talisker was quietly grateful for this. 'It is Jahl, her lover. No one knows where he came from only that his darkness is spreading quietly across the land while he plays and flirts with Regan.'

'No,' Talisker groaned, 'No . . .' He leaned forward and buried his head in his hands.

'Duncan. Are you all right?' Sandro crouched down and tried to comfort the stricken man. Eskarius looked away, embarrassed by Talisker's apparent weakness. When Talisker looked up again, his lined face was wet with tears, his gaze held by the light of the flames. 'I can remember her dancing, Sandro,' he whispered, 'dancing and laughing. She was always so full of spirit wasn't she? My girl . . .'

'I remember,' Sandro replied quietly. 'But Duncan, she's a woman now.'

'I know. I went to see her, to ask about Tris. Jahl was there, but she seemed strong still. She's in love with Jahl, Sandro, but I don't believe she's afraid of him. Maybe she doesn't know about the Scoor.'

'Maybe she just doesn't want to know.'

'If that's true, Sandro, her denial is costing lives. And if it's not true, she's guilty of murder.'

He was still in shock when they found Morias. The old man had begun to travel back towards them and they came upon him almost unexpectedly a couple of days later. He was walking across the snow-clad moorlands leading his mule. He wore a cloak of bird feathers over his tattered robes and the wind which was rushing across the moors tugged at his clothes and straggly beard.

'Ah, there you are,' he beamed as though he'd only seen them yesterday. 'Talisker, you look terrible. I knew you'd find him, Sandro,' he nodded towards Sandro and Eskarius. 'Let's go then.'

'Where exactly are we going?' Sandro asked.

'Don't you recognise the area? That's the western fringes of Or Coille just over there. We're heading back through the forest to Light of the Sky. Appropriate isn't it? Since that's how you first came.'

The travellers fell into step with Morias and began to walk towards the tree line. Talisker moved as though in a trance; since the evening in the Sidhe settlement, he had continually fretted about his children, his mind a whirling mass of reproach. What kind of father turns his back on his children in the way he had – simply because they were living somewhere he could not face going? he berated himself. Could there be other reasons? Regan had always been different, wilful, and Tris his own person. But what could have happened to them in the last nine years to bring them to this? To turn Regan into something unrecognisable . . . If only . . . If only . . .

'Morias,' he reached out and grabbed Morias's cloak slightly more roughly then he intended. The old man was swung around fairly forcibly but his expression, although surprised, contained little indication that he might be afraid of his old ally.

'What's wrong, Duncan?' Sandro and Eskarius stopped a little distance away, Eskarius looking faintly worried for Morias. Talisker did not let go of the feather cloak but pulled Morias nearer.

'Tell me. Tell me what you know.'

Morias frowned, 'You're not threatening me, Duncan, are you?' he asked mildly.

'Duncan?' Sandro stepped to Morias's defence as ever, but Talisker motioned him back.

'No, no I'm not threatening you, old man,' he growled. He didn't release his grip though and shook Morias lightly. 'I just need some answers. What's happened to my children? Where did this Jahl come from? Who is he?'

Morias blanched visibly so Talisker shook him again for good measure. 'Look, I know you know something. The gods know you don't they – so tell me what. . . .'

'Put me down,' Morias's mood suddenly changed, the faded blue eyes sharpening, his façade of vague benevolence slipping away. Talisker – realising suddenly that he had in fact lifted the old man off his feet – did as he was told and backed away slightly. Morias tutted and began smoothing down his ruffled feathers. When he next spoke, he watched Talisker's reactions closely.

'I suspect Jahl is the son of Phyrr. Although . . .' he locked Talisker's gaze in his own, 'I am uncertain who may have fathered such a child. It must have been a mortal – she would be unable to perform such an act of creation herself.'

Talisker's expression was one of stark horror. 'This just gets better, doesn't it?' he muttered. He glanced away, unable to meet Morias's gaze. Before the battle for Soulis Mor, Phyrr had sought Talisker out and seduced him; he had never been able to fathom why – Phyrr was capricious, playing games at the time which he was not party to. He looked back to Morias knowing that if Morias had not already guessed, his expression told the old man everything he needed to confirm his suspicions.

Morias stepped forward, gently took Talisker's shoulder and turned him away from the enquiring gazes of Sandro and Eskarius. 'Talisker,' he said softly, 'I suspect you have another son.'

Knox was trying to wake himself up. He didn't want the dreams tonight but part of him knew somehow that Daniel was coming . . .

A sudden jolt of sensation and then he is there. On the grass. With Daniel beside him. Like the first time. The sun is shining, but its light is a frightening, sickly yellow casting eerie, unnatural shadow.

'Have you thought about it?' Daniel asks.

'Huh?'

'What I asked you. What are you going to do?'

'Don't know really . . . I'm just taking it one day at a time.'

Daniel leans back on the grass and tilts his head back as though soaking up the sickly yellow rays. 'Don't know much really, do you?' he says airily.

'What do you mean?'

'Nathan. You're growing in power and status in a religious group – I believe you want to go all the way. They are leaderless without me and they know it. The Elders won't be able to act in harmony for long. But not only do you not believe in God but you know nothing about the Tribulations or The Rapture – have you read your bible recently? No. Have you prayed recently? No. What

are you going to do as the world starts to crumble?'

'But it's not going to crumble, Danny. You made it up, remember?'

'Did I?' Daniel starts to laugh raucously as though Knox has said something hysterically funny. The sound seems flat, trapped within the airless confines of the dream and Knox feels his chest tighten as panic grips him.

'You made it up, you liar. You're not real anyway. Get lost. Piss off . . .' he feels himself kicking and writhing but the dream Knox cannot move. 'Stop it. Stop laughing you bastard.'

Daniel does stop, quite suddenly and pulls Knox towards him so that they are entwined on the grass like lovers. For a moment Knox thinks Daniel is going to kiss him and he tries to pull away, pushing back with his neck, craning every muscle; 'No, no . . .' he is panting. But as Daniel's beautiful face fills the whole of his vision and his lips part to begin the kiss, a bright light issues from his mouth, bathing Knox in searing fire. There is no pain, just a golden, aching, bliss.

'Do you not know me, Nathan?' Daniel's voice seems to come from behind the light but Knox can see nothing else but the brightness. 'I am the First and the Last . . .'

'I – I don't know what you . . .'

'You killed me,' the voice is calm, holds no reproach, 'so now it's up to you to prepare.'

'Prepare?'

'Don't you see? It's all true, Knox. The End of Days . . . It's really coming . . .'

* * *

'It's coming . . .' the words were on Knox's lips as he woke, covered in sweat and tangled in his sheets. He said the words again, weighing them, making sense of what Daniel had said. Daniel . . . was Daniel an angel then? Reality began to reassert itself and he caught sight of the dim shape of his reflection in the long thin mirror on the wardrobe at the end of the bed.

'An angel?' he grinned slightly self-consciously into the darkness. 'A frickin' angel?' he laughed quietly and began to rummage in his bedside drawer for his tobacco tin. 'Yeah, right.'

'It's coming . . .' the last vestiges of the dream scuttled spider-like through his mind, taunting his trusting pragmatism as he lit one of the roll-up cigarettes he'd made earlier in the evening. With a soft hiss, his petrol lighter flared in the darkness of the room casting flickering shadow and illuminating his reflection as though he was still staring in wonder at the light in his dream. For some reason the big bed and the big, high-ceilinged room suddenly felt cavernous and empty. Knox pulled at the tangled sheets, arranging one around his head and shoulders like a loose tent. He supposed Daniel was right in a way – if the End was coming or not, Knox should be seen to prepare for it, and doing that would require some knowledge of the problem. He sighed and cast his gaze around the dim recesses of the room looking for a bible but there was none to be seen. Still determined to do the research, he stubbed out his cigarette and padded over to the door with only the sheet wrapped around himself; he'd go and look downstairs, there had to be a bible in The Ark somewhere.

* * *

'What did you think you were doing?' Regan was furious. 'Tristan loves that girl . . .'

Jahl smirked, 'Yes. Fairly frequently, I'm told.'

'That's not funny, Jahl. What's he going to say when he returns and finds her in this state?' Regan glared across the recesses of the gloomy dungeon room. On a narrow pallet bed a young woman lay unconscious; her name was Grace and she had been stripped and flogged to within an inch of her young life. Jahl had had his sport with her the night before and Regan's anger was partly because she knew his sadistic rages usually began with sex.

'You've gone too far this time,' she raged. 'I should have you flogged for this.' She turned to storm from the room.

'Really.' Something cutting in Jahl's tone made her pause. 'Would you like to know why I beat her, Thane Regan?'

'Why?' she asked coldly.

'She told me her secret. As a woman I'm sure you'll agree that telling a new lover all of your secrets is most unwise . . .' Jahl began to stride airily across the room and then paused, waiting for her to ask him.

'What was her secret, Jahl?'

'Something I should have guessed from the meeting with your father. You see, Grace was born here at Soulis Mor. Her mother was in the tower during the battle for Soulis Mor and guess who delivered her? Yes, your "adopted" mother Una Talisker. Grace's mother told her that your alleged mother, Brigid, did not in fact give birth to the Twin Thanes. Only one, a boy who was hideously disfigured but nonetheless, sole heir to Soulis Mor. Interestingly enough, Una confided to Grace's mother that she, herself, was pregnant at the time. Grace's mother didn't know what Una gave birth to but . . . I'm guessing it was a girl. Heir to nothing.' Jahl stopped his pacing and smiled disarmingly towards Regan.

Regan's face turned pale with fright or fury – Jahl cared little which it was – and she stood rigidly upright as though someone had tied her to a pillar. There was a long moment of silence in the chamber but Jahl, a past master of such gamesmanship, simply waited patiently for Regan to speak.

'Such lies are treasonable,' she said eventually. Her voice was completely controlled. 'I trust you had her tongue removed before you flogged her.'

CHAPTER NINE

'Light of the Sky' reflected the leaden winter light, its surface shimmering like a slightly dirty mirror. At this time of year the surrounding forest seemed to close in on the great stretch of water, its red leaves rotting around the shores, turning the still loch to stagnant brooding quiet. Past the fringes of the shore, half submerged platforms of ice sealed the secret of the water as though awaiting the spring, suppressing the sound of the waves beneath their freezing blanket. No bird call issued from the forest except for a distant curlew. Talisker and Sandro remembered the air of gloomy quiet well; both men stood staring out into the middle of the loch, each lost in their own memories. Finally, as though coming back to awareness, Sandro let out a long sigh.

'Thanks, Duncan,' he said.

'What for?' Talisker continued to gaze into the distance, unable or unwilling to let go of echoes of the past.

'Fishing me out,' Sandro grinned.

'Ah, well, that wasn't really my call. More Malky really . . .'

'Call me a killjoy,' Sandro replied, 'but I don't fancy getting back in there in a hurry. I was drunk the last time and it wasn't frozen then.'

'That won't be necessary, *Seanachaidh*.'

Both men turned to look back at Morias. He stood near the largest of a ring of toppled stones; the *Fir Chrieg*, the 'False Men'. These were the standing stones from which Sandro had successfully reclaimed the souls of the heroes of the Fine over twenty-five years earlier. The stones were overgrown with nettles and brambles and Morias had set Eskarius to work already clearing a pathway through to inside the circle.

'What do you mean, Morias? Like you said, that's how we came.'

'Yes but it is not necessary this time. The circle was bound up then by the magics which held the *Fir Chrieg*. This time we can simply use the stones.' He gestured towards the crumbling remains as he spoke.

Both Duncan and Sandro looked unconvinced; the stones had toppled outwards at the time of Sandro's intervention and most of them had broken apart. Morias's use of the word 'circle' seemed optimistic at best. Morias tutted at their expressions and turned away to start fussing over his mule.

'You could give Eskarius a helping hand if you like,' he called back over his shoulder. 'We have to be ready by tonight. Oh, by the way, there's something you should know. Time works differently in your old world to the way it does here. When you get back, it won't be very long since you left – if you see what I mean,' he gesticulated absently and began to rub down his mule with a handful of dry grass.

'How long?' Talisker demanded. He walked up to Morias glaring at him, irritated by the ancient bard's habit of releasing such information on a 'need to know' basis.

'Yes, how long, Morias? It would be useful to us to know. We left under a bit of a cloud.' Sandro – slightly more indulgent of his old mentor – tried to mediate between the two as ever.

Morias shrugged, 'About two years.'

'Two years! Sandro gasped.

'Well that's it then,' Talisker moaned. 'I can't go. I'm probably still being hunted for murder.'

Morias stopped and returned Talisker's glare. 'Need I remind you that we are looking for Tristan?' he snapped. 'He could be in trouble.'

'And whose fault is that?' Talisker flared. 'You sent him there, alone. He could be dead by now, damn you . . .'

'I had no choice. It was a life or death situation right then.'

'Duncan,' Sandro took Duncan by the shoulder and stepped between the two, 'this won't achieve anything.' Talisker said nothing but shrugged away his friend's hand and stalked back to the shore.

'Will he be all right, do you think?' Morias muttered.

'It depends. Is there anything else you've neglected to mention?'

Morias looked away and busied himself again.

'Morias?'

'Nothing that I know for sure, Alessandro,' the old man grudgingly admitted. 'It's just that I don't know how this transition will affect your bodies.'

Sandro sighed, 'Yeah, we're not as young as we used to be.' He glanced back to where Talisker stood pensively by the water. 'Don't be too hard on him,

Morias. A week or so ago he was in his little cabin communing with nature or whatever it is he's been doing for the last nine years.'

'It's not me that's being hard on him, Sandro.'

They continued their preparations until darkness fell.

Knox had had a bad day, a really bad day. First of all, he'd had a disastrous meeting with the Elders, the three remaining Elders (all in their twenties) were somehow . . . different than he had expected when he first came to power. They discussed the museum demonstration as if it had been a complete disaster. Knox, still biding his time and evaluating his position, said little although mentally he railed against their weakness. They had real faith though – at least they seemed to – and as far as Knox was concerned that put them at some intangible advantage. Sometimes, in his weaker moments, he wished he had faith, he wished he wasn't just pretending because . . . because Daniel had shown him the first true kindness he'd ever experienced. And living with the Children was warm and comforting and ultimately, better than being alone.

After the meeting he planned to go to bed for an hour, partly because he had a headache but mainly because he was feeling sorry for himself. As he walked past the main double doors of The Ark, he noticed a young girl of about sixteen loitering uncertainly in the hallway. She was blonde and very pretty, her blue eyes darting uncertainly around as though it had taken all her courage to come in.

'Can I help you, miss?' he said.

'I hope so.' Her voice was high and trembled slightly. 'I'm looking for my brother.'

He knew as soon as she said it. He knew who she was. As he spoke, he could hear a crashing sound as the blood coursed faster through his ears. 'Who's your brother? Maybe I can get him for you?'

'Daniel. Daniel Reilly.'

'Oh. Daniel.'

'Do you know him? Is he here? We're worried about him. He hasn't been in touch for months now and that's not like Danny.'

'You must be Rachel. Daniel often mentioned you.'

'Mentioned?'

'I'm afraid he's not here now, Rachel. Daniel left us in October.'

'I thought – I thought he planned to stay here . . .' her gaze flitted around the hallway taking in the dark, imposing woodwork which had once been grand looking but now was rotting. 'He liked it here, really believed in what he was doing. Did he say where he was going?'

'Not really. Mind you . . .' a spark of hope flared in Rachel's eyes, '. . . we did discuss missionary work, just between ourselves. You know, Third World countries. Daniel was keen to spread the word there. Perhaps he'll contact you when he gets settled if he's gone abroad.'

'Okay,' she sounded disappointed. 'I don't know how my mother's going to take this. Look, here's our number,' she handed Knox a card. 'If he gets in touch, could you let us know?'

'Of course.'

She turned to go, and as she did so, the filtered sunlight from the glass panels of the doors caught her blonde hair making a halo around her head, so that she looked like an angel; just like Daniel.

'D-don't worry, Rachel,' he tried to smile reassuringly but the vision of Rachel as an angel had unnerved him. 'He'll be fine. He's doing God's work.'

She smiled slightly but made no reply as she left. She couldn't hide her disappointment, her eyes were brimming with tears.

Once she had gone, Knox stood staring at the doorway for a moment, caught up in the idea that Daniel's family were all angels and perhaps they would come and avenge him. A sound escaped him, somewhere between a sigh and a laugh and he put his hand to his mouth as though to deny his mirth.

'Why did you tell her that?' It was Esther. She had been watching.

Knox fought to look unflustered. 'Do you think she would have believed me if I'd told her the truth?'

Esther shrugged. 'I suppose . . .' but there was something accusing in her dark eyes.

'Is there something wrong, Esther?' Knox frowned.

'Can I speak to you in private, Knox? In your room?'

Once in his room Esther had broken down. In floods of tears she told him she wasn't coping, that she had started looking for help. He frowned at first, not quite understanding until she rolled up her sleeve and showed him the track marks inside her forearm. Knox was no stranger to drugs even now, but he'd never been able to face injecting himself. The red scars on Esther's porcelain-white skin unexpectedly shocked him. Worse, he'd always imagined her to be so self-possessed but now it seemed she was more like him than he had known; weak and self-destructive. Drugs were strictly forbidden in the Children and Knox knew Esther was expecting his censure.

'Why do you think you're depressed, Esther?' he asked gently.

'I miss Daniel. I really miss him, Knox . . .'

'Still?'

'We – we were lovers. How could he have just left without telling me?'

Daniel, he thought bitterly, *why did it have to be Daniel? – I'm glad I killed you, you bastard. You can never have her again.*

'I can't believe he's gone, Knox . . .' she sniffed.

'God has taken him up, Esther. He has work for him to do . . . listen, where are you getting the stuff?'

'J-just on the street.'

'It's not safe, Esther. It could be anything. I want to help you yeah? But while you're working through this, come to me. I'll get you something safe.'

She stared at him for a moment, disbelievingly, 'W-what methadone?'

'Em . . . yeah, if I can.'

She sniffed, pulling herself together although she still seemed relaxed in his arms. 'I don't believe it,' she smiled tremulously, 'I thought you'd throw me out. Daniel would have. He wasn't like I thought . . . It seems to me, he's just conveniently gone. Maybe he just didn't have the nerve to dump me.'

'No, Esther, no. You mustn't think that. I was there remember? I saw.'

When she left, he sat there on the edge of his bed, his mind reeling, his shirt and hands smelling of her perfume. Then he started drinking.

He didn't even like whisky but it was the only thing left in Daniel's stash after the months he'd been gone. Knox had worked his way through the gin and the brandy – even some Jack Daniel's – but the whisky was last. He wondered what they would say if they knew their precious saint had kept such a well stocked booze cabinet. Whisky made him feel like a child, his eyes stung and his throat burned when he drank it but all he wanted now was the solace of the alcohol and the soft blurring of reality that drunkenness promised.

All around his chair scattered pages littered the floor like so much confetti. He'd been reading his bible again as he drank; he knew it all now, Acts, Thessalonians, Revelations, all the choice bits which prophesied the End of the World and the Second Coming. He'd ripped each page out as he finished just to prove to himself that he'd read it, feeling more and more pleased as the pattern on the carpet became obscured. The day turned into evening and the evening grew darker but Knox read on, because each time he stopped he thought about her and it hurt him. He was past the nicely drunk stage by eight-thirty, the room was lurching around and he felt nauseous. There was a quiet knock on the door.

'Knox? Are you in there?' It was LearnToFly's voice.

'Woe unto you, LearnToFly,' Knox whispered, still in the thrall of Revelations.

'Knox?'

He stood up and further ripped pages sloughed down his front, a few sticking to his clothes. This amused him tremendously, to be 'clothed in the Word of God'. He moved to open the door, fighting for calm or at least the vaguest appearance of sobriety as he did so.

'LearnToFly,' he smiled. 'What can I do for you?' It was little use, he realised, LearnToFly could probably smell the alcohol.

'Are you coming to the evening prayers, Knox?' LearnToFly kept his tone fairly neutral but he couldn't disguise the fact that he could smell the whisky, also he was trying to crane his neck to see past Knox into the room.

'Ah.'

'L-lookingUp suggested you might like to r-read the blessing tonight.'

'Tell you what, LearnToFly . . . why don't you do it? I'm not feeling too well. I'd really appreciate it. Here,' he grabbed one of the pages at random which had somehow stuck to his shirt and thrust it at LearnToFly, 'this will inspire you.'

LearnToFly frowned but then looked at the page, 'Ah, Acts 2:42 The Fellowship of the Believers . . . g-good choice, Knox.'

'Yeah well . . .'

'Are you s-sure you want me to do it?'

Knox reached out to pat LearnToFly on the shoulder but then realised this would bring him, and his alcohol-laden breath, closer. He nodded reassuringly. 'You'll be fine, LearnToFly . . . honestly, I have complete faith in you.'

'Thanks, Knox,' LearnToFly beamed, 'th-that means a lot to me.' He walked slowly back down the corridor, his gaze fixed on the page Knox had given him. 'G-good night . . .'

'Good night.'

As he closed the door, a wave of nausea hit Knox; the nervous energy used to appear sober to LearnToFly dissipated and he bent double, thinking he was going to vomit. When nothing happened he straightened up again laughing quietly to himself. Staggering back to his chair, he slumped forward across the desk, reaching for the whisky but instead his hand closed over something cold and sharp.

'Knife,' he said into the empty room. 'Hey Esther, lookit this . . .' His voice trailed off as he stared at the knife. He'd been thinking about Esther all day, a kind of unconscious thinking which ran through the back of his mind like a hurt, even as he read. Holding her while she had cried for Daniel . . . that was harsh. What would she think of her comforter if she knew? And what would she say if she knew his offer of support stemmed from the fact he saw the opportunity to control her? She would be repelled. Because Knox knew that his need for Esther wasn't a bright and shining thing; it wasn't love, it wasn't beautiful in any sense. Something in Esther spoke to the darkest part of Knox's being, the craven frightened part of him which no one could love, not even himself. Her helplessness as he held her had only served to arouse him, which in turn, fed the constant fire of his self-disgust.

He groped around for his whisky glass with his right hand, keeping his gaze fixed on the knife as though frightened the perfectly inanimate object was going to come alive. This time the whisky didn't sting his eyes, he knocked back the glass without blinking and wiped his mouth with the back of his arm. A sudden thought seized him as he felt the faint tingle of the alcohol on his skin. She wouldn't do it, would she? She wouldn't censure him even though he deserved it, he deserved to be punished. Punished for everything, even the stuff she didn't know, for Daniel, for the lies, even those he had inherited . . .

Without even stopping to analyse his drunken reverie, he picked up the knife and pulled it suddenly across the back of his arm. He made no sound, no exclamation of pain; there was no pain, just the strangest, sharpest adrenalin rush. Knox stared down at the beaded line of blood that issued from the fine cut. Why wasn't it flowing properly? He slashed again, more strongly, and this time the blood came freely; welling out, in the darkness of the room robbed of its scarlet, simply dark liquid. He slashed once more but this time the adrenalin was subsiding and a hot stab of pain caught Knox unaware.

'Ahhh,' his vocalisation of the hurt caught him as unaware as the pain had done and he gasped as though taking the sound back. Flinging back his chair he rushed to the window and, pushing it wide open, he stuck his arm out into the chill air. It was raining; the sound had seeped into his consciousness and his instinct was similar to sticking a burn under a running tap. The rain beat against the old house and was blown in through the open window, soaking Knox's white shirt and plastering his hair to his cheeks and forehead. Everything seemed to slow; he watched the chill water disperse the blood, the sensation in his arm like cold fire. Raindrops flew smoothly towards his face and chest leaving trails of light like minute silver comets. His mouth was still open as though he was still screaming his hurt, although no sound now escaped him, and he threw his head back as the cold wetness invaded his mouth and throat, letting sensation refresh and burn him. As he stood reeling in the blast of wind, for a few moments Knox felt a dizzying sensation like flying.

'Speak to me.'

He thought the voice was in his mind at first, had the smallest spark of self-possession left, enough to know he was drunk, injured and well capable of imagining such things. He turned back into the room grabbing a towel from the end of the bed, which he wrapped around his arm, ignoring the fact he was soaked. He stood there dripping and panting for a few moments, listening to hear if the voice came again. Nothing. Pouring another drink, he began muttering to himself: 'Woe! Woe, o great . . . great . . .'

'Speak to me. I know you are there.'

Perhaps he would have denied it longer had he been sober. Knox stared around the room, searching for someone in the shadows but he could see no one. He picked up the glass again, now smeared with blood and finger marks, but as he reached it to his mouth his hand

and arm began to shake violently; grabbing the glass with both hands he raised it to his lips like a drowning man but just as he was about to drink, he saw it.

Hanging over the end of his bed-head was the necklace he'd stolen from that woman, Beatrice. He'd only taken it on a whim – it looked as though it might be valuable enough to finance a luxury which Knox could ill afford to become a habit – if he sold it, it could potentially keep him in cocaine for up to a year . . . Now, it was glowing, a faint greenish colour. As he staggered towards it, Knox distantly considered that perhaps one of the gems in it was catching the light from the bedside lamp but he dismissed this idea almost immediately; the glow was spreading outwards from the gem evenly, like a nebulous sphere, on the outer edges of the sphere, soft tendrils of the light were reaching out, questing for something. Knox stopped at the end of the bed.

'Did – did you . . . say something?' He felt stupid, ridiculous even asking the question aloud. Perhaps some of the Children were trying to trick him, sending him over the edge . . . perhaps they knew about Dan—

'Yes. I spoke to you. What is your name?'

'Knox.' Knox's mind was reeling, dizzy with alcohol and the adrenalin rush from the cuts on his arm. He was light-headed now but sure of what he was hearing. Steeped in the apocalyptic visions of Revelations – of which he had not believed one word at the time – he felt sure that the voice could only have one source. He fell to his knees at the foot of the bed, realising that the knife he'd used on his own flesh had been deemed inadequate punishment. Divine justice was a reality.

'Are you . . . ? Are you God?'

'God?' The voice seemed to consider this a strange question. There was a slight pause, during which Knox imagined he might be struck down for his impertinence. Finally, after what seemed an age, the answer came.

'Yes.'

'I'm sorry. I'm really sorry for everything. I mean, I repent of my sins . . .' Knox garbled. 'The thing with Danny, I mean, well you can see, you know how he was, a f-false prophet, leading your Children into . . .'

'Yes, yes . . .' the voice sounded dismissive. *'Get off the floor. I do not require you to grovel. Come closer.'*

Knox did as he was bid, sitting on the side of the bed and almost sidling up to the top until he sat at the level of the pillows, staring down at the green light. 'C-can you see me?' he asked nervously.

'Yes.'

Without warning the green glow began to shift, tendrils of the light reaching forward, questing for Knox's face. He squirmed as they touched his cheek although the sensation was not too unpleasant; warm but sharp, rather like the cuts on his arm.

'Be still,' the voice cautioned. *'I am simply looking to see what is in your heart and mind. Ah . . .'* There was silence for a few seconds and Knox felt a strange calm as the green tendrils shifted and moved, bathing his wet bloodied face in their glow.

'I do not understand,' the voice came eventually. *'Where are you, Nathan Troy?'*

'You know my real . . . of course you do. Where? Edinburgh. Scotland.'

'. . . of course. No matter. Listen to me, Nathan. When you wake up, your first instinct will be to deny me. Do not do it. Await my word. Do you understand?'

'Yes.'

'This will serve to remind you.' The light flared suddenly and though Knox tried to look away, he could not. There was a sharp smell of burning flesh and he pitched forward on the bed. Then there was nothing but the blissful blackness he had sought so hard all evening.

Jahl flung himself on his bed. It had been an exhausting night and if his guess was right, it wasn't over yet. In light of the new information he possessed, plucked from the warped mind of the stranger, Knox, there were yet things to consider before the dawn. His mother would be proud of the duplicity of his new plan, except that it involved her and actually she'd kill him without regret if she knew. He considered having a sleep before giving Soulis Mor back into time, but it seemed a waste of his resources, he was about to end the suspension, had his hands raised to begin the incantation, when he noted an earlier, lesser spell was coming to fruition.

In the corner, near the dark space of the window, hung a web, made purely from light. No spider lived there, Jahl had woven the complex maze himself and it was merely an echo of the web he had lain over the northern territories of Sutra. But just like a normal arachnid snare, his own would move, vibrate, in reaction –

not to a fly – but to magic. Jahl moved across the room and gazed thoughtfully at the tiny motion of the threads, which even now was increasing as the magic became stronger. If his sense of direction was true, magic was building, gathering, by the shores of Light of the Sky.

'C'mon, can't we just go?' Talisker moaned. 'How much longer, Morias?'

Morias looked up from where he crouched by the fire. It seemed to Talisker that all he'd done for the last hour or so was crouch there, muttering and throwing occasional weeds into the flames. Sandro shifted uneasily, a storm was coming; the clouds, visible by the stark light of the full moon, were skimming across the sky to the eastern side of the loch where a huge cloudbank was building. The air had become noticeably different in the last hour, previously damp and snow laden, it had acquired an unnatural dry quality and Sandro imagined he could almost taste the breeze. Eskarius seemed to be suffering from the atmosphere worst of all, he'd transformed into his Sidho form and sat wordlessly hunched by the fire, his keen senses obviously besieged.

Now he was here, beside the stones, it didn't seem that long ago to Sandro that he'd performed the 'Ur Siol', the one act of magic he had ever done, which almost cost him his soul. Of course, it had been over twenty-five years ago, he rubbed the rough granite of the crumbling stone – which had trapped one of the *Fir Chrieg* – almost affectionately. If he remembered correctly, this one had been Kentigern's stone . . .

'It's not an easy task, Duncan,' Morias muttered. 'These stones are weak now. I used a stronger entry for Tristan. There now. We are ready.'

Talisker looked at the space between the stones. 'It looks . . .'

'Exactly the same, I know,' Morias snapped impatiently. 'Why men must always require flashes and bangs with their magic, I'll never know . . .'

Sandro laughed nervously and Talisker shot him a look.

'Remember,' Morias cautioned, 'You must return as soon as you can or it may be that months will pass here. Jahl . . .' he glanced at Talisker, 'and Regan, may do much harm in that time. Gods willing you find him.'

'Perhaps you could have a word with them, Morias.' Talisker's remark sounded slightly harsher than he intended. 'Sorry,' he mumbled. 'I'm slightly on edge.'

Morias nodded in acknowledgement of his apology and let the remark pass. 'I may be gone when you return. I will go where I can be most help in the current situation. But Eskarius has agreed to wait here.'

'Thank-you wol . . . Eskarius,' Talisker smiled a tight smile. They turned to go.

'Wait! Something is coming!' Eskarius was pointing across the loch. The storm had broken, and a hissing sheet of rain churned across the water towards them. For a moment Talisker could only see the grey diffusion of the storm but then lightning illuminated the scene, five creatures flew on the edges of the storm. Talisker felt a sick sensation in his stomach as he drew his sword, it had been so many years since he had seen any combat but a blaze of adrenalin reminded him he could survive this.

'Naba Scoor,' Eskarius hissed. On the edges of his vision, Talisker noted the Sidhe transforming into his wolf form, Vermesh.

'You must go,' Morias urged. 'Do not wait with us. We will be—'

'Don't be ridiculous,' Talisker snapped.

The Scoor attacked from the skies; there was a sudden lurching rush as Talisker was flung forward onto the ground as the leader of the five raked across his back with some kind of spear. He rolled over quickly in the wet grass and came up cursing with a mouthful of rainwater. The Scoor had lifted back up into the air with a light motion of its scabrous wings and as Talisker stumbled to his feet it dropped back down to press its advantage. Hacking out with more luck than judgement, Talisker managed to lop off two of the creature's insect thin legs but the Scoor seemed to feel no pain, in fact, barely glanced at its dismembered limbs which twitched and moved on the grass. Talisker was aware of Sandro yelling and the snarling of Eskarius Vermesh but had no time to react to his friend's plight as the Scoor advanced on him from above, jabbing with its barbed spear.

'Talisker, get down!' Morias's voice barked. Without waiting, simply reacting to the command Talisker dived to one side just as a bright flare of white light hit the Scoor in the centre of its iron breastplate. Whatever powered the light was strong; it pierced the armour and exited the other side, impaling the creature for the seconds it took to die. Looking round in slight bewilderment, Talisker saw Morias ducking back behind one of the stones, his hands still glowing with the discharge of whatever magic he had flung at the beast.

'Don't just stand there, get Sandro,' Morias yelled above the din. Without waiting to see if Talisker complied with his instruction Morias turned his attention to Eskarius Vermesh who was in difficulty as he was being attacked from above. Two other Scoor circled overhead out of reach, seemingly confident of their victory. Talisker ran towards Sandro who was backing away from his opponent which had landed but was charging towards him; Sandro had been right, the noise of the creature's wings was a sickening brittle whine, audible even above the lashing of the now torrential rain. The momentum of the wings carried it forward as if it still flew across the grass and, as it came, the Scoor opened its strange mouth and screamed a horrible, sharp screech which was so alien and frightening, Talisker felt as if his bowels were turning to water.

'Sandro!' Talisker stood beside his friend and prepared to help fend the creature back. 'We've gotta go. Morias can . . . c'mon . . .' As the Scoor reached them both Talisker and Sandro pulled unexpectedly aside as though reading one another's thoughts with that strange synchronicity which battle situations often created. The Scoor's own swift momentum carried it ahead, and before it had time to turn Talisker and Sandro attacked its back, chopping into the hard chitin of its wings. Talisker's sword severed one wing completely and Sandro's left the other hanging by an ichor dripping thread. The Scoor screamed and convulsed but the two men didn't wait to deliver the killing blow but began to run back towards the stones.

As they ran, the scene appeared to blur into a frightening tableau. Morias was only just striking out at the Scoor which was attacking Eskarius Vermesh; the creature had almost latched onto the wolf's back and Morias was frightened of killing the wrong one. Eskarius was rearing up, snarling and yelping until the Scoor lost its hold and was thrown back, pulling great lumps from the wolf's pelt. As the Scoor fell back, Morias struck immediately and the scene was lit by the bright lightning of his magic which was caught and refracted by a million raindrops. The Scoor they had injured had fallen to the ground, its insect-like limbs thrashing and spasming as it died. The two which had been circling in reserve immediately dropped lower and began to fly swiftly in pursuit of Talisker and Sandro. Eskarius, freed of his attacker, ran to catch up with the two men, to run alongside them for the last few yards.

'Good luck, Duncan Talisker.'

Talisker had little breath or time left to reply.

It was not like before. Had Morias had the time, he could have explained the dynamics of the gateways to Talisker and Sandro. Perhaps he thought it was better they didn't know. Twenty-five years earlier they had passed through water, arriving beneath the surface of Light of the Sky. This time, they ran through fire. As they entered the circle at a run Sandro reached out and grabbed Duncan's wrist; Morias had cautioned them to stay together. Both stopped dead as a wall of flame appeared before them as if from nowhere. Talisker glanced back; he could see the scene outside the circle as a frozen, blurred image. Right outside, the remaining two Scoor were poised as though ready to push into the circle. He looked back at the flames, they burned silently at first, without any discernable heat.

'I guess we go on,' Sandro's voice seemed to come from far away, although Talisker could see him speaking the words, they arrived in his mind like a disembodied echo. He gripped his sword before him as though it could be of some use.

'Keep walking,' Sandro's voice came again, 'Morias said to . . .'

Then the brightness of the flames is all around him and it begins to burn.

'Keep going. Don't stop . . .'

It burns, but it doesn't burn. His clothes are not on fire. He can see himself running through the fire, his legs and his sword. And he can hear a sound. It's like the noise his running feet should be making. Or maybe it's his heartbeat. That's bad. He doesn't want to hear his own heart. Hopes it's his feet . . .

The burning is like . . . it's not like he imagines. It's not pain although he knows it should be. It's more like, melting, dissolving, leaving nothingness. He listens for his feet/heartbeat again. Hopes he is still moving. He can't tell . . .

'Sandro . . .' He calls out. Tries to look around for his friend. He's frightened now. He can see something behind the flames and it's darkness. He remembers the

void. Remembers that each time he crossed through the darkness . . .

. . . he was dying.

'Keep going.'

Who said that? Is he just thinking?

I don't want to die . . .

. . . again.

Then the flames are gone. The darkness is gone. Replaced by darkness which was entirely natural.

'Aw shhhit. Why can't it ever be easy?' Sandro's voice sounded strange and flat within the confines of the little dark room. He gave a rueful laugh. 'How was it for you, Duncan?'

Talisker sat up, rubbing his face which still felt strange, his skin felt hot and prickly; probably imagining it, he decided. 'I hope Tris appreciates this,' he muttered. 'D'you think we're in the Close, Sandro?'

'I guess so. Don't think there're any other gateways into Edinburgh . . .'

'Yeah, like Morias tells us everything . . .' Talisker's journey had not left him in the best mood.

'C'mon,' Sandro stood up, a hazy silhouette as Talisker's eyes adjusted to the darkness. 'Let's head towards some fresh air eh? I feel like someone's skinned me alive.'

Talisker stood up also and wordlessly began to follow Sandro towards the dark outline of a doorway. Sandro carried on chatting, his nerves well and truly jangled by the crossing.

'D'you know what I'm going to do? I'm going to have an espresso coffee,' he mused. 'I haven't had coffee for years. Not just a wee espresso cup though, a great big mug. Huh, I probably wouldn't sleep for a year . . .'

'Is that the best you can do?' They had come out into a long corridor now, somewhere Talisker was sure he dimly remembered. The first faint greys of daylight trickled in. 'I'm going to the pub,' he smiled. He was feeling slightly better already and the realisation that they were, in fact, in Edinburgh made him feel unexpectedly happy.

'Oh yeah. And what are you goin' to use for money?' Sandro chided.

'Jeez, do you have to spoil everything?' He looked ahead as they came to another door which Sandro tugged open. Relative daylight flooded in. Enough to see by.

'Oh my God.'

'Sweet Christ.'

Both men stared at one another's face in complete disbelief. Sandro reached out and touched Talisker's skin.

'Ow,' Talisker complained, 'Still sore.' Then he broke into a wide grin. 'Always was a handsome devil eh?'

Sandro let out a whoop of joy and they hugged one another in a great bear hug, reeling and dancing in the cold, joyless space of Mary King's Close.

The years had burned away. Duncan and Sandro were young men again.

'Wake up, Knox.'

'Wha . . .?'

'Wake up. You do remember, don't you?'

It was mid-morning. Weak sunlight filtered through the gaps in the heavy blackout blinds. Knox sat up and looked around blankly, vague memories of the night before creeping in. The room stank of sweat, stale whisky and something else . . . blood. A surge of hot pain from his arm seized him at the same moment he remembered the knife and the cutting. He let out a quiet groan, his gaze fixating on the red-stained bed sheets wrapped around him. His head hurt. His head really hurt . . . as if . . . Reaching up, he felt his forehead: it was clammy and sticky. In the middle was a tender raised bump. Knox struggled free of the sheets to walk over to the mirror to examine the strange injury.

'Knox!' There was nothing imagined about the voice. It wasn't only in his head but in the room. Like a normal voice, but not . . . The slap of memory was immediate and Knox sat down heavily at the end of the bed staring at the necklace in renewed disbelief.

'Yes, Lord,' he whispered. 'I am here.'

'Good. There is something I need from you, Knox. As a sign of your suitability to lead the Children . . . my Children.'

'Is it true, Lord?' Knox was rubbing at his eyes as though still trying to waken himself from a dream. 'Are you going to end the world?'

'Not exactly. Only those who displease me. You have read your scripture, have you not?'

'Yes – I . . . but why me?' Knox rallied slightly. He frowned at the necklace as if facing down an opponent.

'You could have had Daniel. Daniel was better than me. He believed. I know that now. I just thought he was tricking us. But Danny was for real. I – I'm not . . .'

'For real? But you can become "for real", Knox. There is time yet before the Tribulations. Do this task for me – prove that you are worthy and . . .'

'No.' Knox stood up. 'I don't believe you. You might be a demon . . . a – a false prophet. Yeah.' He felt nauseous and light-headed as dehydration from the night before caught up with him. His legs began to tremble.

The voice paused for only a few seconds before it continued almost as though he hadn't spoken.

'. . . and I will reward you. I will reward you well. You would like power, would you not? Power to do good of course.' Something in the voice's tone made it seem perfectly clear to Knox that it – He – knew doing good was not high on Knox's agenda. But He didn't seem to care. Perhaps it was right after all that God would choose someone who was flawed. A sinner in fact.

'All right . . .' He shifted, a line of sweat trickling down his back.

'Look, Knox. Look at the image I am showing you. You may close your eyes if it helps. There. This being is lost to me. Fallen. You must find him.'

Knox closed his eyes as he was told and a picture appeared in his mind, the image was grainy, slightly distorted perhaps . . . Then he realised the picture was not distorted; it was a boy, or a young man, whose body was cruelly twisted, his neck held at a strange angle giving him the appearance of a slightly hunched back. He wore strange clothes too and a circlet of gold around his head. 'Is – is he the Antichrist?' Knox whispered.

'Possibly.'

'Possibly?' Knox had somehow imagined God would be more definite.

God sighed, but once again simply ignored Knox's doubts. *'You will need help to find him. Put on the necklace.'*

They walked out into the afternoon sunshine of the Royal Mile and stood for long minutes, their senses reeling at the noise and chaos of the city. If Morias was right, only two years had passed and certainly the scene looked much as they remembered it. The Royal Mile, also known as the High Street, was the main tourist street in Edinburgh. At the top end, the huge edifice of Edinburgh Castle squatted on the basalt plug of an extinct volcano, down the other end of the steeply sloping street was Holyrood Palace and the grounds of the Queen's Park. Between the two lay a mile of shops, cafés, pubs, and every strata of Scottish history the visitor required. It was really there, seeped into the ancient stones although many visitors did little but buy a tin of shortbread and drop money into the case of the ubiquitous bagpiper. Sandro and Talisker had both missed the city to some degree; for Talisker, the years in Sutra with Una had dulled the bitterness of association and now he saw the stark artistry of St Giles Cathedral as though through new eyes.

'So how old do you think we are then?' Sandro mused, fiddling slightly self-consciously with his hair.

Talisker smiled to himself almost fondly, the memory of Sandro's vanity suddenly coming back to him. It was something the Sicilian had seemingly lost in Sutra, but it occurred to Duncan that given a week back in the city, Sandro would revert to fastidious type.

'Well, I'd guess I'm thirty-four, so that must make you thirty-six. They're the ages we were when we left.'

Sandro shrugged, 'Makes sense,' he agreed. 'Though I feel like I'm eighteen again.' He grinned broadly and Duncan almost blanched; it wasn't the grin of Alessandro the *Seanachaidh* but Alessandro Chaplin, DI; it was as white, as wolfish as Eskarius but laden with arrogance, vanity and wit. After all these years then, the city was still in his blood.

'What?' Chaplin frowned.

'Nothing. What do we do now? Surely Tristan wouldn't have gone far . . . unless he had no choice . . .'

'We need help, Duncan,' Sandro nodded.

'We don't know anyone who'd help us. Sandro, we can't go within a mile of your police buddies. How do we explain our absence? We don't even know if they put the murder case to bed and . . .'

'Hey, mister,' two young lads of about ten or eleven sauntered over to where the two men stood. They were dressed in baggy shorts, T-shirts and trainers. It seemed to Talisker that the children of the 'real world' were scrubbed, almost chemically clean-looking.

'. . . my mate says your swords are plastic.' The taller boy nodded at Talisker's leather scabbard and Talisker cursed inwardly, realising he and Sandro had made too little effort to prepare for their arrival.

'Is it, mister?' the younger boy asked. 'Can I hold it?'

Sandro stepped forward, curtailing Talisker's awkward response – he'd never been good with children.

'What's your name, kid?'

'Peter . . . Pete.'

'Well Pete, me and my mate here are appearing in a show at the Castle. If you want to see our weapons, your mum'll have to bring you to see the show.' He gave an exaggerated bow as he imagined an actor probably would. Pete frowned.

'See, I telt you they was plastic,' his friend jibed. 'C'mon, let's go and see if we can make the soldiers laugh at the Castle . . .' He pulled at Pete's sleeve but the boy seemed reluctant to go. Talisker suppressed a smile; he could remember trying to make the sentries at the Castle laugh when he was a kid. They weren't allowed to move or speak, making them the object of torment for every bored kid on school holidays for miles.

''S'not plastic, is it?' Young Pete seemed to take the matter of their weapons rather personally. Talisker glanced around and then drew his sword slightly out of the scabbard. The sunlight glinted off the blade in a rather satisfying manner.

'See, see Thomas . . .'

'Cor . . .'

'I can't take it out here, lads,' he glanced at Sandro and smiled slightly, 'the polis'll arrest me.'

'Aye right mister . . .'

'Come and see us at the Castle eh?'

'Okay.' The boys turned to go, seemingly satisfied with a mere glimpse of the sword. Duncan and Sandro watched them, slightly bemused. At that age, they too had been inseparable friends, perhaps had been together on the day they had made the sentry laugh – neither could remember, although it seemed likely – now, they had shared a lifetime and a half of experiences. Sandro glanced at Talisker, his eyes only resting briefly on the medicine bag Talisker wore around his neck, the glance was immeasurable.

'Bea will help us,' he said. 'She was probably my closest friend after Diane passed away. She had a bit of a thing for me really . . .' he smiled again, suddenly considering the possibility of flirtation.

'But she's police too,' Talisker objected.

'She's a friend first, I'm sure.'

'Let's hope so, eh?'

'C'mon.'

'Where?'

'Well she lives in Colinton. It's about five miles that way,' Sandro nodded. 'I'm assuming you haven't kept bus fare in your pocket for the last twenty-five years.'

Deep within the confines of Mary King's Close the dank air becomes drier, harsher. In the room where Duncan and Sandro arrived, flames appear from nowhere, burning silently, flickering shadow on the old stone walls. In the midst of the flame, two figures appear. It seems they are not running but flying and as the figures grow larger, a sound like buzzing pestilence fills the silent, subterranean streets.

CHAPTER TEN

It was early evening by the time they arrived at Beatrice's little cottage. Because it was almost winter the skies had been dark from around four and the faint sting of frost hung in the air. Talisker was glad of the cover of night, his and Sandro's clothes had attracted more attention the further away from the city centre they walked. People assumed they were part of a show while they were within the Old Town but as they reached the outskirts a few people did a double take when they saw them. Luckily the dusk curtailed people's curiosity; that, or the cold expression Talisker fixed them with if they seemed about to approach.

Colinton was one of the more 'well-to-do' suburbs of Edinburgh. It still possessed the air of all slightly resentful villages which have been swallowed up by the encroaching city. There were few shops and the houses nestled quietly into the sloping landscape of the river valley which bordered the Pentland Hills. Some of the buildings had a faded Victorian gentility and it was easy to imagine that when they were first built, the unobstructed views to the hills beyond had been truly tranquil. Now, the orange tungsten glow of the city bypass was reflected in the night sky and the constant hum of traffic in the middle distance was enough to remind the residents that their refinement belonged to a bygone age. It was pleasant though, quiet by city standards and the comforting smell of wood-smoke from a hundred desirable wood-burning stoves drifted into the still air.

'I think it's that one at the end.' Sandro pointed. 'I seem to remember her garden backed onto the road. I think . . . I might have helped her put up the arbour.' He shrugged, 'I could be wrong though. Are you all right, Duncan?'

Talisker had stopped and was staring around frowning, his instincts, honed in Sutra, had caused him to drop his hand to the hilt of his sword. This was not lost on Sandro.

'Remember . . . remember my sight, Sandro?'

'Sight? Oh, yeah.'

'Something's wrong. Something's here.'

'Like what? Like a demon?' Sandro cast his gaze around also, Talisker's mood making him nervous. There was nothing unusual to see. A dog barked in the distance, the sound carrying over the neighbourhood like a wave of normality. 'C'mon, Duncan. God knows what I'm going to say to her,' he laughed, his tone slightly edgy.

'Go ahead.'

Sandro opened the gate and started up the path, his feet trampling and crushing the fragrant herbs Bea had planted there, releasing the soothing scent of camomile and lemon balm into the cold air. He breathed deeply, trying to be calm. 'Here goes,' he muttered. He glanced back as he said this and realised Talisker was backing up the path behind him, his sword drawn. 'For God's sake, Duncan,' he hissed, 'that's hardly going to put her at her ease.'

He stopped. The front door was open. 'Look,' he breathed.

Talisker nodded to indicate he should go in. 'But what if she doesn't live here any more?' Sandro whispered. 'All right, all right, I'm going . . . Bea?'

The first thing he knew was that Bea still lived there; even in the gloom, he recognised her habitual clutter, but in fact, his senses told him before his brain caught up: Bea's scent pervaded the house, a sense memory over twenty-five years old – orange blossom.

'Bea? Are you there?' Sandro edged into the living room which was in darkness except for the light from the fire. As his eyes adjusted, picking out the shapes of the furniture and the piano Bea loved to play, Sandro realised the room had been trashed; broken glass littered the floor and earth from a smashed plant pot was strewn across the carpet in a chaotic splash where someone had thrown it. Duncan switched the light on and walked across to the far window, his feet crunching on the glass.

'Look at this, Sandro,' he fingered a gash in the plaster of the wall, 'someone's been using a sword in here.'

Sandro said nothing, he was staring in abject disbelief at something he had found on the carpet beside the couch.

'What? What is it?' Talisker frowned. He walked over and looked also.

'Ye gods,' he gasped. It was the bottom forelimb of a giant insect-like creature, someone had hacked it off at the joint and a small pool of blue ichor surrounded the limb. Talisker knew from recent experience that this would not disable the creature it came from.

'Scoor? Here? No, surely . . .'

There was a sound from the bedroom and both men raced to the door, their hearts pounding and minds racing at the impossible questions raised by their find. Talisker snapped on the light but there was nothing to be seen, the room was untouched by the chaos which had invaded the living room. A tiny noise came from inside the old pine wardrobe against the far wall. Sandro moved silently over and flung the door open with a sudden movement. There was a short scream, and then as Sandro flung himself to the floor, a loud bang. Talisker stood as though rooted to the spot, his hand still on the light-switch as someone tumbled out of the wardrobe still waving a pistol in front of them.

'Bea! Bea, it's us!' He knew he was talking to her but after the gunshot his ears were ringing with white noise as hers would be. Bea's mouth was open as though she was still screaming or gasping but no noise was distinguishable above the strange buzzing in his head. Talisker moved towards her frantically waving his arms in a 'don't shoot' gesture. She was hysterical, waving the weapon wildly, her normally smart severe hairstyle plastered to her face by tears.

'Bea, don't . . . put the gun down,' he was mouthing, he could almost hear himself now but was pretty sure she still couldn't. Just as she pointed the pistol directly at Talisker, Sandro pulled her legs from under her, grabbing her around her knees; she toppled to the ground with a shriek, dropping the gun as she did so. Sandro caught hold of her and shook her by the shoulders, 'Bea, look at me. Look at me . . .'

Talisker could only just hear Sandro's voice but it was clear from Bea's expression that she had become abruptly aware of who was shaking her. Her green eyes widened in a mixture of relief and incredulity.

'S – Sandro?' He could hear her now, her voice shook as she reached forward and touched Sandro's face. 'No . . . it can't . . .' Sandro seemed unexpectedly moved by this reunion and his eyes were bright with tears as he smiled and nodded at her.

'You're alive,' she said. 'I knew it. I always knew . . .'

'Bea.'

She looked back over to where Talisker stood slightly awkwardly and smiled a tremulous smile. 'Duncan.'

Sandro helped her up and she stood for long moments gazing from one to the other as though not trusting what she was seeing. 'Oh God,' she whispered. 'Oh God.' She hugged Sandro tightly, burying her face in his chest, her shoulders shaking as though she was sobbing. Sandro glanced over at Duncan and smiled almost apologetically, then he hugged her in return and made quiet 'shh' noises. Suddenly she pushed herself away with a gasp and turned to speak to Talisker.

'Duncan. I'm sorry. They t-took Tristan.'

'Tristan? Tristan was here?'

'I was looking after—'

'Who's "they?"'

'They . . . don't you know? Knox – he's called

Knox and . . . Don't you know what those . . . *things* are?'

'Yes but . . .'

'Oh Christ. We've got to go. We can't stay here.'

'It's all right, Bea. We're armed.'

'No, no, you don't understand. I called the police. Callum – you remember Cal, don't you? They'll be coming.'

Talisker and Sandro exchanged frantic glances. 'You're right, Bea, we've got to go,' Sandro agreed. 'How long ago did you call them?'

'Not long, maybe five minutes.' Bea was slowly calming down, her breathing was returning to normal and she picked up a pillowcase off the bed and wiped her eyes on it, leaving a long black streak of mascara. 'But don't go.'

'Bea, we can't explain things,' Sandro said gravely. 'Trust me. No one will believe us.'

'I'd believe you, sweetie,' she smiled slightly ironically and reached for the packet of cigarettes on the nightstand. 'I've seen those things. And talked to Tris. What I meant was – let's all go. So we can talk. Come on.' With remarkable self-possession she walked back into the living room and picked her car keys off the bookcase.

'Maybe we should . . .' Talisker gestured towards the mess.

'No time,' she sighed. 'Maybe we'd better get rid of that thing though.'

Sandro picked up the Scoor's limb, it was extremely light in his hands. After casting around for a few seconds he hastily folded it into the fire. After a brief hissing sound, the limb burned away with a bright sulphurous flame.

'Yeeuk,' Bea muttered. She patted absently at her hair, realising what a mess she was in. As she reached for the door Sandro took hold of her hand.

'Bea,' he said gently, 'are you all right? Are you all right to drive?'

Her chin trembled slightly as she fought back fear and emotion. 'I could murder a gin right now,' she admitted. She gazed at their worried expressions and smiled slightly. 'It's so good to see you both. So good.'

Tristan was cold. In the attic rooms of The Ark there was precious little heat. Knox had fetched him a blanket as an afterthought. Above his head he could see sections of the night sky where the old slates had slipped slightly over the years. A chill night breeze whistled through these gaps and puddles on the wooden floor gave evidence to the fact that, when it rained heavily, the attic was less than weatherproof. Tristan shivered and pulled the thin blanket tightly around himself.

He had been only marginally less surprised to see the Naba Scoor than Beatrice. Although from a world where such things were not only possible, but probable, Tristan had never seen a Scoor before. Rumours of such creatures had reached him before he left Soulis Mor, from those few Sidhe friends which he maintained contact with behind Regan's back. With bitter irony now, he recalled his unwillingness to believe Regan would sanction such things. He knew it was Jahl's doing but his sister . . . surely she could have stopped him if she chose? And now, for some strange reason, Scoor were here in this world. It seemed obvious that they didn't belong here much like himself.

It also seemed as though Knox was acting alone. When they had reached the grounds of the house he had bundled Tris through a side door and up a narrow dark stairway, afraid of being seen. The sound of singing was coming from somewhere in the house but no one heard or paid any attention to Knox's entrance. The Scoor had apparently vanished once Tris had been put into the van, at least he hadn't seen any more of them since they left Bea's house. He wondered about Bea, she had probably been more frightened than he, and yet she had fought, screamed and thrown everything she could lay her hands on at Knox. When Knox had managed to grab her by the arms she had spat in his face before kicking his shin hard enough for a cracking noise to be heard. There was little doubt in Tristan's mind she came from warrior stock, if only she'd had a sword, perhaps they would have stood a chance.

Knox was almost more frightening than the Scoor. There was some intensity about the young man that Tris had only encountered once before; Jahl had a similar demeanour except, behind Knox's gaze was something else . . . something empty, more fragile. Falling off a cliff . . . that's what it was like, what Knox was like; poised, ready to step into oblivion.

Despite his cold and fear, Tristan felt his eyes begin to close. Hunching up into a ball on the floor, he felt his lashes flutter against the skin of his forearms. What had Knox been saying?

Stuff about god . . . which god he wondered? It was apparent there might be only one on this world. One god and all these people . . . He must be pretty powerful . . . He wouldn't be watching for Tris though, one tiny soul from a distant world. No one would be watching for him.

Tris slept as the night frost turned to snow, muffling the ancient house, enveloping the cold space of the attic in a blanket of lonely despair.

In the end, they drove all night. Through the darkness and the snow. There seemed to be no real reason for this, the mood in the car was sombre and for a long while no one spoke. Bea's mood had changed from relief and fear to sullen agitation. She smoked three cigarettes in quick succession, filling the car with greasy yellow smoke and stubbing the butts out in the overflowing ashtray. Sandro coughed and tried to open the window but the handle was broken; Bea wordlessly opened the driver's window a tiny crack without looking at Sandro.

'Are you angry with us, Bea?' Sandro frowned eventually.

'What do you think?' she snapped.

Further silence. Talisker stared gloomily out of the window although there was nothing to see except the silver-white tracks of the snowflakes which appeared to be attracted to the car like shining ephemeral moths. The car's windscreen wipers made a tired, grudging sound and Talisker felt himself drifting into sleep in the relative comfort of the back seat.

'. . . think we've been gone a couple of years . . .' Sandro's voice drifted into the back of the car on warm eddies of smoke and recycled air. He was trying to explain Talisker guessed; he remembered what Sandro had said earlier. 'Trust me, Bea. We can't explain this. No one will believe us.' She had said she would, and Talisker really wanted to stay awake to find out but . . .

'. . . So, you just decided to stay? What about all the people who care about you both, Sandro? What about . . .'

She sounded hurt. What about me, Sandro? That's what she really meant, Sandro, you idiot.

'There was no one really.'

No one. It's true.

'I can't accept that. What about your job? All the good work you did? Do you think Diane would have wanted you to leave the world behind?'

Oho. Don't bring her into it.

'Let's leave Diane out of this . . .'

'And for what? Some weird, fucked-up place where they can have those . . . those things.'

She's angry, isn't she?

'Why are you so mad? Sutra's a beautiful place. I have a life there. Duncan has children. Those things – Scoor – aren't what Sutra's about.'

'I'm not mad. *(Nah.)* Not really. Well, not much. Maybe I'm just frightened for Tristan. And for us. As the first woman in the world to encounter Scoor, I would say I'm entitled to be mad . . . or something.'

'Can't you just say you missed me?'

'Arrogant bastard . . .'

Yeah, she missed you, Sandro.

'Yeah pumpkin, I missed you.'

She's smiling now, I bet. Smiling in the darkness . . .

He woke as coldness cramped his toes. Gentle snoring was coming from the front seat; Sandro and Bea were propped up against each other under a travel rug. In sleep Sandro's face looked younger still, the line of his brows softened. Bea, talked-out and driven into exhaustion, was leaning onto his chest, her hand curled unselfconsciously amongst the dark hair at the opening of his shirt. Talisker smiled and rubbed at the steamed-up window with the edge of his plaid, it didn't change the view however, the window was snowed over from the outside. He pushed open the car door and stepped out into a dazzling white landscape.

They could be anywhere, he realised. He'd been paying little attention to the roads they were taking the night before, the road to nowhere had never seemed so pertinent; all around the blazing white of freshly fallen snow softened the contours of the landscape. They were in a long valley which stretched off into the horizon, a few feet away from the car a narrow stream trilled along the valley floor, a relentlessly optimistic sound. The sky was a clear fresh blue, the snow obviously spent. He could have been back in Sutra except for the electricity pylons which stretched across the hillside – Talisker wished his mood could match the freshness of the morning. He stumbled disconsolately down the road away from the car, breathing the fresh, almost stinging air into his lungs, his mind working on two levels at once: instinctively looking for the ideal, slightly private spot to relieve his bladder, and, more insistently, worrying about Tris. How were they going to find him now? How in hell did the Scoor get here? Tris could be dead by now for all he knew, his only comfort was the fact that they hadn't killed him immediately. Perhaps they needed him alive for some reason. The need to see his son gripped him so suddenly that he felt as though someone had tightened a steely band around his chest.

His thoughts were distracted as he emptied his bladder, he stared ahead at a bank of snow, vaguely watching the little white dots which always swam in his vision like errant tadpoles whenever he suffered from glare. When he'd finished, he moved to turn away and then realised he was being watched. It was a hare; some emotional recognition triggered in Talisker's memory – he had seen a hare the day everything had changed, the day he met Malky. And later, in Sutra, a hare had led him to Mirranon as she lay fatally wounded. This hare was white rather than brown, its pelt only slightly creamier coloured than the snow, it was watching him closely. Talisker wondered whether all hares turned white in the winter, or just a certain species.

'Hi,' he muttered.

The hare did a slow double take glance as if to check he was watching and purposefully began to move along the bank. It seemed clear to Talisker that the creature wanted him to follow it. He glanced back at the car –

no sign of life yet – and began to walk slowly along behind the hare strangely enjoying the sense of *déjà vu* it brought. The hare gained speed and Talisker had to speed up until he was almost jogging. Just as he considered stopping, not wanting to lose sight of the car or become disorientated, the hare veered off into an adjoining field where the bank sloped lower to the road. Talisker stepped off the road after his quarry but his feet sank deep into the snow plunging his bare legs into the freezing whiteness up to his thighs. He staggered forward a few steps before deciding to give up and return to the firm ground of the tarmac road; the hare had vanished from sight anyway. Just as he turned however, he realised his leg was against something solid, buried entirely in the bank. Crouching down, he brushed back the snow, digging a small trench away from the surface of the thing he had found. It was a rough stone pillar about three feet tall but too wide to be a fence post, there were letters cut into the front surface. Talisker wiped away the snow which left the letters picked out in a pale tracery where flakes had compacted into the grooves. He sat back on his heels.

'Oh,' he smiled, slightly puzzled, slightly sad. The letters spelled 'McLeod'. There was no further explanation; no particular McLeod, no reason why the stone was there.

'It's a battle-site, ya plum.'

Talisker looked up. It had begun to snow again, the wind was whipping up the loose flakes from the newly fallen topcoat. The whirling white flakes blasted across his vision, catching on his lashes, making him unsure of what he saw.

There was a man standing only a few feet away; he was dressed similarly to Talisker but his plaid would have been more recognisable to tourists and ex-patriot Scots as 'proper tartan'. He carried a short silver sword sheathed in a rough leather scabbard, his ropey red hair straggled down his shoulders to his back and he stood with his hands on his hips watching Talisker with quiet concern.

'Malky? Malk? Jesus! Is it really you?' Talisker laughed. He rushed forwards to hug his old friend but somehow ended up grabbing at thin air and falling on his face in the snow. When he looked up again Malky stood the same distance away as before although he had not registered the Highlander moving at all.

'Sorry, Duncan. It's me all right but I canny stay. I'm a proper ghost this time.'

'Oh,' Talisker felt inordinately cheated about this. The fleeting idea that Malky might have returned by some magic of his indomitable spirit – sheer bloody-mindedness in fact – had rushed over him like a wave of reassurance. If Malky was there, things would somehow be all right. Childish really, just because he, Sandro and Malk had saved a whole world together . . .

'So what is it, Malk?' He pulled a wry face. 'Are you a harbinger of doom this time?'

'A what? Oh aye . . . no, no' really.'

Talisker stood up again, brushing the snow off his plaid and cloak. 'Are you . . . at peace, Malk?'

Malky grinned, time and otherworldly existence had not improved the sight of his gums. 'Oh aye,

Duncan . . . it's peaceful all right.' He paused as though considering his next statement; something of an admission. 'It's a wee bit boring sometimes really. Ah've been allowed tae come an' see you cos you and Sandro are in trouble again eh?'

'I get the feeling we're opening a whole can of worms,' Talisker nodded in agreement, then laughed as Malky looked completely blank at this expression. 'Yeah, we're in trouble.'

'No' as much as your bairns though . . .' Malky looked serious. 'You've got to help them, Duncan.'

'I know Malk. I'm trying.'

'Try harder, Duncan. If ye dinny get Tristan back tae Sutra soon . . .'

'What?' Talisker frowned. 'What do you know, Malk?'

'Jist that Jahl is big trouble – you know he's your son, Duncan, don't ye – well, he's drawing power from whit you caw "the void".'

'And? What does that mean? The void is just that isn't it, empty . . . void?'

'It's no' that simple. There's all kinna stuff in there. Stuff like the Scoor an' the demon Corvus sent here before. There's stuff that wiz put there deliberate like, so's it'll never be free again. Jahl disnae really ken what he's meddlin' with. But so far . . . naebody kens what he's after.' Malky shrugged.

'I should've just killed him when I had the chance. It would've been so easy.'

'Aye. But I suppose ye didnae want tae upset Regan. I tell ye, that lassie needs a good smack.'

'It's gone beyond a good smack, Malk,' Talisker

sighed. 'Can you tell me anything else, like where Tristan is?' he asked hopefully.

'Oh aye. That's mainly why I came. He's in a big hoose in Edinburgh somewhere . . .' Talisker waited patiently, remembering with exasperated fondness Malky's complete inability to prioritise information. '. . . it's got those trees in the grounds, you ken, those ones that are cut into funny shapes . . .'

'Yew trees.'

'Aye, yew trees. An' it's really old, probably aboot from my time. And it's got a name . . .'

'A name?'

'The Ark. Aye, I think that's what it's cawed, The Ark or Ark House.'

'Brilliant Malk, brilliant. I'll go and get Tris and take him back to Sutra today,' Talisker assured his friend.

'That may not be a bad idea,' Malky looked serious.

'Is something wrong, Malk?'

'Naw, well, no' exactly, yet. Jist remember about the time difference, Duncan.'

'How long have we been gone?'

'Almost two weeks already.'

'Shit, I'd better go and sort this out.' Talisker turned to go and then turned back again. 'Thanks, Malk. It's good to know you're still . . . around.'

Malky looked faintly embarrassed. 'Well, like I said, ye dinny get rid o' me that easily. Oh Duncan . . .'

'Yeah?'

'Give my regards tae Sandro eh? The great lummox . . .'

'I will, Malk.'

''Bye.'

The snow blew harder for a few moments and Talisker watched the space where Malky had stood, unable to distinguish the moment he vanished. He stood for long moments as though frozen, his hand on the hilt of his sword, his head bowed, staring at the plain granite stone which it seemed marked the passing of other clansmen, just as remarkable in their way as Malky. Then he turned and began to run back towards the road, sliding and scrambling across the uneven surface of the field and banks. When he reached the car he rapped on the steamed-up window on the passenger side.

'Sandro! Sandro, wake up!'

There was mild cursing from the inside as Sandro tried to open the jammed window. Then the door opened with a blast of warm air.

'What's up?' Sandro blinked owlishly in the glare.

'I've just seen Malky.' As he said it, Talisker broke into a wide grin as the realisation struck home.

'Malky?'

'Who's Malky?' Bea's slightly drowsy voice carried over Sandro's shoulder.

Sandro nodded and rubbed his eyes fighting the last vestiges of sleep. 'What did he say?'

'Who's Malky?

'He's a ghost, Bea. What did he say, Duncan?'

'Oh.'

'Tristan's in an old house called The Ark or Ark House. We've got to get him back, Sandro, there's some kind of trouble brewing in Sutra. And we've been gone about two weeks already.'

'Two weeks!'

'Well look, the first thing we've got to do, is drop me off to work.' Bea smiled brightly as both men looked at her uncomprehendingly. 'Think about it, sweetie,' she said to Sandro, 'if I don't turn up with some kind of explanation you'll have every policeman in Midlothian on your heels.'

'But no one saw us,' Talisker objected.

Bea pulled a wry face and raked her gaze pointedly up and down his plaid. 'Trust me, you may just have attracted some attention on the way. Anyway, I can get you some proper clothes.' She lit a cigarette and puffed the smoke into the fresh morning air with great gusto. 'Get in darling, I think we can get back to the city in time for the morning shift. Oh yes, I know where The Ark is by the way – it's a squat – and I did know that's where my pal Knox hangs out. He's part of a religious group called "Children of the Deluge" – fundamentalists – believe in the Rapture, End of Days, that kind of stuff. Never done any harm up till now . . .'

She started the car, almost kicking the accelerator to bring the reluctant engine to life. The car produced almost as much smoke as its owner but after a few worrying noises from the exhaust, began to move quite smoothly, skimming lightly along the snowbound roads.

'Maybe we didn't really need divine intervention from your ghost, Duncan.' She said it with good humour and Talisker couldn't help himself but laugh.

'I don't think anyone's ever called Malky divine before.'

* * *

Knox's emotions veered wildly between elation and fear. He didn't think God was tracking his thoughts now; he could feel it when He was, a kind of prickly itching sensation in the back of his head. Earlier, when he had gone as directed and found the Scoor hiding in the dark reaches of the High Street alleyway everything had just clicked into place. Here were the creatures of Revelations, a vanguard of the army which, according to St John's book, would cause men to suffer such agonies for five months that they would long for death. Except for those who were saved of course, like himself and the Children. Here was irrefutable proof of the Word of God and the fact that the time of Tribulations was truly upon the world. That he alone in the world knew that the Scoor (God had told him their name) were here, that was power. He thought of the other Elders and their shining acceptance that their faith demanded no proof, and he felt a mixture of scorn and pity. Ironically, Knox still had no faith, or belief; he knew, and that was different altogether.

Still, Knox was far from stupid, and only a fool would not have been afraid of the creatures, even if he was supposedly in charge of them. The Scoor could become invisible on command (God had told him, and Knox only had to think it for the Scoor to obey) which was just as well because he had parked the transit van about half a mile away from the alley. It had been dark, but Knox still ran to reach the vehicle, glancing back occasionally and sensing the passage of the Scoor following him which was almost as frightening as actually seeing them. The creatures did not speak, although their faces were human and technically they would be capable of speech, only a faint, keening noise, like someone blowing on a reed, came from their mouths when they made any sound. When the Scoor became visible again at the house where they had abducted Tristan, Knox almost lost control, his natural fear threatening to overwhelm his command of the situation. Perhaps the only person who did not show any sign of real fear was the object of the whole exercise, Tristan. For some reason, the little man accepted the idea of something which could only be described as supernatural with a kind of wry stoicism. Unexpectedly, Knox found himself admiring Tristan for this and, when he bundled him into the van, it was perhaps done less roughly than it might have been. He knew he'd find it hard if God commanded him to kill Tristan – but he would do it of course.

Once again, he found himself alone, the Scoor invisibly banished and Tristan captive in the damp attic of The Ark. Alone and drinking, more than a little bit afraid of what was to become of him.

There was a knock at the door.

'Knox, it's Esther. Can I come in?'

A dark tremor ran through him at the mere thought of her, and for a moment, he considered pretending not to have heard.

'Knox. You have done well. You desire her, do you not?'

'Y-yes Lord,' he whispered.

'You may take her then. Do not be afraid. Women

despise weakness. Here, I have a gift for you.'

Knox opened his mouth to respond when an explosion of senses wracked his frame; energy crashing through his veins as though his blood suddenly carried something other than oxygen. Within the space of seconds he felt different, somehow other than himself. Pausing before the mirror he stared closely at his own reflection; he was gasping, his body reeling with warming fire.

As his breathing slowed, he noted something different about his eyes perhaps, some bright echo of a light which had not been there before. A slow smile spread across his features and he ran his long fingers through his hair, suddenly wondering why he had been so . . . afraid of women in the past. Afraid of their good opinion of his pale slim body and gaunt features which he had always feared to be weak but in fact, he decided now, were refined and smouldering.

He grinned. 'Yeah, smouldering . . .'

'Knox?'

'Esther. Hold on.' He opened the door and smiled into her upturned face. 'Hi.'

'I – I need . . . something, you know, soon and . . . are you all right?'

'Never better. Why?'

'You look different somehow.'

He laughed, not his usual rusty tin can, self-deprecating laugh, but a low, melodious sound. Esther smiled in response, slightly uncertainly, but the pupils of her eyes were growing larger by the moment, not entirely in response to the gloom of Knox's bedroom.

'I'm fine, honestly, just in a good mood. How are you though, Esther?' he reached forward and lightly squeezed her shoulder. 'How are you bearing up?'

'I'm . . . fine too, except . . .'

'No, you're not,' he fixed her with his penetrating gaze and she looked away, misery etched on her beautiful features. 'Look, I can get you something later, I promise but come in and talk to me for a while, eh? Come on.' He slipped his arm around her shoulder and ushered her into the room.

'Are you sure about this, sweetie?' Bea peered over her tortoiseshell glasses at Sandro. They were sitting in the car beside the eastern wall of The Ark gardens. 'Maybe there's some other way.'

'Like what? Sandro frowned.

She shrugged, 'Dunno really,' she admitted. 'Maybe I could get Stirling to do a drugs bust on them . . . sneak up the stairs . . . no, you're right. It'd never work.'

Bea had had a hard day. She had called into Ladyfield as soon as they arrived back in Edinburgh and 'explained' to Cal that she'd had something of a 'turn' the night before due to a slight overdose of the antidepressants she was taking. Cal, who had been worried sick after arriving at Bea's home and finding the chaos there, had lost his temper and blasted her for wasting police time and behaving like a lunatic. She realised that this was a response to his concern, but worse, she sensed also, that something which had been in the fragile process of germinating between them was irrevocably lost. Perhaps now, Cal would believe the things said about her; unstable, edgy, alcoholic. Perhaps he'd think she had lied about her tremor . . .

'Bea?'

'Sorry?'

Talisker was looking at her expectantly. 'Could you just run that by me again, pumpkin?' she smiled.

Talisker sighed. 'Are you all right, Beatrice?'

'Yeah, fine.'

'All right, give us about thirty minutes. We'll go up the back fire escape,' Talisker pointed out the route on a floor plan Bea had managed to photocopy from the library. Unfortunately, it was around thirty years old and it was obvious from their vantage point that new extensions had been added to the building. They could only hope the basic layout was still the same. 'If we're not out by then, come and knock on the door or something. Cause a diversion.'

She nodded and watched them go, almost smiling at the fact that Talisker's dark trousers were loose enough to droop at the waist and sit on his hips and yet, short enough in the leg to leave his ankles exposed to the chill night air. She had 'requisitioned' the black clothes they wore from the Salvation Army bin at the station. They looked, and smelled, like distinctly second-hand ninjas.

'Be careful,' she whispered hoarsely. Sandro waved back distractedly and they slipped through the back gate, disappearing instantly into the shadows.

Regan woke for no reason she could tell. Her eyes snapped open, focusing instantly on the empty space beside her, the bolster pillow where Fraser had so often slept. Outside, a slow, creeping mist held the silent city in its thrall and Regan's disquiet owed much to a pervading sense of unease which many had felt in Soulis Mor in the past few weeks but none would give voice to, least they invite a disaster which, as yet, was only imagined. The night was achingly still in these hours before the dawn; the hours when those who were grieving felt their pain afresh, if unable to sleep through it. And it would surprise many to know that Regan was grieving for Fraser.

It wasn't that she had loved him really, she had been nowhere near to loving him in fact, but he had made life a little easier. Life as Thane of Soulis Mor was harsh in many, subtle ways; to be constantly watched for one, and to be surrounded by people saying yes to her every demand. In truth, Fraser had been one of those people, eager to please and so obviously besotted by her. Regan had had no qualms about ordering him to her chambers and then her bed, she knew it was what he wanted. Her only condition was that he tell no one. Fraser was simply easy in all senses of the word, he demanded nothing from her – which was as well – he didn't stretch her intellect like Jahl, didn't challenge her. In return for occasional bouts of passion, he made her laugh and smile and took the edge off her loneliness. Now, like Tris he was gone too and his death, in contrast to his striking beauty, had been a hideous and bloody affair.

She sighed and reached across to rest her hand on the pillow, feeling almost sore with weariness and sorrow. She hadn't been sleeping well since the night when . . . she shuddered. Night-sweats left her sheets cold and damp so that she awoke feeling like an invalid, her hair sticking to her chilled shoulders. Someone would pay for this. Someone was dispensing of her friends and lovers one by one, leaving her isolated. It had come to her attention that two of her favourite maidservants had disappeared in recent weeks. Perhaps Jahl would be next, she should warn him . . .

'I wouldn't bother if I were you.' The voice came from the bottom of her bed and she sat bolt upright, a cry of alarm trembling on her lips.

An old man stood there. He was dressed in tattered grey rags and held a long, gnarly staff of wood; the bare arm which held the staff was thin in the extreme and in the darkness of the room Regan almost imagined he was a spirit or ghost visiting her. This impression was immediately dispelled however, as the stranger sat on the end of her bed, causing the mattress to sag where his skinny frame rested.

Regan had a sudden sharp memory of a bright summer's day when she was a child of around ten years old. She had been playing with Tris and he'd made her really angry by breaking something of hers so she'd lashed out, unable to control her temper. Caught off balance on his ever unstable legs Tris fell and hurt himself badly. The man who was sitting on the end of her bed had been visiting that day and the soft blue eyes held the same expression of foreboding then as they held now.

'You read my thoughts then. Are you . . . who I think you are?'

'And who might you think I am?'

'Morias,' she said. 'I remember. But you look the same as then . . .'

'Yes, I do,' his voice was quiet in the room but he gave no sign of furtiveness. 'But you, Regan. You are no longer content with simply hurting your brother. Now, Sutra stands on the edge of a precipice to which you have brought it.'

'Have a care what you say,' she remarked coldly.

He smiled, but the smile did not reach his eyes. 'Do you know what magics it took for me to get in here? I'll tell you; more than you would know. Soulis Mor is bounded by markers and wardings so strong that nothing of magical origin can survive here. Even the lay-people who work in the city cannot use their simple earthbound cautions . . .'

'I don't know what you mean,' she frowned.

'No. You don't. Regan, you have been a fool . . .' Morias stopped suddenly and looked around the room as though expecting to see something in the shadows. There was a sound outside in the stairwell and antechamber, like a wind rushing through the city; quiet at first . . .

'What is it?' she whispered, affected by his mood.

'I must hurry. He sees me. Tristan is alive . . .'

'I know . . .'

'No. You only think you know. I cannot tell you where he is in case *he* reads it in your mind. But your maidservants – the ones you have been wondering about – they are dead so you may cease looking for them. They were killed by the same hand as Fraser. Only great sorcery made their deaths silent and unremarked in the city . . .'

'Who?' she demanded, 'who could do such a thing? I was here. I saw it. One moment he was alive and the next . . . I never saw the blow, or the assassin. It was as though the knife just appeared in his throat . . .'

Morias had risen from the bed as though preparing to leave. Outside, the sound of the wind grew louder, gale force. He glanced towards the door and then back at Regan, disbelief and anger in his gaze. 'How is it possible you *do not know*?' He stared closely at her face as if trying to read the expression and beyond it, to her soul. 'It is—'

The door burst open and an enormous blast of air entered the room; but not only air. Carried in the storm were strange insects, beetle-like, the size of a man's fist. Their wing casings glowed a dark vermilion in the dull light cast into the room from the antechamber and they made a rasping sound which was at once deafening – due to their number – and terrifying. Regan screamed, and pulled her bedcovers up around herself but the whole force of the insect squall was not directed at her but at Morias, the terrifying creatures flew past the end of the bed, contained within the tunnel of wind, towards the old man who had retreated into the corner of the room.

'Get back!' he yelled, his voice surprisingly loud and commanding. He held his staff before him and a faint blue light was visible, enveloping Morias's form. The wind and the beetles halted before it, hitting some invisible shield and within moments, the outline of Morias's protective barrier was crawling three or four deep in the beasts which continued to make their whining, clicking noises. From where she sat on the bed, Regan could see that the effort of maintaining the barrier cost Morias dear; his features were ashen, sweat ran down his face and neck and the arm which held the staff wavered and shook as the aged muscles convulsed with the power he was somehow directing. She knew instinctively that his strength, both magical and physical, would fail against the onslaught soon. There was nothing she could do but watch helplessly, she knew the beasts had been sent for the old mage but she dared not touch them.

'Morias . . .' she groaned. Soon, he would fail. And be consumed.

He turned his agonised face towards her. 'I will not be denied,' he gasped. 'He has done this . . . surely you must see . . .' As if sensing his intention to say their master's name, the insects' din grew louder and sparks flew outwards from Morias's staff as his flare of power began to fade.

'. . . it is Jahl. He is your . . .'

There was an abrupt noise like an implosion and Morias vanished, the wall of beetles fell to the floor like a discarded cloak, spreading outwards across the slabs, covering the stone and rugs in a moving, hissing sea of insects. Regan screamed and stood up on her mattress gathering the covers and her nightgown around herself as though trying desperately to seal herself in.

'Majesty! Regan!' Jahl stood in the doorway, his face a picture of horrified concern, but even as he looked the shimmering mass of beetles vanished in a soft glow of green light, leaving behind a noxious sulphur smell and a stricken, disbelieving Thane.

'I was dreaming, Jahl,' she quavered. 'Please tell me I was dreaming.' She could feel the violent tremor of reaction in the pit of her stomach and she slid back down into a sitting position on the bed, her knees curled up to her chin and her eyes still round with terror. Her hands moved spasmodically, tucking the sheets beneath her feet and her gaze darted to and fro across the room looking for the telltale movement of any remaining insect.

Behind Jahl, two of Regan's personal guards and one of her maids were peering into the room, having all run to her aid when awakened by her screams. They had arrived after Jahl, too late to see the mysterious creatures.

'The Thane is correct,' Jahl snapped, 'she has had a bad dream. You there, go and get your mistress a warm drink. The rest of you are dismissed. I will tend Thane Regan.' The bodyguards left immediately, recognising Jahl's authority and within moments of the vanishing of Morias and his strange aggressors Regan was alone with Jahl.

He sat beside her and took hold of her hand, his touch was cold, his long thumb making a soothing repetitive motion across the back of her palm. 'You saw it, didn't you, Jahl?' she whispered.

He nodded, staring intently into her eyes, locking her gaze into his own, so that it seemed the rest of the room dwindled away into darkness and Regan's whole world consisted of just his face. His beautiful face . . .

'But listen, Regan . . .' he kept his voice quiet and soft. Regan felt the tiny spasms of hysteria seep away. 'Sometimes, our fears can take form, become real . . . you must be tired . . .'

'. . . it is Jahl. He is your . . .'

'Is my what?' she wondered. He continued stroking her hand, his touch growing warmer, as though he was stealing her warmth. But it was not an unpleasant feeling.

'No,' she said. 'My fears . . . my fears are not . . .' She lost the thought somehow, was aware that her breathing had begun to slow, that Jahl had brought her down from abject terror to this malaise very quickly . . . too quickly. He frowned, but it was a pretend frown, such as one might humour a small child with.

'It doesn't matter,' he said. 'Nothing matters.' Then he smiled.

She stared at him. Something like a silent scream was beginning to build inside her, she felt as though she was helpless, drowning. She found herself wishing he would kiss her, could almost feel the warm sensation of his kiss on her lips. But she knew he wouldn't . . .

'. . . it is Jahl. He is your . . .'

She was sleepy now. Could feel her eyes drifting shut.

'Jahl?'

'Hmm?'

'Will you stay?'

He did kiss her then; a slow deliberate kiss on her forehead. Reassurance . . . and something more, something unsettling. Again, the thought slipped away.

'Of course I will,' he said.

CHAPTER ELEVEN

It almost seemed too easy. Talisker and Sandro were halfway across the ornamental section of lawn, ducking behind the strange, clipped outlines of the yews, when Sandro beckoned Talisker over to where he stood.

'Duncan,' he whispered hoarsely, 'look up at the roof.'

Talisker frowned at where Sandro was pointing. At first it seemed there was nothing to see. The outline of the old slate roof was simply a darker blotch against the overcast sky. But then he realised what Sandro meant. Every few feet in a seemingly random arrangement, the slates had slipped as frost and thaw had weakened their hold over the years; this left small cracks and gaps between them which would normally be unnoticed – unless a light was burning in the attic as it was now

'It might not mean anything,' he whispered back, unwilling to let himself hope. 'They might have had a . . . what's it called . . . a loft conversion.' As with many 'real world' words, this sounded strange to Talisker's ears, obliquely making him wish for a speedy return to the sanity of Sutra.

'If they'd had a loft conversion, they would have fixed the roof,' Sandro insisted. 'C'mon.'

'I wish I had my sword,' Talisker muttered.

*   *   *

Tantalisingly close, Tristan shivered in the cold of the attic. Near to his feet a camping lantern was burning, the gas making an almost subliminal hissing which the young Sutran disliked and distrusted. The blanket which Knox had given him smelt as dank and musty as the attic itself but Tris pulled it tightly around himself. He knew he was feverish, it was something which had plagued him since his youth and he recognised the prickly, barbed heat which was already causing cold lines of sweat to trickle down the centre of his back. Perversely, the familiarity of the feeling was almost comforting except that this time there would be no one to nurse or care for him if delirium set in. He gazed around the attic as the faint traces of panic churned the pit of his stomach and he wondered what was to become of him and why he wasn't dead already. As tiredness gripped him, his eyes flickered shut.

A sound, coming from the far wall startled him into wakefulness. Tristan's eyes snapped open again and the hair on the back of his neck stood up. The sound was like something scraping across the outside wall, clinging on and pulling itself across. Every few seconds there was a sudden whooshing sound as the thing lost its grip and slid back down. Tristan's first thought was Scoor and he cast around for a weapon to defend himself with, sure that the creatures were coming for him. He found a metal tool – a wrench – near the water tank and stood by the tiny casement window where it seemed they were trying to break through. Despite the cold of the room, he felt slick with sweat due to his fever and he stood with the wrench raised in a trembling, wavering hand, feeling violently sick. There was another, quieter sound from outside which he recognised, a whispered curse as someone fumbled with the latch and then slid the window open.

'I hope you're right about this,' a disembodied voice drifted in on the thin icy air and was immediately followed by the dark outline – which was at least human – of someone struggling to fit through the narrow space of the window. Tristan backed away, unsure if his eyes were deceiving him in the gloom or even if he was, in fact, asleep or delirious. The figure was dressed in dark, loose-fitting clothes and had a strange woollen garment on its head which covered the whole face except for two holes for the eyes. Landing in an undignified heap on the floor with yet more curses, the first intruder was followed immediately by a second, dressed in a similar manner. Tristan knew he had the advantage as the disoriented pair picked themselves up and looked around, blinking in the light of the lantern, and yet, he didn't strike while they were vulnerable. Something about them seemed, impossibly familiar . . .

Tris met the gaze of the first man just as a wave of nausea struck him; he wavered slightly, lowering the wrench as he did so.

'Tris? Tris, it's me . . . us . . .'

Tristan groaned in response, all sense of reality slipping away from him as the fever took hold. Perspiration dripped into his eyes which felt as though the very orbs of his eyeballs were on fire; he blinked rapidly and gasped his answer, his voice like a weakened child.

'I – I don't know . . .'

The man took a step forward and removed the black face covering. 'It's me, Tris. Talisker . . .'

'F-father?' He stared, grimly determined to cling onto the strange vision before unconsciousness took him. 'No . . . you're not him . . .'

'Duncan.' The other man removed his face covering also and although it was equally impossible, Tristan had seen this face more recently and knew its lines more clearly than the fading vision of his father.

'*Seanachaidh*?'

'Yes, Tristan,' the man smiled. 'Duncan – it's the age thing remember? Tris thinks we should be sixty.'

Tris nodded, still fighting the pull of the fever. 'Yes,' he agreed, 'sixty.'

Talisker looked distinctly unhappy, perhaps he had imagined a different reunion. 'Why should he remember?' he said bitterly, 'Whatever age I am – he hasn't seen me for years. Tris,' he stepped towards his son, 'it is me. Beatrice is with us. We've come to . . .'

Tristan collapsed and was only vaguely aware as his father caught him. Talisker gripped his son to him, his face almost blank with confusion and anguish.

'He didn't know me, Sandro.'

'He's ill, Duncan.'

'I know, I know,' Talisker nodded gravely. 'But he should have known . . .' he stared down at his son, wishing for things to be different, wishing he could go back and change almost everything. 'We've come to take you home, Tristan,' he whispered.

It began to rain as they left the attic room, the sound of water as it hissed against the tiles and gurgled along the ancient guttering was amazingly loud. Rainwater began to drizzle through the gaps in the roof, pooling onto the floor in small puddles.

'You know, you'd think for people expecting a flood, they'd take better care of their building,' Talisker observed. He was hefting the semi-conscious Tristan onto his back.

'They don't think they'll be here to worry about it, Duncan. God will take them before the End of the World kicks in. That's what The Rapture is.'

'I don't see where enlisting the Scoor and kidnapping people fits in with this scenario,' Talisker frowned. 'It's amazing what people will believe, eh?'

Sandro shrugged as he prepared to climb back out the window. 'It doesn't seem that unreasonable to me, saints, angels, miracles . . . it's all part of faith really. You can't cherry-pick, Duncan.'

'Yeah, but . . . maybe we should discuss this later.'

Sandro grinned in response just before he disappeared from view. 'He's enjoying this,' Talisker thought, 'It's the old Sandro . . .'

'Hold on tight, son,' he instructed Tris.

The climb down – mercifully short to the flat roof of the extension and then down the fire escape – was harder with the added weight of Tris and the rain causing the pipes to be slippery. Talisker missed his footing and fell the last few feet but managed to land slightly on one side and avoided injuring his semi-conscious burden. Fortunately, the rain and cold air began to revive Tris somewhat and he climbed down the wrought iron stairs of the fire escape with little assistance.

'Come on . . .' Sandro's anxious stage whisper was

barely audible above the sound of the rain which was now a deluge even the Children might find worthy of notice.

'Come on, Tris. It's not far,' Talisker said, 'Bea's car is just over there . . .'

They began to make their way across the lawn, Sandro ahead and Talisker following more slowly whilst attempting to support Tris who was still weak. As Tristan's head was only at the height of Talisker's chest this was far from easy and he wasn't really sure if his grip under Tristan's arm was particularly helpful. Just as they ducked in behind the first of the ornamental yews – clipped into the shape of a peacock – Talisker heard Sandro call back to him again, it sounded urgent.

'Tris, stay here till I call you,' he cautioned. Sandro's voice came again, almost a shout this time, and as Talisker caught up with his friend he cursed aloud. It was Scoor; two of them. But both Sandro and Talisker were unarmed.

'Oh my God!' Sandro had turned and was running back towards Talisker before he had a chance to react. 'Duncan, run! We've got no—'

There was a strangely flat banging sound as the first of the Scoor caught up with Sandro and, reaching out with its uppermost arms, grabbed him by the shoulders and pulled him back towards it, yanking him off his feet like a rag doll. Talisker froze for long seconds, terrified. The bang was the sound of the creature's sting as it connected with Sandro's back.

'Duncan!' Sandro's whole body arched forward in the creature's grip and his cry was filled with anguish and pain. Spurred into action, Talisker raced back through the line of the yew trees, his feet splashing and slipping in the sodden grass. Behind him, the sound of the Scoor's wings could be heard above the noise of the rain as it pursued him. It seemed as though the Scoor were having difficulty flying between the trees; the level of the sound rose and fell like a struggling biplane engine. Talisker began to weave amongst the yews, hoping to slow them further but after a minute, he had effectively disorientated himself. He couldn't call out to Sandro or Tris without alerting the Scoor to his position; he stopped, gasping for breath behind a yew which was clipped into the shape of a windmill. Stilling his breathing, he listened for the sound of the Scoor's wings trying to evaluate their distance, but for the moment there was nothing, just the sound of the storm. They must have landed – the idea of the bizarre creatures scuttling across the ordered green of the lawn through the yews was somehow nauseating and Talisker recognised that, despite their human features he saw them as large insects. Still no sound, no lights had come on in the house, just the rain and the creeping sensation of a silence which was not quite empty.

As he cast his gaze around Talisker realised he was almost back to where he had left Tristan but slightly to the right of him – he reckoned Tris was around three trees to his left – but perhaps more importantly, just ahead of where he stood, someone had left a wheelbarrow full of tools. Cold moonlight glinted off the sharp edge of a pruning blade and was echoed by the frozen humour of Talisker's grin.

Lurching forward, he ran towards the barrow which was a mere hundred yards or so ahead. He guessed the Scoor were waiting for his move and he was right, the instant he left the black shadows of the tree, they took to the air again; he didn't even look but raced ahead. Almost there, and he reached his hand forward as though to grab the nearest tool, then, disaster. A sudden slip and he was on the grass, breathing in the cold wetness.

'No,' he groaned. He pushed himself up, aware as he did so, of the sickening sound of the wings coming closer and closer, and the fact that his back was a vulnerable target for their stings; ready for the insect embrace of their strange arms. Sheer force of will overcame his dread – 'Keep moving. Keep moving.' – The phrase came from nowhere and played through his mind like some disembodied mantra; simple, meaningless, but enough to keep the sick terror a heartbeat away. Louder and closer they came, behind him now. Right behind him, their wings causing the raindrops to explode outwards. They made their strange, almost sad noise which grew more insistent as he reached the barrow just ahead of them. There was no time to choose a weapon; in one motion, Talisker flung himself forward, almost falling again on the slick grass, but grabbing the nearest handle, turned and struck.

It was a scythe. The first Scoor was simply sliced in two. As it fell dead, it was still reacting to the blow, its features contorted in a wild helplessness. As recognition of what he held came to Talisker, he adjusted his grip on the handle and jabbed upwards, slicing open the lower abdomen of the second Scoor up to the metal breastplate. It fell back, its limbs flailing, making the voiceless keening sound again apparently unable to scream. Seizing his advantage and quelling any vague sympathy for the creature's plight Talisker lunged forward and beheaded it with his third blow. The silence of the night reasserted itself and Talisker stared for long moments at the fallen bodies of his foes and then at the bloodied scythe.

'Wow,' he whispered. It had been so fast. 'I've got to get me one of these . . .'

'Father,' the hoarse whisper came from up ahead. Talisker glanced back once at the Scoor as he sprinted towards Tristan's voice and noted that they had vanished. There was no glow of light or anything remarkable about it, they were just gone.

Tristan had made his way over to Sandro, who was lying face down in the mud where the Scoor had discarded him. Weakened by his fever, he was attempting to turn Sandro over but was struggling with the weight of the bigger man.

'Oh no,' Talisker breathed. 'Here Tris . . . let me . . . Sandro, Sandro . . .'

Kneeling in the muddy grass he flipped Sandro over with relative ease and was relieved to notice the Sicilian's eyes flicker open as he struggled for consciousness. As he held Sandro around his middle, he couldn't fail to notice a huge lump on his back which was emanating a fierce heat.

'He's alive,' he muttered. 'Tris, can you walk now?'

Tris nodded, the cold air had revived him somewhat although he still felt weakened.

'C'mon Sandro,' Talisker stood up slightly unsteadily, carrying Sandro's limp body in his arms. 'Let's go.

They ran back through the lych gate to the car where Bea was waiting, anxiously scanning through the rain for signs of life.

'Tristan, thank God,' she smiled. Her smile vanished as she saw Talisker. 'What happened? Did someone shoot him? Is he alive? Oh my God—'

'Bea, stop babbling and help me get him in the car,' Talisker snapped. As the car was a three-door model this was easier said than done and it took the combined effort of all three of them to get Sandro slumped into the back seat beside Tris. Bea gunned the engine and the fan belt squealed as the car sprang reluctantly to life. Talisker, dripping wet and shaking with exertion, laughed an exhausted husky laugh.

'What's so funny?' Bea frowned.

'That's more noise than we've made all night. And we've killed two Scoor.'

'I'm sorry,' she sniffed, obviously slighted by his remark.

'No, I didn't mean it like that, Bea . . . I'm sorry, stuff just strikes you like that when you've been in a battle situation, kinda . . . never mind . . .'

She sighed, 'Looks like we've got two invalids in the back.'

'Yeah.'

'What's that blue stuff on you?'

'Scoor blood.'

'Jeez, thank God there're no more of those things, Duncan. D'you think they'll be all right?'

Talisker glanced back at his son and Sandro. Tris had immediately fallen asleep.

'I think Tris just has a fever. It used to happen when he was a boy all the time. Sandro . . . I don't know.'

'You mean he might die?' Bea's voice was sharp with alarm.

'It's possible, Bea. I'm sorry.' He kept his gaze fixed on the darkened streets outside, knowing she'd be embarrassed if he noticed her instant reaction. 'You really care about him, don't you?' he said. 'It must have been hard on you when we disappeared.'

She shrugged, not really knowing how to respond, but when she answered him, her voice was thick with tears.

'Yeah. Yeah, it was. But Sandro was never mine . . . You know about Diane, don't you?'

'Diane . . .' he shook his head. 'Well, I suppose there's some advantage in the fact we've been gone for twenty-five years. He's had a whole lifetime to get over her. I'd say he cares about you, Bea, more than he realises. You were the first person he thought of when we came back.' He glanced back at Sandro again and sighed. 'I'd say you're in with a good chance . . . if he survives.'

Regan woke as the first light of the dawn entered her room. Her memories of the evening before were hazy, confused. She had had a nightmare she knew . . . something about beetles. A sharp image of insects scuttling across her floor played in her mind, causing her to gasp. She gazed around the room as though seeking answers but there was nothing out of the ordinary in the hazy grey light. It felt strange to know that something of major importance had occurred last night, but her memory of it was as blank as the sky from her window; heavy with snow and foreboding.

Never one to give in to the pull of inertia mentally or physically, Regan dressed quickly in her warmest clothes without summoning her maid. She had to get out into the fresh air, she had to walk and think alone.

Outside, Soulis Mor was quiet; only the first stirrings of servants and tradespeople working in the kitchens of the castle compound or the marketplace disturbed the last vestiges of the night. Perhaps because of the bleak grey weather, people's moods seemed affected, they moved virtually silently, no one called or whistled. Regan frowned, unable to fathom the silence. She slipped out of the city through the hidden gateway she and Tristan had discovered early in their reign to walk amongst the small patch woodland which for some reason clung to the back of the northern city wall. Beyond the woodland lay the empty spaces of the Badlands, scene of the battle for Soulis Mor twenty-six years earlier. Tris had remarked that the blood of the fallen Fine had enriched the soil behind the walls which had caused the wood to spring up where nothing would have grown before and certainly there was always a melancholy atmosphere in the little tunnel of trees. Regan, ever more pragmatic, was sure that Isbister had had the trees planted as an informal farewell to her kinsmen although she had found no record of it amongst her papers. Today, the sombre ambience of the city carried out into the woodland, the denuded branches of the trees reached into the empty winter sky like a silent, unanswered plea. There was no pathway amongst the trees and Regan picked her way between them with no real goal, her thoughts unfocused, grasping at the faint strands of memory from the night before which slipped from her conscious mind in the same taunting manner as dreams on waking.

A movement, high amongst the trees caught her attention, jerking her into alertness. She knew in a fraction of a second what had caused the motion, every nerve in her body reacted strongly to such movement; it was a bird, a large, black bird, a crow or a raven. Regan froze where she stood, her fingers gripping tightly to the lower twigs of the tree which she had casually pulled on moments before to aid her progress. She stared long and hard at the crow, and the bird, emboldened by little experience of people, stared back, its head at the strange, crooked angle all birds were capable of. Despite the cold freshness of the air, Regan felt beads of sweat forming on her brow. She could not walk on beneath the glare of the crow if her life depended on it, or so she thought, she must make the bird fly away despite the fact she feared the creature's flight and sound of its wings even more, or she must turn back.

'No,' she whispered. 'My fears are not . . .'

She frowned, clutching at the memory, glad to focus her attention away from the crow.

'My fears are not insects.' That's what she would have said. To Jahl. Last night. He had been sitting on her bed as she fell asleep . . . she had a sudden image of his face; his heavy eyes full of concern, his lips moving – although she could not make out the words he spoke – as he reassured her. But she had tried to tell him – it could not have been a waking dream because insects were not her biggest fear and it didn't make sense that . . .

. . . It didn't make sense that Morias had come. As the thought crystallised in Regan's mind the floodgates of her subconscious opened and she remembered everything. Every word the old man had said. Everything which happened after. With the clarity of the morning she saw that Jahl had arrived at the door of her room before her maids and bodyguards which should have been impossible, except that he had obviously been on his way before Regan's screaming had woken her attendants. He had been coming to make sure the old man was finished, that he had silenced him before Morias could tell Regan what he had come for. But he had failed.

'. . . it is Jahl. He is your . . .'

Regan heard a strange sound; a kind of choking, rasping noise, and then realised it was herself. She was a strong woman and it had been years since she had made that sound. She was crying, not gentle, ladylike tears but a heartfelt wailing which ripped through her frame like a physical torture. Because now she knew. Not what Morias had actually been trying to tell her – that Jahl was her enemy – but that she loved him. It was the most painful epiphany she would ever know; despite the fact they had been playing mind games and wearing masks with one another, despite the fact (or perhaps because of it) that Jahl was still a fascinating enigma, she was passionately in love with him.

She found herself gasping for air and sat down heavily on a snow-covered log fighting for calm, listening to her own ragged breathing. Closing her eyes, she buried her face in her hands to stifle the sound of her sorrow but for long minutes she could visualise nothing but his face; so full of contradictions, his features so delicate but so strong, his dark eyes so warm and yet so intense and clever, the tattoo, high on his cheekbone which he had told her symbolised infinity. It had been so long since he first came to Soulis Mor, he had helped her, he was the only one who seemed to understand her feelings about the Sidhe, and now, Regan realised she had desired him since the first moment she saw him.

And he was a traitor. And traitors must die.

'This can't be right. I can't be dying here.' Sandro's voice, weak and faltering belied the truth of this statement. Talisker bent his head closer to his friend's mouth in order to hear the whispered words.

'I'm sorry, Sandro,' Talisker's face was drawn with tiredness and grief. He was still wearing the black clothes from their night's escapade and he knew he stank of sweat but he didn't care; he had been at Sandro's side all night. Tristan was sleeping off his fever having taken the first aspirin he'd ever had, which worked miraculously fast in a body which had never had chemical medicines in its life.

Bea was also asleep but her battle with fatigue was finished after half a bottle of gin. Talisker had held his counsel but remembered enough of his father to know a hardened drinker when he saw one; Bea clutched at her smudged glass as though it were a lifeline, although to be fair, in the current circumstances, it probably was. She hadn't wanted to leave Sandro alone either but had been overtaken by the emotional strain of watching her friend dying. It must have been heart-breaking, Talisker thought, to have been reunited one day and have to let go again the next. Perhaps it would have been better for Bea if they had never come back at all, at least then she had hope.

From the site of the sting which the Scoor had injected into Sandro's back, a strange transformation was taking place in his fevered body. Radiating outwards from the site of the injury, the skin of Sandro's back and torso had changed colour and texture, turning a dark blue and thickening into a brittle, chitinous layer. This change was slowly moving upwards to his chest and downwards into his thighs. Talisker had noticed it when Sandro had thrown his covers back in delirium an hour or so earlier but he wasn't sure if Sandro himself realised the changes that were happening to him.

Over the years Talisker had lost many people who were dear to him, but Sandro's apparently inevitable demise was almost too bitter to bear. Unspoken between the two men was the unique experience of their shared connections, the highs and lows of a friendship unlike any other. At some point in the long hours before dawn, both men remembered their transformation into one unified being to bring about the defeat of Corvus. There had been three of course, them and Malky McLeod.

'You'd kind of think he'd come, wouldn't you?'

Sandro whispered. 'You'd think he'd at least show if I'm dying.'

Talisker gazed almost blankly at Sandro's face, knowing at once who he was talking about and wondering if Sandro could somehow read his mind.

'Yeah . . .' he grated.

'Duncan. I want to tell you something . . .' Sandro struggled to sit upright but rather than help him, Talisker looked faintly annoyed.

'Sandro, I swear, if it's another apology about . . . before, I'll kill you myself.'

Sandro laughed hoarsely, his throat was dry. As his quilt shifted to one side, Talisker noted the thin tracery of blue beneath his skin, spreading upwards and he glanced away, unable to look somehow. 'I'm sorry, Sandro,' he tried to smile. 'Here, I'll get you a drink.'

'No, no, I'm fine . . .' Sandro pushed the cover back deliberately and stared in horrified fascination at his own body; the central band around his waist was transformed into something completely alien looking. It was reminiscent of the hard casing of a wasp or dragonfly.

'Does . . . does it hurt?' Talisker frowned. He knew it was a stupid question.

For a moment, Sandro didn't respond but when he looked back at Talisker, the fear was undisguised in his face.

'Duncan . . . you know when caterpillars become butterflies they make a cocoon—' He broke off, leaving the rest of the statement unsaid because he couldn't give voice to what was happening to his own body. He closed his eyes and Talisker thought for a moment that he had lapsed back into sleep but then he spoke again, his voice a low, sickened groan. 'They become all mushy inside, don't they . . .?'

'Stop it, Sandro. Don't even go there.'

'Just because it's disgusting, doesn't make it not true.' It appeared Sandro was giving in to the pull of unconsciousness which was a blessing given the way his mind was working.

'What were you going to tell me, Sandro?' Talisker murmured. He absently patted his friend's hand which was freezing cold despite the heating being on in the cottage.

'Doesn't seem right . . . dying here.' Sandro rallied for a moment, his eyes opened and he managed to fix Talisker with a determined gaze due to sheer force of will. 'My death . . . you have it. It belongs in Sutra.'

'Yes. You're right,' Talisker agreed. But the thought seemed to end there. Sandro sank back down on his pillows, his face ashen against the pinks and lilacs of the pillowcases and quilt. This time he didn't have the strength to return to consciousness and Talisker was relieved to see his chest still moving as he breathed deeply. He took the medicine bag from his throat and stared in at the gem nestled amongst the soft leather seams. Sandro was right, Talisker did have his death in his hands but it was his death in Sutra, not Edinburgh . . .

'Whassup?' Bea stood in the doorway to her room not looking any better for a couple of hours sleep. She wore a fluffy orange dressing gown and her long fine hair straggled across the shoulders, full of static; her features were still red and puffy from where she'd been crying.

Talisker sighed. 'I think we're losing him, Bea.' As he allowed himself to say the words, Talisker had the realisation that he had never wanted Sandro dead – even during the times it would have seemed easy to think that way – and that was because he admired the Sicilian. He always had, ever since they had been boys; Sandro's poise, easy charm and confidence (mistaken for arrogance by some), a certain quiet dignity, only truly recognised in Sutra when Morias had named him *Seanachaidh*. Sandro – almost the antithesis of Malky – was a hero. His hero if he was honest . . . He realised he was crying soundlessly and he lowered his head, crushing the medicine bag in his fist.

'What is that?' Bea had sat down in the easy chair at the head end of the couch. It was possible that she just didn't know what to say and was casting around hopelessly for something to distract him, but haltingly, Talisker explained about the medicine bag and Sandro's death gem, almost expecting scathing scepticism from Bea who was after all, a scientist. He was forgetting however, that he was preaching to the converted so far as Bea was concerned.

'Can I see it?' she asked when he'd finished. He took the gem from the little pouch and placed it in the flat of her palm. Bea peered closely at it but there was nothing to indicate it contained anything mystical. 'What about . . .' she began, then she frowned as though unable to make sense of the idea she was having. 'Look, if we give this to Sandro to hold, what would happen?'

'He'd die,' Talisker noted dully. 'It would be the death that Morias saved him from – apparently an excruciating, agonising one.'

'But what if he's already dying?' Bea persisted. 'He is dying, Duncan, isn't he?'

Talisker stared for long moments at Sandro's prostrate body. The bizarre blue shell formed from his thickened skin was now as high as his underarms, the blue tracery ran up his neck, just touching his cheeks like cold blue flames. Sandro's breathing was extremely shallow and Talisker had seen enough death in his time in Sutra to know that the end was close for his friend. 'I don't know,' he admitted. 'He'd probably die horribly rather than . . . peacefully.' He looked down at Sandro as he spoke, at least this death, frightening as it was, would allow the Sicilian to sleep away.

'Just suppose though, if they cancel each other out? Maybe we can save him, Duncan, maybe we could . . .'

'No, we can't . . .' Talisker expected some response to his words and when none came, he looked up, just in time to see Bea taking the decision into her own hands. She was reaching forward with the gem obviously intending to place it on Sandro's chest.

'No!' Talisker's hand shot out and he grabbed hold of Bea's fist. 'What do you think you're doing,' he yelled. 'Doesn't he deserve to die peacefully?'

Bea was gasping, tears starting afresh in her eyes, 'You're hurting me,' she snapped back, 'let go.'

'He's my friend. Let him go, Bea.'

'No.'

Talisker began to pull back Bea's extended arm and prize open her fingers. 'No, Duncan,' she groaned. 'He doesn't deserve to die at all.' There was a short, futile struggle which both knew Talisker would win. Although he didn't want to hurt Bea, Talisker couldn't face the thought of giving back Sandro the death Morias had cheated. She didn't understand what that death would be like . . .

'What's going on?' Tristan stood blinking in the doorway of the bedroom watching their struggle with a confused scowl on his face. Distracted by the interruption, Talisker turned towards his son, realising it might appear as though he was attacking Bea.

'It's not how . . .'

Seizing her moment, Bea knocked his hand away and dropped the gem onto Sandro's chest.

'No!' Talisker roared, he pushed Bea aside and reached to grab the stone from where it had landed between Sandro's ribs. But it was too late; already, bright light was spilling outwards from the stone which was disappearing from view, melting into the surface of the shell-skin.

'What have you done?' Talisker hissed, his eyes wide with horror. Bea – her hands still buried in the wool of Talisker's jersey as she tried to pull him back – froze, staring at the tendrils of purple light which issued from the hole in Sandro's skin, sliding across the surface of his transformed body to begin to form a glowing web.

A small whimper escaped Bea's throat as she realised what she might have unleashed. 'He deserved a chance,' she whispered. All eyes were fixed on Sandro but Talisker's features were contorted by fury and helpless rage.

There was silence in the room, Talisker, Bea and

Tris stood motionless, watching as the shimmering purple strands wove a web around Sandro's unconscious form. There was something about the movement of the lights which had a deliberate, sentient air as though, once unleashed from within the gem they must perform this task as Morias had bid them do. Once Sandro was encased within the lattice-work, all motion ceased, the web complete. The watchers held their breath, Bea and Talisker sinking back down into their seats with no further thought for their argument.

Suddenly, eyes still closed, apparently unconscious, Sandro began to scream, long and loud. The sound, bereft of any emotion but pain, was unbearable. His body, wracked by invisible torment, writhed and convulsed, his features a mask of slack-jawed suffering, spittle drooling from the corners of his open mouth.

Bea picked up a cushion from her chair and began to sob into it, unable to even look at Talisker. Tristan stood rooted to the spot, his features ashen. Talisker, leapt up from his chair and moved to the far side of the room as though irrationally hoping to get away from the sound.

'Goddammit, Bea,' he shouted, 'Goddammit, what have you done?' He struck out, punching his fist into the kitchen door which crashed back against the wall like a gunshot, then he rested his forehead on his arm which was against the lintel of the door. Bea didn't respond, making incoherent sobbing noises into her cushion.

'Can't you see he's suffering?' Tristan's comment appeared to be directed at no one and for long moments neither Bea or Talisker sensed his intention as he stepped into the room. Only as he neared the still screaming, convulsing Sandro, dropping his hand to his waist, did something about the movement catch Talisker's attention.

'Tristan! No!' he yelled. In a split second it seemed as though Talisker's heart and mind reacted in opposition to one another; even as he raced back to the couch, as Tristan raised his sword to release Sandro from his agonies, he recognised his son's reaction was right. But even then, he couldn't let him kill his friend.

'No, please, Tristan . . .'

Tristan turned on his father and Talisker was amazed to see such quiet strength in his son's anguished gaze. 'It is right, Father. You know it is . . .'

'You can't do that.' Bea's voice was garbled, distraught, her face red with tears. 'Tell him Duncan. Tell him. We don't do that here . . . can't just kill people. Please . . .'

But although Sandro's voice was failing him, his screams becoming almost soundless as his straining vocal cords failed, there was no doubt that a man was not intended to survive such agony. Talisker glanced once at Bea and, holding his arm out ready to fend her back, he gave Tristan the tiniest nod, closing his eyes as he did so. Tristan raised his blade once more.

Then, before the blow could strike home, as abruptly as they had begun, Sandro's screams ceased. Tristan only just managed to stop the chopping motion of his sword within half an inch of Sandro's neck, a gasp of amazement escaping him. Sandro's face, twisted with pain a mere second earlier, had turned to calm serenity; his eyes remained closed but his features suddenly relaxed, his mouth settling into an almost beatific smile. Tristan's sword clattered onto the wooden floor as a shock tremor ran through him realising how close he had come to ending Sandro's life prematurely.

'Look, Father,' he whispered, 'the *Seanachaidh* lives.'

CHAPTER TWELVE

Regan loved dancing. She always had, since she was a child. The dances of the Fine were like a controlled fury, their steps traditional, called over and over through many years. And yet within those confines, an energy of purest joy. At Soulis Mor, Regan ordered that there be dancing once each month for no particular reason – and not just within the palace walls – the whole city must dance. She maintained it was good for the body and soul, and in truth, it was one of her more popular edicts.

Tonight would be difficult, Regan knew. Sitting on her throne, beside the empty chair where Tristan should have sat which now, symbolically, held only his circlet crown, she watched the dancers assemble in the Grand Hall ready for the flautists, pipers and drummers to begin. Even before they danced they moved in swirling eddies of colour, the women in their delicate but simply tailored gowns and the clansmen in their dark green plaid – the colour of the Soulis Mor clan.

The Grand Hall was decked out in its finery also, with huge evergreen branches suspended from the vaults of the ceiling and hundreds of lanterns making the space at once intimate and warm. However, there was still something subdued about the city; Regan knew now she had not imagined it, in fact, wondered how she could have failed to note it earlier.

Before coming to the Hall she had stood for long minutes before her silvered mirror staring pensively at the extraordinary woman she had become; she had allowed Jahl to influence every area of her life she realised, he had been silently chipping away at her for the last five years or so, sculpting her from ice some might say. She wasn't sure, but she thought that the lines of her face had hardened into stern aloofness – that's what all these people saw when they looked at her. She had their respect, she realised, for all the wrong reasons, because they feared her wrath and the persecution of their kinsmen. She had become a Dark Thane as if from legends told by the *Seanachaidhs* – few of whom visited Soulis Mor these days – fierce and vengeful. In recent times she had sanctioned torture, assassination and, to some degree, genocide of the Sidhe but to say that she had regrets about this would be to miss the essence of what made Regan prideful and strong. The few regrets she had were all focused on Jahl, because she had allowed him to use her to his own ends, she had fallen willingly into an abyss of his making and not her own.

And yet, her heart was beating slightly faster as she gazed around the room, watching the doorways and arches of the antechambers for his entrance. She clenched her fingers tight around the stem of her wine goblet, digging her nails into her palms to punish herself for her reaction. Glancing to her right, she noted the small group of Sidhe tribesman of the wolf clan to whom she had granted an audience earlier in the day, she was sure Jahl would have found out by now, could imagine his cold disdain as he wondered what game she was playing. In truth, there was no game, the outlaw status of the wolf Sidhe was well known, they could almost be assumed neutral in the ominous conflict which was ready to erupt between the Fine and the Sidhe. Neutrality was not to be confused with trustworthiness of course. Behind the Sidhe a tall figure leaned nonchalantly against the wall, almost indistinct in the shadows cast by the arches of the stone lintels. Regan's gaze rested on the man for a mere second and he gave a tiny nod of acknowledgement and readiness; his name was Finnbar and he was a mercenary from far south near the lands of Thane Huw.

And then, there he was: Jahl. As he strode straight across the dance floor those few couples already dancing made way for him as if he were some force of nature, a wind which bent leaves and branches before him. He smiled and bowed, small and polite, to a few people, his gaze flickering back and forth before reaching forward for Regan.

She knew he was angry, as he drew nearer she could see the tiny vein pulsing on his temple. Just for a second she saw his mask of civility slip away and he flashed her an ice-searing gaze which gave little respect to the fact she was his Thane. As he approached the throne dais, Regan reached out imperiously and he paused for what seemed like a dangerously long time before he paid her homage by kissing her hand lightly. 'Is something wrong, Jahl?' she enquired.

'No, Milady. As ever your radiance lifts my spirits.' His tone belied the statement and she wondered if he somehow knew her plans, she wondered if he could read her very thoughts. Still, she held his gaze steadily and stared back at him tilting her chin. He smiled unexpectedly, disarming her. 'I have brought you a gift, Majesty. May I present it to you now?'

'Of course,' she smiled back. Glancing around, she watched the colourful whirl of people dancing, the music was loud and relentlessly cheerful so that it seemed she and Jahl might share a private moment despite the crowd. She leant forward to see her gift, keenly aware that it would be the first and last gift he would give her as this night was destined to be his last, but still, she was swept along by him as ever, riding the adrenalin rush she always felt when he was near her; addicted to him. *If this night marks his end,* she thought, *it will be an end of sorts for both of us, because without him, I will surely return to shadow.* The candour of her own thought surprised Regan but she dismissed it as a result of tiredness and the tension which seemed almost palpable in the air.

Jahl held forward a small wooden box which he opened with a dramatic flourish; inside, something glinted warmly in the light of the sconces. Regan reached out but then suddenly, instinctively, recoiled. It was a feather, finely wrought in white gold with a large diamond near the base of the quill. Did he know? Was he taunting her, she wondered?

'Don't you like it, Thane Regan?' His face was a picture of innocent consternation and he lifted the feather from the box to better show her the fine craftsmanship. The brooch was so delicate and cunningly made it seemed as though it could be as light as the object it represented.

'I – I . . . yes, Jahl. It is beautiful.'

'Will you wear it?' He reached forward to pin it to her gown and she almost recoiled once more but she stilled the impulse. *It's just pretend after all, a pretend feather; no bird has moulted it out or used it to line its nest.*

'Yes,' she whispered. But for a moment, she could not meet his gaze as before and she fought not to tremble as he pinned the vile thing to her gown. How bitter that his final gift should be so strangely inappropriate. She felt a sharp warmth and realised he had scratched her with the pin but as she looked up into his eyes, a storm of reproach on her lips, he bent closer to her so that their cheeks were almost touching. His breath was warm and sweet against her skin as he spoke quietly to her; in a moment of weakness she wished she had not ordered his death this very day, wished she could sleep with him just once and wake beside him.

'You're trembling,' he said. 'Some strange mood is upon you tonight. Would you do me the honour of dancing with me?'

She nodded, frightened to speak least she betray her fear. Jahl led her to the dance floor, making a tiny, prearranged signal to the musicians as he did so. The music slowed, became softer, until only the high, haunting sound of a *Feadan* and flute could be heard. All around, couples made way for Regan and Jahl to dance, a slow measured waltz. Jahl reached to take her lightly by her waist and they began to dance, it seemed to Regan their footsteps were but an echo of her heartbeat. She looked at his face, her emotion threatening to overwhelm her and she was just about to speak to him, to make polite courtly conversation, when a movement from high above caught her attention.

At first she jumped slightly, thinking a bird had somehow gotten into the Hall, although she had people whose job it was to make sure that never happened. But then she stilled her fright: it was a white feather and it fell in a slow, elegant swirl quite far from where they were dancing. For a second she began to relax but then she realised there were more feathers, hundreds and thousands more . . .

It was as though someone had shaken a feather bolster out somewhere high overhead – all over the Hall a white, silent rain began to fall. Regan stiffened in Jahl's arms, her breath catching in her throat.

'Regan,' he said quietly. 'Is there something distressing you?'

'Jahl – I . . .' She could hardly breathe, her chest was so tight, her heart hammering between her ribs. All around people continued dancing, oblivious to the falling feathers even though they landed on their clothes and settle in their hair like unmelting snowflakes. She didn't understand, how come they could not see them? She knew they were beautiful, that other people at least would think so, and yet, no one even remarked on their strange presence. They just kept dancing. She could not breathe, her throat was constricting, her eyes burning. She heard her breath rasping through her chest, a broken, wheezing sound . . .

'Regan?' Jahl stopped and shook her by the shoulders, his face an artless picture of concern. Feathers which had clustered in his dark hair were shaken loose by the movement and caught further down in the folds of his shirt. She was drawn closer to him as he shook her and she panicked.

'No, no, let me . . .' she knew they were in her hair too, she could feel the tiniest crawling sensation as one brushed against her face. A sudden high pitched scream ripped from her throat as she could bear it no longer. The music stopped and everyone in the Hall froze to look around for the source of the sound. She was gasping now in fear and panic, trying to pull away from Jahl, who for some reason had tightened his grip around the top of her arms.

'Regan, Regan, calm down. What is it?' The whiteness covered him like a thin dusting of snow and the Hall now seemed predominantly white, in the clutches of some strange winter.

'Let me go, Jahl.' He didn't let her go so she screamed it again into his innocent bemused face. 'Let me go now!' Her voice, hysterical and high carried across the Hall, spurring her bodyguard into action. Jahl released his grip and Regan immediately began scrubbing her fingers into her hair in a frenzied, obsessive motion. 'Get them out, get them out,' she sobbed.

A ripple of concern passed through the crowd. It appeared the Thane was in the grip of some sorcery or madness but no one moved, unable to identify any real assailant.

'Oh gods,' she began to moan, a low helpless sound. 'They're on my gown . . .' she made little darting brushing motions to her skirts and then stopped, overcome by the sheer number of the feathers. Crippled by indecision, she clutched at the neck of her gown as though for a moment considering ripping it off; her eyes were wide and unfocused. Then she ran towards the doors of the Hall through the silence of the stunned crowd, her ragged breathless sobs filling the reaches of the Great Hall with despair. As she departed, the musicians quickly began to play cheerful music but the pall of shock in the Hall was immovable. No one had even seen a feather, only their Thane losing her mind.

Jahl ran after Regan, calling out for her but she was swift on her feet, her fear giving her wild energy. She ran through the echoing corridors towards the imagined safety of her chambers holding her skirts up to allow her legs unimpeded movement; her feet making a soft slapping on the stone floors. She could hear someone following her and knew it was probably Jahl but she didn't want to stop, even though the feathers had gone now, even though there was no whiteness . . .

As her thoughts clarified her shock began to abate, although she was still shaking with reaction she slowed down, reaching her hand to her dishevelled hair; as she did so, she brushed against the brooch . . . the feather brooch.

She turned just as his footsteps drew near. He was standing only a few feet away but he didn't try to come any closer or offer her any sympathy. A look passed between them which told them both everything they needed to know. Regan ripped the brooch from the breast of her gown – crushing the delicate filigree as she did so – and flung it at his feet. It made a strangely flat sound as though it was in reality some cheap piece of bronze or pewter, its magic spent. Distantly, she knew she was still crying, her face and chest red with the rush of hysteria, her hair tangled and matted as some old crone where she had scrubbed it, but she drew the last vestiges of her dignity about her.

'Why, Jahl?'

He stepped forward slightly into the brighter light of a sconce and she could see before he spoke that he was still playing his game. Whatever that game was. As she felt her breath slow and the faint, creeping dawn of calm began to take hold, she wondered if he was doing something now, at this moment, some other charm to quiet her. She thought if he was to tell her everything and throw himself at her feet begging for mercy, perhaps she might spare his life. But she knew that wasn't going to happen.

He contrived to look crestfallen. 'It was a gift, just a small conjuring. I thought . . . I thought you would like it . . . think it was pretty . . .'

Her face contorted in ugly fury, her lips drew back from her teeth in an animalistic snarl. 'Liar!' she shrieked. '*You're a liar!* You knew, you must have known! Stay away from me. Just stay away.' She backed away a few steps as she spoke and then, turned on her heel and ran once more.

This time, Jahl did not attempt to follow. He kept his expression carefully contrite until he heard her footsteps die away, then, he allowed a malicious smile to creep across his features.

'Why?' she had asked him why. Well, if the Thane should now mysteriously fling herself from the ramparts of Soulis Mor, few would question the fact

it was insanity. But mostly, because Regan's subjugation would be all the more sweet if he could reduce her to drooling insanity first, he shrugged. It was just more fun this way; he'd thought she, if anyone, would understand that. Reluctantly though, he had to admit that Regan was nearing the end of her usefulness – it would be all the better if she now took to her rooms for a few days.

He continued his walk to his own chambers, noting almost absently, the clumsy way in which the pursuing assassin allowed an unnatural silence to fill the sound of his muffled footfall.

Holyrood Park was freezing. Under the baleful glare of a new moon, a spiteful cold breathed across the empty expanse of manicured grass until each blade stood stiffened, as a tiny sharpened dagger. Knox walked across the silent parkland in his bare feet, knowing subconsciously that his legs were absorbing the coldness of the ground and he was losing all feeling. He wore only his grey cotton robe which appeared similar to a long, loose nightshirt as he had failed to put the belt around it before leaving The Ark. Knox was in a strange trance; if anyone had asked him how a trance might feel, this waking dream would not have been it: he could still think his own thoughts, they ran behind the *other* thoughts with the frightening clarity of a silver stream. The other thoughts were not God's thoughts either, rather, they were a seed God had planted into Knox's unsuspecting mind after he awoke to find Tristan and the Scoor vanished from The Ark. God had been displeased, very displeased . . .

Knox stumbled slightly but kept his gaze fixed on the sight ahead of him; Salisbury Crags, the cliff area of Arthur's Seat, which jutted from the plane of the ground level like the legs or paws of some huge lion. Behind the crags, the slightly softer, rounder outline of the hill, clad more kindly in long grass and heather, was over eight hundred feet high. Now, in the bright light from the full moon, it was almost possible to make out the iron red tint of the exposed rocks whose expanse covered the secret of what had once been an active volcano. The sense of 'awareness' of the great hill was something deeply ingrained in the psyche of the people of Edinburgh, its outline the first thing they looked for if returning home by train or car; a sense of homecoming which only such a guardian could provide. Knox, however, knew in his own thoughts that what God had sent him to do might be resented by any real guardian spirit of the hill and so, as he approached through the northern end of Holyrood Park, he imagined a sentience which was far less kind, in fact angry and vengeful.

But Knox would not, could not stop. Inside his compartmentalised mind the other thoughts held a picture of a place he had to find. It was what God wanted. If he found it, God said that he, Knox, could take the Children there in times to come. Knox imagined He meant the Tribulation but something bothered him about the fact God didn't quite speak in the terms he would have expected. His feet were bleeding now, he had the weirdest sensation of hot blood against frozen skin, also, the torch he had brought with him which was inside the voluminous pocket of his robe kept hitting against his leg as he trotted along. He'd like to slow down but God was angry. So angry in fact, that He had done something to Esther . . .

. . . At the mere thought of her, Knox felt a rush of warm adrenalin. She was his now; whether she had given herself to him, as she probably told herself, or whether he had simply taken her against little resistance. In Daniel's great big bed he had fulfilled every fantasy he had ever held about Esther; he'd scratched, bitten and bruised, twisting his fingers into her sweet scented hair and yanking her closer, ever closer, until he felt she was tiny, insubstantial against him. Had God seen him then, he wondered?

She had sighed and whimpered when he caused her pain; pliant and submissive, she had spurred Knox into a frenzy of selfish passion. And yet, if he was honest with himself, as he looked into her wide unreproaching eyes just before he fell asleep, Esther was the victor of the day. She now held the secret to Knox's soul, she just didn't know it; his passion, his rage in her arms, made him weak before her, his loss of control had frightened and amazed him. The last thing he saw as sleep claimed him was her smile and the uneasy feeling that it contained a hint of self-satisfaction stayed with him as he slept, making his dreams restless. When he awoke, the feeling remained with him and he watched her sleeping, frightened by her innocent beauty, shamed by the bruises he had marked her with, and fighting the urge to wake her by slapping and beating her – punishment for her disarming of him. Did he love her? He didn't know. Knox knew nothing of love. But he had wanted to hurt and hold her for ever.

But Esther didn't wake up. He hadn't realised at first, thought she was only sleeping, exhausted from the night before. As realisation struck home, he shook her limp body in a useless effort to rouse her, sobbing and promising never to hit her again. It seemed he had somehow killed her, but then, God had come into his mind . . .

'This is a warning, Knox. If you fail me again, I will take her and I will make you outcast from the Children . . .'

'F-fail? Have I failed you, Lord?' He was confused at first.

'Tristan is gone from this place. The Scoor destroyed.'

'No,' he was aghast, 'that's not possible.'

'It has happened, Knox. My enemies have taken him while you slept.'

Knox had fallen to his knees and begged for another chance and God had granted him the chance to prove himself once more. As he babbled, rocking back and forth as he had when he had been a child, a sudden torment had seized his mind as though God had placed some jagged, poisonous flower in there which opened slowly in a blossom of vibrant pain. He lay prostrate on the floor, unable to move or react, simply consumed by the agony. Then, just as he felt he could bear it no longer and began to entertain thoughts of dying, the pain stopped, and in the afterglow of suffering, his forgiving God had sent him the vision of the place he must find now. He had come to consciousness to find Esther crouched over him, examining him with an oddly dispassionate air.

'Esther! Thank – thank God . . .' He reached up to touch her and she recoiled. 'What's wrong?' he frowned.

As if displaying her wounds to him she reached up and touched the bruise on her own cheek, her eyes held a dark light he'd never seen there before. 'I'll say when you can touch me, Knox,' she had said simply. With that she got up and left the room, carelessly walking down the corridor from his bedroom in her dressing-gown, making no attempt at discretion. She was angry, he knew, probably she had realised on awakening exactly how much damage Knox had inflicted on her aching body.

She would forgive him though, that was the thing, she knew it and he knew it, it was like some new, strange sickness which would kill one of them eventually; need, weakness and anger. It didn't have to be like this, Knox was sure. Trouble was, he couldn't see another way of being – she would forgive him, and then he would hate himself all over again . . .

He was on the rocks now, the sensation of cold hardness on his feet felt as though it was happening to someone else, someone whose steps followed a path determined by the thoughts. The rough sill of rocks would bring Knox up to the level just behind the upper part of the hill called the Lion's Head; there must have been an easier route, the climb was arduous and dangerous. It was as though God was combining punishment with pilgrimage and Knox had no real argument with that, it was what he deserved.

Finally, he stood gasping for breath looking across at the outcrop God had planted in his vision, in the almost harsh light of the full moon, the colours of the rocks were bleached and flattened, the strata, which ran vertically, appeared as though someone had simply scraped the rock-face with a huge rake.

'There're no caves or nothin' here,' he muttered. He wasn't really expecting an answer; although he still wore the necklace, since presenting him with his vision, God had been silent. Knox knew this was make or break time, if he failed in this, he might never hear His voice again . . .

Cursing quietly, he ran his fingers up and down the rock surface, questing for some gap or lever even. There was nothing for long minutes and Knox paused, glancing behind him to where the first faint warmth of dawn would creep across the Firth of Forth towards the sleeping city.

'Fuck,' he hissed.

As he turned back he slipped slightly which lowered his level of vision; that's when he saw. Not far to the right of where he stood there was a narrow opening in the rocks. The opening was obscured by wiry bushes of heather which clung to furrows in the rock-face where the most meagre amounts of soil collected. It was easy to see how the opening could be missed; the rocks jutted inward making a thin, elbow shaped gap. Knox squeezed himself around the bend and once past the initial cramped space he was plunged into complete and utter blackness. After fumbling for a few moments to find and use his torch, he stared forward into a shallow cave no more than ten feet in depth.

'But this is no good . . .' he whispered. It wasn't

like his vision at all and for a dizzying moment, doubt assailed him; he slid down the wall of the cave and sat on the ground his knees hunched up to his chin. His lips moved as he muttered to himself; it was a habit he'd had since he was a boy.

'Hey, Danny, I bet you're laughing now, bet you're havin' a right laugh . . .' He stopped whispering and began to crawl across the frosted ground towards the far side of the cave; something over there had caught his attention.

Where the rock-face disappeared into the ground, a dark line of shadow indicated a ledge where a gap had opened under the wall. Knox stuck his torch down into the hole; the light vanished underneath into some space beyond.

'Aw no,' he groaned, but without pause he climbed down into the narrow trench and ducked beneath the sill. For a moment, the yellow tungsten of the torch could still be seen in the tiny cave, wavering and flickering like a lost soul. Then, it was gone, swallowed up by the volcano, and the cave returned to still darkness once more.

'I can't go back.'

'What d'you mean, you can't go back?' Talisker stared aghast at Sandro who was still sitting propped up on Bea's couch. It was mid-morning of the day after Sandro's 'cure' and the Sicilian was looking almost his normal self again. Talisker had been toying with the idea of returning to Sutra that evening, well aware that around forty-five to forty-eight days may have passed during their short sojourn in Edinburgh.

'Anything could have happened by now,' he pointed out.

'Things are happening here, Duncan,' Sandro replied calmly. He handed Talisker the morning edition of the *Scotsman* newspaper.

'There's nothing . . .'

'Page five,' he sighed.

At first, Talisker couldn't decide which article Sandro was talking about and he was just about to say so when a small, three-column box at the bottom of the page caught his attention. It was headed: '*Driver Blames Bus Crash On Apparitions Of "Monsters"*.'

The article took the tone of laughing up its sleeve but to Sandro and Talisker there was obviously nothing to laugh about.

'"It's like something out of *The X-Files*," thirty-five-year-old Graham Flockhart exclaimed. "I know folk won't believe me but I know what I saw. There were about five of the creatures and they half-ran and half-flew across the High Street from the direction of Jeffery Street down towards the Holyrood Palace end. They were like giant scorpions crossed with men . . . and they had wings. Horrible they were. I only saw them for a few seconds before they disappeared – I don't mean they went behind a building or anything but they vanished into thin air. I know how Mulder feels now." Mr Flockhart admitted he had done a longer than average shift driving on LRT buses and was very tired. There were three passengers on the bus when it skidded into a brick wall but none were seriously hurt . . .'

'More Scoor?' Talisker groaned in dismay. 'I thought

I'd killed them all yesterday. Where the hell are they all coming from?'

'That much we do know,' Sandro remarked sourly. 'But why has Jahl sent more? If he sent them to kill or retrieve Tristan why does he need more in Edinburgh now? It just doesn't make sense . . .'

'No, but you can't stop him from here, Sandro. It's all the more reason to go back and get him.'

Sandro sighed again, 'I've given it a lot of thought, Duncan. Bea and I can look for answers here and at least we're in a position to do something about it. If Scoor start popping up all over the city, there'll be panic. That Knox, the cult guy, he's a good starting point, Jahl was controlling him when he grabbed Tris and . . .'

'You don't want to go back, Sandro, do you?' Talisker sat down heavily on the end of the couch. 'Everything you're saying makes sense but you just don't want to go back to Sutra. I do understand.'

Sandro grinned slightly shamefacedly, 'I feel as if I've come home, Duncan. And to get those years back again, it's a bonus. Don't misunderstand me, I love Sutra, but I'm a different person there, I'm a *Seanachaidh* and that means loneliness. When I first went, it was what I needed, to rediscover myself and have pride in what I was – it was a whole different, creative me that Morias saw. But now I know that the old me was just as valid . . . I had just lost my way after Diane died. If I go back now, I'll feel as though I'm in exile.'

Talisker laughed softly. 'That's how I feel here.' He rubbed his brow as though wiping the emotion from his features. 'Just give it some more thought, Sandro, I'm pretty sure me and Tristan will need you on the other side.'

There was the sound of a key in the lock of the front door and Bea came in looking breathless and flushed. She had gone into the office, supposedly to hand over the files she had completed as a favour to Stirling but mainly to try and make peace with Cal.

'You'll never guess what's happened,' she said. 'I think the Scoor have done a murder.'

Knox arrived back at The Ark at eight-thirty in the morning, exhausted by the night's events. It was still dark and, being Saturday, which was the day many of the Children spent away with their families, there were few people stirring in the house. Knox had a brief glimpse of James, one of the newer and younger members of the Children – he muttered 'blessings this day' as he passed, thankful the lights from the downstairs hallway only cast a dim glow up the bend in the staircase. James seemed half asleep anyway, which was just as well; Knox's foot, tingling now as the blood rushed back into them, were cut and bloody, his robe was ripped and wet. It had been a night like no other; grim and exciting, confirming Knox as a prophet for the New Age of Christ's Rule . . . his head was throbbing with tiredness and anxiety and all he wanted now was the warmth of his bed for just an hour or so, so that he might have the strength he would need to tell the Children . . .

As he opened the door of his room a tiny noise made him look down at the floor. Just beside the door Esther lay sleeping, curled up in a blue sleeping bag.

'What the hell . . . ?' he muttered. He bent down and gazed at her sleeping face, one side was badly bruised, the eye puffy and sore looking. Knox sat down beside her on the floor and stroked her hair aside from her cheek, she stirred slightly in her sleep and then opened her eyes quite suddenly.

'Knox,' she whispered, in her sleepy state she seemed not to notice his cold disarray. She smiled sadly. 'I'm so sorry I made you angry.'

He stared at her in mute disbelief. 'I don't know why I get like that.'

'You have a lot of responsibility, Knox. I understand.' She reached out and touched his face and he kissed the palm of her hand. 'Do you forgive me, then?' she smiled.

Something tightened within Knox's stomach as he instinctively recognised the cycle of her vulnerability and his violence. 'Of course I forgive you,' he said. 'Why don't you come to bed?'

'Isn't it morning?'

'Just for an hour or so.'

She struggled to get up in the sleeping bag so he picked her up and carried her back into the room.

'Where were you going?' she asked once he curled up beside her on the bed having taken off his robe and put on his warm dressing-gown. She had mistakenly thought he had been in the room all night.

'Oh, to get a bible. I – I think I need to study some more. It can wait though.'

Esther was still sleepy and snuggled against him. Knox felt himself drift into sleep, his mind almost numb, his fingers tangled in her hair.

'Knox?'

'Hmm?'

'Do you think about Daniel very often?'

'All the time,' he breathed.

'Do you miss him?'

'Yeah.'

But sleep eluded Knox. As he listened to the slow sound of Esther's breathing, images played through his mind as though projected onto the back of his helpless eyelids in black and sepia. The chamber, deep within the hillside, glowing with weird, cold light. The rock formations which appeared to have erupted from the ground to the high ceiling of the chamber like a jagged cry of vengeance. The altar stone, the huge organic sweep of twisted basalt pillars behind the altar stone like a cathedral organ gone insane, which terminated in something which looked strangely like a throne. But most of all, the fact that, when he had clambered into this silent frightening world, six Scoor had been there, waiting for his arrival, standing as stiff and still as the stones beside them.

'L-Lord?' Knox whispered. His voice carried across the great space as weak and frightened as a child. The reply came as before, through the necklace, but it was magnified and sharpened by the rock walls so that the sound was all around him.

'I am coming soon, Knox. Here is the place you must bring My Children. I will appear to them as a sign of My love.'

'Why are the Scoor here?'

'They will not harm the Faithful, Knox, those who

are watching for the day of My return . . . You will be their leader. Command them and they will do as you say.'

Knox glanced at the nearest Scoor nervously; the creature was impassive, staring straight ahead, the phosphorous light in the chamber reflected dully on the iron of its breastplate. 'Will they be invisible again?'

'If you command it so.'

Knox thought for a moment. It occurred to him for some reason, that Daniel should be here, not him, he was an impostor in the situation somehow. What would Daniel do, he wondered if God gave him an instrument of revenge? Probably nothing – Daniel was a being of light and love – perhaps that was why God had chosen to work through Knox. The time of Tribulation would require people to make harsh choices. His thoughts settled on the day he had stolen the necklace, at the museum . . . the Evolution exhibition . . .

'You,' he said to the nearest Scoor. Its gaze flickered towards him. 'Take two others,' he signalled towards another two, 'and destroy Professor . . .'

'You only need think it, Knox.'

'Oh yeah.' Knox formed a picture in his mind of Professor Ian Galbraith standing on the steps outside the museum's old building. 'Destroy this man. He teaches against the Word of our God.' The creature seemed to hesitate for a moment but then, abruptly, vanished with the nearest two of its companions.

Knox walked forward towards the throne, his bare feet making an empty slapping noise on the smooth stone floor. As he reached the throne he paused, looking around the chamber for some reaction from the Scoor. None of the remaining three moved or even flickered their eyes towards him so he sat down hesitantly on the seat, a slow smile of satisfaction spreading across his face. Still, he did not have quite enough nerve to settle back into the deep recess of the chair, but rather perched on the edge.

'There are others, Lord,' he announced into the rocky silence, 'other scientists and politicians who teach against Your Truth. If I may, I will use the Scoor to kill them all.'

'There is little time for such diversions,' the voice boomed, *'but as you will, Knox. If it serves your purpose.'*

Knox nodded his head in a small, courtly bow, 'My only purpose is to Glorify You, oh Lord,' he said, slightly self-consciously.

There was a sudden green flash of light in the chamber and the three Scoor appeared again only feet away from the throne. The middle one of the three carried something in the claw-like hand of its uppermost limb which it tossed onto the floor at Knox's feet. Without thinking Knox recoiled with a disgusted yell as a warm splatter of blood splashed across the toes of his frozen feet.

The object lolled to one side slightly and a pair of broken glasses tinkled to the floor; it was a human head, ripped without any hesitation from the shoulders of its most unfortunate owner, Professor Ian Galbraith. The expression on the face was indescribable horror and it seemed to Knox that death had been so instantaneous and so recent that somewhere within the dying cortex of the man's brain, the last traces of thought were recognising their own end. Galbraith's eyes blinked once as the eyelids spasmed and the jaw suddenly dropped into slackness as though he was about to scream. A dark spreading stain of blood pooled around the mess of the severed neck.

'Oh God,' Knox garbled, all composure gone. 'Oh God. Get it out! Get it out of here . . .' He lifted his feet onto the chair as though the blood was actively pursuing him. The Scoor, puzzled by his strange reaction to their obeying his command so promptly and efficiently, gathered around the head and one of them reached out with its short spear and stabbed the head through the back of the neck so that it could lift it up. Knox groaned and covered his mouth in case he vomited. With another, shorter, green flare, the Scoor's trophy was disintegrated at the end of the spear and the Scoor returned to their strange posture of silent vigilance once more.

There was laughter then, cruel mocking laughter filled the cavern. God was mocking his weakness and Knox, rocking back and forth on the throne, fighting nausea, could not believe that God was truly so spiteful.

'Stop it!' he yelled. 'Stop laughing at me!' The laughter stopped and a hush ensued for long moments. Finally God spoke once more and his tone was apologetic, raising the hairs on the back of Knox's neck.

'But this is only the beginning, Knox. Be strong. You must prepare yourself for the blood of the Tribulation. Many will die soon.'

* * *

Tristan watched in bemusement; it must have been the twentieth time they had said 'goodbye'. 'You're sure about this aren't you, Sandro?' Talisker reached out to shake Sandro's hand once more, the question nothing more than rhetorical, 'It's not as if you can just change your mind.'

Sandro glanced at Bea who smiled warmly in response. 'I feel as though we've got work to do here, Duncan. I hope we can stop the Scoor getting out, people will panic. Magic . . . just doesn't belong here.'

'Yeah,' Talisker grinned broadly, 'and the rest, Sandro.' Sandro looked mildly embarrassed but didn't deny the obvious strength of feeling which was growing between himself and Bea. 'Anyway, clean slate time, *Seanachaidh*,' Talisker touched the medicine bag which was back around his neck, 'I'm taking this back with me. I don't know if it has any power left, but it can't touch you there.'

'No.'

'No . . .' Both men seemed to have the realisation there was little left to say, this time their worlds were parting seemingly for ever, and they, who had shared a common bond, had made a choice which left them on opposite sides of some chasm – in reality.

'You have an extra lifetime,' Talisker nodded solemnly, 'make it a good one.'

'Father. We should go,' Tristan reminded gently.

They were standing in the dark confines of the Close and Talisker had already reactivated the gateway by use of a gem which Morias had given him. A warm haze had begun to emanate from the far side of the room and a faint smell of woodsmoke carried with it.

It didn't occur to any of them that the smell could indicate disaster; gateways seemed an imprecise phenomenon on the whole.

'Yeah. 'Bye Bea.' Talisker hugged Beatrice again. ''Bye Sandro.' He made to pump the Sicilian's hand again but Sandro pulled him into a hug. 'Sandro, you're such a big jessie,' he joked tearfully, yanking on Sandro's pony-tail. Then he turned to Tristan, the laughter and tears dying in his eyes.

'Son,' he said gruffly, 'we should go and get your city back for you. Looks like our campaign is short of a hero though . . .'

Tristan smiled in return; it was a shy but somehow imperious smile. He'd already said his goodbyes. 'You will do just fine, Father,' he enthused.

'Let's go then.' Talisker didn't look back again but waved his hand towards his friends as he began walking towards the heat of the gateway. 'Look after him, Bea . . . Sandro, maybe the polis'll take you back eh . . . ?

They vanished in a brief flare of flame.

As the blackness of the gateway surrounds them, Talisker realises he hasn't told Tristan what to expect. Tristan came a different way, a stronger way, Morias had said. In the distance, he can see a sheet of flame like before. He turns his head, realising as he does so, that everything is slowing down as before.

'It won't hurt you . . .' he tries to say but the sound is distorted and amplified, an odd, flat bellow which comes from all around. He cannot see Tristan's face because of the angle at which Tristan holds his head – it seems as though he is deliberately looking away

from his father. For some reason Talisker wants to see his face before the fire engulfs them both. He knows – remembers – from when Tristan was a boy that it's difficult and painful for Tris to try and move his neck to look back over his right shoulder and so he steps behind him to the left.

'Don't be afraid, Son – I'm here . . . I . . .'

But then, the flames are right before his face, burning silently, their heat making a solid, breathless wall. He remembers; it does hurt, it will hurt . . .

'I mean it won't kill . . .' he turns his head to look at Tristan, the movement exaggeratedly slow almost as though he has acquired his son's disability. Tristan has gone. Somehow from being by his side, he has vanished into the fire. Talisker opens his mouth to shout his name and so, when the flames take him, their brightness reaches down into his throat, down into his belly.

It's like drowning. Drowning in the fire. But this time, the flames are in him and he is part of the burning. He knows he's still moving, can feel his legs walking forward into an oblivion he cannot see for flame. Just ahead another figure is moving through the fire and his heart knows it is Tristan. He tries to call out again but fear and fire robs him of all sound.

After long moments the flames die back slightly and Talisker mutely allows himself to hope it is finishing. He can see the encroaching darkness on the other side of the fire and the shadowy outline of Tristan moving bravely ahead.

But then there is a third figure moving through the gate. It is tall, as tall as himself, and dressed completely in strange white robes made of animal skin. On its face it wears a mask of leather which is fashioned into a face like the sun; the expression of the mask is alien and sad denying its wearer any emotional opinion. Before it reaches Talisker whose covering of flames is dying away, it stops before Tristan. There is silence in the breathless space but the two regard one another and it seems to Talisker that something passes between them. Finally the figure approaches Talisker whose relentless footsteps cause their paths to cross. He tries to look into the eyes in the slits of the mask but he knows he cannot pause for long or he may be lost between worlds; in fact he continues to walk but without moving – treading fire instead of water. Something about the figure is known to him but his mind slips away from the knowledge as though it is the enigma of a dream. His chest is tight and his heart sore for no reason he can tell.

'Thank-you,' the voice comes into his mind as their paths cross briefly and, instinctively he reaches out his hand to the figure which, still moving, has gone slightly past him. The figure also reaches its hand back towards him and for the briefest moment of sad sensation, their fingertips touch.

The voice comes again, almost fading now. 'I love you.'

He turns back then, his body dangerously close to losing its pathway. But the figure does not pause, although its demeanour seems strangely stiff as though its admission has cost it dear. The vision of the strange being is swallowed up by shadow which obliterates the whiteness of its form by degrees of darkness, which is not unkind. The last thing Talisker sees is a large white feather the being holds in its right hand.

'What . . .?'

No answer. He can hear his heartbeat now as before and knows he is nearing the end. He begins to move forward again but realises almost instantly he is lost. It's not as simple as turning around and retracing his steps; by turning back, he has somehow invalidated an agreement between himself and the gateway . . .

'Father . . . Father, can you hear me?'

'Yes . . .' his whisper is amplified as before into a strange, low bellowing sound. He turns back towards the sound of Tristan's voice.

'Keep moving, Father. Don't stop . . .

. . . Don't stop . . .'

Panic. He's beginning to panic. It's never taken this long before.

'Tristan . . . Tris . . .'

'Keep moving . . .'

It finished abruptly. Talisker stumbled and fell to his knees, suddenly gasping for breath and realised that daylight was blinding his exhausted senses.

'Try to breathe slowly and not too deeply, Father. It's the smoke.'

Despite this sensible warning, Talisker drew a deep, shuddering breath and then dissolved into a storm of coughing. Eventually he opened his eyes – which were stinging and filled with hot tears – once more. Tristan was watching him, his expression a picture of concern.

Talisker wiped his face with the back of his sleeve and stared around himself in anguished disbelief.

'Where the hell are we?'

Sandro stared at the blank wall of the chamber where Talisker and Tristan had vanished. He felt unexpectedly bereft, almost empty. 'Sandro,' Bea touched his arm lightly, 'they're gone.'

'Yeah,' he nodded almost too vigorously as though to shake himself out of his trance. His emotions conspired against him however and tears spilled out of his eyes. 'Yeah, yeah, I know. It's over, Bea . . .' Still he felt unable to look away for the moment. 'God, you must think I'm stupid.'

'No. Not stupid,' she shrugged, 'just slightly sentimental. And Sandro, it's not over. Like you said, we've got work to do here. We've got to get rid of the . . . What is it?'

Sandro didn't reply, just nodded towards the gateway wall. Tiny tongues of flame had reappeared and begun to ripple outwards.

'Oh no,' Bea whispered. 'Scoor . . . it could be more Scoor, Sandro.'

Sandro nodded, casting around for a weapon but there was nothing. Talisker and Tristan had both taken their swords back with them and Sandro had left his back at the house. Instinctively, he reached his arm out, gently pushing Bea behind him, unaware of her annoyed expression. She tutted and tapped him on the shoulder.

'Here, this might help,' she handed him her pistol.

'Ah. Thanks.'

They watched in silence as the pool of flame spread outwards across the expanse of the wall. A figure appeared in the centre of the pool, in silhouette at first and then more discernible. The figure was running towards them, flames sloughing off its white robes as though it ran through water, beads and feathers which adorned the mask it wore dancing in the flames.

After a few seconds there was a sudden blast of hot air which filled the chamber, pressing Sandro and Bea back against the far wall. The figure stepped out of the gateway and into their reality; tiny remnants of fire clung to the fringes of its mask and cloak. No one spoke for a moment and Sandro raised the pistol and pointed it at the stranger.

'Who are you?'

To their surprise, a low chuckle came from within the mask; the sound was distinctly feminine. Reaching up, the stranger undid a clasp and threw the mask aside, 'I am an exile, *Seanachaidh*,' she smiled.

Sandro's hand shook, the pistol wavering in his line of vision.

'Ohmigod,' he whispered, 'Ohmigod . . .'

'Sandro,' Bea frowned, 'what's wrong? Who is she?'

CHAPTER THIRTEEN

The void was dangerous. Jahl knew that, he had known that since his mother had warned him at the age of eleven when – during his informal lessons – he had asked her why she had failed to mention it to him before. Her reply was etched on his mind for ever: *'Because it's dangerous, Jahl. Because it's everything and nothing. All souls will cross this space during their existence . . .'*

Of course most mortal souls were dead at the point they came here and to come in any other state was an act of supreme confidence or foolishness. Jahl was currently concentrating too hard to decide which it was on his part. He spoke quietly, unnerved slightly by the way his words were swallowed up by the distance. It was a Summoning; the first he had done since that fateful childhood day, but Jahl had learned the error of his ways. Rather than endangering himself by descending deep within the void he planned to summon a more minor creature to act as his envoy – he could do this from his entry point without having to move around which required great skill and self-control.

Something was moving in the darkness ahead of him. Jahl stood rigidly still, sweat beading on his brow. He continued to speak even as the object grew clearer, looming out of the darkness like the great silver whales of the Northern Ocean. Initially, it looked like a heap of grey-brown rags, but then, as the last words of the Summoning were spoken, it moved; a spasmodic movement, twitching like the legs of an insect. There was a hollow, rasping sound and the creature stood up. It was a large man-like being whose skin and robes hung in grey leprous tatters. Its eyes were red with tiny black pupils which contracted and dilated constantly, giving a flashing appearance like a bird; its claw-like hands further enhanced this impression as did the scabby, denuded wings which sprouted from its back. These wings were never intended for flight: one need only look at the bizarre appearance of the demon – for such he was – to know for sure that the gods of Sutra had a sense of humour and it was purely malicious. There was something intelligent in its gaze however, and just as Jahl finished the next stanza of words – the Binding – it spoke.

'Grell,' it said.

'Grell?' There was a pause as Jahl considered the degree of formality required to address a demon. 'Grell. I – I need your help.' Grell did not respond, the red eyes flashed and flickered disconcertingly. If Jahl tarried much longer in the void, he could be trapped. 'I will explain . . . later. Come with me.' He turned to go but Grell did not move. Jahl felt a small surge of panic which he bit back. 'Come, Grell,' he said patiently. His heart was racing, anxiety threatening to overwhelm his calm.

'Grell.' The demon said again.

There was no time for this. If the creature didn't understand him it was no use. Reluctantly, Jahl turned to leave the void. He had failed, and failure had never sat easily with him. He didn't bother with a Banishment – let the creature suffer the pain of existence, he fumed – it would be trapped here in the upper reaches for ever . . .

'Lee-ving. Grell lee-ving.' It was like the voice of some strangely ancient child, its glassy, strangled tone coming from far away. Jahl turned. Grell had taken a step towards him and somehow, this effected his release from the inertia of the void. As the creature took its next faltering step, its lethal looking talons flexed involuntarily, opening and shutting – Jahl suppressed a shudder and grinned.

'Yes. Leaving Grell. I have a job for you.'

There could be no more lies. No more pretence that she was in control. Regan had built herself a fragile house of cards and when they fell it was pain and fire. She had woken to find something – some being – so bizarre standing over her that, for a second, she believed herself still asleep in the grip of a nightmare. By the time she had opened her mouth to scream, shining black talons had gripped her throat and her waist, and lifted her from her bed. The creature held her at arm's length, regarding her from strange red and black eyes which betrayed no expression. Regan felt her breath escape her in a thin wail of fear but then, unable to breathe air back into her lungs, she began to suffocate. The pressure behind her eyes and in her chest was enormous – the pain like searing daggers in her lungs. Her vision began to fade as she came close to unconsciousness but even as the black heat overwhelmed her, she heard a voice, *his* voice.

'Don't kill her yet, Grell . . .'

And she knew everything. The realisation, the absolute undeniability of the truth was so clear and bitter that as her breath failed her, her lips moved in soundless accusation. 'Jahl. You bastard . . .'

When she awoke she was in the deepest dungeon of Soulis Mor, so far into the bowels of the mountain that the walls seeped water through the bedrock. The cold was gripping. As consciousness returned Regan remembered the creature and thought it still had its strange talons wrapped around her neck, but in fact the sensation was caused by bruising. She drew a long deep breath as she opened her eyes. In fact, she need not have bothered to open them, there was hardly any light at all and it was a minute or so before her eyes adjusted enough to discern shapes in the gloom. She was half-lying on the ground in a crumpled heap as if she had been tossed there, and she felt little surprise as she pushed herself upright to realise there were chains around her wrists. Groaning at the pain of the bruises the creature had inflicted, she attempted to stand up; her legs trembled, her cold muscles spasming, her numbed feet feeling no contact with the ground. Eventually, she teetered upright and stood, swaying slightly, peering into the darkness. It seemed possible that Jahl was watching her from the darkened corner of the room but there was no way of knowing.

'Jahl? Jahl? Why are you doing this?' Her voice echoed back to her from the rock walls but elicited no reply. However, almost immediately, a door opened in the far wall – light spilled inward causing Regan to shy backwards as her eyes brimmed full of dazzled tears. Jahl and his strange new ally entered.

'Regan. My Thane . . .' he gave a mocking bow. He couldn't disguise the look of delighted smugness on his face – in some respects, Jahl could be extremely childish. 'I see you've met Grell.' The creature shuffled up behind him; it had an unsteady, lurching gait and something in the movement nauseated Regan.

'Jahl . . .' Regan's voice escaped her in a juddering sigh; the cold of the chamber was causing her to shiver violently. 'Why would you do th-this?'

'Oh come now, Regan. It is only a week since you signed the order for my assassination. He was useless, by the way – I'm surprised at you. Don't be offended, it's not really about you. It's just that my plans don't really include you any more . . .'

'Is it S-soulis Mor you want? You could have had it, Jahl – we could have ruled together . . . I don't understand why you—'

He laughed. 'Is that what you think? That my plans are limited to your damned city? I have *had* the city for weeks but you have slept through my rule and, once you are gone, it will be mine to dispense with. And that's what I'll do, Ree . . .' He walked towards her and took hold of her face so that she had to look at him. 'I know you don't understand but I have little time or patience to explain myself to you. But let me tell you this, Ree – I lied. Tristan is probably dead in a ditch somewhere and your father by now . . .' He pushed her back against the wall and, unprepared for the shove, Regan thudded against the rocks. She gasped, unable to reach her head to rub it as instinct demanded. Jahl let go and strode back towards the door.

'I like you, Regan, I really do,' he said airily. 'If things had been different, who knows? In fact, I find you quite fascinating. So, *I* don't want to kill you, don't worry . . .'

Rather than reassure, the threat of his tone belied his words. Regan felt her stomach turn over as fear tightened its grip on her. 'Look, here's the thing,' Jahl continued, 'I've been trying to get some of this stuff for years – it's called *Stiglame*. Ah, I see you've heard of it – it's secreted by some maggot or other – anyway, I've finally got some and I want to see how it works.'

'No!' Regan panicked and began thrashing uselessly at her bonds. She knew what *Stiglame* was, self-inflicted torture; it did something heinous to the mind of anyone who took it, causing horrible hallucinations, but not only that, the results of whatever were imagined were enacted on the body. The victim inevitably died in some bizarre suicide. 'No, Jahl . . . don't give me . . .'

'Too late.' He grinned nastily. 'It's absorbed through the skin.' He held up his hand to show her the thick glove he was wearing.

Regan screamed. It was too late. She was going to die. And for what? For being stupid enough to trust a craven . . . Her mind reeled suddenly as the *Stiglame* made contact with her brain, her vision shifted and the whole room seemed to buck and move. 'No, no, no . . .' she could hear her own voice as though it was someone else's. She fell back to her knees, retching dryly. Raising her head she saw Jahl and Grell standing a few feet away – Jahl laughing and Grell, watching her expressionlessly, shifting from foot to foot. Closing her eyes to stop the sensation of movement Regan tried to soothe her thoughts – how bad could it be? If she thought of nothing . . . but the drug didn't work that way. A picture came into her mind and she screamed again, drowning out the sound of Jahl's laughter.

It was her. But she was changing; she could see reddened lumps all over her skin, her face, her arms – and as soon as the thought was there, the pain began, a thousand needle points beneath her skin, pushing, pushing . . . she convulsed, howling in pain and horror. She opened her eyes (or thought that she did) and held her hand as near to her face as the shackles would allow. The pinpricks had burst through, minute waxen blades. Some tiny lice-like creature scuttled up the length of her arm amongst the bristles which grew longer and longer. But before she had time to react, another pain crashed in, along the underside of her arms the points were closer, larger, the pain, excruciating.

'What's happening to meee?' she wailed. 'Jahl . . .' but the sound changed became mangled, her tongue unable to form the sounds. Within the next few seconds Regan, transfixed, was transformed and although she knew the full horror and sick irony of it, she was unable to express anything.

Regan became a bird.

Perception was the key: Jahl, laughing himself sick, saw Regan rolling, writhing, screaming on the floor of the black stone chamber. He saw the manifestation of her hysterical mind ravage her body, her white shift blossoming with the pinpricks of blood as weals burst open on her skin; he saw deep lines of blood etch a strange outline on the delicate skin of her face – a deep, almost triangular mark which described the shape of a beak. He saw her legs twist and cramp, her feet and toes stretching and twisting in agony.

What he did *not* see, however, was what Regan saw: the feathers, black feathers complete with lice, the beak, the talons. He clapped his hands in delight and turned to leave the chamber.

'Grell. Watch her. Come and get me if she recovers. Or dies.'

Grell nodded, his expression blank as ever, earthing the dichotomy of horror and laughter in the chamber. 'Grell,' he said. Jahl paused and glanced back at the creature. It seemed when his tiny vocabulary was exhausted he simply said the word to show he acknowledged his master.

She flew. She knew she did. Not a graceful gliding flight, but rather she railed against her captivity – panicked, traumatised, disgusted. She was a *bird, a bird . . .* She had no thought of Jahl. Pain and shock overruled all. She opened the grey cartilage beak and screamed, '*a bird . . .*' and the sound was the sound of a crow. Somewhere deep within her mind a duel awareness reigned, a sense-memory of her old body, cracked and bleeding, blood everywhere . . . She screamed and screamed and screamed, beating her wings.

And then, as she felt her heart near exhaustion, as the pain threatened to overwhelm her, something happened. Grell.

He stood before her staring in a strange distant way, his bird-eyes *(oh gods, hers might be like that!)* flashing, black/red black/red. Could he see the bird or the blood? It was impossible to tell. He came closer. Peered at her. She stopped beating her wings.

'Grell?' he said.

She could hear her own heartbeat, the pain, the pain was . . .

'Pain you?' The sad/blank face grew closer. She made a sound in response – *a bird sound, not a word, was her body dying then?* – 'Grell pain.' He nodded to himself as if distantly acknowledging his own thought. 'Pain knowing.' This last was said with an almost triumphant air having managed to compose the thought: she was in pain and he knew how she felt.

Reaching out, he touched her face. 'Go,' he said sadly. The pain subsided. And, perhaps more importantly, the effect of the *Stiglame* stopped. Regan became herself again.

She stared down at her wrecked body. Her loose nightdress, previously white, now hung in bloodied tatters, all over her body were almost a thousand of the ghost quill marks which were bleeding profusely. Her face was strangely cold as the air chilled her wounds around her nose and mouth. She realised she was crouching on the ground and struggled to stand on her damaged feet.

'Grell,' she whispered. 'Thank-you so much.' Grell said nothing in return, his features had returned to his usual impassive state. Regan limped towards the doorway expecting the demon to grab her again at any moment but he merely watched her painful progress. 'I'm going,' she mumbled, 'back to . . .' Suddenly Grell lurched into motion. He scooped her up effortlessly and began to march surprisingly fast back along the corridor.

'No,' she kicked ineffectually but he ignored her. She felt faint and dizzy and vaguely realised she was leaving a trail of blood behind her. She had no idea if the demon was simply returning her to his master but for now, she was too weak to do anything about it, and the cessation of the worst of the pain was strangely liberating . . .

'Go,' Grell said suddenly. 'Go away Ree-gan.'

'When the Creator made Lysmair, He sang and danced. He moved across the empty lands striking the ground with His spear, making lakes and oceans and all the creatures of the Sidhe. Except one. In the great darkness of the sky, a bright star became curious to see the world that the Creator was making. The star flew down to the world and formed itself into such a form that it could run tirelessly for many miles and see far across the great plains. In such a way, the first wolf Sidhe came to Lysmair; different, separate from other creatures, a wise observer of creation . . .'

The grizzled bloody muzzle of Eskarius Vermesh twitched in his sleep as he dreamt of his mother's voice. She had been considered the most beauteous of the wolf clan Sidhe and Eskarius's father the most blessed of men to have captured her heart. As Eskarius Vermesh drifted back towards waking he considered the wisdom of his tribe with a candour which came with the comfort of sleep. '. . . different, separate from other creatures . . .' It was something the wolf clan took great pride in, their status as loners and wise creatures. But Eskarius felt unease as the thought and voice, flitted through his mind. His mother had been speaking of times past, the Sidhe mythology belonged to another world entirely . . . here on Sutra, the Sidhe were dwindling away, persecuted by Regan and Jahl but still divided physically and emotionally by their differing allegiances with the clans of the Fine. Although there was some harmony between the other Sidhe, the only meeting place which all respected and held them together, however tenuously, was the Council of Tema and that had not met for five years . . .

Eskarius was coming to wakefulness now although he stubbornly refused to open his eyes, unwilling to look at the scene he knew awaited him. A deep frown, which appeared almost as a snarl, furrowed his brow, running from the centre of his muzzle across the bridge of his eyes. His thoughts, however disjointed, seemed to be racing towards a conclusion he was reluctant to reach; unless something was done soon, the Sidhe might vanish from Sutra for ever, and the Fine would mourn the loss of their '*Fair Folk*' even though they had done nothing to stop that loss.

At last Eskarius opened his eyes. All around him the land was red and black. Red with fire, black with ashes and a few scattered corpses of Scoor. Smoke had drifted across the scorched land overnight and settled like a thick greasy mist a few feet from the earth, choking the life from the creatures who lived in burrows and holes in the ground. No freshening breeze had come and nothing moved amongst the jagged outlines of the denuded trees. At first it seemed there was silence, and yet, as Eskarius listened closely, he could hear a tiny, insistent sound like a stifled whisper. He knew the sound was fire, travelling wickedly, treacherously beneath the ground. With nothing left for miles to consume, the fire was moving through the peat, breaking cover occasionally like a flaming talon which grasped the roots and lower braches of any tree which had so far escaped, and destroying it from within.

The wolf breathed slowly, his chest moving in a shallow rhythm to avoid inhaling the smoke as best he could. He stood up on top of the slab of granite he had slept on, which had become warmed by the fires in the earth, and stretched, arching his back, juddering the stiff muscles beneath his fur. As he limped slowly onto the ground he felt the tense pull of the skin around the wounds on his hindquarters; one of the Sooor had been lucky and raked its short spear across the wolf's back as Eskarius had pinned down its companion and ripped the foul-tasting flesh from its throat. There had been too many for Eskarius to stop, though – perhaps ten – and in the end they had simply ignored the great wolf and continued their noisome flight.

Eskarius stopped and stared ahead to where they had gone, his expression almost wistful. The smoke was affecting his eyes now, causing them to sting and water, giving him the appearance of weeping, and in truth, his heart was sore. Ahead, impervious to the flames, the black shapes of the stone of the *Fir Chrieg* lay, smoke curling around them, the first touches of the winter daybreak catching the yellow curls, making them seem almost solid, like golden ropes or creepers which sought to topple those few still standing in the circle. Behind the stones, the silent mirror of Light of the Sky was clouded by a shroud of smoke. Or Coille, the Great Forest, which had covered the land for almost a hundred miles to the south and west, was no more. Destroyed, burned and ravaged by legions of Scoor and other, stranger creatures, whose like had never been seen before in Sutra. It was a death, as profound as any mortal death, Sidhe and Fine alike were in the first stages of grief and there could be no doubt that retribution would be harsh.

'Where are they?' Eskarius thought, 'Salkit's teeth, where are they?' He had promised to wait by the stones and wait he would, but he never imagined it would be like this. The pads of his feet were already uncomfortably hot and he stared down at the tiny wisp of smoke issuing from the fur between his paws with an almost disconnected air. Sighing, partly in order to gasp more air into his toiling lungs, he climbed back slowly onto his own rock which was one of the toppled monoliths and, sitting back on his haunches, he threw back his scarred, tearful muzzle and began to howl. The mournful yipping carried across the suffocating expanse and was distantly answered by another of Eskarius's kind. After a few minutes, exhausted by lack of clear air, Eskarius sank back into a lying position and was about to put his head down to sleep again, when a distant movement caught his attention.

A rider was moving slowly through the blasted landscape. Instinctively Eskarius froze, tracking the movement with unblinking eyes. The horse, a tall, elegant bay, was struggling to walk through the ashes of the forest, even from the distance Eskarius could see its progress was deliberate but faltering, every now and then the beast would stumble slightly but the rider made no attempt to correct its path. It seemed the rider must be injured or even unconscious; the figure, concealed in a heavy red cloak which was beginning to smoulder at the edges, was slumped over the pommel of the saddle. Each time the horse lurched, the rider rolled precariously forward or to the side and it only seemed by some small miracle he was not pitched into the smouldering remains of the forest.

Eskarius Vermesh did nothing for long moments; the hackles of his back were raised and he growled softly under his breath. Finally, as the rider grew nearer, curiosity overcame caution and he dismounted the rock once more, creeping forward in a low crouch, growling in a long continuous noise. The horse stopped almost ten feet in front of where Eskarius stood and the two creatures surveyed one another. A wolf Sidhe, equivalent in size to a small pony, was a natural source of fear to the horse and only the fact that it was numbed with tiredness stopped the mount from shying and galloping off with its unconscious burden; instead it stood still, its eyes bulging and ears flat in miserable panic.

Just as Eskarius was about to investigate further, the

rider gave a low groan and slid gracelessly from the back of the mount, landing in a crumpled heap and lying still amongst the ashes of the undergrowth. It was clear that if he did not get up, the rider's clothes would soon catch fire but he made no attempt to rise.

Eskarius snarled in annoyance and transformed into his human form in order to aid the stricken rider. He ran across to the prostrate body and flipped it over, almost assuming it was dead.

It was a woman; that much was immediately obvious from the moment he grasped hold of the delicate body. It was difficult to see her face as her hair had fallen across and stuck to the sweat and grime which covered it. Eskarius picked her up carefully and carried her back to his vantage point rock; there he wetted a soft leather cloth from his pack and bathed her face, propping her up on his knees. She was completely covered in drying blood which stuck her thin garment to her frame. He wet the cloth three times and each time, blood from deep wounds to her face turned the fabric red. Strangely, her body was covered in a lattice of small blisters, a few of which were still bleeding. Eskarius muttered to her gently in hushed tones using the Sidhe language as he would to a small child, but, quite abruptly, as her face became clear of soot and grime and she opened her eyes which were still delirious, he stopped. He knew her.

The last time he had seen her, these cold eyes had scoured across him without noting him in the crowd. It had been Samhain two years earlier and Eskarius had gone to Soulis Mor to exchange news with the few contacts he still maintained within the Sidhe tribes. She had ridden past beside the cripple, Tristan, in procession to light the winter fires. It was Regan.

Eskarius hissed, his teeth drawing back in instinctive imitation of the wolf he often was. His hand dropped to his waist where his dagger was sheathed; in one swift motion he drew his weapon back for the kill. And stopped.

She was watching him. Her gaze held no trace of fear, only a sad acceptance. 'Go on,' she whispered, 'Kill me. A swift death is more than I deserve.'

Eskarius paused. Could it really be this easy, he wondered, to rid the land of the woman who had caused so much despair? And could it be up to him, a wolf Sidhe, to decide her fate? She was right in one thing; if he killed her now, it would be too easy a death. The Sidhe, the Fine and the land must know of her passing, and why should retribution be taken when none was there to witness it?

'No,' he murmured dully, 'You are right, Lady. The Council must be told.'

She did not react to the removal of the threat to her life as he sheathed his dagger again. Eskarius gave her some water from his flask and then she lapsed into sleep or unconsciousness.

Jahl stared across the frozen expanse of the Great Hall. If he was honest with himself, he supposed he would have to admit he'd gone about things in the wrong way, but honesty was not something that troubled him very often. Now, he had trapped himself in a course of action which was, at the very least, unsatisfactory. Regan was gone, escaped from her own dungeons,

Gods knew how. After her escape, to buy himself time to think, he had frozen the fortress in time once more. It had been late at night and the Great Hall full of rather subdued courtiers, supposedly just drinking and listening to the music, but actually speculating wildly on why no one had seen the Thane for over a week. Soulis Mor and the Northern Clans were currently leaderless, something which would not continue for long. Jahl already knew messengers had gone out to Thanes Ulla, Huw and Lachlan and although he had sent pursuing Scoor, he had yet to have confirmation that they had killed the riders. If the riders had reached their destinations it was only a matter of time before the Southern Clans rode out to confront him.

He sighed. Regan's loss was regrettable, possibly with far-reaching consequences but she just made him so angry; after their confrontation during the ball, Jahl had lost perspective – he knew she knew him now – she recognised his true power and the threat he represented. When he returned, by some miracle, she was gone and Jahl experienced a brief instant of relief that he could no longer hurt her. After that, he froze the city once more, to lick his wounds and think ahead.

He had new allies now; while the Scoor were expedient, frightening the Fine by tapping into their most primal superstition, once at close quarters they were easily killed. Grell had proved surprisingly useful in that regard. Jahl had briefly considered releasing the demon after Regan's inexplicable escape but then curbed his anger; Grell was merely literal-minded like one of Jahl's hounds and possibly Regan, or some ally, had tricked him into releasing her. In the past week Grell had managed to enlist many bizarre and dangerous creatures from the void through a mixture of telepathic threats and promises which Jahl was happier not knowing about; he suspected the loss of his soul was the least of it . . . His simple quest for power had turned into something far worse and, as far as Jahl was concerned, with far more potential.

Then there was the matter of his foray into another world. He had fledgling power there, he just hadn't decided what to do with it yet – Knox was fanatical and frightened sufficiently to be extremely useful. So many loose ends . . . he sighed again.

'It can't be . . . This can't be Or Coille,' Talisker stared around him aghast, his eyes streaming with burning tears. Tristan said nothing for the moment but the shock was evident on his face. 'Maybe, something happened in the gate,' Talisker mused, 'maybe a hundred years have passed or something . . .'

'I don't think so, Father, unless the Scoor have survived that long,' Tristan nodded towards the smouldering outlines of corpses amongst the ash of the forest floor which had to have been Scoor originally; the shape of their strange bodies and wings was unmistakable.

'What happened to Eskarius? He promised to wait,' Talisker was thinking aloud more than anything.

'Who's Eskarius?'

'Wolf clan Sidhe . . . I know what you're thinking, but he gave his word and I had no reason not to believe him. Something must have happened . . .' Tristan almost laughed at this obvious remark but his father's anguished expression stopped him. 'I mean, I hope he's all right,' Talisker muttered.

'Is he related to the Eskarius who . . .'

'His son,' Talisker nodded. 'But he has his own integrity, Tris.' He was surprised to hear himself say so, having had the same reservations Tristan obviously felt. 'The wolf clan believe they acted with honour,' he shrugged, 'it's a bit of a moot point now . . .'

Tris looked about to argue and Talisker was suddenly reminded of his son's love for discussion of such things; ethics, morals, laws. In all senses but the physical, Tristan was truly born to be Thane of Soulis Mor.

'But they murdered . . .'

'Tristan,' Talisker interrupted gently, 'did you see someone else as we came through the gateway?'

Tris looked slightly surprised to be asked. 'Well, yes . . . but I don't know who it was. I think it might have been a woman – or a rather delicate man.' He chuckled, a mild, pleasant sound in the wasteland, 'maybe we'll be lucky and Jahl was leaving for a new world.'

'Did she say anything to you?'

'I'm not sure . . . not with a voice as such. I got a definite kind of feeling though . . . regret I'd say, more than anything. Who do you think it was?'

'I don't know,' Talisker said. But he didn't meet his son's gaze and his eyes were troubled.

It began to rain. Large, impossibly slow raindrops spattered onto the floor of the dead forest. Talisker leaned back on the rock as though sunbathing, his palms outwards, gazing up into the sky letting the cooling droplets of the rain rinse his eyes. After a minute, a strange sound could be heard, the forest began to hiss and smoulder as the water seeped into the peat floor. Talisker, still gazing upwards into the dizzying tracks of rain, couldn't lose the notion that the land was sighing, sighing because he had brought Tristan back perhaps . . . He felt little inclination to move, strangely fascinated by the simple calm of the deluge. Just as he was beginning to feel cold from his rain-soaked clothes, he saw the black shape of a great eagle Sidhe moving from the west.

'Tristan, look.'

The eagle seemed to be looking for them, at least its flight was purposeful, it flew towards the standing stones as though homing in on a target. Talisker and Tristan both stood up, watching it come. It alighted on another toppled slab which had once formed part of the standing circle; it was huge. Talisker was suddenly acutely aware that he had had no dealings with the Sidhe, except for Eskarius, for a long time. He remembered Prince Makhpiyaluta, Grey Ghost Stalker Eskarius had named him, the anguished conflict he had carried within him . . .

As the eagle began to glow, a familiar transition between beast and man, Talisker became aware of Tristan, standing beside him, drawing himself up and straightening his clothes; not preening exactly, but becoming ready – ready to be Thane. He felt a pang of conflicting pride and pity for his son, knowing how hard it must have been for him to earn any respect as Thane. Consequently, when the Sidhe had finished its transformation, Talisker took a single step backwards so that he stood just slightly behind his son.

The tall, imperious man who stood before them a few feet away as though marooned on another island gave a small bow to Tristan, his glance flickering briefly over Talisker but missing nothing. 'Highness,' he said. He allowed himself a smile which crept cautiously across his features as if somehow prohibited. Tristan's response was warmer.

'Prince Tecumseh. It's good to see you.'

'Who is your companion?' the Prince frowned.

Tristan glanced at his father and they both realised in that moment, that Duncan had not aged again while coming back to Sutra. 'This is my father, Duncan Talisker. Your legends speak of him, I believe. He came to the other world through the gateway of the *Fir Chrieg* to find me again, who was lost and a world away from the danger of my kingdom.' Tristan had lapsed into his formal speech on his return; he spoke with the gravitas of a Thane.

Prince Tecumseh nodded towards Talisker again, giving him a more considered look this time. Talisker could see the questions burning on the man's lips but he held his peace for the moment.

'Where is Eskarius of the wolf clan?' Tristan asked. 'He was oath bound to wait here.'

'It was he who sent me to find you, Highness. There have been many grave developments since you have been gone and the Sidhe are gathering at the Council of Tema . . .'

Tristan glanced around at the dampening remains of the forest; it would be a black, ashen journey through a hundred miles of devastation. Tecumseh guessed his concern. 'I will carry you both, Highness,' he bowed again, lower this time, as though hoping to impart the sacrifice this represented to an eagle Sidhe. Also, his voice was quiet, almost as if he wished to make sure no one heard his offer. Tristan looked surprised, he'd never heard of such a thing.

'My thanks to you, Prince Tecumseh,' he bowed in return. 'You do us great honour. Let us leave this place soon then. Already, my lungs feel sore . . .'

The Prince nodded in agreement – although the expression on his face clearly said they should not plan to make a habit of such transport – and began to transform once more.

Tristan had no idea he was frightened of heights until he was a thousand feet up in the air for the first time. At first, the relief of escaping the pall of acrid steam which would encase Or Coille for weeks to come overwhelmed all else; the air above was almost freezing but fresh and pure because of it. They rose up through the blanket of the rain above the dark threat of the clouds into a strange, sun-warmed place where the topsides of the same clouds formed a frosted golden floor. Talisker had warned Tris about the coldness of the air and so he had wrapped part of his plaid across his mouth and nose. Even so, breathing was difficult at first as his ailing lungs accustomed to the change of air. Prince Tecumseh had come prepared to carry them – he had brought a rope which they had passed behind their backs and crossed over the breast of the eagle. Tristan gripped the rope tightly as he stared down at the clouds below and, as they cleared the cloud-cover and the landscape of Sutra appeared below him, he gave a strangled gasp of awe and fright. Behind him, he heard his father chuckle quietly and wondered with a hint of annoyance whether Talisker was ever frightened of anything.

Tecumseh had found a thermal to ride and, to Tristan's concern, he flapped his huge wings only occasionally; it seemed unnatural to Tris that they could stay up in the air, flight was something he'd never considered before and it would be little comfort to him now if anyone was to try and explain it.

Fear however, can only peak for so long, and after the first ten minutes, Tristan felt himself begin to relax a little. He stared in wonderment at the land below; they were flying south-west, out towards the ocean and down the coastline. The rolling monotony of the dead brown bracken – taken by the winter frosts – gave way to a rugged landscape of dark rocks – scarps and cliffs – which fell dizzyingly into the steely expanse of the grey winter ocean. Here and there, clusters of houses nestled amongst the contours of the landscape but they were few, clinging to a harsh salt-blown existence; most of the inhabitants of Sutra held to the great cities for protection and those who did not were a hardy breed. Further south where Huw and Lachlan ruled – the flatlands as most of the northern Fine thought them – it was warmer and more people lived amongst a gentler landscape.

Both Tristan and Talisker were unaware of the location of the Council of Tema of the Sidhe but just as it seemed their journey would take them far enough south to see the fringes of Lachlan's realm, Tecumseh veered sharply west and before they knew it, they were above the sea, with the coast of Sutra disappearing behind them.

'Do not worry, Duncan Talisker. It is not far . . . Eskarius told me you have the talent to hear the mind-speech of the Sidhe . . .' The voice of Tecumseh arrived in Talisker's mind unexpectedly, the tone flat and authoritative. Talisker was reassured and passed the message on to Tristan who nodded grimly in response, still gripping tightly to the rope reins.

In fact, they arrived at the Council of Tema only ten minutes later; a barren looking island of red rock jutted from the depths of the ocean, the colour of the stones warm, almost incongruous looking amongst the grey waves. At its northern end a mountain of giant red columns rose almost a mile high into the clouds and as they swooped nearer the riders could see that the scale of the rock-face was massive. Halfway up, at the bottom of the fluted columns, was a plateau with a cluster of low, organic looking buildings – Tecumseh adjusted his wings and circled gently down to land.

'What is this place?' Tristan asked wonderingly. As a Thane, with access to more knowledge than most of the Fine, he knew this island to be on none of the maps of the western seas. He spoke the thought aloud without expecting an answer but after a moment, Talisker replied. It seemed his father was listening to the mind-voice of Prince Tecumseh.

'Yeah, right . . .' Talisker muttered. 'He says it's magical, Tris. It's called . . .' There was a slight pause as the soundless conversation continued, for some reason Talisker snorted derisively, 'Have the Sidhe learned nothing about letting go?' he said almost bitterly. 'It's called Lys, Tristan – don't ask . . .'

As they landed Sidhe, in human and animal form, came forward to greet them. Tristan recognised two of the Elder Councillors from a time when relations between Soulis Mor and the Sidhe had been happier: Markomete of the Bear clan and Tsali of the lynx clan – both currently in human form. Tristan smiled, slightly nervously, and brushed his windswept hair back from his face. Talisker gave him a pat on the shoulder which was wordlessly reassuring.

'Welcome, welcome, Thane Tristan,' Markomete boomed in his sonorous tones, 'would that our meeting be in happier circumstances.' He bowed low, leaning his weight into a long staff he had propped into the ground before him.

'Perhaps once we are rested from our journey, you can appraise me of exactly what the circumstances are,' Tristan said smoothly. Behind them, Tecumseh transformed into his human state once more and he came forward, assuming command of the Sidhe delegation by virtue of his stature and bearing.

'Markomete,' he nodded, 'Thane Tristan's companion is his adoptive father, Duncan Talisker . . . Tal-ees-ker.'

There was a stunned reaction from the small group. 'No, no, it's not possible,' Markomete frowned. 'My cousin, Tayna Ashka saved Tal-ees-ker and his companion in the snows over twenty-five years ago. This man is only thirty summers or so.'

'Thirty-four, actually,' Talisker bowed, a slightly formal bow. 'I . . . I have been back to my world to find Thane Tristan and my renewed youth is the result.' He was about to shut up, unwilling to take attention from Tristan but he gave a small smile to Markomete. 'Tayna Ashka was a courageous young woman – she gave her life for us and I'll never forget her. Your clan must be proud of her memory.'

Markomete nodded, his faded blue eyes showing pleasure at Talisker's compliment to the Sidhe. 'Indeed,' he said gruffly. He turned his attention back to Tristan, 'I am afraid there is little time for you to rest, Highness. The Meeting of the Council is tomorrow. Judgement will be soon after.'

'Judgement? What judgement?'

Markomete glanced at Prince Tecumseh, a mixture of alarm and annoyance. 'Have you told them nothing?'

'I had little time. They were suffocating in Or Coille – what would you have me do?' Tecumseh frowned, 'wait until they were dead while I gave them a report?'

Markomete sighed and looked at the ground, apparently unwilling to meet Tristan's gaze once more. Beside him, Tsali patted Markomete on the shoulder as though seeking to reassure him.

' I – I think you should come with us, Highness,' he mumbled.

They walked into a labyrinth of vast chambers hewn into the red rock-face. Tristan knew something was wrong but held his peace for the moment. Talisker's expression was grim, and as they entered into the comparative darkness of the troglodyte dwellings his blue eyes began to rake back and forward uneasily, watching the shadows which were illuminated with only few lanterns. He said nothing to Tristan but kept him near, within the reach of his sword-arm.

Once they had crossed a succession of the chambers, Tristan became aware of a different light up ahead, a warm, organic green. Up ahead a narrow, unadorned doorway led into a further chamber, and it was from there the light issued. Outside a huge wolf was sitting as though on guard, although as they first entered, it seemed as though the creature was dozing slightly.

'Eskarius?' Talisker called.

Eskarius looked up, his eyes wide in surprise. It was clear as they grew closer, that he had suffered many wounds in some skirmish or other. Tristan remembered the outlines of the Scoor corpses etched in ash on the forest floor.

Without a sound, the wolf stood up and began his change; moments later Eskarius stood before them in his human form. Although he seemed quietly pleased to see Talisker, he said nothing to them but turned to the Sidhe delegation of Markomete, Tsali and Tecumseh.

'I will take them,' he said.

Tecumseh nodded. 'Very well. We will speak later.' Without further discussion, the three Elders left, leaving Tristan and Talisker alone with Eskarius.

'Eskarius,' Talisker frowned, 'what's going on?'

Eskarius did not reply immediately but addressed Tristan. 'I will take you in first, Highness. Talisker, you must wait here. Only one must enter at a time.'

Talisker's eyes narrowed dangerously and his hand clenched and unclenched uselessly beside his sword. 'If I hear any trouble, I will come in, Eskarius . . .'

'I assure you, there is no danger,' Eskarius replied.

Talisker nodded; he was still reluctant to trust a wolf clan Sidhe, even though the other Elders had left them in Eskarius's care. He watched as Eskarius and Tristan entered the narrow doorway but although he craned his neck to see beyond there was only the green shimmer of the light and darkness beyond for seconds, then, Eskarius pulled some hide curtain across, obscuring the view entirely.

Tristan shuffled forward in the shifting light of the chamber. Because of his disability, his legs were inclined to feel almost disconnected at the best of times. Now, the darkness was such that he was unable to see his own feet and this unnerved him. Up ahead the green light became a huge dazzling mass which he could not look at directly without his eyes watering and afterimages flaring in the blackness of the chamber which was otherwise unlit.

'W-what is it?' He shielded his eyes and tried to stare into the light looking for something in the centre of the mass but it was impossible to make out any detail from where he stood.

'You must go forward,' Eskarius pointed to a narrow pathway which extended in towards the light. As Tristan's gaze tracked along it he realised that after the first twenty paces or so the pathway became a bridge – on either side the floor of the chamber dropped away into an abyss. 'When you reach the stone statue at the end, you must stop,' Eskarius continued. 'You will know all then.'

'No. I cannot.' Tristan shook his head.

'You are afraid?' Eskarius frowned.

'No. Not afraid,' Tristan glanced at the Sidhe who was regarding him with some distain. 'It's my legs, Eskarius, they . . . well, they're not reliable and the path is very narrow.'

'I am sorry, Thane Tristan, it must be difficult.' Eskarius sighed, 'I will carry you over.'

'Is it so important that I see what is there?'

The Sidhe did not reply but changed once more into his wolf form, Vermesh. Tristan had the distinct impression that escaping further discussion was partly his motivation, but he climbed gratefully onto the wolf Sidhe's back once the change was over. Tristan's legs were still shaking – the muscles spasming and twitching – from his flight on the back of Tecumseh. Eskarius was as broad as a horse and Tristan's legs and hips ached, but at least he was in touch with the ground; as long as he kept his nerve and didn't fall off as they passed over the bridge he would be fine. Tristan stared resolutely ahead between the soft shaggy outline of the wolf's ears, but nothing could prepare him for what he saw once within the glow of the lights.

The green dazzling glow was caused by three separate beams of light which were directed towards a huge gemstone suspended from the roof. These rays mingled within the gem and were refracted outwards where they were caught and reflected by thousands of tiny mirrors. The whole effect created a living, glowing cage of light and within that cage – tied to a stake with her arms behind her back – was its prisoner. Her head was bowed, once lustrous black hair cascaded in filthy rat-tails, the dress and cloak she wore was burnt and torn. Tristan did not need to see the prisoner's face, however, to recognise instinctively someone he'd known his whole life.

'Regan?'

She lifted her head then and fixed him with a steady gaze. 'Tris? You've come back then . . .'

'What happened?' he whispered in horror. 'Who ordered this?'

To his dismay, a look of accusation crossed Regan's face and she laughed bitterly. 'Come now, little brother, let's not play games. When you left you ran to the Sidhe for help. My demise is just what you've been waiting for. I could have respected you more for it had you stormed Soulis Mor and captured me honestly . . .'

'But it wasn't me, Ree . . . I know nothing of this. I have been to Father's world and . . .' he stopped; she could always do this to him, make him feel childlike and weak. He felt a surge of resentment and sat up as straight as he was able on the back of Eskarius. 'You have brought this on yourself, Regan. The Sidhe have suffered much at your hand.'

She laughed at him, less bitterly this time but still mocking, still as though she held some invisible moral victory. That was Regan; more than cornered, defeated, but still defiant. As though for the first time, Tristan saw her as others did and understood that her strength could be seen to come from sheer arrogance. Her laughter stopped abruptly and her gaze flickered nervously across his face. 'The Sidhe will have their vengeance, little brother. They plan to execute me whatever happens. The trial will be for show only.'

'I am sorry,' Tristan said quietly, 'but there is probably nothing I can do.'

Regan pulled forward on the leather ties which bound her to the post; she seemed surprised and furious but Tristan held his ground. '*Sorry? Is that it?* When are you going to act like a Thane, brother? Command them to release me!'

'Acting like a Thane begins with oneself, Ree,' he said. 'There cannot be justice for some and not for others. Accountability is part of being a Thane.'

'But Tris . . . Trissy . . .'

He scowled in response to her use of one of her pet names for him, the colour in his cheeks was high, emotion tightening his throat. 'Come on Eskarius, let's go.' Eskarius began to turn around in the narrow space. 'No, wait,' Tris said suddenly. He turned back towards Regan, twisting his body across the wolf's back. 'Regan. Is Grace still in Soulis Mor?'

'Grace? Your serving wench?' Regan giggled, an unpleasant, ironic sound. 'She's dead, Tristan. Jahl was bored one night, you know how it is with servants . . . he said she screamed . . . a lot. So, he had her tongue removed.' Her expression changed as she expounded Grace's fate, almost as though she remembered, quite suddenly, what the young woman had suffered, and that Jahl, like a wild dog had turned on her, who had thought herself his mistress. Regan's eyes glazed over, assuming the glass-bead look of someone who was retreating from the world.

'You whore!' Tristan yelled. He could feel a torrent of grief ready to swamp him but he held back long enough to spit forcibly in his sister's direction. 'She never hurt anyone! Jahl's whore, that's what you are . . .' A sob escaped him as it seemed his frame could contain his shock and fury no longer, leaning forward he buried his face in Eskarius's fur and gave in to the tide of emotion. Eskarius didn't wait for Regan to respond and Tristan didn't see her reaction – in fact, there was little, Regan had subsided into her dark, injured soul once more – the wolf sped back up the path towards the light shape of the doorway, hoping his sobbing burden would have the presence of mind to hang on.

'Regan?'

'Father? This is a surprise.' She smiled brightly as though she still stood in the doorway of their cottage holding a bunch of wild flowers or some child's prize she had picked up on her walk. 'They're going to kill me, you know, Father . . .' the look which Talisker had dreaded seeing when she was a child, slid across her face like an avaricious moon hiding the brightness of the sun. It was a look he had denied seeing to himself until the day she had come to tell him of the accident which had killed her mother; sly, malicious, something which infected Regan like a cancer . . .

'What did you say to Tris? Why is he so upset?'

'I had to tell him that a dear friend of his had died while he was away from Soulis Mor.' She contrived to look sad. 'He didn't take it very well. In fact, I think he blames me. People always hate the messenger, don't they, Father?'

'Yes.'

'Will you come to the trial?' She smiled again, the bright, sweet-Regan smile. It was as if she was commenting on the weather or an impending party. He nodded, at a loss for what to say, conflicting emotions battling within him. He saw before him a proud, spiteful young woman and he was well aware that Regan being 'nice' to him would not be without reason. And yet . . . it was still Ree; and what made her so powerful and threatening to people was part of the same personality that had enough courage to face down a wild boar with only a short spear when she was twelve. But Talisker was angry and he couldn't let go.

'I told you he was poison, Ree. Goddammit, why didn't you listen to me?'

'It was already too late by then, father. But don't blame Jahl . . . at least not entirely. I was a willing accomplice . . .' This time she looked genuinely saddened, 'You know, if he had put a sword in my hand and said "go and kill some Sidhe women and children" . . .' she paused, 'actually, I guess I would have done it – if Jahl had asked me himself. I can't go out on trial tomorrow and pretend I am blameless – I suppose Tristan is right about that,' she grinned disarmingly. 'Accountability. I can't claim I didn't know what he was doing. Turning a blind eye can only take you so far . . .' she sighed, 'You can fool the heart gladly, but not the head.'

'But why, Regan?' Talisker's voice echoed around the chamber sounding plaintive and pained. 'Make me understand. I need to understand.'

She looked at him as if he had asked something so rudimentary any fool could see the answer. 'They're only Sidhe, Father. They – they're dirty animals. They are suffocating the Fine, their population is growing, some are even interbreeding with Fine women. We need to be rid of them, that's all. Look around you, this island was made with great magics . . . can you say you feel easy that the Sidhe have such power?'

'*Only Sidhe*?' he gasped, 'Only Sidhe? Ye gods, how did I sire such a hateful little monster? The Sidhe are a peaceful people . . . how could . . . Where does the hate come from, Regan?' He broke off, incoherent with rage. Regan was watching him with an expression of surprise and amusement and suddenly he felt unable to speak with her any longer. He turned to go.

'Father. Don't go. Don't leave me like this. I need to know, will you speak for me at my trial? Will you tell them I'm a good . . .' He turned back, his face wet with uncontrolled tears of fury. For long moments he said nothing and Regan flinched under his gaze. 'Tell them I'm a good girl,' it came out as a whisper which echoed like a sigh. She stared back at him, her large green eyes brimming at last with honest tears. 'I don't know,' she whispered, 'I don't know how I got here, Daddy.'

He seemed to look straight through her. 'I will tell them I don't know you,' he said. 'I will tell them my daughter . . .' his voice trembled, 'my Regan, is dead.'

As he left the chamber he could hear a sound which would have broken his heart if it had not just sustained that damage. It was the sound of Regan weeping.

CHAPTER FOURTEEN

Far, far to the north, past the badlands, past the point where legends of the Fine died, a storm was raging. The storm was violent and chaotic; a huge, shining tornado which ripped up what few plants grew there, and burnt them to dust with the hot fire of its own lightning. Beneath the epicentre of the tornado was an 'otherworldly' structure: a dome – comprised of something which might have been glass (unknown in Sutra) – that reflected and repelled the fury of the storm, and which had in fact been created for the mild amusement of the dome's occupant. The sound of the tempest, if heard by men, could have been thought to hasten the end of the world; it struck against the dome in impotent fury but, as if the circular form was indeed the iris of the eye of the tornado, inside the structure, there was stillness and quiet. It looked like a forest glade in autumn – which is exactly what it was – Phyrr had transported her favourite spot here and simply covered it over to protect it. But the seasons never changed within this space, the leaves were always golden and red, always on the verge of falling. It satisfied the Lady Phyrr somehow, such a state of potential ending.

Across the expanse of the glade, a large black bird flew like a silent shadow, its outline rimed by the blue-white of the lightning outside. It landed on a branch of an ancient looking tree and, hunching its head forward, intensely watched the lower branches where Phyrr stood, gazing into a mirror she had suspended from the tree.

She was bored with being in human form; she had experienced everything. Phyrr stared at her own reflection listlessly. Still, after twenty or so years, she had the damage on her face that her brother had inflicted on her in a fit of rage; she smiled distantly and touched her cheek just below her blind eye which shone in the semi-dark like an iridescent opal. When Jahl had been younger, he often reminded her of Corvus, he had the same dark looks and the same emotional intensity . . . also, he could not be trusted. But Phyrr didn't care about Jahl any more, she had decided what she wanted – peace, oblivion. She drew a long silver dagger from a sheath at her side, keeping her gaze fixed on the reflection of the thing as though she could not bear to confront the reality of the actual object.

She was not afraid. For those who possessed the blood of the gods, death held little to fear. Indeed, self-inflicted dissolution was their most common end when the almost infinite charms of true power come to an abrupt halt. This realisation that nothing meant anything anymore was rather like a tale told by a *Seanachaidh* which stopped in mid-sentence, everything becoming meaningless . . .

'I can see you, Sluagh,' she muttered absently. She looked up at the raven, meeting its cold gaze with the same mixture of contempt and empathy as ever. Sluagh, her brother's long-time companion, had appeared to her the day after Jahl's birth. She had always hated the raven, vaguely jealous of the high regard Corvus had had for the miserable creature, and yet her heart was not without vague pity. Sluagh was lost and directionless without his master and so, rather than kill him, as she had always imagined she would given the chance, she had allowed him to stay, tolerating his presence perhaps because he was a reminder of her lost twin. 'If I am to go, you must go also,' she smiled sadly. 'You have no purpose in the world any more, old bird . . . you and I are both remnants of a simpler age.'

She walked to the comfort of her low bed and lay down, holding the dagger up, pointing away from her body for the moment. Phyrr had ever been one to cherish anticipation and saw no reason why her dissolution should be an exception. She should have gone when her brother did, she mused, even though he went unwillingly, killed by Talisker and the warriors he merged with . . . Phyrr sighed and lowered the weapon, laying it aside for the moment.

The distance of time allowed her to remember Talisker with some vague affection; even now, if she closed her eyes, she could still hear the quiet sound of the rain on the roof of the tent, still feel the coldness and fire of that night. And that moment he had made a connection with her as their eyes met during a struggle for the blade she had been carrying. She had wanted the kill for herself, so that she might take his head and throw it at Corvus's feet, but instead, she had met his gaze and there had been . . . something between them. Later, she had come back, her curiosity unsated, and seduced him by means of deception, disguising herself as his lover, Una. But he had won over her in the end, he had defied her, planted a seed within her womb, making her capable of the only act of true creation she had ever been able to perform. Talisker had fathered her son, Jahl, but, if she were honest, the essence of their connection was always in that first look, that transient, indefinable moment, and it was to that moment her memory returned her each time she thought of him. Talisker might have been shocked and surprised to learn that the goddess Phyrr had thought of him often over the years.

But now it was over. She said the words necessary to empower the kill, and she planned to make her last journey in spirit form to tell Jahl that his mother was dead; she wasn't expecting any tears from the boy. Loyalty and filial feelings were not something the gods – or even halflings – were particularly bothered by. Still, she felt a vague pang of regret that Jahl had become the ambitious young monster that he was, she wished now that she had followed her first instincts and adopted him out to a mortal family before he even had the chance to dabble with magic; now an adult, Jahl was still a misfit in every sense.

She raised the dagger and smiled up at the blade as though absolving it of its impending crime. She had been cut before, it didn't hurt for long. She must strike through the throat with a single blow . . .

'Phyrr? Why haven't you come yet? You said you'd come . . .'

She dropped the dagger with an exasperated sigh. 'I lied,' she said. 'I'm not coming to Soulis Mor, Jahl. I've had enough.' She looked around the chamber until she saw him; his image was sharp and detailed, almost as if he was actually standing before her rather than projecting himself from his fortress. Phyrr was momentarily impressed, his skills were growing stronger. His expression – as ever when dealing with Phyrr – was petulant.

'But you've got to come and see what I've done,' he argued. *'I have Soulis Mor now, it is mine for ever . . .'*

'Very good,' she sighed. She had 'seen' Soulis Mor already, had checked up on Jahl, the city was encased in ice and overrun by such demons that Jahl would soon struggle to control them. He was only a halfling and had already overreached himself . . . Phyrr's thoughts tumbled over one another, abruptly stumbling over a suspicion which arrived as if from nowhere. Her eyes narrowed as she focussed on the ethereal form of her son, 'Very good, Jahl,' she said, trying to sound more enthusiastic. 'But what will you do now?'

'N-nothing.'

He never could lie to her convincingly. Phyrr could not help smiling a satisfied smile. 'Nothing? How will you live? How will Soulis Mor sustain itself once the food is rotted in the stores and what about when Cernunnos comes to claim the souls you are denying him? You cannot keep the people suspended for ever . . . You will have angered him greatly.' She watched closely for his reaction. Jahl's features flushed with a mixture of consternation and anger.

'It is all arranged. I have plans. I – I have sent messages to the Thanes calling for their surrender and allegiance and I . . .'

'Yes?'

'Nothing . . . nothing important. Why are you not coming?'

'I have had enough, Jahl,' she repeated. 'I am weary. Being immortal, godly, it palls eventually. Forever is a long time.'

He frowned, understanding the implication of what she was saying although unable to conceive that she could be weary of something he longed for. *'No. I won't let you,'* he said. *'Now is an exciting time, Phyrr. You must come and be my consort. We shall rule over all of Sutra – such a rule that . . .'*

She sighed again, cutting off his enthusiastic rant. 'Trust me, Jahl, I've seen it all before. I'm going.' She raised the dagger and prepared to strike.

'Noooo!' His anguished yell surprised her – Jahl's voice became like a wind which rushed around her position on the bed, whipping her hair and clothes and blankets, shocking her with its force and fury.

'Get back!' she yelled. The dagger was wrested from her grasp by sharp, spindling fingers and thrown across the room. Although the sound of the wind was deafeningly loud Phyrr's scream of rage was louder; losing control of her aspect she grew larger, towering into the treetops so that the blast of the gale played only around her legs.

'I decide!' she screamed. 'I decide when I go – not you!' She lifted her leg and swatted at her ankle as though Jahl's spirit visitation was a mere irritating insect. Jahl – whose essence had transformed into simple light and energy – wrapped himself around her hands; curling her fingers, Phyrr stared at the light, her fury beginning to ebb slightly.

'It's not as if you care, Jahl. It is not for us to love. You know that.'

'I am not a god, Phyrr. I love and hurt. I . . . I need you . . .'

Phyrr was momentarily touched and she shrunk back down to her more usual size. 'Why?'

'What do you mean?'

'Why do you need me?' She could feel the faint touches of suspicion arising once more but allowed herself to hope she was wrong. The lights detached themselves from around her hands and the image of her son re-formed – sight of his expression was all she really needed to tell her what she already suspected; Jahl was plotting to kill her himself. He required her energy for some dark deed . . . She could tell this because he was smiling his most endearing smile and in that moment she imagined there was something of his father in his features. Phyrr smiled back, playing along with the game although his betrayal touched and injured a heart she was surprised to know could still feel such pain.

'I just do . . . Mother. My victory means nothing to me if you are not here.'

She wanted to look at the dagger which was on the floor, to locate its position precisely in case she had to run to reach it. If her son actually stood before her physically it would have been easier, she could have bound him with a simple spell, but there was nothing she could do to affect his Sending as his body was safe in Soulis Mor. Phyrr fought the impulse to look, but noticed the tiniest movement of his gaze and knew he was anticipating her movement.

'All right, Jahl. All right. I'll come to Soulis Mor.'

'Really?' He laughed and clapped his hands in delight like a small boy.

Phyrr smiled indulgently. 'I will be there in three days. I have things to attend to here first.'

'Oh. All right then. I – I'll prepare for your coming, you can have the best rooms, Phyrr.'

She nodded in response, afraid to say much in case her voice betrayed her. 'Goodbye then, Jahl.'

'Goodbye.'

The image of Jahl began to fade and Phyrr watched as the last motes of light dissipated amongst the dark outlines of the trees. Then, she raced across the chamber.

She knew she was too late even as she reached for the knife. He was coming back, just as she anticipated; the sound of the wind screamed back through the chamber and she recognised the mindless, hollow sound of chaos which consumed the soul of Jahl. But Phyrr was more powerful than her son and as she grabbed the knife she turned around into the face of the storm.

'*Stay back, Jahl!*' she screamed. '*Stay back or I will take your soul into oblivion with me!*' She could not release her anger through her aspect this time, needing to remain her mortal size in order to kill herself, but she blasted a furious discharge of energy from her left hand towards the centre of Jahl's – now unformed – Sending. There was a howl of rage from all around her but Phyrr ignored the sound and without any hesitation, plunged the dagger hard, into her neck.

It hurt. It hurt. She staggered forward, blinded by the searing pain, her mind reeling with shock; this could not be dissolution . . . why did it hurt? Why was she not leaving her pain-wracked body?

'Jahl . . .' as she voiced her last, she didn't know whether she was forgiving or condemning him and it hardly seemed to matter. But he was still angry, thwarted, the icy wind tore at her clothes and hair. *Gods forgive you,* she thought. She pitched forward onto her bed as, at last, oblivion beckoned.

It was not as she had imagined. She could see her own hand, limply outstretched on the bed, and as it began to dissolve into a cloud of tiny, beautiful lights Phyrr smiled. *It's coming. Peace. Oblivion.* She closed her eyes and the pain began to drift away. *It's coming . . .*

But then, something was pulling her; not the physical her, but the disembodied shards of light which constituted the soul of the goddess and were soon to dissolve to the ether. Somewhere in the bright mass there was still a diminishing consciousness which had been Phyrr and it knew the pulling sensation was caused by Jahl swearing his deepest curses in order to trap her soul, to deny her dissolution. With her last awareness she pulled away as hard as she was able, willing herself to scatter, to be lost in the ether, speeding up and outwards to the blankness of the uncaring heavens. Thinner and thinner, the motes of light spread as though to echo the brilliance of the stars but still, the awareness was there, and as long as it survived it knew that Jahl had won.

The lights ceased their journey, causing the night sky to flash and glow in bands of pink and gold brightness. Below, amongst the solitude of Phyrr's forest, the lone figure of Jahl could be seen; it burned with the ethereal brightness of a Sending. Jahl stood observing something lying on the bed before him, an object which appeared at first glance to be a normal branch off the nearest birch tree. On closer inspection it could be seen that the branch was glowing from the inside as though the light trapped within was fighting for release still. Jahl's expression was one of shock at the realisation of what he had done; he'd reacted on pure impulse and the result was more than he could have expected. Any sense of remorse he might have felt certainly did not show on his features as he reached down to pick up the branch – he held it at arm's length at first, unsure of how much of the goddess was trapped within – and then wrapped it carefully in his cloak, his lips moving, chanting the words he needed in order to be able to handle physical objects whilst projecting a Sending.

'Set me free, Jahl. Please . . .' The distant sound of a voice whispered through the treetops like a sigh and Jahl stared around the forest for long moments fearing Phyrr could punish him somehow. He knew she was watching in some way, could still sense her presence, but allowed himself to think it was only proximity to the branch which caused the sensation.

'Goodbye, Phyrr,' he muttered absently. Then, he

vanished, the brightness of the Sending flaring briefly before it disappeared. In the sky above, the remaining lights which had comprised the soul of a goddess flared as if in response, there was something of distress in the pulsing illumination, something pathetic; it seemed as though the stars were screaming a silent, anguished scream.

Tristan wanted to speak with his father to somehow reassure him, but, in truth, he knew anything he might have to say would be useless. Both men sat silently, lost in thought whilst eating their morning meal in the cave they had been shown to by Eskarius the night before, after their talks with Regan.

Talisker had the appearance of a man in great pain; it seemed almost as if someone had struck him a heavy, physical blow. Tristan, still angry and grieving for Grace himself, had tried to make conversation with Talisker. 'What did she say to you, Father?'

Talisker had stared at him from within an implacable mask which was at once frightening and piteous. His lips moved soundlessly for a moment before he seemed to find the emotional strength to speak. 'Nothing,' he whispered. 'Nothing really . . .'

They had lain down to sleep shortly afterwards but sleep was a long time coming for both of them. Tristan, turning and fidgeting until his blankets were wrapped snake-like around his listless form, had turned towards Talisker's pallet bed just before dawn and noted his father lying straight and still as a corpse, staring up at the roof of the cave with unblinking, red-rimmed eyes.

Now it was the morning of the first day of Regan's trial. Tristan had decided to plead for mercy on his sister's behalf. It seemed clear to him, who knew her better than anyone, that Jahl had somehow affected her mind. While it would be hard to forgive Regan, Tris had decided in the small hours of the night that he would rather she was alive at least. He glanced over at Talisker again, unsure of his feelings.

'I will speak for her, Father,' he said.

Talisker nodded. 'She is nothing to do with me,' he said sourly.

Tristan paused for long moments, observing the tick of a muscle in his father's jaw. When he spoke, he kept his tone as neutral as possible, watching closely for reaction. 'She will probably be sentenced to death.'

A tiny spark of something flickered briefly in Talisker's gaze but then, it was gone. He said nothing, probably aware that Tristan was trying to provoke a response. 'She is your daughter.'

'No, I have no . . .'

'Talisker!' A sharp voice cut the space between them. 'Be careful what you say.'

They both looked over to the entrance of the chamber: it was Morias. He looked as frail as ever, but he wore an intense expression. The sight of the old man at least brought a slight smile to Talisker's face. 'Morias. It's good to see you.' He walked forward and shook Morias's hand and then kept hold of him, supporting some of the elderly man's weight as they walked back across the room. Morias didn't wait to be seated before continuing however.

'I understand your anger, perhaps you are even reproaching yourself for being her parent – for siring such a monster. And it's true, Duncan, it's all true, she and Jahl together have murdered many, many people. Not by her own hand of course, but her responsibility is undeniable . . . But she is still your daughter, Duncan.' He sat down on the bed, slightly winded, but affixed Talisker with a serious look. 'And you must save her. Much depends on it.'

Talisker sighed and rubbed at his brows. 'I'm not even going to ask you why much depends on it, Morias. Because I'll just get the usual half a story, and this time, I'm not interested. I don't care any more. I've stopped caring. She . . .' he pointed in the general direction of Regan's prison '. . . that woman in there . . . I don't know who she is.'

Morias sighed also, and was about to speak again when Tris interrupted. 'It's Ree, Father. It's still Ree . . .'

Talisker looked over at his son's worried expression. For a moment he thought Tristan had taken him literally but soon realised that Tris was again trying to goad him into defending his sister. 'I understand, Tris. It's hard for you, I know, but she—'

'I will not turn my back on her.' Tristan's tone made it clear he would brook no further argument. Both he and Morias glared at Talisker as if he had committed some awful crime.

'Where's Sandro?' Morias demanded, 'He could always get through to you.'

'Sandro?' Talisker's intense annoyance faded instantly. He realised it would be hard on the old *Seanachaidh* to lose his protégé. 'He's not here. He didn't come back with us, Morias. He stayed in Edinburgh.'

'Oh.' Morias looked surprised but then nodded his approval. 'It is for the best. His death cannot claim him there. I will miss him though . . .'

The heavy fur which covered the entrance to their chamber was pulled back and Eskarius stood there, resplendent in his finest silver grey robes; he had plaited his hair back from his face which accentuated his wolf-like features. He bowed.

'The Council is ready to see you now.'

Both Tristan and Morias looked expectantly at Talisker who shrugged. 'I can only say what's in my heart, old man. I'm sorry, Tristan.' He turned to walk from the room but Morias reached out and grabbed his arm in a tight grip.

'Talisker,' he hissed. 'Remember who sent you to us from your seclusion. It was Una. Her soul is not at rest . . .'

Talisker jerked his arm back. 'Una would still be alive if it wasn't for Regan . . .'

Tristan groaned aloud to hear his father voice what he had always suspected, 'No, Father . . . it was an accident.' Talisker ignored him.

'It was an accident,' Morias repeated. He had scrambled to his feet and now placed himself between Talisker and a rather confused Eskarius who stood in the doorway. 'Listen to me, Duncan. Regan had no chance of resisting Jahl . . . she was affected in the womb by—'

'Get out of my way,' Talisker snarled, his patience snapping.

'It was Corvus.' Morias reached out a bony hand and placed it on Talisker's chest as though to restrain him – although it would have done little good had Talisker decided to push him aside.

'Corvus?' He stared disbelievingly at Morias. 'That can't be true. Corvus was dead by then. I killed him myself.'

'The Council is waiting,' Eskarius interrupted. Talisker held up his hand in a gesture designed to still the Sidhe.

'The gods do not die so easily, Talisker . . .'

'Easily?'

'I mean, it takes time for their spirit to retract from the land. Corvus was at the height of his power when you killed him. Imagine if you can, as his awareness faded, the opportunity to do one final, spiteful harm to the man who had destroyed him.'

Talisker's expression was grave. 'If that's true, Morias, Regan is evil. She's little better than Corvus and she deserves to die.'

'No,' Morias groaned. 'She was born with that seed of darkness within her, Duncan. I watched her as she grew – never fear – the love which you and Una gave her was not wasted. But she was always going to be easy prey to Jahl's influence . . . Please, do this last thing as her father. Plead for clemency. She can be exiled . . .'

'Exiled?' As Talisker said the word, his eyes widened in surprise.

'Yes, Duncan, exiled . . . Is something wrong?'

'No . . . it's nothing.'

'Father?'

'Let's go then.'

'What will you say, Duncan?'

'If they ask me I can't lie and say she's innocent. My guess is, she will condemn herself in her arrogance. But I will ask for clemency.' He pushed past Morias this time and strode towards Eskarius. 'It's more than she deserves,' he muttered.

He had a plan now. And although there were a few small problems Jahl knew that the situation contained the seeds of his ultimate victory. He stared around at the empty Great Hall. The dancers, the flames of the candelabra and the fire, the hounds which lay before the hearth, they were no longer simply frozen in time; they were frozen, encased in ice. Something had happened to his spell, the effects he had thought he could maintain forever at a constant rate had begun to intensify. Soulis Mor was encased in walls of ice so thick that even sound could not penetrate from the outside world. Physically it mattered little to Jahl, he simply refused to feel the cold, his mastery of his own body was accomplished enough for that, and yet, he was irked by his own loss of control and sure that the gods were somehow involved; sabotaging his plans for the sake of a few meaningless souls.

Still, victory was within his grasp. He had his mother's trapped spirit now to heighten his magics, and he knew the location of the artefact which he believed was the key to the whole thing. True godhood was approaching at last . . . but not here . . . Jahl's original plan, had been unwittingly thwarted by Tristan taking the artefact to another world entirely . . . Something moving distracted his reverie and he glanced at the floor where a delicate object whirled against his feet: it was a white feather which had drifted in on a slight breeze from somewhere. He smiled coldly and picked the feather up, staring at it lying flat in his palm and thinking of Regan.

She could have been so perfect if not for her all too human vulnerability. Even her stupid phobia was almost charming. But she was gone now too, just like his mother, she had deserted him when his plans were coming to fruition. So be it – he blew the feather from his palm and watched disdainfully as it drifted back to the ground – he didn't need either of them. Women were ever unreliable and he resolved in that moment to do without them in future.

There was a creaking sound from the dance floor as one of the icy dancers collapsed; the ice was eating through their flesh gradually, reducing them to heavy statues whose weight became unstable. As the dancer fell it shattered on the black slate floor, its body parts reduced to sharp red splinters. The dancer – a young woman – had been reaching forward to take the hand of her partner, and now the disconnected arm with its outstretched hand pointed accusingly to where Jahl sat. He scowled at the body, disgusted and enraged that the gods of Sutra should see fit to interfere with his plans.

'Grell' he yelled. 'Come here.' Grell obediently appeared. 'I am leaving for a while.' Jahl said.

'Where going you?' Grell enquired mildly. The creature stood slightly tilted forward in a position to suggest intense interest, its head cocked to one side.

'Just away,' Jahl snapped. 'I will return soon. While I am gone, protect Soulis Mor, use as many creatures as you need. I will show you how to make more.'

'Am powerful I?'

Jahl's eyes narrowed and he stared at the demon thoughtfully. It seemed absurd that such a creature should possess ambition. Many years ago his mother had shown him how to conjure such beings correctly and she had warned him they were dangerous; 'As long as they exist in our world, they are in pain . . . in agony in fact. Much can be achieved by simply promising their release and return to oblivion.' It seemed Grell was somehow different but Jahl did not have the time to wonder about it. He walked slowly over to the creature, stilling his disgust at its appearance, and stared into the expressionless fidgeting eyes.

'Yes.'

'Where going you?' Grell insisted again. Jahl hissed through his teeth in annoyance at Grell's persistence, but he answered him anyway.

'I am going to collect souls, Grell. Blood and souls. For great magic . . . You are in charge of the Scoor until my return.'

Grell said nothing but rocked back and forward slightly as if congratulating himself.

The trial lasted almost a week. It seemed strange to Tristan that the Sidhe still treated himself and Talisker with such simple courtesy while his own sister stood trial for the mass murder of their kind. Each morning was the same: Eskarius would lead them out into the large amphitheatre where the trial was being held before taking up his position as representative of his clan. In the very centre of the circular space, Regan was seated, bound with leather ropes and wrapped in a red cloak which was symbolic of the accusation against her; she was not required to speak in the beginning but appeared to be listening intently to the testimony of the various witnesses, most of whom could barely stand to look at her. She defied them, fixing her gaze on their faces, scowling as though constantly denying the truth of their traumatic recitations of the killing of their children and partners.

Around the edges of the great circle, as though stationed at points of the compass, groups of different clans were seated. Facing due north from Regan Eskarius stood alone, the wolf clan, disparate and spread throughout Sutra with no affiliations, were making no claims for justice. Because of this supposed neutrality, Eskarius had been deemed a suitable mediator although the power of passing judgement was not his; behind him sat a Sidhe neither Tristan nor Talisker had been introduced to – a tall figure, dressed in ceremonial robes whose face was obscured by a large mask. The mask had the appearance of a creature which seemed to be a composite of all the clans of the Sidhe: eagle, bear, lynx and wolf, all were represented in a bizarre image whose expression was strangely passive. In one hand the Sidhe judge held an eagle feather and in the other, something wrapped in soft leather; Talisker was sure it was *Braznnair* although he never actually saw the gem.

To Eskarius's left and right groups of lynx and bear

Sidhe were positioned – these clans had suffered the most persecution, their tribal lands shared with Regan's own Fine and the Fine of Thane Ulla's clan further south-east. The eagle Sidhe were also aggrieved and sat to the right of the lynxes. Witnesses such as Tristan and Talisker sat to the left of Regan at the westerly point of the compass.

By the third day when neither Tristan nor Talisker had been asked to speak and Regan had been given no opportunity to make any representation on her own behalf, Tristan was growing impatient. He understood how important it was to each of the Sidhe speakers to present their evidence and claims; the raw emotion was written on their faces as they spoke, but as horrific tale followed horrific tale and Regan's imperious, remorseless expression did little to help her cause, the situation became less and less retrievable. One of the eagle clan was holding the large staff they used to signify it was their turn to speak without interruption. He shook the staff angrily towards Regan as he described how Scoor had attacked a flight of young eagle Sidhe and burned them from the skies – the tassels and bells on the staff jangled acidly in the cold, still air but Regan remained impassive. Tristan could stand it no longer.

'Is there to be no defence?' He stood up. 'Is this the justice of the Sidhe?'

'Thane Tristan, you must remain quiet until you are asked to speak,' Eskarius rebuked. 'The eagles have the floor.'

Tristan's brows drew together in a scowl which twisted his normally pleasant features into something entirely un-Tristan. 'Am I a prisoner here, Sir?' he demanded. 'I am a Thane and I may speak as I please.'

'Tristan.' Talisker reached up and took his son's arm. 'This is a Sidhe court . . .'

'It's no court. It's a farce,' Tristan railed. 'We all know she will be executed. We all know she deserves it . . . where is the dignity in this? Just do it . . .' he choked back on his words suddenly, 'Just kill her . . .' his voice wavered, and his next words could only be heard by Talisker and Morias who was sitting close by. '. . . my sister . . .'

Morias got up and stood before Tristan, wisely blocking him from the view of the confused Sidhe observers. He whispered urgently, fixing his gaze on Tristan's grief-stricken face. 'The trial is not for Regan. Do you understand, Tristan? The trial is for her accusers . . . so she may show some remorse and perhaps ask their forgiveness—'

'Before she dies?'

Morias nodded sadly.

'Then I cannot watch it, Morias. I will not watch it.'

'Your loyalty does you credit, Tristan. But remember, you are still Thane of Soulis Mor. When this . . . is over, the Sidhe may or may not remain your allies.'

Tristan drew himself up as straight as he could. 'If you are suggesting that I be seen to condemn my own sister for political expedience, Morias, then you underestimate me greatly. I know what she is. But I will not use her death for my own ends.'

'You need do nothing, Tristan. Just remain seated and quiet,' Morias said firmly.

'No. If they will condemn her with or without me,

they can bloody well do it without me.' Tristan turned to walk from the amphitheatre. 'Will you walk with me, Father?' he asked.

Talisker's voice was thick with emotion. 'It will be my honour, son.'

They walked back to the caves in silence without taking leave of any of the Sidhe dignitaries. Behind them there was a buzz of agitated voices but both men ignored it. Once within their own quarters Tristan broke down, flinging himself onto his bed and sobbing. Talisker sat uselessly by, patting his son's back as though he were still a child.

'W-why does she have to be like that, Father? Why can't she throw herself on their mercy? Did you see? Did you see the way she just sat there?

'Yes,' Talisker replied. 'It's the only way she knows how to be, son.' He couldn't fathom his own feelings – the image of Regan sitting straight-backed and dignified in her chair was so absurdly painful. In some indefinable way, both of his children had made him proud within the last few hours, but with Regan, that foolhardy pride would cost her her life.

It must have been an hour later that Morias came to get them. He seemed excited and tired in equal measure. 'Well, it seems we have effected something of a change in Sidhe tradition,' he beamed. 'I have been given permission to act as an intermediary. I will call you to speak this afternoon, Tristan, and then you tomorrow morning, Duncan. Regan is to be given an opportunity to speak also – although her words must remain within strict guidelines – she must not be seen to justify her actions.'

'What's the point if it will not affect the outcome?' Tristan frowned. 'What difference do mere words make?'

'Need you ask a *Seanachaidh* such a thing? Words are all. Words are memory, young man.' Morias smiled without rancour in response to Tristan's dismissive shrug. 'These words will matter whatever the outcome – history will judge your sister – but the Sidhe Council have also agreed to consider clemency. If we can convince them Regan was in the thrall of Jahl and was . . . unaware of certain key incidents—'

Talisker laughed bitterly, 'Can we sell them the lie, Morias?'

'And what makes you so sure it is a lie, Duncan?'

'I'm her father, Morias, and my heart remains cold when I look at her. Yes, she was influenced by Jahl – she imagines that she loved him – but love doesn't excuse this . . . This word has probably never been used on Sutra before and it makes me sick to my stomach that I'm in any way responsible – Regan is a racist, Morias – she hates the Sidhe just because they are different from the Fine. There is no real reason except fear and insecurity and . . .' he stopped, Morias was frowning. 'See, I can't even make you understand, perhaps it's really a human flaw.'

'No. I don't believe so; if, as you say, such "racist" feelings come from fear and insecurity, then Jahl – and probably his uncle before him – planted and fed this fear – not you or Una. And surely, Regan is more to be pitied than blamed?'

'Ohboy,' Talisker laughed weakly, 'You haven't seen the damage such ignorance can do, Morias. You must study my world sometime.'

'Do you think Regan would survive in your world, Duncan?' Morias asked.

'Yeah, she . . . no . . . wait a minute. You're not suggesting—'

'What do you think?' Morias regarded him coolly. 'You say your heart is cold when you look at her but I cannot believe you would not prolong her life.'

'What do you mean?' Tristan frowned.

'It may be acceptable to the Sidhe, especially with their history of resettlement, to agree to exile Regan to your father's world,' Morias watched closely for Tristan's reaction as he spoke.

Tristan gasped and stared at his father who nodded as if in agreement.

'What do you think?' Morias asked, realising he was missing something.

'Well . . . I think you've already done it, Morias.'

'What?'

'Father and I saw someone as we crossed back into this world – she was wearing a mask and ceremonial robes but . . .'

'It was her. Regan.' Talisker finished. 'I wasn't sure before, but it makes perfect sense now. It must be because of the time difference between here and Edinburgh – she would be going backwards in time slightly – whereas we were coming forward . . . relatively . . .' he threw his hands up, unable to express the strange intricacies of the gateways.

'Oh.' Morias looked grave. 'I wish you had told me this earlier.'

'I thought you'd be pleased,' Tristan said. 'It means we win. Regan will be alive in Father's world.'

'It doesn't mean we win – at least, not automatically. It means we had better win.'

'Well, what happens if we don't? If Regan doesn't go through the gateway as we've already seen?'

Morias shrugged, his expression bleak. 'I'm not sure. Such a thing has never happened. But changing a timeline like that . . . it could only be disastrous.'

'Disastrous,' Tristan echoed, 'great . . .'

'Well we'd better do our best to make sure we win through,' Morias glanced at Talisker, 'whatever our feelings on the matter.'

In the end, Tristan's and Talisker's testimony made little difference. Later that afternoon Morias called Tristan and asked him to describe the changes in his sister since Jahl had come to Soulis Mor. Then he asked about the breakdown of their relationship and how much Tristan held Regan responsible. Tris, who couldn't quite see the direction Morias's questions were taking, became more and more agitated. 'You know what I don't understand, Morias,' he said. 'I cannot understand why I am not on trial here, that's the truth . . .'

Morias looked surprised and gave Tris a hard look. 'Just answer the questions please, Thane Tristan.'

'But it's true. I'm the one that could have done something about the whole sorry mess before it started. I could have had Jahl arrested before he got his hooks into my sister. I turned a blind eye – isn't that worse than anything? Isn't there a word for it – complicity? I let Regan have her head in matters of the kingdom and it was my responsibility. I wasn't particularly interested and she was so good at it . . . all the laws, functions, running the city . . . she was a natural.' He gave a short, bitter laugh and Talisker, suddenly sensing where Tristan was going with this thought, sat forward in his seat, a look of dawning alarm on his face. Unfortunately Morias was standing with his back to Talisker and was not so quick to realise Tristan's testimony was about to spiral out of control.

Talisker glanced over at Regan: she did not meet his gaze but there was a strange expression on her face as she fought to contain her fear. Did Tristan realise, Talisker wondered, that his admission would rob his sister of something that meant everything to her?

'. . . and it's ironic really,' Tristan was choked with emotion, 'because she has no royal blood at all. Regan is the true blood daughter of Duncan and Una Talisker.'

As he spoke the words, Morias's realisation was written on his face – too late – and a growing ripple of consternation amongst the watching Sidhe travelled around the circle. Regan's head dropped forward onto her chest and although she did not speak or cry out, it was clear she was devastated. Morias waited for the noise to die down before speaking to Tris again. 'Why, Tristan? What makes you say this?'

'Dammit Morias! You know it's true! Regan is a commoner. It was to protect me – we said we were twins – because . . . because . . .' he held himself together as well as he could but Talisker could see tears tracking down the side of his cheek unremarked. 'Look at me,' he said quietly, 'the Council of Thanes would never have accepted me as Isbister's only heir. Regan . . . Regan has the best quarters on the top floor because . . . because I can't manage the stairs. But I could have changed that – people's view of me I mean. I know I'm not stupid just because I look the way I do and I could have done something, anything, to change what has happened.' He glanced at Regan and smiled a fierce, humourless smile. 'At least she's done something with her life other than hide away. She has passion and fire. She's strong, she just wasn't strong enough to withstand Jahl, who – least we forget – you yourself believe to be the son of the goddess Phyrr.'

There was a further ripple of consternation amongst the Sidhe. Morias leaned in towards Tristan. 'Did we have to tell them everything?' he glowered in apparent disbelief.

'I have little left to lose, Morias,' Tristan muttered. 'At the moment, you still have a kingdom.'

Morias tried to pull things back together the following day when Talisker was giving his testimony. It would have been impossible to demonstrate Regan's character as being anything other than it was; if anything, her expression was more severe, more distant than previously. As Talisker came out, he smiled nervously towards her but she ignored him as though determined not to throw him the smallest crumb of her fragile decorum.

'Talisker, can you tell the Council why the decision was taken to lie about Regan's lineage?' Morias began mildly.

'It's just as Tristan said. It was to protect Tris. They were both much younger and more vulnerable at the time. But you should be aware that the idea was Regan's. She was always protective of her brother. When they were children she looked after him without being asked – they were very close.'

'Which makes it strange that years later, she allowed Jahl to send his hounds after her brother to hunt him down and kill him?'

'Yes . . . I cannot believe Regan could have given that order.' Talisker glanced over at his daughter who gave the tiniest shake of her head.

'So what about the order to send Scoor to eradicate the clan of the lynx Sidhe?'

'No. She has never been . . . that way.' Talisker felt his throat tighten as he swallowed hard, wondering if they could sense the fact he was unsure.

'You tried to warn her about Jahl didn't you?'

'Yes. But she imagined herself . . . she was, in love with him. What could I say to dissuade her? I was unaware then of the extent of Jahl's malice – as was Regan I believe.'

The next question hit Talisker like a thunderbolt. 'The accident that killed Regan's mother – her true mother – your wife, Una . . . do you believe your daughter deliberately caused the accident or contributed to her mother's death?'

'What?!'

Morias didn't blink. 'You must answer the question, Duncan. Why don't you look at Regan as you do so?'

'I can't believe you're asking me this. What do you hope to achieve?'

'Honesty. It's what the Council of Tema demands.'

Talisker turned to look at Regan. For the first time in the whole of the proceedings her face registered complete shock; she stared at him, her eyes huge, her mouth hung slackly open as if she had just taken a huge gasp.

'No . . . I . . .' He was suddenly aware of the silence; no one moved. A wind had blown up from the ocean and a fine reddish dust blew across the amphitheatre. Regan's red cloak and Talisker's own robes whipped and snapped in the breeze. It felt as though they were alone and Talisker realised just how short their time was. He wanted to deny his feelings as he had for many years now, but he could not. 'How could you have let go? You let her fall . . .'

'No.'

He saw Regan mouth the words but couldn't hear her voice so he stepped closer to the centre of the circle. The two Sidhe who guarded Regan throughout the proceedings crossed their spears before him to warn him off, but they remained where they stood when Talisker brushed them aside to stare at his daughter. 'Why didn't you hold on?' he groaned. 'If it was me . . . I would never have let her fall . . . never . . .'

Regan was crying now, silent tears tracked through the thin layer of dust on her skin. 'No,' she said again, 'No . . . I couldn't hold on . . .'

'You killed her, Regan.' Talisker turned away, unable to face her any longer.

'No . . . Daddy. I was just a little girl. I was only twelve. I was slipping too . . . I was frightened. I didn't want her to fall – she was my mother . . .' Regan sat forward and cradled her head on her knees to cry.

Talisker began to stalk from the circle. 'Happy now?' he hissed at Morias. Morias said nothing, his features ashen. If his intention had been to show Regan's vulnerability, he had certainly succeeded, she was weeping inconsolably.

'Please stay, Talisker,' he pressed. 'I feel we are making a difference; the Sidhe must understand that Regan was not to blame—'

'The Sidhe do not care, old man. They see a woman before them who is responsible for the deaths of their loved ones – they don't care what kind of girl she was or whether her father loved her. They will condemn her. There's nothing left for me to say.'

He was right. Later that day, the Council of Tema delivered their verdict: Regan was to be put to death in a traditional Sidhe manner. She would be tied to a post and impaled by many spears thrown by riders chosen by her accusers. She took the verdict calmly although Talisker was not present to see it – Tristan, still shaking violently with reaction, told him soon after.

'She is so brave,' he whispered. 'Morias, will you please make sure she is drugged or something. I can't bear to think of it—'

'I cannot, Tristan.'

Tristan looked up sharply. 'At least speed her passage into the next world, Morias.'

'Well, that's exactly what I intend, Tristan. She

cannot die. We must rescue your sister and send her through the gateway as foreseen. I can see now that it is of the utmost importance she go to Edinburgh.'

CHAPTER FIFTEEN

In the gloom cast by the candles, the tall-backed wooden chairs cast sombre shadows. Outside, evening traffic could be heard, endlessly travelling the ancient road homeward but here, in the cramped sepia and shadow of the old meeting rooms, an air of waiting pervaded. Knox had not been here for a while – his mind reeled away unexpectedly from the reason for his last visit – and he'd forgotten how the muffled quiet of the place could turn a man's thoughts inward. He walked to the front of the hall, his eyes habitually fixed on the empty, unadorned box of the pulpit; in a few hours he would preach from there, telling the Children about God's new plan for them. Knox's sense of unease was not because of the approaching task, but because someone had slipped a note under his door demanding they meet here. The irritable scrawl of the writing had caused him to suspect someone but he wasn't completely sure and he'd had little time to check the handwriting of the various Children. Someone had begun to watch him over the last day or so, he felt sure, the sensation of being watched was strong – crossing the parkland towards Arthur's Seat the last two nights had felt oddly disjointed – as though he was an actor in some movie and he was watching himself . . .

'Knox.'

Then he knew immediately: it was LearnToFly; Gordon. Although unsure what LearnToFly thought he knew, Knox felt himself relax slightly – with his Scoor allies there wasn't much he couldn't deal with.

'What's wrong, Brother? Why all the secrecy? If there's something you need to speak to me about in private I can assure you of my discretion.' He kept his tone deliberately light and placatory as this always seemed to fluster his old adversary.

'I b-bet you c-can,' LearnToFly responded. He was standing just behind the steps to the pulpit which was why Knox hadn't seen him on his arrival. 'D-discretion m-must be imp-portant to you.'

Knox sighed. LearnToFly's combination of stammering and a continually outraged viewpoint on the world could be extremely tiresome. 'Look, I'm very busy. Just tell me what you want, LearnToFly.' Knox sat down in the front row of the congregation chairs and observed LearnToFly coolly.

'I've opened the carpet, Knox.'

Knox didn't hesitate. 'So? Is that why you called me here – you want help laying the carpet?'

LearnToFly stared at him for a moment and Knox kept his gaze steady; this unnerved his accuser somewhat.

'I f-found the b-body.'

'Body?'

'D-Daniel's body.'

There was a pause as each man considered their position; LearnToFly's confidence was shaken but it wouldn't take much deduction to realise Knox was bluffing, he had been the only person to have anything to do with the carpet. Briefly Knox considered summoning the Scoor to dispose of his accuser but then dismissed the idea; LearnToFly would be missed if he disappeared.

'LearnToFly . . . how would you feel if I said I could show you irrefutable proof that God is working through me?'

'I don't see w-what that's got t-to do with murder,' LearnToFly replied doggedly. 'Our God doesn't c-condone murder.'

'Hate the sin but love the sinner, LearnToFly,' Knox replied, 'That's what our God demands, is it not?'

'But D-Daniel . . . you k-killed Daniel!' LearnToFly sat down heavily on the steps which led up to the pulpit, his eyes full of earnest tears.

Knox sighed heavily, 'not exactly, LearnToFly. We all loved Daniel and he found that responsibility just too much in the end.'

'Are you saying Daniel killed himself?'

Knox didn't respond immediately but buried his head in his hands; he wasn't so stupid as to pretend to cry but he scrubbed at his face as though fighting with emotion. 'I tried to turn it into something positive, I thought that's what Daniel would have wanted . . . and then, God forgave me . . . He sent me a sign that I was still worthy of His grace and that Daniel had been right about living in the End Times . . .'

LearnToFly was looking less than sympathetic, the next few moments would determine whether he listened to his rational mind asking him why Daniel's mummified body had its head caved in; fortunately for his continued survival, his curiosity got the better of him. 'W-what was the s-sign?'

Knox clicked his fingers and a Scoor appeared. The creature scuttled lightly up the central aisle of the meeting place, its wings buzzing at half speed, knocking the wooden chairs at either side of the narrow space flying. LearnToFly screamed, his eyes round with terror, and then flung himself to his knees. 'The sound of their wings was like the thundering of many horses . . .' he garbled, '. . . tails and stings like scorpions . . . angel of the abyss . . . Abaddon . . .' He could not bring himself to look at the Scoor and kept his gaze fixed on the floor. Once he had exhausted his memory of descriptions from the book of Revelations, he simply cowered, whispering, 'Oh God, Oh God, Oh God,' in a meaningless litany.

Knox felt a certain amount of unexpected sympathy for LearnToFly. The Scoor were bloody frightening to look at, in fact, Knox tended not to look at them himself unless it was strictly necessary. The Scoor, meanwhile, had stopped just behind Knox, waiting for his orders.

'Get up, LearnToFly. You have nothing to fear from the Scoor. They are merely servants of our Lord, just like ourselves.'

'Th-they? You m-mean there're lots? Oh God, has the whole army come from the abyss while we slept?' LearnToFly wrung his hands in true biblical fashion. 'W-why have we not b-been Raptured?'

'No man may know the hour, LearnToFly,' Knox said smoothly. He grinned wickedly. 'Kinda settles the Pre-Trib–Post-Trib argument though, eh? But now we can be sure it's close.' He patted Gordon's shoulder and smiled slightly more reassuringly. 'Look, this is going to be hard on those of the Children who are not as strong in their faith as they should be. I have to witness to everyone this evening. I trust I can depend on your support?'

LearnToFly seemed to calm slightly, he straightened up and adjusted his glasses which he had managed to knock awry while in the grip of his fear. For a moment, Knox thought it was going to be fine.

'It doesn't change the f-facts about D-Daniel though. They'll have to be t-told.'

'No. I will deal with it – it's not really important in the bigger picture, is it?' He moved slightly to one side, allowing LearnToFly a full view of the Scoor again. LearnToFly paled instantly.

'No, I suppose it's not,' he muttered. 'Knox, does this mean God intends you to lead the Children into the Tribulation – I mean since we haven't been Raptured?'

'Oh yes. That's what He told me.' Knox smiled again, all sweetness and light.

'He told you?'

'Trust me, LearnToFly. His plan is only just beginning.'

'So much for the redemption of the wolves,' Eskarius muttered. 'It seems each generation must repeat the mistakes of the last.'

'Not so my friend. I can assure you, this is the right thing to do. In time, the Sidhe will come to understand.'

They stood on a narrow peninsula where the Sidhe's displaced island ended, swallowed up by the grey reality of the Northern Ocean. Eskarius was carrying Regan who had been drugged when they had entered her prison – presumably by someone on the Council as an act of apparent mercy. She already wore the clothes in which she would be executed; white buckskin and beaded robes. The mask which Tristan and Talisker had already seen her wear as she walked through the gateway, hung loosely behind her head momentarily resembling a strange sunhat.

Morias had worked magics, the strength of which surprised Tristan, freezing the inhabitants of the island, suspending them in time. It was something which, had Regan been awake to see, may have made her laugh at the irony of it. Jahl had kept her awake, unfrozen, while he performed his strange torture before her escape and she had become briefly aware of the state of her city.

'In fact, it's not my spell,' Morias said. 'There's only so much magic in a world . . .'

Tristan frowned. 'What do you mean, Morias?'

'I've . . . borrowed the spell – from Jahl actually – so we must hurry . . .'

'Do you mean the people in Soulis Mor will be restored?' Eskarlus asked. He grinned as he considered the possible implications of this for Jahl.

'It's not necessarily a good thing,' Morias sighed. 'The last I heard, Soulis Mor is inhabited by demons and Scoor – I'm not even sure Jahl is still there. No, we must act quickly and "give the spell back" so to speak. More lives will be lost the longer we delay.' He turned to Tristan and Talisker who stood looking bereft. 'I'm truly sorry she is not awake so you can say your goodbyes,' he said, 'but you must take comfort in the fact she will survive.'

Tristan was crying silently, his tears felt like ice against his skin in the gale which whipped water from the tops of the waves. Talisker put his arm around his shoulder to comfort him. He spoke quietly as he gazed at Regan's cold, deathlike face. 'I judged her too harshly, too soon. Perhaps I could have made a difference to her . . . Ree, I . . .' His voice broke as he used her childhood name, and he and Tristan clung wordlessly together.

Morias ignored their obvious misgivings and continued in a brisk manner. 'Remember, if possible, the Sidhe must believe I acted alone. Tristan, you must ride to meet the Southern Clans – I know they are coming. Now, give her to me, Eskarius. Stand back.'

Eskarius handed over Regan's sleeping form and Morias buckled slightly at the knees but then recovered, placing his feet wide apart to better distribute the weight.

'I will tell her to seek out Sandro as you suggested, Duncan. Farewell.' Morias vanished, in his usual simple undramatic style; one moment he stood there struggling under the weight of Regan's body, and the next he was gone – the watchers were left staring at the bleakness of the ocean.

'It's not going to be easy,' Tristan noted distantly, 'telling the Sidhe he acted alone.'

Eskarius shrugged, 'as far as we know, the Grey Oak owes no allegiance to Fine or Sidhe.'

Talisker said nothing but he remembered many years earlier the goddess Rhiannon speaking of Morias with something akin to affection; it seemed Morias was more like a force of nature than anything else.

'Come on, Father,' Tristan nudged him, 'we have only a short time to get back before the spell is returned to Soulis Mor.'

'You go on, Tris. I'll catch up in a moment.'

Tristan frowned but did as he was asked, he and Eskarius walked silently back over the rocks. Talisker remained where he stood for long moments, staring out at the ocean whose restless gale seemed to be subsiding.

'She's gone, Una,' he whispered. 'Regan is gone from the land. Rest easy, my love.' He watched the deep velvet of the night sky for long moments as if for some sign; there was nothing, the stars were as immutable as ever, but, he did feel a deep sense of serenity. Perhaps he had expected Una to come and tell him he had done the right thing, perhaps he just wanted to hear it from her. But somehow, it didn't really matter now, Regan had been his daughter too after all, and he had done the best he could. Sighing to himself, he followed the others back towards the sleeping encampment.

So, this was 'Edinburgh'. The world Knox believed a great, vengeful God was about to destroy. Jahl smiled quietly to himself; the fool was more correct than he knew, although, perhaps 'destroy' was too strong a word – there would be some inevitable devastation, but at least Sutra would escape most of it. In the silence of the chamber, around twenty Scoor stood at statue-still attention, what little light there was coming from the sconces mingled with the lurid green shimmer from the object Jahl carried and played like reflected water on their breastplates and the gold circlets they wore. Jahl had brought reinforcements with him, unsure of what awaited him in Knox's world, but so far, sealed within the hillside, it seemed there would be little need for them.

He walked forward to the flat altar stone and lay the delicate tracery of the birch branch he carried into the middle of the space. For a moment he stared at it as though considering something; there was perhaps, the tiniest expression of regret on his features, but then, it could have been a trick of the light. He hoped the power contained within the branch was strong enough to start the incantation now; Knox would come soon with the necklace but Jahl was far too impatient to wait. Clambering up onto the flat coldness of the altar, he sat cross-legged, sweeping his black hair back from his face then rubbing his eyes, cursing to himself that he should be weak enough to feel tired now. The situation at Soulis Mor occupied his thoughts still and he tried to push it from his mind. If anyone saw Jahl sitting on the altar, they may have thought he looked like a young boy preparing for a picnic, his face becoming a blank, guileless mask, only his heavy-lidded eyes betraying the weariness he was feeling. In fact, he was preparing to become a god.

Taking a long, deep breath he began the incantation without further hesitation.

Knox stared out of the window into the little alleyway which led up to the High Street; it had snowed during the last couple of hours while they railed and argued, the quiet whiteness outside almost gave the impression that God, or someone, had tried to shut them up with some kind of white muffler. From the aged brown frame of the window, the scene outside looked like a painting in which nothing was actually happening, the snowfall had landed in a narrow strip between the walls of the adjoining buildings and the white strip led away from the meeting house up to the intersection with the High Street, where every now and then a car crossed, its lights and sound softened by the snow. The only telling thing about the curious brown and white picture was that a line of footprints in the new, white pathway, led away from the meeting house, a detail which informed any careful observer that around ten people had left the building within the last hour and that the empty picture in fact told a story of abandonment.

Knox sighed, it was called a 'schism' he thought. That's what they said when church groups split into factions – except the groups in question were usually a lot bigger – he glanced back at the remaining faithful who sat around in small, dejected clusters speaking in hushed tones. Twenty-two of the Children had remained after Knox's announcement; the others, led by an unexpected leader, FaithWarrior, a woman to whom Knox had never paid the slightest bit of attention, had gone back to The Ark. The question on everyone's lips was, did they intend to stay in The Ark, or did they intend to leave and let Knox's faithful take over the house? It seemed unlikely that they would leave, and so, the almost farcical situation of the two factions vying for ownership of the decrepit old building seemed inevitable.

'Why didn't you just sh-show them, Knox?' LearnToFly spoke quietly as he leant against the opposite side of the window. His normally open expression was guarded and grave-looking. There was something else also – it was as if knowing had robbed LearnToFly of some invisible flame, his zeal was no longer required – it changed him somehow, made him ordinary. 'Y-you could have just shown them a S-scoor.'

Knox nodded wearily. Actually, he'd been asking himself the same thing. 'It just didn't seem right,' he shrugged. 'It wasn't the right time . . .'

LearnToFly did not respond but nodded as though he could easily understand such an ephemeral idea. Walking over to the nearest chair, he sat down, folding his large hands together and closing his eyes. For a moment, Knox assumed he was only deep in thought, but as his lips began to move soundlessly, he realised LearnToFly was praying. This realisation came with something of a small shock, prayer seemed somehow irrelevant to Knox, but then, he was the only one with a direct link to God . . .

'He's not God . . .'

The voice was loud and strong, no whispered suggestion or insinuation. It was also immediately obvious whose voice it was. Knox blinked rapidly and shook his head as though to clear it, none of the Children had reacted in any way so it seemed only he could hear the sound.

'Go away, Danny,' he muttered. 'Not now.' He looked back out of the window so no one could notice his confusion. Outside, there was a faint shadow on the snow, a transparent thing which flitted across his vision.

'*I'm telling you, Nathan. He's a false prophet . . .*'

'Here, I've made some tea.' Esther was standing beside him, a chipped mug in her hand. She smiled slightly nervously as Knox took the drink and he noticed she almost flinched as their hands touched. He had known their relationship was futile from the start and now he had used Esther, all Knox really felt when he looked at her was self-disgust and anger. She seemed oblivious to this however, anxious to please him still, even if it was to ensure her next fix – there was only one set of footprints in the snow which stopped and turned back to the hall and they were Esther's.

'What happens now, Knox?' she asked.

He is about to answer when 'it' happens. The unthinkable, unbelievable thing, so outside the experience of Edinburgh's citizens that it is almost over before any lips in the entire city can utter the word 'earthquake'. There is a sound, a deep, almost subliminal rumbling, accompanied by long seconds of awed incomprehension from the million souls caught within its range. It's as if the city holds its breath for the first few seconds, a long, futile denial of some hidden pain which assails it. Holding, holding, holding . . .

Then, the scream, the city moves, splits, buckles; the glass in thousands of windows shatters as compression grips the buildings with some invisible hand, causing them to creak and groan. Car alarms squeal. People shriek in terror but the sound is mainly lost in the cacophony of the city.

In the meeting rooms the Children are thrown across the floor as if they are on board a ship riding a storm; the wooden chairs are scattered. They scream also, and shout prayers begging God for forgiveness. Knox is thrown into the doorway, his arm crumpled beneath his body, pain searing into his chest.

Tell me he's not God now, Danny boy, he thinks.

Then, after a final, smaller shudder, the earth stills once more. Again, there is silence for long seconds as everyone waits to be sure it is finished. Human sounds creep back in tones of disbelief; muted sobs, groans and sighs.

'Dear God.' Knox has said the words before even considering them. The meeting rooms are ruined. The chairs have scattered around the edges and look even more like the jagged debris of a nest than ever; plaster and the two old crossbar chandeliers have fallen from the ceiling. Most remarkable of all, the pulpit, the simplest, severest of wooden boxes, has fallen forward from the wall and, by chance, where it has landed, the floor has split apart with a crack that buckles upwards, splitting the wooden floor against its grain. The jagged line of the crack ends where Knox is leaning under the lintel of the doorway. He stares down into the basement, looking at where the carpet is lying, knowing Daniel might be thought to be accusing him should anyone else know the truth.

Esther has been thrown to the right side of the room, banging her head against the wall. She sits up, her expression dazed and frightened, and looks back towards Knox. The others are picking themselves up – none are seriously injured although there are a few cuts and bruises. It's darker now and they are all coated in plaster and dust, ghostlike in the gloom. One by one, they do the same as Esther; they turn and look to Knox for guidance.

Knox is speechless for long moments. *It's real,* he thinks. *Shit. It's really happening . . .*

'I th-think we should pray,' one of the plaster saints whispers. It's LearnToFly. Knox, still as dazed as the rest of them, feels a pinprick of annoyance that LearnToFly should steal his thunder and this brings him back to full awareness.

'Yes,' he says. 'We must pray for strength in the coming times. And then . . .' he looks around the frightened, huddled group trying to make eye contact with as many as possible whilst his own heartbeat struggles to return to normal. '. . . And then, I will take you all to God's Temple . . .'

Dressed in grey they wander like shadows through a scene of devastation made monochrome by the night and the snow. The High Street has some of the oldest buildings in the city; some are virtually untouched by the earthquake by virtue of their squat shape and solid walls, but others are less fortunate and have collapsed, killing and injuring their incredulous occupants. People are in the streets already, shocked and bewildered for the most part. Perhaps the Children would have been gratified to realise they were not the only ones who considered that God's judgement had come. At St Giles Cathedral, Knox paused to stare; all around is chaos and madness but the plight of the building is picked out by night-lighting which now serves to show its damage.

The main spire of the cathedral is gone, a heap of rubble lies all around the building; the shell that remains is open to the sky and the snow, which has begun once more, drifts into that defiled space as though comforting its wounds. Fires are burning in the old building of the Sheriff's Court and shards of glass from the great, coloured windows of the cathedral lie scattered amongst the snow, catching the firelight, like jewels. Knox stoops to pick one up, it has the face of a saint painted on, the face is serene, but his halo destroyed, shattered by the explosion as the glass was flung outwards when the windows buckled and tore.

The Children walk on. Knox has given instruction that they cannot stop to help anyone – '*God's purpose for his Tribulation Saints is far more important*' – and so, they only look forward as they trek through the snow, down the steep incline of the ancient hill, their gaze focussed on the darkness at the end where the outline of Holyrood Palace and behind it, Arthur's Seat, blots out the stars. Just before Jeffrey Street, their progress is slowed by a collapsed building and they clamber over the rubble without question, following Knox who only pauses briefly to frown at the plaque which marked his namesake's house but now simply bears the word 'Knox'.

'What is it, Knox?' Esther asks.

'I suppose you could say it's a sign,' Knox remarks, his mouth twisting into a weird expression which might have been a smile. He tosses the plaque back onto the heap.

'Oh.' She doesn't seem to understand he was being

ironic and nods mutely, her tired features almost blank, blood still drying on her forehead.

That's the trouble with Christians, Knox thinks. *No sense of humour . . .*

Regan was fuming. She hated this place. It stank, she could taste the air, especially when there were those 'car' things around. She put her feet up on the bench, bunching her knees under her chin and staring moodily into the darkness of the park. They had come to the park to see if Knox would show up here again as the *Seanachaidh* had said he had previously, but she'd squabbled with Beatrice and left the car, slamming the door behind her. At least the park was quiet, apart from some dog which was barking frantically somewhere in the distance, and she could think for a few minutes. Sandro would come looking for her she was sure, then she'd have to go back and apologise to Beatrice. Just who did that woman think she was anyway? Just because she and Sandro seemed to know one another from when the *Seanachaidh* had lived here before, she seemed to think that gave her the right to order Regan around as though she were a child . . .

It had begun to snow. Regan tilted her head right back and stared up at the white flakes spiralling silently towards her. If she was honest with herself she was lucky to be here, at least she was alive. But the thought of living the rest of her life here filled her with a dread which felt like a leaden weight in her chest. The people were so strange; no one knew or cared who she was, so no one treated her with any deference. She wished she had a sword or at least a short dagger, so that next time someone in a shop called her 'hen' she could slit their throat as a message to others. She sighed, that wouldn't be right either, matters of honour counted for little here. Sandro was fast losing patience with her, she could tell . . . She wished she had had time to talk more with Tris and her father before she left; she had been so wrapped up in her posturing, so intent on appearing strong and proud that she had neglected to speak frankly – she supposed it was only human nature to imagine there would always be more time to come, even on the evening of the day before one's execution when the minutes stretched into hours. What would she have told them?

Tris was easy; she loved him as fiercely as ever and was shamed by her failure to protect him from Jahl – she would probably have asked his forgiveness if she had been really honest with him. Her father? That was different; she would never forget the look on his face when Morias had asked him if he blamed her for Una's death . . .

'How could you have let go? You let her fall . . .'

She sniffed and wiped her nose – with some satisfaction – on the sleeve of the puffy jacket she had borrowed from Beatrice. Perhaps if she ignored their coldness she could deny the fact that tears were mingling with the snowflakes on her face. Why should she care what he thought anyway . . .

'Regan?' Sandro stood a few feet away from her, an exasperated frown on his normally mild features which softened when he saw that she'd been crying. 'Are you all right?' he asked.

She scowled at his concern. 'Of course I am, *Seanachaidh.* I just wanted to be alone – away from Beatrice's infernal chatter . .'

'I told you, you don't have to call me that here,' his frown deepened. 'And you shouldn't be so hostile to Bea either, she's just trying to set you at your ease. She's trying to help, Regan.'

'I don't need her help. Or yours.'

'Yes, you do,' he had begun to walk towards her to sit down beside her when the earthquake started. Sandro fell forward, caught off guard, grabbing onto the bench to steady himself. This was little help however as the bench lurched aside, throwing Regan to the ground which was heaving and moving as though it were liquid waves.

'Oh my God!' Sandro yelled. 'Bea!' He turned back towards the car but was knocked from his feet and lay there for long seconds, stunned and unsure which way was up, as the earth continued to shake. The trees behind them were uprooted and fell forward with a splintering squeal which sounded like a scream. Sandro glanced around but Regan was nowhere to be seen.

It lasted for over a minute and a half. Later, people would know that the quake was force six on the Richter scale, had killed five hundred and fifty-three people by virtue of its sheer unexpectedness and caused hundreds of million of pounds worth of damage. Right now, as the shock wave subsided, there were other, more immediate concerns.

Sandro had twisted his leg somehow as he fell but

other than that was uninjured; he realised he was clinging to the ground almost as if he thought he was to be shaken off the surface of the world like a flea from a dog's back. The smell of grass and earth was in his nostrils and his mind reeled aimlessly, unable to shape a coherent thought. He sat up and stared around. In the darkness, Holyrood Park was relatively unscathed; the line of trees around the edges had toppled like dominos, but the outline of Arthur's Seat remained a constant, blotting out the starry sky. Only the continuing sound of collapsing masonry gave the reminder that Holyrood Palace, a historic building hundreds of years old, was falling apart behind them, crumpling into the now still earth which had betrayed it.

They had been waiting to see if Knox was going to show again but that hardly seemed to matter now . . . Sandro stood up shakily and tested his leg, pressing the weight onto it slowly and wincing as a warm flash of pain surged up through his torso. For a moment he wondered who he should check first, Bea or Regan? He couldn't see either of them. Bea was still in the car by the side of Holyrood Palace when the quake hit and Regan seemed to have vanished – the bench lay upturned a few yards away on the grass but Regan was nowhere near it. Slowly, his leg paining him, Sandro hobbled towards where he thought she had been thrown; he found her tangled amongst one of the fallen trees, fortunately she had been just at the limits of the tree's height and only knocked down by the lighter branches. Regan was unconscious, but, after checking her pulse, Sandro left her where she was while he went to find Bea, reasoning that she was fairly well shielded by the branches in the case of any aftershock and he was unable to carry her with his leg as it was. A sickening thrill of shock ran though him as he reached where he had left the car: Bea's old Sierra was on its roof, a tree had fallen across the upturned body.

'Bea?' he broke into a hobbling run. 'Beatrice!' He could hear sirens now, a haunting, disconnected wail that echoed from across the shattered city, as though his anguish had been vocalised by something else. On reaching the car however he almost laughed with relief – Bea was upside down but unhurt, in fact she seemed more frustrated than anything else. She saw Sandro coming towards her, rolled down the window and stuck her hand out.

'I've broken my nail on this fucking seat-belt, sweetie.' In his confusion, Sandro thought she might be serious for a moment, but as he looked at her outstretched hand he could see she was shaking violently and her upside down face was completely pale with fright. He laughed softly in response, 'C'mon, let's get you out of there.'

After a short struggle the seat belt gave up its captive who crumpled ungraciously onto the upturned roof of the car. She crawled out, cursing as she snagged her tights and almost lost her shoes amongst the assortment of debris which had fallen from the glove box and the doors.

'Is Her Highness all right?' she asked as she scrambled to her feet.

'She's fine,' Sandro nodded. 'She's just over there.'

They walked slowly back to Regan. The sound of the city's distress was louder now, sirens, voices, screams, but to their right, the snow-covered park was an oasis of silence and darkness, the fallen trees which now lined its edges formed a wall within which the chaos of the earthquake held no sway.

'I can't believe it,' Bea sniffed, holding back tears. 'We never have earthquakes here . . . well, nothing like this . . . nothing remotely like this . . . What's wrong?'

Sandro had stopped. 'She's gone,' he muttered. He turned around a few times, checking, trying to orientate himself.

'Are you sure?'

'Yeah . . . yeah she was . . . she was here.'

'Oh.' Bea didn't seem overly concerned. 'She must have wandered off somewhere.'

'Well, she can't have gone far. I was only at the car for a couple of minutes. Stay there.'

Sandro ranged around up past the perimeter of the palace where various alarms were ringing. A burst water main was shooting an elegant plume of water twenty feet in the air which sparkled beautifully amongst the devastated rubble of the palace walls. He shouted for Regan a few times but it was difficult to make himself heard against the background of increasing noise. Eventually, he returned to Bea.

'She's not th—' he stopped, staring at Bea's fixed expression and then turned to follow her gaze.

From where they stood they could follow the line of the High Street which stretched away uphill towards Edinburgh Castle – the ancient heart of the city – and now it was ablaze. Gas pipes had ruptured during the quake and the fire had caught the tightly packed buildings within minutes. And at the top of the hill, although they could not see it from their viewpoint, the biggest, brightest fire reached bright tongues of flame into the night sky; the castle was on fire. It seemed some iniquitous salamander had gripped hold of the street's cobbled spine and spread outwards through the buildings, burning as it went. The sky reflected the blaze, so that it glowed an ominous, heavy mixture of smoke and ash.

'I think we're walking home,' Bea whispered.

Regan was good at pursuit, light-footed and slim, tall and silent enough to merge with most backgrounds. She had discarded Bea's orange puffy jacket as it was not exactly camouflage type material, but regretted her action within minutes as the cold began to numb her back and shoulders.

Ahead, her prey were walking silently across the open space of the park – Sandro would miss them by a minute – they seemed frightened and subdued except for their leader, the one called Knox. Some of them appeared to be muttering some kind of incantations, their eyes downcast, lips moving almost silently. They were nearing the hill now and Regan knew this was where Sandro had lost sight of Knox when he had followed him the night before; there was no more cover at this point as the line of trees finished. She was already stooped over as most of the trees had toppled, the tangles of roots and mud on some provided almost as much cover but, in some sections, the profile was much lower than when the trees had been upright.

Knox was leading them onto the hill. Regan watched closely and, when she was sure they were all concentrating on their climb, she ran across the snow-covered ground at full pelt and then crouched behind a large boulder which had probably been shaken loose by the quake. As she tried to still her breathing she watched Knox, she could see him quite clearly from where she was. Sandro had told her about the enigmatic youth but he wasn't what she had expected; he was handsome in a poor looking way, poverty had marked his features and marred an intelligent expression but Regan knew better than to observe only the surface from harsh experience. Small white lines around his mouth and eyes, silver in the reflections of the moonlight and the snow, spoke further about bitterness and cruelty. She ducked back behind the boulder as he glanced directly towards her but in that second she saw that he wore the necklace which had caused so much trouble between herself and Tristan. The thing was cursed, she was sure. She held her breath for a few moments trying to ensure no telltale steam escaped into the air and, when she was sure he would have turned back to his task of directing his followers, she peered back.

It seemed they were gone. They had been standing in front of a solid rock wall and now they had vanished. Regan sneaked forward and ran her hands over the freezing sandstone; living in Soulis Mor for many years had completely prepared her for the idea of hidden doorways so where others may have faltered, she simply looked for the entrance. She grinned in the darkness with some self-satisfaction as her hand disappeared behind a deep crack in the rock – Sandro would never have found it.

* * *

It took them almost three hours to reach Bea's house; it seemed the quake had had a fairly small radius of around three miles but this was sufficient to devastate the city centre. Sandro and Bea staggered through the rubble, their expressions bleak. Sandro was increasingly sure he had fractured his leg and he knew if he stopped to help anyone else the pain would take over. His relatively minor injury would be the least of the problems for the city's hospitals so the best he could do would be to reach Bea's and take some painkillers.

At the corner of Lothian Road a small girl of about seven did stop him, she wasn't crying but her face bore a grim tightness, her little brown eyes like bullet holes.

'Mister. Hey, mister. I can't find my mum.' She grabbed his coat with urgent ferocity. Sandro turned back, a strange helpless anger rising in him.

'I can't . . .' he stopped. She was looking at him as if he had an answer. Bea smiled down wearily at the girl. 'Where do you live?' she asked.

'In there. Number five,' she pointed at a block of low-rise flats which had sustained some damage – the top two floors appeared to have caved in and it didn't take too much intuition to guess where number five was. Sandro crouched down in front of the girl.

'What's your name?'

'Melanie.'

'Well Melanie, this is very important. I want you to wait right here by the stair, okay?' She nodded solemnly in response. 'You see the . . . the police or the fire brigade will come in a while to check your building, I'm sure. And it's very important that you can tell them which house your mum is in, yeah?'

'Yes.'

Sandro glanced at the backdrop of the burning city centre. 'It might take quite a long time, but they will come. So you must wait, eh?'

'Here, Melanie,' Bea wrapped her cashmere coat around the girl's shoulders, 'this'll keep you warm while you wait. There might even be something nice in the pocket.'

Melanie slid her arms into the sleeves and delved into the pockets which were around the level of her knees. Sure enough, Bea had some chocolate in there.

'Thanks missus.' Without further ceremony Melanie turned and went back to sit in the doorway of the building, chewing happily.

'C'mon, Bea . . .'

'But she's only little. What if there's an aftershock?'

'We've done the best we can. Look, she's sitting in a doorway now – that's where you're supposed to go isn't it? She's eating chocolate – that will keep her sugar level up if she goes into shock . . . What can we do? We can't help everyone . . .'

She knew he was right and so they walked away. There was nothing else to do.

Colinton was relatively unscathed. The only visible damage to Bea's cottage was a large crack which ran through the brickwork, floor to ceiling. Neither of them commented on this, it was three-thirty in the morning by then, the first tinges of dawn were touching the eastern sky and both of them were just desperate to sit down. Once inside the house Sandro gave in to the pain of his leg and took some painkillers washed down by a straight shot of whisky.

'Do you want me to check you over, Sandro?' Bea asked as she slumped down on the couch beside him.

'No, no, I'll be fine,' he shook his head as he poured another whisky. 'I've had worse than this, much worse . . .'

'Yeah, you really are the most unfortunate man,' Bea managed a small ironic smile and knocked back the drink he had handed to her. She winced slightly as she felt the alcohol burn its way down her throat and into her belly. 'Do you think many people were killed, Sandro?'

He nodded wearily. 'We're not prepared for earthquakes, are we? Some of the buildings . . . well, you saw, they just disintegrated.' Closing his eyes he leaned his head back on the softness of the couch cushions. He heard Bea get up and then, after a few moments, the radio came on. Bea came back and cuddled up against him.

'. . . *massive earthquake has rocked the city. Emergency services are stretched to the limit. Anyone listening to this broadcast with cuts, sprains or even minor breakages of limbs are being asked to please stay at home at least until tomorrow lunchtime. Fire crews and ambulances are fully occupied freeing those trapped in the rubble. Priceless buildings and national treasures have been irretrievably damaged in this event but the main concern for the next few hours is the saving of lives . . .*'

Exhaustion crashed over Sandro and Bea as the instinctive realisation of warmth and security numbed their senses. Bea fumbled for the blanket which was thrown over the back of the couch and pulled it across them. Sleep was calling.

'. . . *of the British Geological Survey says there was no warning or natural indicator that this event might occur . . . not on a tectonic plate boundary . . .*'

'. . . *epicentre appears to be Arthur's Seat . . .*'

'Where's Regan?' Sandro wondered exhaustedly.

'. . . *a tiny miracle baby . . . parents will name her Hope . . .*'

He slept.

Knox no longer knew what he felt. It was that strange sensation, that splintering of his consciousness which had been happening to him for the last few days. Deep down he felt sure the amulet was to blame; the power which God channelled through it was unravelling his mind. He knew he should feel afraid, it would be reasonable to be afraid, the world, after all, was effectively ending for most people. But not the Children, they would be saved and live until the end of The Tribulation as God had promised . . . some of them were praying now, rejoicing, giving thanks, but Knox didn't feel that way either. It was as if he could only watch other people feeling things – perhaps that's what true power did after all – if so, it was a sham. He had wanted the same adoration and loyalty that Daniel had inspired, not this emptiness of emotion where only echoes of his directionless hatred could be felt.

He stared around the antechamber of the caves at the dirty, bedraggled people who were talking amongst themselves; he realised now in his unassailable numbness that they had all been like him all along – lost, abused, ex-addicts, drop-outs, rejects – they just lived their pain, showed it to other people as if it was a badge they wore. Knox despised them. But he still needed to lead them as much as they needed to be led.

'Are you ready?' he asked.

'Should we pray once more, Knox?' Esther said quietly.

'No.' He shook his head. 'The time for prayer is past because . . .' he paused as his thoughts drifted away for a moment, his mind unfocused.

'Knox?'

'. . . because God . . . Jesus . . . walks amongst us again. Come. Follow me.'

He walked into the chamber as confidently as he could. He thought he knew what to expect; he was wrong. The caves were encased in an ice-like substance which radiated a deep vermilion green, it covered the floor in a smooth slick sheet and dripped from the walls in sharp rivulets. Scoor – more than he had seen so far – were enveloped in this green ice also, frozen still in their habitual statue-like stance. It was cold; colder than outside in the snowbound city, an unnatural cold which he could almost taste. Behind him, he could hear gasps of amazement and exclamations of fear from the Children but he ignored them, walking across the icy chamber towards the altar stone, his footsteps small and measured, his heart hammering in his chest.

What now? he thought. *He promised he would come. What if he doesn't come?* He glanced behind him, just in time to see one of the Children reach out to touch the frozen Scoor.

'Don't touch! You must not touch them,' he commanded. He didn't even know why he had said it.

'He is quite correct. You will die if you touch them.'

At first, there was just the voice and the light, a blinding brightness which issued from above the altar stone. The Children clung together, clutching at one another's robes before falling to their knees. Knox stood where he was, blinking owlishly into the light, refusing to look away even though the tears were streaming down his face.

So, this is religious experience . . . Am I supposed to feel reverent or something?

There was the same quiet laughter which Knox had heard before. And then, He appeared. Jahl stood, or rather, hovered in the air above the altar stone staring imperiously down. He wore a simple white robe which clung to his body and billowed in slow-motion waves in some non-existent breeze. His long dark hair was swept back from his face and the only surprise Knox felt was the fact that God had some occult-looking symbol drawn or tattooed across the sweep of his right cheekbone. He had dark, heavy-lidded eyes which glittered in the reflected light from the green ice.

'Knox. We meet at last,' he said. Knox nodded mutely in response. 'You are correct, I often feel religious experience to be somewhat overrated.' Jahl's eyes flickered towards the cowering Children and he smiled a pale smile, 'We all know what is in our hearts, do we not . . .?' He stepped down as if stepping off a stair and stood, barefooted on the cold surface of the alter slab. 'Come here, Knox.'

Knox walked forward until he stood within arm's reach of the altar but Jahl beckoned him closer still. As he neared the stone Jahl sat down on the edge of it. Finally, they stood nose to nose. Knox's heart was still thumping in his chest, and fear, or the effects of the amulet, heightened his senses, his thoughts slowed and his whole world consisted just of God's face, that intense, beautiful, cruel . . . face.

'How can God be cruel?' The voice, Danny's voice, flitted around his brain like a persistent gnat. Danny was here . . . in him . . .*'Shut up. He'll hear you . . .'* Knox's eyes widened in surprised innocence but God seemed unaware of Danny's presence – if indeed it was real and not a product of Knox's beleaguered consciousness.

He could feel the warm touch of God's breath now, he watched the lazy ripples of God's fine black hair as it moved like a vision, like it was underwater . . .'You have done well, Knox.' God smiled.

He wanted to wake up. Be aware. Something . . . something amazing was going to happen . . .'I'm afraid.' He heard his own voice without knowing he was forming the words. *'No,'* his mind raged, *'Don't say that . . . Never say you're afraid . . . never . . .'*

'Do not be afraid, Nathan Troy.'

Then it happens. God reaches out and grabs the necklace. It shouldn't have mattered, not really. But it . . . it feels like . . . steel fingers, imbedded in his body are being snatched out of his flesh. Knox groans involuntarily. It burns.

'Peace.' God reaches out and touches his head lightly, with just one finger, and the pain vanishes immediately. Knox, not yet registering the absence of pain, almost lurches forward and crashes into God, but steadies himself at the last moment. 'What did it . . .' he gazes at the necklace draped in the long fingers of God's hand. 'It hurt me . . .'

'It doesn't matter now.'

'Yes it does.' Danny again.

God's next demand takes Knox completely off guard. 'I need a sacrifice.'

CHAPTER SIXTEEN

'W-what?' His own voice sounded so small, so weak within the chamber; a familiar sick twisting of his gut telling him his body had acknowledged what his mind already knew: he had lost control of the situation. In fact, he was stupid to imagine he ever had any.

'Gods demand sacrifice, Knox. And I need one now.' God's eyes flickered almost lazily to where the Children were standing. 'You choose.'

'No. This is not right. Tell him, Knox. Tell him!'

'I – I can't.'

God frowned but then waved his hand impatiently. 'Very well.' He snapped his fingers and two of the Scoor moved into action, their icy cocoons fading quickly. Knox heard a scuffle behind him but he didn't turn around.

'Please . . . don't. These people are your believers. There are so few . . .'

'It is necessary,' God said dismissively. He nodded towards the Scoor who were drawing level to where Knox stood, half-dragging, half-carrying someone between them. Their captive was fainting with fear but they propped her up between them as they awaited Jahl's next command. It was Esther.

'No!' Knox yelled.

But it was so quick. Undramatic really. And she

seemed so afraid she was out of her mind. One moment, alive and afraid – the next . . .

They slit her throat with grim efficiency. She made no sound although there was a tiny moment of horrific realisation before she pitched forward onto the altar stone, her limbs contorted, robbed of her dignity. Red plasma pulsed out onto the waiting slab, made brown in the green ice-light. She twitched a couple of times – not big convulsions – enough to know that Esther felt something in the seconds before she lost consciousness.

A scream split the chamber, a long drawn out, tortuous scream which seemed to come from the very pit of Knox's soul. Even when it seemed he could have little or no breath left, the sound continued, until it became a dry, cracked noise. He did not reach out for Esther but rather held onto himself, his arms wrapped around his chest, as he sank first to his knees and then curled into a foetal position on the ground. The remaining Children, shocked beyond belief, were galvanised into action and began to rush forward, perhaps with the intention of comforting their leader. With an impatient 'tut' and a wave of his hand Jahl froze their motion and that of the Scoor, so that only he and Knox were left alone with Esther's rapidly cooling corpse.

Knox was beside himself with grief and rage. It seemed that all this time of not feeling anything had conspired against him – now he felt *everything*: Esther, Daniel, his own miserable, loveless existence, the cheap emptiness of his soul – it crashed in on him in a crippling, self-pitying wave. He was unaware of what Jahl had done to the Children, he wouldn't have cared even if he had known, Knox was consumed by himself. He cried like a proverbial baby for what seemed like the longest time until his ribs hurt as if with sick laughter. Mucus and spittle trailed across his cheeks but he made no attempt to wipe them, he had given himself over; his eyes were open but he saw nothing.

'Knox. C'mon . . . C'mon Nathan.' Danny's voice, consoling his own murderer. *'He's a false prophet. It's not your fault . . . he was sent by the Deceiver himself . . .'*

Knox did not reply. Even his thoughts were silent. But he stopped weeping. His mind drifted in a comforting void but he heard Danny's voice. He heard it . . .

. . . eventually, a thought did form – 'I'm sorry' – but he didn't really know what for, and, even from within the comfort of temporary madness, even though every nerve in his body was so blasted it was unable to communicate with his mind, he only had to reach out his hand to touch the hem of Esther's grey and bloodied dress to know that such a word was obsolete.

It was far, far too late for sorry.

In Sutra, it had been over a week since Regan had left. The Council of Tema had grudgingly accepted Tristan's and Talisker's feigned innocence, especially since Eskarius assured them he had slept by their door all night. For the first couple of days neither Tristan nor Talisker did much but mope around; they didn't want to talk about Regan and both kept their thoughts to themselves. After that, Talisker saw Tris in earnest conversations with Eskarius and Markomete but didn't ask what was going on.

Talisker walked alone for miles around the shoreline of the island, looking out at the ocean towards Sutra. In the years since he had been here he'd often thought about the fact that what he thought of as 'Sutra' was in fact a country, rather than an entire world, adrift in the ocean. There must be other lands in this world and yet, he'd never before had the desire to explore them. The Fine were not great mariners, they fished the waters off the coastline but, as far as Talisker knew, they did not trade with anyone else. In a world where 'far away' was defined by how far a horse could travel in the space of a day, this was reasonable enough, but Talisker did wonder about such an ingrained lack of curiosity . . .

'Father, Father . . .' Talisker squinted into the sunlight to see Tristan hurrying up the beach towards him; the rough shingle made it difficult for him and he was panting for breath despite the freshness of the air. To make Tris's arduous journey shorter, Talisker began to walk towards his son.

'What's wrong, Tris?'

'Nothing's wrong. The Council of Tema have agreed to give me the aid of the Sidhe tribes. I thought you'd like to know.'

Talisker frowned. 'What aid? What for, Tristan?'

'It's an alliance, Father . . . you know . . .'

'But what for?' Talisker persisted. 'I thought . . . well, I thought you'd come back home with me.'

Tristan looked surprised and angered at his father's apparent lack of faith in him. He drew himself up as straight as he could stand and his reply, when it came, stung Talisker's heart.

'Regan is gone and I know it pains you as it does me, but she was never truly Thane – I am the Thane of Soulis Mor lest you forget and I will regain the throne your daughter lost me . . .'

'*My* daughter?' Talisker's tone was reproachful but not angry. 'She was your sister too, Tristan. Have we lost everything which bound us? Did our family die with Una?' As he spoke, Talisker realised he didn't seriously expect his son to answer. Regan was indefensible, and they both had had to come to terms with that idea. His grief was still directionless, unformed; his reproach of Tristan more sorrowful than anything else.

Tristan shook his head. 'Family? And what did that mean to her at the end of the day? Maybe she did set out with the intention of protecting me but she lost sight of that as soon as power and lust ruled her. There is no forgiving her, Father. When I regain my throne I will ensure she is erased from the history of the Fine for ever – no *Seanachaidh* will ever tell Regan's tale.'

'Even Corvus is accorded his history, Tristan . . .'

'It's my decision . . .' Tristan stared out to sea, his normally mild features set into bitter lines. He was taking Regan's betrayal harder since he had said goodbye but this sadness seemed to have brought a new determination to him. There would be no more tears for his sister.

'Yes,' Talisker agreed quietly, 'but first of all you must take your throne back from Jahl. How do you propose to do that with only a few Sidhe?'

'I may be a cripple, father, but I'm not stupid . . .'

'I would never—'

'The Sidhe have been watching Soulis Mor for some time. They suspect – as did Morias – that Jahl is no longer in residence there.'

'What? Who is there? Where would Jahl go?'

'We don't know. We don't know his plans. We do know that he has left someone . . . well, something, which appears to be in charge. Another thing is, the army Morias mentioned, the Southern Clans, it's pretty small, perhaps two thousand men. We think Thanes Huw and Lachlan must have sent them but again, we don't actually know . . .'

'Two thousand men,' Talisker echoed despairingly, 'that's not enough to take Soulis Mor.'

'No,' Tristan agreed, 'I know. But that's the least of my problems. If I can't intercept the army and get Huw and Lachlan to acknowledge my sovereignty, they won't even be fighting for me. If they won – by some miracle – it wouldn't be on my behalf. They probably think I'm as bad as . . .'

'. . . yeah.' Talisker sighed. 'They may even attack you, son.'

Both men were silent for a while, listening to the breakers as they crashed relentlessly on the shore. Talisker walked over to a large rock and sat down, Tris followed and they spent a few moments listlessly throwing stones into the water.

'Are you cold?' Talisker asked finally. 'The wind's getting up . . .'

Tris squinted up through the brightness of the sunlight and smiled. He chose to ignore his father's awkwardness.

'I'd very much like it if you were with me, Talisker,'

he said softly. 'The Sidhe and the Fine have great faith in you – you're a hero to them . . . and to me.'

Talisker was about to respond but Tristan continued. 'Mother told me what my real father was like, how he tried to kill me because of what I am. You and Mother – Una – you were the best parents I could have had in preparation to be a Thane. You taught me everything my own blood would have denied me. But it's not over . . .'

'No, I know. I don't think it's ever over – being a parent, I mean.' Talisker smiled wanly and tried not to think about his other children: one who was lost to him, and the other who had no idea he was his father, but was threatening the whole existence of Sutra. 'Of course I'll come with you Tris. It seems I'm responsible for this whole mess. What's the plan?'

Tris frowned, not quite understanding. 'Well, I thought we'd fly over Soulis Mor and see what's happening there . . . and then, once I've devised a stunningly brilliant plan, we'll ride to meet with the Southern Clans.'

'A stunningly brilliant plan, eh?' Talisker chuckled. 'Any ideas?'

'Nope.' Tris shrugged, laughing also because there seemed little else to do at the hopelessness of the situation. 'I'm kind of hoping it will come to me.'

'Where's old Morias when we need him, eh?'

'I think the point is, we – or rather I – have to prove I don't need him,' Tristan said. His determination was plain and Talisker could see there was little he could say to talk him out of it even if he had wanted to.

'All right, Tris. When do we leave for Soulis Mor?'

'In the morning. It's all arranged.'

'You would have gone even without me, wouldn't you?'

'If necessary, yes.'

The next morning dawned with a grey mist creeping in off the sea. Tristan was already outside when Talisker finished gathering his few belongings and went to find the waiting scout party. Tris was talking to Prince Tecumseh and another Sidhe who was dressed in identical green and brown robes as the prince.

'Ah Father, I'm glad you're here,' Tristan smiled. 'Let me introduce you, this is Prince Tenskwa, he is the brother of Prince Tecumseh and he has offered to fly you on this journey.'

Talisker bowed low. 'My thanks, Prince Tenskwa. I am greatly honoured.' The Prince returned Talisker's bow but said nothing in return.

'My brother has relinquished vocal speech, Talisker,' Tecumseh explained hurriedly least Talisker be offended. 'He is a spiritual leader amongst our people and uses only mind speech.'

Talisker tried to clear his mind for a moment. *'My thanks, Prince Tenskwa. I am greatly honoured,'* he thought. A look of almost comical amazement crossed the Prince's features and then he broke into a broad, white smile.

'What's so funny?' Tristan asked, slightly worried that he was missing something.

Tecumseh laughed, 'Your father is an amazing man, Thane Tristan. It is very rare that the Fine can understand our mind-speech.'

'Indeed,' Tristan replied slightly stiffly. 'Are we ready then?'

Both of the Sidhe Princes bowed once more and moved back from Tristan and Talisker to effect their transformation. Talisker took his chance to speak with Tristan alone.

'Are you all right, Tris?'

'Fine. Why should I be otherwise?' Tristan's demeanour was as if he and his father were departing for a picnic.

'It's just . . . I know you don't like flying. Last time—'

'This is different. If I am to reclaim my throne, I have no time for fear.'

Talisker nodded, sensing his son's words were in fact bravado. 'Fear is useful, Tris,' he cautioned. 'It heightens our senses, helps us to survive . . .'

'Or cripples us,' Tris said flatly. 'Let's go.'

The mist which had enveloped the island extended for many miles, the winter sunlight too weak to burn it away. As they passed over the coastline of the mainland Tristan could see only occasional patches of brown and green which gave way to dismal blackness over the remains of Or Coille. The mist cleared as they ranged further north and Tris could see the black outline of strange riders, hunting parties or scouts, moving south across the moorland. The eagles passed unnoticed by these figures, their height allowing them to dip in and out of cloud cover.

As they neared Soulis Mor it became noticeably colder, bitter winds lashed the eagles' feathers but the

Princes continued onward without apparent discomfort. 'Look!' Tristan yelled. He wasn't certain if Talisker heard him or not, but when he looked over to his father Talisker's grim expression confirmed he had also had first sight of Soulis Mor. Tecumseh and Tenskwa glided lower for a better view.

Soulis Mor was no longer the 'Black Guardian' of legend. The city was frozen, encased in white, shining ice so thick that tunnels had been hewn outwards from the doorways as if the ice were more bedrock. Tristan gasped in amazement and then gave way to coughing as the freezing air burned his lungs; he could see the stable yards and the brewery yards from his vantage point and the people who had been frozen in a snatched moment of time. Talisker, who had in his previous existence seen such instants of time in the shape of photographs, was less shocked by this than Tris; he was more immediately concerned by the figures that were moving below. He recognised the shapes of Scoor – from here they appeared more like giant scorpions than ever – but there were others, more outwardly human-shaped, a few on horseback. Could it be the Corrannyeid had returned to Sutra and mimicked the bodies of the unfortunate victims of Jahl's icy spell?

'Take us lower, Tenskwa, maybe we could land on the north tower.'

'It is too perilous to land, Duncan Talisker. We cannot risk the Thane. Look there . . .'

'Where?'

'In the gardens near the north wall. I will take us closer.' Tenskwa didn't wait for Talisker's assent but

began to spiral downwards. When Talisker glanced back Tecumseh and Tristan were following, flying as if on the same curve.

It was a body. But what marked it out from the other frozen forms was that this one – a young girl – had been thrown away, discarded like a piece of rubbish. It was impossible to know whether the unfortunate girl had been dead at the point she was frozen but the chaotic positions of her splayed limbs suggested that unconsciousness was the best that could be hoped for.

Talisker heard something like a howl from behind him and he twisted back to see an expression of sheer rage on Tristan's face. *'I think we should go and get her,'* he thought. *'Ask Tecumseh to stay back and keep the Thane from harm.'*

'Salkit's blessing, Duncan Talisker,' Tenskwa replied. This appeared to be agreement as, without further warning, Tenskwa banked steeply and folded back his wings. It was like falling, free fall, as smooth as silk, the speed dizzying; Talisker let out an involuntary yell of exhilaration which was left behind in the wake of the eagle. As if snatching a salmon from a river, Tenskwa gripped the frozen body in his talons and began to lift up once more with little or no pause, working the backdraught with his wings to regain speed. There was a sound from behind them, a kind of snarling roar, and Talisker glanced back to see what was coming.

'Go, go, go,' he yelled aloud to Tenskwa. There was fear in his voice and with good reason. Not Corrannyeid then, not Scoor, the creatures now attacking them were completely unknown in Sutra. They were extremely large, human in general form but with black horny-looking skins and yellow, tusk-like teeth. The word which sprang to Talisker's mind was 'troll' – except that was to ignore the speed at which they ran. Some were still running towards Tenskwa even though he had left the ground already, but others had stopped and were notching arrows into clumsy, rough-hewn bows. Talisker flung himself forward, burrowing his face in warm feathers as an arrow the size of a throwing spear whizzed past his ear. He could hear the curious rasping noise the creatures were making but the sound faded swiftly as Tenskwa rose higher and higher.

Finally, he looked up. There was silence for the moment and clear blue sky. Quite far ahead he could see Tecumseh flying south-west.

'Are you all right, Tenskwa?'

'I am uninjured, Duncan Talisker but I suspect our passenger may have been hit by an arrow.'

Talisker tried to look down but couldn't see directly beneath the eagle's body. *'She's probably dead anyway,'* he thought, *'poor girl. I don't know why we picked her up really.'*

'Tecumseh told me that she is known to Thane Tristan.'

'Oh.'

They had their backs to Soulis Mor now but were flying below cloud level. Talisker saw everything that happened next extremely clearly although he literally could not believe his eyes at first. It was the sound which made them turn back to look at Soulis Mor, a low rumbling which seemed to have its focus under the fortress city, but their attention was caught by a group of Scoor which had set out in pursuit of the eagle Sidhe. *'Do not worry, Duncan Talisker. They are unable to fly at altitude, their wings are feeble,'* Tenskwa remarked scornfully. *'The Scoor have not yet killed an adult eagle Sidhe and yet it is we Thane Regan feared the . . .'* he stopped, *'I am sor—'*

An explosion ripped through the plains in front of Soulis Mor – a blast of freezing air shot upwards with the force of a geyser and Tenskwa, caught in the updraught, was whirled around, his flight feathers damaged, Talisker clinging on for dear life as the great eagle battled for equilibrium. They were losing altitude and Tenskwa cried out in alarm knowing he would have to let go of his burden as the girl's body was hampering his struggle. He let go of her as he plummeted but Tecumseh, who had turned back to aid his brother, snatched her from the air beneath him.

On the plains below, devastation had come to Sutra as the earth first trembled and then split and distorted. From beneath the ground, huge stalagmite structures of rock and ice were thrust violently upwards, propelled by some unnatural force. Freezing air accompanied this traumatic birth; the rocks screamed and squealed and crashed. Soulis Mor itself was pulled apart as a huge fissure tore the bedrock asunder. Jagged sheets of ice burst from the ground at chaotic angles making platforms and instant miniature mountains.

Tenskwa had levelled off his flight but now he flew amongst a landscape which railed against him, sought to bar his way; his talons and underbelly were chilled to the bones and in the back of his mind he feared his death was imminent, if not by the freezing of his heart, by being stabbed as one of the massive icicle structures was thrown high into the air.

'What the hell's happening?' Talisker screamed. There was no answer from Tenskwa as he seemed to brake in mid-air as a huge sill of ice reared up before him. Talisker closed his eyes, bracing for impact but the eagle veered aside at the last moment, his left wing just brushing the ice as he went by.

'Duncan Talisker – the air – it's too thin – cannot climb – cannot fly much longer . . .'

Talisker glanced back towards Soulis Mor, it seemed there was less ground-wrenching activity going on there. *'Turn around, Tenskwa!'* he thought urgently, *'Head north, behind Soulis Mor . . .'*

'To the badlands?' It was a rhetorical question given the desperate situation; Tenskwa was failing, his wings rimed with ice. Another ice mountain erupted forth behind them and they were buffeted by a freezing back-draught which whirled the great eagle around as if he were a mere single feather. After another few heart-stopping moments Tenskwa managed to gather himself together and headed north as Talisker suggested. Below them, amongst the transforming blue whiteness of the plain, the Scoor who had attempted to follow the Sidhe Prince lay dead on the ice sheets; one unfortunate had in fact been skewered by an erupting stalagmite, its tail still twitching as it died.

As they reached the back towers of the city, the rumbling which had accompanied the strange ice-quake ceased abruptly, the sound of falling, smashing rock continued as an echo, and now, shouts could be heard from the city below as the creatures which inhabited it communicated their pain or terror. Once past the northern wall, Tenskwa and Talisker were free of the ice cloud which had accompanied the eruption and Tenskwa's wing beats grew steadily stronger, more sure. Behind the fortress the signs of devastation were less marked but there was nowhere for Tenskwa to land which was not covered in thick ice.

'Do you need to rest, Tenskwa?' Talisker queried.

'No, Duncan Talisker. I will be well. I will circle west and out to sea. My wings are recovering.'

'I hope Tecumseh and Tris are all right. I didn't see what happened to them after your brother caught the girl—'

'What is that?'

'Huh?

'Look there. Ahead and to the east . . . Do you see that thing?'

At first, Talisker couldn't see what had caught the Prince's attention; the terrain ahead was similar to that on the other side of Soulis Mor – bleak plain – which was now covered in ice. He knew it was the plain he had ridden out over with the *Fir Chrieg*, Sandro and Malky years before to confront Corvus and it gave him no pleasure to be here. It was as desolate now as it had been all those years ago. *'Let's go, Tenskwa,'* he urged.

'No,' Tenskwa insisted, *'I want to see it.'*

Ahead there *was* something. As they flew over Talisker realised the scale of the thing; it was a black disk-like object around a mile in diameter. Its surface appeared to have the consistency and look of tar – it glimmered coldly in the light that was reflecting from the ice sheets – and it was surrounded by low outcrops of rock and ice.

'What the hell is it?' Talisker muttered. Tenskwa did not reply but circled around the strange new landmark, climbing higher and higher.

'Why are we climbing?'

'I thought perhaps some scale might help, Duncan Talisker.'

Below, the rocks which clustered around the perimeter of the pool were moving slowly inwards; as they did so, something in the movement became chillingly familiar. Lines in the rocks on two opposite sides of the black pool crushed and cracked into fine fault-lines and a thin film moved across the blackness from left to right.

'Oh my God,' Talisker hissed.

It was an eye. And it was blinking.

Sandro awoke to a familiar sound, completely out of context: horse's hooves. A horse was coming up the pathway of Bea's cottage. As awareness returned, he remembered the earthquake and sat forward burying his face in his hands. How many dead, he wondered? Bea was snuggled up against him and he stood up slowly, moving her gently onto the cushions without waking her. Then, he went to the window to look out at the city.

From here, at first glance, one could almost imagine it hadn't happened. The epicentre of the quake was confined to the Old Town and the only real sign from this distance was the dismal wail of sirens, and helicopters buzzing overhead. Plumes of smoke curled lazily into a bright, winter-blue sky.

'Good morning, *Seanachaidh*.'

He turned. Regan stood in the doorway. She was holding a thin piece of rope which she had attached to the bridle of the shire horse behind her. Something had happened to her, she looked . . . different. It was strange to think that trauma such as the one which had overtaken Edinburgh could bring someone alive, but that was how it seemed with Regan. She grinned towards him and there was no mistaking the light in her eyes – Sandro had seen it too many times before battle.

'Where did you get that?' he nodded towards the horse.

Regan patted the beast's flanks with a loud slapping noise. 'Oh, I found him wandering around the back of the parkland. He was a bit confused . . . weren't you, boy? I've never seen a horse like this before. Look at his feet!'

Sandro nodded and smiled thinly. He was pretty sure it was one of the horses the brewery used to pull its old-fashioned drays – a tourist thing – but he was more interested in what had happened to Regan during the night. He folded his arms and tried his best not to sound like a nagging parent. 'Where have you been, Regan? We were worried about you.'

'There was no need. I'm fine. But Sandro . . .' the horse nudged her back. 'I'll put him in the back garden, then I'll tell you everything.' she wandered off without waiting for a response. 'We've got trouble . . .' she said over her shoulder.

Sandro stared out towards the skyline of the city – he realised now it was like a familiar smile with teeth missing – buildings which people passed every day without even knowing what they were, anonymous low-rise tower blocks, tenements that had dotted the city since Georgian times, historic but unremarked – many were simply gone, with the equally unremarked people who had inhabited them. 'No kidding,' he muttered.

Like many of Edinburgh's inhabitants this morning, Sandro felt so stunned by what had happened that his mind felt hazy and unfocussed, almost as though someone had hit him on the head with something; the feeling was not dissimilar to the worst hangover ever. He shuffled through to the kitchen to make coffee for himself and Bea but as he did so, his attention fell on his stone; it was the stone Morias had given him all those years ago to signify he was a *Seanachaidh*, a large plain pebble which fitted in the palm of his hand. When Jahl had had him tortured, it was the only thing he'd managed to keep, his weapons and jewellery had been taken, but the stone, so plain, so innocuous, had been left around his neck by his torturer who probably deemed it worthless. Sandro picked it up, caressing the smooth surface unthinkingly as he had many times – it was certainly calming. He was walking towards the kettle when his expression changed quite suddenly. A warm sensation was radiating up his arm and into his chest: it was something he was familiar with, something he had felt many times over the last twenty-five years or so, but not in this world. His stone was active. He frowned down at it. 'Not here,' he muttered, 'There are no stories here . . .'

Still, the feeling was strong within him; as he boiled the kettle – faintly surprised that there was still electricity in this part of the city – he enjoyed the sensation, which was like no other, the physical channelling of the words waiting for release, the satisfaction to come.

'Bea. Bea . . . wake up.' He put her coffee beside her on the table. 'I've got to tell you something . . .'

Bea sat up, groaning softly. 'What time is it, Sandro? Oh God, it's real isn't it? I didn't dream it or anything—'

'Wait. Listen. We can talk about the quake in a minute. I've got to tell you a tale . . .'

'A tale? A story?' Bea arched her brows and sipped her coffee. 'Sandro, it doesn't seem appropriate somehow. I want to know how everyone is . . . Cal, Stirling . . . my parents are okay, they're in Fife visiting . . .'

'Bea, listen,' Sandro crouched in front of her and took her hand. 'You know about me being a *Seanachaidh* . . .'

'Well, yeah, sweetie but—'

'It's difficult to explain, Bea, but sometimes, the words just come and demand to be spoken. It's happened now. I've got to tell you because there has to be someone to listen.'

'What now? Here, in the real world?'

'Can I listen too, *Seanachaidh*?' Regan had returned from the back garden having settled the horse in Bea's arbour.

'You're back.' Bea smiled tiredly, unable to summon

enough energy to continue the argument she and Regan had fallen out over the night before – it seemed such a long time ago now. Regan gave her a withering look but sat beside her anyway, eager to hear Sandro's tale.

'This is my tale,' Alessandro began. *'It is a tale of King Euan, first and wisest ruler of the Fine. King Euan inherited Sutra when the gods had tired of their sport and many strange and troublesome creatures were left behind in the world. Euan had no city to rule, so, with the help of his clan, he built a beautiful city amongst the lush valleys of the south. Its like had never been seen before, its walls of white marble sparkled in the daytime and, at night, thousands of torches lit up the night sky. Scattered people, artisans and farmers alike, moved into the great white city of Kirris Dira.*

'However, after ten years, King Euan's happiness was ended when one morning, a terrible noise began. It sounded like a rushing, roaring wail and it echoed through the streets of Kirris Dira and out into all of Sutra. So terrible was the sound that many people killed themselves, women who were pregnant miscarried their babies and the fabled white towers of the city began to crack and crumble.

'The sound did not stop. It continued for many months and the people who lived in Kirris Dira fled to the furthest places of the land. Finally, King Euan was left alone amongst the deserted streets of his city and, in despair, he took himself to the highest tower to throw himself to his death.

'But then came his salvation in the shape of a small white bird. It was like a sparrow whose feathers had

been painted with snow. It sat observing Euan as he tried to summon the courage to jump. "What are you staring at?" Euan demanded.

'"Ruler of none," the bird replied. Euan was so angered by this response that he reached out and snatched the bird from the sill on which it sat, intending to squeeze the life from its form. The bird became frightened and said, "Spare me, wise King and I can help you stop the sound which is destroying your city."

'"What can a small bird do?" he asked, still angry at the creature's impudence. To his amazement, the bird transformed itself into a beautiful woman. It was the goddess Brigantia. "I will help you, Euan," she said. "But first you must promise that when all the people return here, they must worship me above all others."

'King Euan readily agreed to this. "Tell me what I must do," he begged.

'"The sound you hear is caused by two dragons named Kivik and Hemmek. Kivik is a red dragon of fire and Hemmek, a white dragon of ice. They live deep underground and fight perpetually and their struggles make the seasons of the world. They are as old as time but time has brought them to just under the surface of the earth and they continue their battle beneath your city unaware that anyone can hear them. They must be caught and contained for ever . . . "

'The goddess outlined her plan: King Euan must gather together one thousand men to dig a massive pit – for the duration of their task Brigantia would make the workmen deaf least the dragons' roaring drive them away once more. Euan did as instructed and it took three years to dig the pit.

'Once the pit was ready Euan went to stand in the middle and the goddess Brigantia appeared beside him holding a silver sword. Before the watching crowd along the rim of the pit, Euan took the sword and beheaded the goddess with one mighty blow, the crowd gasped in disbelief. The blood of the goddess spilled out across the soil in a dark tide; more blood than can have possibly been contained in any human body. Euan ran from the pit – which he had been warned to do – with a tide of rich dark blood lapping at his heels. When he was safely up on the side he looked down to see that the blood had soaked the rocks beneath making them black as coal.

'Holding his arms up for silence, he spoke the words Brigantia had told him and, as promised, the dragons appeared in the pit, entangled as ever in their struggle, roiling over and over. Flame and fire flew from the red dragon and hissing, cracking ice from the white, until the pit, and all the ground around it glowed and turned to liquid forcing the watchers on the rim to retreat.

'Finally, after many days, the land fell silent once more, the pit cooled, and Euan and his men crept back to look for the dragons. There they found them, coiled for all eternity, neither burned nor frozen, but encased in shining metal. Euan knew it was time to say the final words of banishing to rid Sutra of the scourge of Kivik and Hemmek for ever. The dragons, still wrapped in their shining shroud, vanished from sight into the void between worlds as Brigantia had promised. Peace returned to Kirris Dira and so did the Fine. King Euan kept his promise to the goddess Brigantia and built a

great temple in her honour. The sound of dragons was never heard again in Sutra.'

When Sandro had finished there was a stunned silence for a moment.

'Dragons?' Regan said.

'What does it mean, Sandro?' Bea frowned. 'How can such a simple myth have anything to do with us? I'm sorry, sweetie but I can't see why it can be relevant. I don't want to offend Sutra's traditions or anything but the idea is preposterous. Perhaps they're an allegory or a metaphor for something.'

'No. It's something to do with Jahl,' Regan said. 'He's here. I've seen him.' Her features acquired a look of bitter ferocity.

'Here? How can he be here?' Sandro groaned.

'Well, you're both here,' Bea pointed out. 'Why shouldn't he be? What's the difference?'

Regan gave her a scornful look simply because Bea wasn't up to speed on the subject of Jahl. 'Well, he's partly a god – from our world – responsible for the deaths of thousands of Sidhe and Fine. He's tortured both Sandro and myself, Sandro not personally, but me . . . very personally.' She glanced down at her hands and then up through her lashes at Sandro, begging him not to tell Bea the full details. Sandro ignored her, but his next comment was not entirely what she had expected.

'He's also Talisker's son.'

'What?' Regan's whole body stiffened, 'W-what did you say?'

Sandro regretted his words instantly. 'God, I'm sorry,

Regan. I – I thought Talisker or Tris would have told you by now . . . I . . .'

'It's a lie.' She shook her head in mindless denial. 'Why would you say that, *Seanachaidh*?' With a swiftness that belied her confusion, she drew a dagger and pointed it to Sandro's neck. 'Tell me it's not true,' she snarled.

Sandro did not flinch at her reaction but rather held her gaze. 'I wish I could, Regan. Duncan was seduced by the goddess Phyrr. She is Jahl's mother.'

Regan's hand shook but she didn't withdraw the dagger, her features were contorted with anger and spite. 'You are telling me,' she said slowly, 'that that worthless, manipulative bastard is my brother. I was in love with my brother.'

'I'm sorry.' There seemed little else to say. Regan dropped the dagger to the floor and stood up suddenly. 'I want to be by myself,' she commanded.

'You can go to my room then,' Bea replied quietly. She was angered by Regan's reaction, less used to the idea of weapons than her guests. 'This is my house.'

Regan didn't reply but stalked into the room slamming the door behind her.

It was dark again when she emerged from the room. Bea and Sandro were watching the television coverage of the earthquake rescue which had replaced almost all other programmes on TV. 'This is what I think,' she announced boldly as if nothing had happened. 'He's up to something here. I know he's using that pathetic youth . . .'

Sandro and Bea sat up. 'Knox, you mean?' Sandro said.

'Yes, Knox. I followed them and saw them go in

the entrance to the caves. He brought all his followers to Jahl's lair inside the hill, and Jahl sacrificed one immediately. He needs power, magical energy, for what he's doing . . . I just don't know what that is yet. I think . . . I think whatever it is he's doing . . . it's not going to plan.'

'How do you know?'

She wrinkled her brow, trying to identify what her gut instinct was telling her. 'I saw him. He's rattled by something – when Jahl is insecure, he hides behind theatricality. Knox and his followers believe he is a god . . .'

'A god?' Bea frowned.

'They have a whole pantheon in Sutra, Bea,' Sandro explained. 'They're real as well . . . Regan, I think they're under the impression he is the Christian God – there's only one.'

'Whatever,' she waved her hand dismissively, unwilling to interrupt her train of thought.

'Is Knox alive still?'

'Yes, Jahl has killed a woman . . . I just can't see how this connects with the dragons of King Euan.'

'And the necklace thing,' Bea added. 'Don't forget that – it's got to be important if he tracked Tristan here because of it.'

'It's a spell, isn't it?' Sandro nodded to himself. 'The necklace, the location . . .'

'And he had something else in the chamber – some kind of trapped energy,' Regan added. 'I say we go back and take another look.'

'It's not possible, Regan. We've been watching the news coverage – scientists are swarming all over

Arthur's Seat, it's the epicentre of the quake,' Bea said. 'They may even find Jahl if he's not careful.'

'No, he's far inside the hill and the entrance is well concealed.'

'You found it,' Bea objected.

'Yes, but I was tracking Knox.'

'I think we'll have to wait until at least some of the initial fuss dies down,' Sandro agreed. 'Don't forget, he's got Scoor in there. We don't want other people hurt or killed.'

'No. We've got to go soon,' Regan insisted. 'We should go now in fact. We can't afford to wait. *Seanachaidh*, being back here is making you soft and witless,' she looked scornful.

'Caution is not the same as cowardice, Regan,' Sandro said evenly. Bea looked more annoyed at Regan's comment than he did.

'Don't you understand,' she stamped her foot impatiently. 'If Jahl is working on a spell, he's not going to stop because of the earthquake—' she stopped suddenly, her features paling.

'What is it?'

'He probably caused the earthquake . . .'

'Why would he—'

'The dragons. What if he's summoning them?'

'Here? Dragons here?' Sandro was aghast, 'No. Why would he . . .'

'Maybe he needs their power – or maybe it was accidental.'

'Oh God,' Sandro stood up, removing his support from Bea. 'You're right. We've got to go now. We've got to stop him—'

'Whoa. Hold on a minute.' Bea grabbed Sandro's hand. 'Regan, can we have a minute *alone please*?' Regan glowered but did as Bea asked and went back through to the bedroom.

'What's wrong, Bea?' Sandro asked.

'For starters, strange flying scorpion things I can just about cope with – I can just about believe because I've seen them – but dragons? And Sandro, assuming it's true – which I haven't got time to debate with you – what if you're injured again?' He frowned, not quite understanding. 'There's no magic here,' Bea's eyes glinted with unexpected tears. 'No Morias, no death gem. If you're hurt or killed . . .' she tried to smile, 'there's only the NHS. It's for real here.'

'I know,' he said gently. 'But that's it, Bea – why I can't pass the problem on to someone else. Telling people would open a whole can of worms. We're the only ones who can deal with it, Regan, me and . . . You're not coming, are you?'

'No. I don't know if I can face it. For the last two years, Sandro, I so wanted the magic to be real. I clung to the idea that you and Duncan escaped the fire by some amazing means because I had evidence that something strange was happening. But now . . . it's not how I imagined. This stuff, it's darker, I was naïve . . . it's too much.'

He nodded. 'I understand.' She looked faintly surprised. 'I do, Bea. But Jahl – dragon or no dragon – has got to be dealt with. I'll – I'll see you when I get back.'

'Yeah,' she was still holding his hand and she stared at it morosely. 'Yeah you will.'

* * *

It was Daniel. He could see him so clearly. It wasn't a ghostly, wraith-like form, Daniel just stood there in front of him, not smiling though – which was unusual for Danny. The really disconcerting thing was that, even when Knox opened his eyes, Daniel was *still there*, exactly the same, standing in exactly the same position. He wasn't saying anything yet and Knox was quietly glad of that but not sure why. He groaned softly and moved his head, which hurt, a lot. 'Esther?' he whispered. Then he remembered. He whimpered as if injured in some small sharp way, a cracked, broken noise.

'Knox?' Danny was speaking to him now.

'I'm so sorry, Danny. You were right,' he whispered. 'Christ came to take us up to be with him. But he was a vengeful God. Esther . . . Esther is dead . . .'

'Yeah, I know, Knox,' Daniel replied. It wasn't like before, just a voice in his head, this time he could see Daniel talking. *'But it's not God, it's not The Rapture. Remember what I told you? He is a false prophet . . .'*

Knox blinked, but the image of Daniel remained still, like the after-flare of a photo flash, imprinted on his vision. 'N-no, it's not true. See Danny, you wanted me to believe didn't you? Well, now I believe – I wish I didn't – I believe that God is here. And now, you're telling me *not* to believe?' Confusion and pain assailed him once more. 'Well, fuck you Danny. You're just a ghost now. And d'you know what? God didn't even care that I'd killed you . . .' He thought about the knife he was carrying in his back pocket, wanted to punish himself again, to show God he was sorry – his arms itched and burned with that peculiar heat beneath the skin which demanded release. 'And there is no fuckin' such thing as angels either . . . just Scoor . . . Wh-where am I?'

'They've thrown you out. With the rest of the trash.' Danny sounded angry. For a moment, his image disappeared and Knox could see as clearly as the darkness of the night sky allowed.

Daniel was right, he had been removed from the chamber along with Esther's body which lay beside him on the frozen ground in a forlorn crumpled heap. They were still inside the hill he imagined; all around him columns of tall reddish rock towered upwards towards a small vent, through which the clear silver and black of the heavens could be seen. It was cold, Knox was chilled to the bone. He sank back to his knees and absently moved Esther's hair back from her face; her blank eyes – as empty as his soul – stared back at him. Daniel reappeared.

'Don't hold back, Danny. Just say what you think,' Knox snarled sarcastically.

'What I meant was, Jahl thought you and Esther were both dead.'

'I might as well be. Yeah, in fact I'm . . .'

'What about the Children?' Daniel frowned. *'You can't just leave them in there.'*

'Yes I can. They got themselves into this mess.'

'By believing in you.'

'Crap. They're not children. They're . . .' Knox stared down at Esther's prostrate form. For the moment, he imagined he could still smell the faint aroma of apple from her hair. His voice trailed off '. . . adults.'

'Nathan,' Daniel sounded weary somehow. *'He's not God. But that doesn't mean he's not powerful. Something is happening here. It could still be the time of the Tribulation . . .'*

'Yeah,' Knox had found the knife in his back pocket. It glinted silver, a welcome clarity in the strangeness of the night. He touched it to his forearm, its coldness above the itching of his skin like a poisoned salve. Cutting would be release of a kind and he didn't stop to question his instinct but slashed across the arm – lightly at first – in criss-cross patterns. It never hurt when he was like this. The blood was black liquid in the moonlit silver and blue of the cave. Knox found himself laughing.

'Nathan? What the fuck are you doing?' Daniel's face was incredulous, it had never occurred to him that Knox, admittedly capable of murder, was also teetering on the brink of insanity. *'Stop it. Stop it now!'*

Knox just laughed more. The cuts were deeper now. Inside, the tiny rational voice of his consciousness told him that these would be the ones which would really hurt tomorrow. Unless he made the final cut of course, then there would be no tomorrow anyway . . .

He could still see Daniel although his eyes were half-closed during this ritual mutilation; Daniel managed to be visible wherever he looked. It was funny that the ghost of a man he had murdered could be so horrified at Nathan cutting himself. Danny was still angry though. He came closer and tried to shake him or slap him but of course couldn't touch him physically – or so Knox thought. He was screaming something about selfishness – about how killing himself would be typically selfish of the loveless son-of-a-bitch Knox was. It just seemed sickly funny.

Suddenly, it appeared as if Daniel had found a way through, a coldness grabbed hold of Knox which jerked him into alertness; immediate sobriety. The coldness chilled the blood and saliva on his face and he knew within an instant what a witless slavering animal he had become. Shame washed over him in an equally frozen wave.

'Leave me alone, Danny,' he gasped. 'Leave me alone. I deserve to die, don't I? I'm just a waste. Look at what happens to people who love me . . .' He gestured to Esther's body. But Daniel was suddenly nowhere to be seen – it didn't occur to Knox to wonder why he had disappeared physically – but his presence was still there. And his voice, which seemed to be all around, was cold and hateful – something which made Knox's embittered heart unexpectedly sore.

'You stupid, stupid bastard. No, you don't deserve to die. It would be too easy. You'll die when I'm good and ready to let you. Get up.'

'What?'

'GET UP!'

He stood up on legs which felt like matchwood. He was quaking with cold and terror.

'You've got to get them out, Knox. D'you hear me? You can't let them be killed like Esther. It's your responsibility . . .' There was a slight pause during which Knox gave a strangled sob. *'. . . and mine. I led them to this almost as much as you. Get them out. Then you can die. I'll even help you, you sad fuck.'*

There was silence for a moment as Knox considered

Daniel's admission. Wild hope flared within the bleakness of his soul. 'And will you be . . . will you be with me, Danny?'

'Does it matter?'

'Yes.'

'Very well. And Knox . . . God will be with you also.'

'I don't care about God anymore . . . Let's go and get them, shall we?'

'Not yet, Knox. There's something you should know before you go back in there.'

'Oh?' Knox was expecting some kind of answer but instead, he was picked up bodily by some invisible force. 'What the . . .?' he gasped.

'Close your eyes for a moment.' He did as he was told and felt himself transported smoothly and coldly, higher and higher through the air. But something else was happening to him also, something was sloughing off him, something like light or fire. *Maybe I'm dying,* he thought, *maybe he's has taken pity and has let me go. He* is *an angel . . .*

'Open them now,' Daniel ordered. He did so.

'Oh my G—'

Below lay the shattered city. Beautiful in its pain. Fires still flared into the night sky and burned through the old buildings, connected like some bright string of diamonds. Snow had already covered some of the rubble as if some beneficent hand had sought to cover the hurt. Lights twinkled with an air of desperation and, because of their colour, even from this height, Knox knew them to be fire engines and ambulances. But none of this was the cause of his amazement.

It seemed he could see other things now. Things

which could not be physically present but were there nonetheless. Overlying the city, spreading out into the distance, brilliant lights travelled, as the souls of the dead, unwilling to leave, circled through the air, dancing and moving in a breathtaking ballet. It should have been a beautiful sight, but beneath the lights, further down, perhaps amongst the earth itself, Knox could see that the city was in far deeper trouble than it knew.

It was a massive beast. The beast of Revelations – he felt his heart lurch as he thought this – and it was wrapped around the centre of the city in an avaricious coil as though Edinburgh was a treasure. Red and scaly, reptilian, its eyes like black pits of iniquity, tongues of flame moved along its length, lighting its scales with gleeful fire.

'It's . . . it's . . .'

'Yes,' Daniel said. *'It's a dragon. Now do you see, Knox? It's not just about the Children anymore.'*

CHAPTER SEVENTEEN

The girl lay in a deep cold sleep for three days. Tristan was beside himself with grief, only able to assume the worst. The Sidhe shamans surrounded her bed, chanting softly, a low resonating sound which made Talisker's head ache within minutes of being in the room. The air was filled with the smoke of burning herbs.

'Who is she, son?' he asked Tristan when they first arrived back at Lys.

Tristan smiled bitterly, 'Just a serving girl, father. Someone unimportant you might say.' He began to walk away but Talisker grabbed hold of his arm.

'No, I wouldn't say, Tris. Why are you angry with me? I didn't do this to her.'

'I'm sorry, father,' Tris glanced around slightly nervously and lowered his voice. 'To be honest, I feel completely useless. She – she's special to me . . .'

'A lover?'

'Yes. Jahl – or Regan – have tortured her. Her tongue has been removed and she has scars and broken bones. It must have been a while ago because the scarring is already well advanced – the bones have knitted badly in her right leg. If she survives, she will have a limp at best.' He shook his head, 'We will make a fine couple, will we not?'

'I'm sure you will, son,' Talisker chose to ignore

Tristan's sarcasm but his anger was not so easily dismissed.

'I wish Ree was still here,' he hissed. His fingers tightened around the hilt of his sword.

'Thane Tristan,' Prince Tecumseh came over, 'your friend is waking up. It seems her spirit is strong but there is much healing still to do and . . .' Tristan rushed off without a word. '. . . and she cannot speak,' Tecumseh muttered. He smiled in the direction of Tris's departing back, though.

'Will she survive, Tecumseh?' Talisker asked.

'Yes, Duncan Talisker. But only as long as the rest of us.'

'What do you mean?'

'The beast. I believe the Fine would name it a dragon . . . the Sidhe have been attempting to make contact with its mind,' he gestured up towards the highest pinnacle of the hill where the red rocks split into columns which reached for the heavens; amongst them, white smoke curled and drifted in the cold air. 'The shamans have up there for two days now . . .'

'I didn't realise what they were doing,' Talisker muttered.

'. . . but they have gained little insight. The beast is trapped between worlds. Someone, probably Jahl we imagine, has made a spell which is transforming the creature's existence in the void to a physical existence. We cannot kill it. But it continues to grow in strength and stature. In time it will shrug off the confines of the earth and its emergence will wreak havoc in Sutra.' Talisker nodded, remembering the size of the creature's eye. 'All we have gained is a knowledge of its name

– Hemmek. It is a creature of extreme coldness – even if the clans of the Fine are able to survive its rebirth, Sutra will become a devastated land of ice. Few will survive such a transition.'

'How long do we have before this happens, Tecumseh?'

The Prince shrugged wearily, 'The shamans cannot say. At the moment the balance of the creature's spirit is equally split, but once it is largely here . . . none can tell when that will be.'

Talisker frowned. 'The southern army are riding straight towards it. They must be warned.'

'Indeed. But that is the province of Thane Tristan and it would seem he is rather preoccupied.'

'I will speak to him,' Talisker promised. He glanced towards the entrance to the caves where Tristan had gone to see his injured maid. 'But ten minutes won't hurt.'

Tristan stared down morosely at Grace's sleeping face. Everyone else had bowed out of the room when he entered, leaving Grace and him alone. When she fully awoke, he would be the first person she saw and Tristan wasn't too sure how she might feel about that; he had deserted her after all – deserted the kingdom – unaware of just how vicious his sister would become. If only he'd stayed, he could have made a difference, not only to Grace but all the people of his clan, most of whom were still entombed in Soulis Mor, their souls trapped in limbo. Could they still see out, he wondered? Were they watching the decimation of their city? He had reached out to move Grace's hair from her face but a bitter surge of anger coursed through him and his questing fingers curled into a tight, impotent fist. He would reclaim his throne – he was sure of that now, not in any conscious way, just as sure as he knew he was breathing, but Regan, and now Jahl, were apparently gone from Soulis Mor. He suspected that revenge was by its very nature personal, and he was to be denied such satisfaction – he could only hope his anger might be quenched by fighting a battle and that his people would forgive him his abandonment . . .

She was waking up. Her pale skin was almost translucent over her eyelids, tiny veins pulsed around her temples as her blue eyes fluttered open.

'Grace?'

She gasped and then turned her face into her pillow as if to hide. In fact, her face was unmarked except for a thin line beneath her bottom lip which extended outwards across her chin. Tristan suspected that this was where some leather strap had been used to keep her mouth open . . . he felt tears prickle behind his eyes. 'It's all right, Grace,' he soothed. 'You're safe now. No one will ever hurt you again – I promise . . .' He saw the haunting images of his frozen people, their days and nights stolen from them. '. . . any of you,' he muttered. 'No one will hurt any of my clan again.'

He smiled down at her and she flung her arms around him, her warm breath raising the hairs on the back of his neck. For a few moments, it mattered little that Grace was unable to talk – words were unnecessary.

* * *

Talisker awoke suddenly, his first impulse to speak stifled by a hand across his mouth. Gazing up wide-eyed into the darkness he could see little but a smudged outline of his assailant but he recognised something in the sharp profile and delicate bearing. When the hand was removed from his mouth, its long forefinger pressed to lips in a gesture instantly recognisable.

'Eskarius?' Talisker whispered, 'Is that you?' Eskarius did not reply but signalled to Talisker to come outside. Talisker glanced back to where Tristan lay sleeping but Eskarius shook his head in warning not to wake him.

'What's going on, Eskarius?' he asked in a low voice once he was outside. The night was freezing, an ominous chill was blowing in on the east wind from Sutra. In the dim light of flaring torches three other Sidhe were standing waiting and Talisker realised with surprise, that they were also wolf clan like Eskarius. It occurred to him how few he had seen in comparison with the other clans. These Sidhe wore similar robes to Eskarius – mid-length grey robes mingled with black and white feathers, soft grey breeches and cloaks or wraps made of animal skin. They stood silently waiting but there was nothing furtive in their bearing, they had the casual self-assurance of their totem animals, predators at the top of the food chain. Talisker felt his instinctive mistrust of the wolf clan come to the fore but quelled it; Eskarius had given him no reason to mistrust him – yet.

'You must come with us, Duncan Talisker.' Eskarius spoke quietly and glanced towards his companions.

'Well, that depends . . .'

'On what?'

'Whether you are asking me, or telling me, Eskarius Vermesh.' Unnoticed by Eskarius, Talisker had grabbed his sword as he had gathered his plaid about him and his hand crept towards the hilt of it now, suspicion rising.

'Please,' Eskarius begged. 'I give you my word we will explain everything. There is no treason afoot if that is your concern . . .'

Talisker nodded shortly but his expression made his feelings plain; if anything were to happen to Tristan, there would be trouble and Eskarius would be its first victim. 'Very well,' he said gravely. 'Where are we going?' In reply, Eskarius pointed upwards and Talisker glanced behind him to where he pointed – the top of the hill, where the shamans had been working – the pinnacle towers were shining luridly red against the night sky.

The climb took longer than he expected, the distance was deceptive from beneath, and although the pathways were easy, Talisker imagined the air was beginning to thin before they reached their destination. Eskarius's companions had said nothing to Talisker, simply bowed solemnly before transforming to their wolf form for the climb. Eskarius remained in his human form and Talisker was somehow glad not to be the only human amongst the small pack.

'Have the shamans made contact with the creature, Eskarius?' he asked, breathlessly. 'I don't understand why they want me. I should be sleeping – Tris and I go to meet with the southern army tomorrow . . .'

'It is better that he go without you,' Eskarius replied quietly. Talisker stopped, grabbing Eskarius's arm. 'Wait a minute, Eskarius, how long will this take? I promised Tris I'd ride to meet Huw and Lachlan with him.'

'I don't know how long it will take, Duncan Talisker, but it is likely that Tristan must go without you . . .' Talisker turned around to walk back down the pathway. 'No wait,' Eskarius said. 'This is of utmost importance.'

'So is my going with Tristan. I cannot let him down, Eskarius Vermesh. I am his father, surely you understand?' Ahead of them, the grey shadow of the wolves had stopped and they sat observing Talisker's and Eskarius's urgent conversation, eyes glowing with dark impatience.

'Yes, I understand,' Eskarius nodded.' And I too would be proud to ride out with my father in any battle. But know this, Duncan Talisker, as the son of a father whose name is as legend in our clan, I have struggled to be myself, to be a warrior and a Sidhe in my own right. I would have people know me – even if they curse my name – as myself. You are such a legend as my father was, you may think that your show of allegiance will make Tristan stronger in their eyes but that may not be so.'

'But it's different for Tris . . . he is . . .'

'Weak? A cripple? It seems to me your natural instinct to protect him has led Sutra here. If Regan had not claimed the throne with him . . .' Eskarius shrugged, aware that his words stung Talisker but unwilling to stop and let him walk away. 'I have watched him,

Duncan Talisker, he can be strong if he is given the chance – not his body no, but,' he tapped his temple, 'he is greatly intelligent – wise for his years . . .'

'That is not something which can be seen, Eskarius. Huw and Lachlan, they judged him on sight years ago, not to mention they think he ran away in the face of Jahl's and Regan's genocide. He needs his allies . . .'

'Yes, he does. And he will have them. In the morning, a guard of almost one hundred eagle Sidhe will form to fly with him. On their backs will be all the Sidhe tribal leaders, Markomete and Tsali amongst them. Such a sight – unity of the Sidhe tribes behind one Thane – has never been seen before. I think he'll manage to impress, don't you?'

Talisker grinned in the darkness and Eskarius smiled back. 'So, you're saying he doesn't need me there?'

'No,' Eskarius patted his shoulder, 'That does not mean he will not want you beside him. But for the moment, Duncan Talisker, you must consider yourself an honorary wolf Sidhe.' Talisker began to walk slowly back up the hillside, his expression still wrapt in thought. 'The wolves are not going,' he frowned.

'No, we have other business.'

At the top of the hillside, more wolves were gathered. A wolf Sidhe was around the size of a pony and Talisker shuddered as he was unexpectedly reminded of the battle for Ruannoch Were years earlier, when the Corannyeid had appeared in the guise of massive dogs. The towers of red stone, which had seemed much smaller from below, encircled a large plateau and the wolf clan Sidhe had made this their enclave. The shadows cast by the tower rocks were thrown inward, knitting together into a shared darkness like the interlaced fingers of an angry fist. Fires flared between each tower and banners snapped in the breeze on thin canes. In the very centre of the space a lodge had been erected which had a surprising air of permanence about it for what Talisker understood to be a temporary camp – there were only small tents and lean-tos dotted around the perimeter, easily recognisable as travelling quarters for the warriors.

Eskarius seemed to sense Talisker's scrutiny. 'Wolf clan Sidhe have no long term lodges, Duncan Talisker. We travel freely.'

Talisker nodded a response but said nothing. There was a deep quietness in the encampment, punctuated only by the wind whistling between the rocks and the low heat-sound of the fires. Snatches of voices seemed to carry with these sounds but they were indistinct, might have been the ocean . . .

Eskarius was leading Talisker towards the lodge and, as they walked, others of the wolf clan filed in to walk silently behind them. He could hear the quiet jangling of their necklets or the snapping of leather fringes but no one said anything to him. It reminded Talisker of a game he used to play when he was at school – '*What's the time Mr Wolf?*' – he almost laughed aloud but swallowed the impulse recognising it as his nerves conspiring against him.

Just as they reached the lodge, the door covering was pulled aside and a tall, stately-looking man stepped out. He carried a long decorated staff which was topped by a gemstone, the sight of which made Talisker's stomach turn over – could it be *Braznnair*? When he spoke, the stranger's low voice had the quality of woodsmoke and leather. 'Welcome Tal-ees-ker,' he said. 'World-walker, we, who walk alone for ever, have much to tell you.'

Hamish was an axe-man as was his father before him. He walked into battle on his own two feet and had learned from a young age that the axe-men were the noblest of warriors, marked by their integrity and fierce pride. But the warriors of the southern Fine had never travelled this far north before and, walking across moorland and down rocky gorges following narrow sheep trails, Hamish reflected sourly that never had a noble axe-man spent so much time looking at a horse's rear. Since the weather had closed in around the column of men no one spoke much, each concentrating on the effort of will required to fight off the snow and a gripping cold that none of them had ever experienced before.

At first, they thought it was just what the weather was like in the north – it was after all famous for being bleak and godsforsaken – it wasn't until they came to Or Coille, or what was left of it, that the warriors began to get nervous. Thane Huw called his column to a halt and they stopped disconsolately, some sitting down immediately, the riders getting off their horses and doing all the fussing around that Hamish could never be bothered with. He sat down on a nearby log and took some dried beef from his purse, nodding slightly smugly at the horseman as he tore a strip off.

'Ho there, young Hamish, doing what you do best I see?' Dairmud came over, grinning his toothless grin. Hamish scowled in response – Dairmud was all right in his way, but he had the sneaking suspicion that his father had asked the old veteran to keep an eye on him. As if he needed the old fool . . .'We makin' camp Da?' he asked.

'Dunno,' Dairmud hawked and spat into the bushes. 'Hope so. Stomach thinks my throat's been cut. Thought we weren't goin' to stop till we reached Or Coille though . . . shelter from the snow an' all . . .' he scratched his head as if this thought was deeply taxing. The horseman, who Hamish didn't know, turned around swiftly as he heard Dairmud's words.

'Keep your voice down, will you.'

'Why? Whassup?'

'This *is* Or Coille . . .'

'Get away,' Hamish frowned. 'Or Coille is the biggest forest in Sutra.'

'Aye. And now it's the biggest charcoal heap.'

Hamish and Dairmud cursed in unison, Dairmud spitting again to emphasise his feelings. 'But why wid they do sic a thing?' Hamish wondered aloud. 'It's their ain self they're burnin'.'

'Some folk dinny need a reason,' Da said softly. They stared around at the empty scene.

Snow had covered the blackness of the fires, softening the brutal reality of the razing of the forest. But now the warriors knew, they could see that the skeletal shapes of the trees which dotted the landscape were just that; skeletons, burned black, their worst ravages hidden by the snow. Underlying the cold sting of the air was the faint, but unmistakable smell of burned wood. Where the ground had been churned by feet and hooves, black tarry earth was revealed. Every now and then as if in defiance, a tall tree had survived the burning, but they were few.

Thane Huw's second-in-command rode back down the line, his face grim, reflecting the mood of the warriors. 'Aye,' he kept repeating, 'this is Or Coille. We ride on in ten minutes . . .'

Hamish was about to get up again when a searing pain shot up his left leg and he fell back. 'Cramp?' Da frowned.

'Nah . . . eiya it hurts.' Hamish's feet had been really cold a couple of hours ago but he had thought they were getting better as the pain seemed to have gone away. Now, he realised that in fact his feet simply had no feeling left in them. He cursed aloud in pain and confusion. An axe-man unable to walk may as well be dead – cursed by Bann himself.

'Let's see yer feet then,' Da frowned. He knelt down and gently removed Hamish's boot, hissing through his teeth at what he saw. 'No, don't look,' he cautioned as Hamish strained to sit forward, 'it's like to upset ye lad.'

Hamish's feet were black and swollen, the skin the texture of tanned leather. Up and down the line of resting men warriors were realising they were suffering the same plight and cries of dismay and bewilderment could be heard. Thane Huw himself came riding down to see what all the fuss was about. 'Ye gods,' he muttered when he saw Hamish's injuries. 'What is it?'

'I don't know, Sir,' his second replied darkly. 'Some sickness of the snow. Some of the other men have the beginnings of it in their fingers but the walkers have it the worst. Perhaps Thane Tristan's clansmen will know.'

'They're hardly in a position to tell us,' Huw snapped. He scowled fiercely ahead to the north. 'The very ground is cursed. Thane Tristan will answer for bringing this blight on the land. Get these men up on horseback – wrap their feet with . . .' he waved vaguely, '. . . something warm.'

'Aye Sir.'

The Thane had turned to ride away, probably to go back and speak with Thane Lachlan who was still at the head of the riders, when the cataclysm happened.

It was the ice-quake. The same moment which was overtaking Talisker and Tenskwa fifty or so miles further north-west. But here, at the furthest reaches of its range, the destruction came in quite a different way: there was a loud hissing, searing sound as an invisible front of cold blasted across the landscape – an ice storm so severe that almost a quarter of the southern army fell dead instantly, frozen to the very marrow of their bones with no time to even cry out. The ground heaved and reared as at Soulis Mor but no ice formations erupted forth, only geysers of frozen air which were bad enough. The dead and the living were thrown together, horses' hooves flailing wildly as the horses screamed in terror. For two minutes, the world was a tumbling, shrieking terror and when it was over, the silence was absolute.

'Something's wrong. Something's wrong with the city.' Regan gazed around her from the shire horse she rode which was progressing doggedly through the dark streets. 'Do you feel it, *Seanachaidh*?'

Sandro, who was sitting behind her on the creature's broad back, almost snorted derisively. He waved his hand around in a sweeping gesture, 'You mean apart from the obvious?'

'Yes. It's something else . . . It feels like . . .' she shivered involuntarily. 'I can't explain, there's something . . . here.'

'Jahl?'

'No. It's whatever he's doing with his spell. This world is very resistant to magics, isn't it?'

'We don't see much of it as a rule, no.'

They carried on silently for a while, the great horse's hooves – although muffled by the snow – making a deceptively gentle clip-clopping sound on the pavement. The horse had proved useful, enabling them to skirt around where streets were blocked and the car would have been useless. But it was slow – Regan had managed to get it into a reluctant trot a couple of times but it soon lapsed back into its stride. Sandro had advised a somewhat circular route to Arthur's Seat, looping around via the outskirts of the city centre where the damage was less. In these residential streets, curtains occasionally twitched as people looked out to confirm they weren't imagining the sound of a horse but there were very few people around. It seemed reasonable to think that most people in the city were shattered by the events of the night before and those who had come through the destruction unscathed were sleeping things off as the shock eased and exhaustion took over.

'I'm going to kill him, you know.' Sandro's train of thought was interrupted.

'Pardon?'

'Jahl. He's got to die and I'm going to do it.'

'Regan, we can't just go rushing in there . . .'

'Oh yes, I can. I've got a weapon now . . .' she lifted something up and the sharp glint of silver was caught in the moonlight. Sandro frowned, he knew the Sidhe had sent her through to Edinburgh with no weapons.

'Where did you get that, Ree? It doesn't look . . .'

'Found it.'

'Like the horse you mean?'

'Hmm.'

'I don't think it's real, Regan. Did you find it in the High Street by any chance?'

'Maybe.'

'It's a replica. People have them to put on the wall for decoration.' He could see the inscription now, it said 'Excalibur' along the top of the blade.

'Doesn't matter,' Regan replied sullenly. 'It'll do the job.'

'No,' he sighed, 'That's the problem. It won't, it's only tin or something. You may as well hit him with a stick.' She cursed angrily but didn't throw the tourist sword away as he'd hoped. 'Look, I'll probably regret this . . . but take this.' He handed her a pistol, the heavy iron glinting dully in comparison to the bright idyll of Excalibur. 'I'll show you how it works when we get there.'

He could see the dark outline of Salisbury Crags now. Soon Regan and he could confront their torturer – he felt his mouth go dry – and Regan was right, they would have to kill Jahl. What had he expected, he wondered? Did he seriously think they could arrest a deviant demi-god?

'Look, *Seanachaidh*,' Regan pointed towards the crags. Ghostly shapes of bizarre-looking creatures were materialising from the side of the hill, blinking into bright, luminescent existence and then vanishing within seconds. They were large and their shapes seemed to flicker and change even for the brief moment they could be seen. 'What do you think it is?'

'My guess is some kind of magical discharge.' Sandro frowned, 'Jahl's in trouble. I guess he's out of his depth.'

Regan urged the horse forward again although both of their gazes were transfixed by the silent spectacle on the cliffs. 'Your world doesn't want either of us, *Seanachaidh*,' she muttered. 'It's resisting him.'

Jahl knows the spell is not working as he planned. He isn't too perturbed by this however, he has enough souls left to drain to complete the spell. Glancing over at the immobilised figures of the Children of the Deluge he decides to wait, to save the remaining eight until the last moments, when the intensity of the magics will require kindling like any fire. He turns to the altar stone; on the shelf, now covered in the lifeblood of three victims, lies the branch which contains the spirit of the goddess Phyrr, it is pulsing and glowing with a frantic air. Jahl removes the necklace which brought him to this strange place and stares at it for a few moments. Now, his suspicions that it contains the fingerbone of Corvus, his uncle, will be confirmed or, the spell will fail spectacularly . . .

As the amulet draws near to the branch, light flares from it which envelops the delicate tracery. The pulsing stops for long moments. Jahl's lips curl back in a sneer. 'Yes, Mother. Can you see him? Your brother, your twin . . . only this tiny remnant remains, but chaos will not be denied.' He puts the necklace beside the branch; moving purposefully he traces symbols in the blood, visible only for seconds before the blood, still warm, closes around their shapes.

Abruptly, the lights from the amulet and the branch combine, shooting upwards towards the roof of the chamber and then trailing down like a spent firework. Jahl's eyes are dazzled for a moment but then he sees that the lights have indeed done their job – that the souls of Corvus and Phyrr are not wasted. Hovering in the air above the altar is the shape of a naked man, still transparent, shifting and shimmering uncertainly. The man looks like Jahl and then some, in much the same way a lion can be said to look like a cat. He is bronzed and muscular but that is the least of his magnificence, something in his bearing marks him out – he is more than a man. He is, or will be, a god. For the moment, however, he is an empty husk because the essential ingredient is lacking: Jahl.

'Hmm, bigger in all respects, I see.' The amused voice rings around the chamber and Jahl, who has been staring in awe at his handiwork spins around, a hiss of fear and annoyance escaping him. When he sees her standing by the entry, smiling a deliciously feral smile, he fleetingly thinks that she has changed – that she has become worthy of him. He shakes his head in disbelief, momentarily lost for words.

'. . . *Regan*?'

Outside, on the hillside at the base of the crags, Sandro came back to awareness with a curse. It wasn't the first time in his life he'd been pistol-whipped but it couldn't have come as more of a shock. His lip was bleeding and he spat into the snow with slightly more vehemence than necessary. Regan was trouble whatever world she was in he reflected sourly. He could understand her need for vengeance – it was reasonable that her unfinished business with Jahl must seem the only thing in this world that was relevant to her – but, as was her curse, once again she failed to see the bigger picture. His world, his city, was endangered by Jahl and whatever he was unleashing but all that was just peripheral to Regan – with her, everything was personal. And, in her infinite wisdom Regan had decided Sandro could only slow her down or perhaps, somehow limit the viciousness of her revenge. Hitting him with the gun he'd just given her was adding insult to injury though.

Still cursing and dabbing at his lip with his sleeve he began to edge his way slowly along the path, which wasn't easy – away from the city the darkness of the hillside was almost absolute. He didn't know the exact location of the entrance to the caves but he hoped that in her eagerness Regan had been careless about covering her tracks. After a few minutes though, it was obvious to Sandro that it was far too dark to find anything. He sat down, leaning his back against the rocks and staring out across the park. It was then he noticed how bright the park was outside the ring of shadow around the base of the hill – the reason for this was people. People were sleeping in the parkland, afraid of aftershocks; a tented village had sprung up, its lights, from hundreds of candles and lanterns, shining defiantly in the darkness. Snatches of sound, music and dogs drifted in towards the crags. In true Blitz spirit people were singing stupid campfire songs – despite himself Sandro grinned fleetingly into the darkness. Perhaps someone would lend him a torch . . .

'Sandro . . .'; someone was coming up to the hill – they had a torch with them which they were waving back and forth to see where they were walking. Sandro's gut reaction was to hide behind a bush or something, he didn't need the complication of other people, but as he glanced again at the figure, there was something about it he recognised – it was a woman and she walked with a long, elegant stride.

'Bea? Bea, over here.' He started towards her and she quickened her pace, they met on the footpath just at the corner where the crags began their incline into the earth. 'What are you doing here? How did you get here?'

She ignored him. 'What the hell happened to your face? Where's Regan – did that poisonous little cow do this to you?' She took out a tissue and made to dab his face but Sandro grabbed her wrist. 'I'm fine. Calm down, Bea.'

She nodded and slipped her hand through his. 'C'mon, we can look together.'

'I thought you'd bowed out of this.'

'So did I, but I couldn't let you have all the fun could I? Look at all these people. It's amazing . . .' He opened his mouth to respond but then changed his mind. They walked on around the base of the hill for a while but there was nothing to indicate that Regan had been there. Bea lit a cigarette as she walked and puffed away at it, leaving great clouds of smoke and steam behind her.

'It's you. You're the dragon,' Sandro joked. She gave him a sour look, knowing he didn't approve of her smoking and was about to make a cutting remark when a low rumbling sound began which seemed to emanate from under the hillside.

'Aftershock!' Sandro didn't hesitate; grabbing hold of Bea, he ran away from the base of the crags just as the ground began to shake once more. There was a loud cracking noise as parts of the rock-face began to break away, the rocks slipping and cracking against one another. As they ran, they were aware of debris falling behind them. Bea screamed as a large boulder shot past them, bouncing and spinning as if someone had skimmed it across the surface of a lake. Sandro could feel his legs pumping hard, frantic heat rushing through his muscles and veins. When he fell, tripping over a rock concealed by the snow, he let out a yelp of surprise and pulled Bea down with him, instinctively shielding her body with his. The ground continued to heave for long moments and then stopped abruptly. Sandro looked up cautiously as Bea rolled over groaning and complaining. They had run as far as the nearest campers – a family of around eight people – who were either hysterical or immobilised with fear. Everyone sat where they had rolled or fallen, personal space made redundant in shock. Sandro jogged Bea's arm to shut her up and pointed wordlessly back at the hillside.

'What the hell is it?' She was still breathing hard, winded from their escape.

'Magic, Bea. It's what you couldn't resist coming to see right?' The animal spirit-shapes were back; rolling down the cliffside in a green silent wave before disappearing back into the earth.

Bea drew in a long, ragged breath. 'Yeah. So can we go home now?'

Sandro stood up and was brushing as much of the snow off his clothes as he could. 'We've got to find Regan,' he said. 'She needs our help.'

'No. I don't think she does,' Bea frowned.

'What? You're kidding right?'

'No.' Bea's hair had come undone as she fell and she tossed it back over her shoulder in a slightly petulant movement. 'Look, I'm not just saying this because I don't like her – which I'm not denying by the way – but think about it, Sandro. Maybe she's right. Maybe it's her problem to deal with in a kind of "bad karma" sense. Her and this Jahl – they have issues to deal with right?'

'Yes but—'

'They're both from Sutra and better equipped to deal with some kind of . . . magical duel . . .' she waved her hand vaguely as she stood up.

'Right. So we just go home and wait for them to sort it out, do we?' Sandro frowned at her.

'That's what people do in the real world, Sandro.'

'Need I remind you, that Regan is Duncan's daughter? Sending her here was the only way of saving her life. Do we just let her die? C'mon, Bea . . . Are you afraid? Is that it? Because it's okay to be afraid and—'

'Arrgh!' Bea had started to stand up but almost collapsed back onto the ground clutching at Sandro's jacket her face twisting in pain. 'I don't think I can go anywhere, Sandro. I think I might have broken my ankle.'

'Have you hurt yourself, dear?' An elderly lady, the matriarch of the big family was gathering people together in a group again so that she could help them. Bea smiled through gritted teeth.

'I'm fine . . . really . . .'

'Nonsense. Come on. That lady over there is a St John Ambulance officer.'

'You should go,' Sandro nodded. 'Just keep an eye out for me, eh?' He squeezed her hand.

'I'll be okay for a while. You go and find madam – bring her back so she and I can fight a bit more, eh? I'll watch the pretty lights . . .' she nodded towards the silent show on the crags.

'All right. I won't be more than an hour.' He kissed her on the cheek and left, wondering what she'd do if he never came back at all. There was no one she could tell – as far as Edinburgh was concerned, Alessandro Chaplin was already dead. He stuck his hand deep in his pocket and groaned aloud as his fingers closed around something cold and square; it was the ammunition clip for his pistol.

* * *

'Surprised?' Regan was enjoying Jahl's horrified expression immensely. She waved the pistol towards him in a threatening manner – she had seen someone doing it in a similar fashion on Beatrice's strange entertainment box.

Her gaze travelled around the chamber, noting there were at least five Scoor – presumably motionless because they were awaiting Jahl's orders – and, huddled together in a bizarre frozen tableaux were a group of eight youths: Knox's followers. Their expressions were almost unbearably terrified, Jahl having released them in order to select the last two victims and then re-frozen them immediately so they could offer their friends no assistance. The girls were screaming in panic, their hands reaching outwards towards the altar in a gesture so pathetic, one could not fail to be moved by it. A couple of the boys in the centre of the group were pushing their way forward in a futile attempt to rescue their friends, others were holding them back, pulling on their clothes, so that it seemed as the moment was frozen, they were like a statue, held in a strange emotional equilibrium.

'Noble, are they not?' Jahl chuckled. His voice was smooth as silk. He had recovered fast, within the seconds it took Regan to assess the situation. He took a step towards her.

Regan did not hesitate; she was not here for discussion. Pointing the gun straight for his heart, she sneered, 'Die, brother.' She fired.

Nothing happened, no bang, no blood, not like she had been expecting. There was a tiny hollow click but that was all. Still, Jahl reeled back slightly as though some invisible bullet had indeed been fired. 'Brother? What are you talking about, Regan?'

Regan lowered the gun, holding it at her side and trying to shake it frantically, thinking that perhaps something inside it had jammed. She tried to appear calm – it seemed Jahl had no idea of the significance of the gun, in fact, he had dismissed it momentarily. She played for time, noting that he signalled to one of the Scoor with an almost idle gesture.

'You remember my father, don't you? The one who warned me you were poison . . .' she laughed slightly shakily. 'Duncan Talisker, hero of the Fine – well, your mother seduced him, which makes us . . .'

'Only half brother and sister. Only one of us is the stuff of the gods – me.'

'Is that what this is about?' she nodded towards the shimmering husk of the inanimate figure. 'You becoming a god?' In the corner of her vision she saw the tail of the nearest Scoor twitch as thought the creature had just woken. 'Are you aware of the damage you're doing here and in Sutra? How can you return in triumph to a world you've already destroyed?' She shook the gun again and then pointed it – less certainly this time – and fired. Again nothing happened. This time, she threw the useless thing aside in disgust. Jahl leaned back on the altar and crossed his arms, an expression of bemused puzzlement on his face that was patronising in the extreme.

'I am already part god,' he grinned, the flickering light of the chamber catching on his canine teeth. 'These people certainly think so,' he gestured towards the Children. 'But you are right, Regan, the spell will make me a full god, combining the energies of Phyrr and Corvus, and I will be the most powerful god Sutra has ever seen – I don't care about this place, it was just a way of hiding my intentions from Phyrr . . .' he waved his hand airily. 'I am already imbued with power from the spell. Did you imagine your curious little weapon could kill me? Now if you don't mind, I'm busy . . .'

She expects him to order the Scoor to attack and kill her – she will be helpless against them. She draws the mock sword awkwardly from the belt loop on her jeans and readies herself for her death, her heart hammering in her chest. Jahl confounds her however – he waves his hand and a bright surge of energy rushes towards her, its vibration a dull roar as it moves within the rock floor. Before she has time to speak, the impact is upon her. She expects death but instead she is frozen like the others; the chill moves upwards from her legs, expelling the breath from her lungs with a hissing sigh. Now, she knows; this is not the same as the frozen sleep Johl inflicted on her subjects in Sutra. These people, these poor frozen statues, can still see out; their eyes cannot move but neither can they close their eyelids. They can see everything that happens, and they can think. They have seen their friends slaughtered by Jahl and they know they are next.

Jahl walks over and languidly caresses her frozen face, she cannot even flinch. 'I don't care that we are related, such delicate morals are the province of your precious Fine. When I am finished, my little sister, you will not be able to deny me. I will make you my consort whether you want me or not . . .' His breath is hot, almost painful on her cheek, she wants to spit in his face, wants to deny him, wants to make him stop the words he is saying but she cannot. His expression becomes thoughtful for a moment as he gazes deep into her eyes as though seeking to make contact with her soul. 'Perhaps it is why I always found you so intoxicating, sister – perhaps chaos is ultimately drawn to itself. Perhaps wanting you was only wanting to possess my own reflection – torturing you was . . . energising.'

He breaks away from her suddenly, as if aware he has made an admission which could make him seem weak before her. Striding back to the figure above the altar he raises his hands in supplication and mutters low sounding words. The image flares slightly as energy courses through it; pulsing light surges outwards surrounding Jahl in its glowing cocoon. He turns around to motion to the Scoor who encircle the captive sacrifices and, as he raises his hand, the figure behind him moves for the first time, mirroring his movement. There is still no sense of animation to the figure, just a connection with its creator, it seems as though some huge inversion of a puppet and puppet-master is taking place. From where she has been frozen, far back near the entrance to the door, Regan can see everything, is helpless not to see.

Jahl releases the captives and the chamber, previously so quiet, becomes filled with the sounds of screaming and supplication. Three of the young women fall to their knees, holding hands they seem to be praying to some god or other – hopefully not

Jahl. The others are making most of the noise, panic stricken; two of the men try to rush forward but the Scoor bar their way with their metal spears. Regan has seen death before and she knows their panic is the mind's trick, a delaying tactic which will keep the denial going until the last second of life. The acrid stench of fear is in the chamber.

The Scoor push them back into their huddled group and Jahl holds his hands up in a beneficent gesture designed to silence them. 'Children of the Deluge,' he says. 'I am your god and I require your lifeblood for my ascension.'

'Antichrist!' one of them screams, 'Deceiver!'

'Bless you,' he raises his hands again stretching his hands outwards at right angles from his sides, he pauses for a second and then dips forward into a deep, graceful bow. Although Regan cannot know he is parodying their god, she recognises Jahl's warped sense of theatre; behind him, the shadow-god raises his arms and bows also, its reflective gesture conveying nothing of Jahl's own iniquity. The Scoor draw long knives from their belts but await Jahl's signal.

There is a scream of rage; something enters the chamber, moving fast, passing Regan in a rush of heat. It is a man, she thinks it's Knox but it's difficult to tell – he is transfigured. A bright, flickering glow surrounds him and inside the glow, the black, stick-like figure of Knox has its own incandescence. His face is a mask of particular rage which Regan immediately knows – he has been deceived by Jahl. The two nearest Scoor move to engage him and he wastes no time, lashing out with a long stick.

What Regan does not know, is that Knox is denied his glory – to the Children of the Deluge he appears as Daniel; a golden saviour, an angel. Heartened by his appearance they attack the three Scoor behind them – all hell lets loose in the chamber but, although they have the advantage of numbers, Regan doubts the Children will survive. A thin scream pierces the air as one of the women is stung and then dispatched by the biggest Scoor; a blow to her head with the metal spear he carries ending the scream with horrible abruptness. The Children at least have the sense not to pause and the Scoor is immediately attacked again.

Regan wonders why Jahl is not freezing them but then realises he cannot move far and perhaps, his magics are being sapped by the waiting God. The spell is taking effect and he is constrained by the bonds which hold him to his creation. If someone had the sense to attack him now . . . a faint flare of hope warms Regan's belly. Jahl is watching the confusion, his expression unreadable for the most part although there is no denying the faint irritation there. A yell of exultation goes up as Knox/Daniel manages to topple one of the Scoor to the ground, exploiting the creature's clumsiness in the confines of the space he has knocked its legs from beneath it and then, without pause, he stabs hard through the neck. The Scoor thrashes around for long seconds, its tail spasming in insect-like frenzy – it dies silently. One of the young women notices the useless sword Regan is holding, runs over and wrenches it out of her from her grasp, taking the skin from Regan's palms but she feels nothing.

'Sorry, thanks . . .' the woman garbles. She turns back

to the fray and, after a single second of hesitation, thrusts the sword into the nearest Scoor – which has its back to her – just above the iron breastplate. The thrust is not hard enough and glances off the hard fusion of bone where the creature's spine and clavicle meld, it spins towards her, but the woman, riding her rush of adrenalin and fear has pulled the blade back again and strikes hard, finding a wide arc. More by luck than judgement the blade hits the creature's neck and even though blunt, it manages to sever halfway through. The woman screams in revulsion, never having seen such carnage before.

There's another movement by the door and the *Seanachaidh* enters. He groans aloud at the scene he is confronted with.

'*Seanachaidh*? Here? This just gets better!' Jahl is amazed.

'You there! Get them out – get these people out of here!' Knox/Daniel screams. Sandro glances towards Regan but can see there is nothing to be done. 'This way, come on . . .' he grabs two of the nearest girls by the arms and begins to push them towards the exit. Once they realise someone has given them permission to put the horror behind them, they break into a sobbing run. Sandro comes back and takes hold of another girl and a young man – but the man doesn't want to come, he is in a frenzy of rage – he pulls back. 'C'mon you stupid bastard,' Sandro has little patience for heroics and forcibly pulls another of the men from the fray and shoves them towards the door.

This leaves Knox/Daniel, Sandro and the three remaining men behind to fight the three surviving

Scoor. Only Knox/Daniel is armed. Although the odds are now better, the Children are unused to violence of any kind and although they fought with as much ferocity as anyone Regan has ever seen, they have little stamina. Knox/Daniel makes another kill with his spear, it seemed his hand *is* guided by some divine force. This time his companions are too breathless to shout or cheer. With only two Scoor remaining it seems as though the Children finally have a chance but, just as Knox/Daniel recovers himself and starts back to the fray, he is grabbed from behind by the scruff of the neck and flung back across the room. It is Jahl; Knox/Daniel has strayed within his grasp. As he is shoved back, he drops his wooden spear and it rolls across the floor towards Sandro.

Jahl is angry now and, for some reason, the fight has gone out of Knox/Daniel. Backing him towards the altar stone, Jahl pushes him down onto it, a grin of triumph on his face. Knox/Daniel has just enough energy left – he turns his head towards the still battling Children and screams: 'Run! Get out!'

Sandro has picked up the wooden spear and jabbing it at one of the Scoor, manages to get the beast to retreat towards Regan's immobilised form. The three Children and the other Scoor are at a stalemate – the men, unarmed, crippled by indecision – the Scoor slow to decide its best target.

'Go on. Run!' Sandro repeats Knox's instruction and two of the men immediately move, breaking away suddenly and running for the door.

'God bless you, Daniel,' one of them shouts. 'God bless you . . .'

The other man is Gordon – Learn To Fly – he has retrieved the sword and this gives him an instant of pause as he glances back towards the altar. His glasses are askew and he is panting hard – but he knows what he is seeing. Too tired to keep up the illusion, Knox is struggling in the grip of Jahl. And LearnToFly can see that it is Knox. He stares. Seconds drop away into nothingness.

'Knox?' No stammer this time. Knox turns his head from Jahl's murderous grasp just as Jahl reaches for a sickle knife on the altar stone.

'Gordon. Run . . . Tell them . . . tell them it was Daniel . . .'

'Oh God.' LearnToFly drops the sword as he is grabbed from behind by Sandro who has chosen that moment to break away. They run together towards the exit, Sandro seeing Regan from the corner of his eye but powerless to stop and help her. It is over – she is lost. As they reach the doorway there is a loud screamed curse from Knox as Jahl brings the knife home into his heart. Could they but know it, there is a smile on his lips.

The hillside begins to shake and tremble once more as Sandro and LearnToFly scramble through the narrow gap. A wave of pure light follows after them. And there can be no doubt that Jahl has succeeded. The sound of the earthquake becomes indistinguishable from deep, rich laughter, which resonates through the very rocks. The sound becomes deafening, and it seems that Jahl is moving outwards through the ground. As they run out from the hillside towards the waiting group of Children, Sandro is aware that

LearnToFly's lips are moving constantly and he distantly assumes the other man is praying as he runs. They stop within a few yards of the survivors, gasping for breath and, just before LearnToFly's friends reach him, enveloping him in hugs, Sandro hears what he has been saying: 'It was Knox. It was Knox.'

Sandro can't see why it matters. The tremor subsides again and he stares back towards the crags. What now? he wonders. Now a god is amongst us . . .

CHAPTER EIGHTEEN

So, this is how a commoner may die beside a Thane . . . Hamish stared at the grey figure of Huw which lay only feet away from him. The Thane's eyes appeared half-open but it was difficult to tell if he could still see. Some of the men had been blinded by the snow but that was really the least of their problems. The army of the Southern Clans was dying . . .

After the ice-quake – three or four days earlier, Hamish had lost any sense of time – those left alive, possibly as few as seven hundred men, had gathered themselves together and marched on. There had been both dissent and desertion but Thanes Huw and Lachlan were as fierce and stubborn as any flatlanders in history. Hamish listened to the mutterings of his fellows but kept his own counsel for the most part. To him, and others of Huw's clan, it was unthinkable to betray his Thane so even if Huw was leading them on a doomed mission and only ten of them survived to knock on the gates of Soulis Mor, Hamish wanted to be one of those ten. But the weather – which even the southern soldiers had come to realise was unnatural – had defied them all. Never had Sutra known such cold; the blizzard was overwhelming enough, but the ground had frozen so hard that the earth was turned to glass-like rock and the air froze the breath in a man's throat and nose. The army had struggled onwards, men falling away, dying unremarked in the snow, partly due to the blizzard but also because none could help, frightened to stop least they disappear, snatched by the whiteness of oblivion.

Last night – at least, Hamish thought it was last night – Huw had halted the army once more; there were around six hundred men left alive and many felt in their hearts that none would awaken the next morning. Still, they built what few shelters they could erect in the solid ground, anchoring them with rocks. Huw supervised this and ordered that the injured, those suffering the worst from the snow sickness and blindness, must sleep in the shelters. The remaining soldiers, who were also dying on their feet from exhaustion, were to camp within the shadow of a long sill of black rock which had been created by the icequake – its shallow height provided only a little shelter from the biting wind but it was better than nothing. Hamish refused his option to sleep in the tent, superstitiously believing that to be amongst the dying would only confirm that he was as good as dead himself. As he lay down to sleep, he dimly thought that in the morning, if he awoke, he would use his battle-axe to sever his leg off – he had seen the black sickness spreading up through the limbs of the soldiers and thought that perhaps such a drastic measure might save his life. Da would do it for him . . . not that he'd seen Da for a while . . . His father had given him the axe before he left for this cursed campaign. It had been made especially for Hamish's height and length of arm, the curved bronze head scratched with the names of his father and his grandfather. The weapon was unused and the first blood it would shed would be its owner's. Hamish stared at the crescent of the axe-head as he drifted into a sleep which was near to unconsciousness and from which he might never awaken, but he was too exhausted to care.

He did wake though. And lying just an arm's length away was the Thane. All around the southern army lay like statues of ice. Many had died overnight, slain by no army, but by a silent invisible assassin. The whiteness covered everything, soldiers cocooned in ready-made shrouds, horses had fallen and lay dead or dying, their stomachs bloating. The tents which had been erected with much pain and effort had collapsed with the weight of snow and tellingly, no one had crawled out or attempted to raise the structures again. The snow had stopped, its damage done. The morning was clear and crisp – somewhere down the line a survivor was playing a lament on a tin whistle. Hamish lay for a long time, immobilised in his cocoon, his chest burning with the exertion it cost him to keep breathing. Both he and Thane Huw had been saved by the angle of the jagged landform which had sheltered them from the chest up, allowing them to breathe as they slept. His thoughts as blank and featureless as the snow, Hamish stared up at the sky, his vision swimming with black spots, tears spilling down the sides of his cheeks . . .

He thought it was the black spots at first, so distant were they. And then birds – crows probably, come to feast on the bodies of the fallen. Some flare of recognition kindled within him and he frowned uncomprehendingly towards the birds. They were big. He sat up – a movement he would have had to persuade himself to without the sudden hope. He'd never seen them before, but he had heard, he knew what they were . . .

'Eagles,' he muttered, 'eagle Sidhe . . . Thane Huw, Sir . . .' he scrambled to his feet, teetering uncertainly on legs which felt like pillars of stone, tears of pain washed unchecked down his face as he tried desperately to push his feet one in front of the other to walk those few yards to his Thane. He lost his balance and fell gracelessly into the snow with a yell. Someone else had seen the birds and was shouting something – but Hamish wanted to be the one to tell Huw. Groaning with exertion, he pulled himself forward across the snow, using his axe as a lever for his weight. 'Huw . . .' he panted, 'Thane Huw, wake up! Wake up man!' He reached Huw's side but there was little sign of comprehension from the Thane, so Hamish scrabbled around on his hands and knees and managed to prop him up; it was too difficult to be done with adequate respect or dignity but Hamish felt sure the Thane would understand. 'Look . . .' He tilted Huw's chin and more or less pointed his vision up at the sky.

One hundred eagle Sidhe filled the whole sky from horizon to horizon. They flew from the west, the light of the newly risen sun streaking their feathers with gold. As they grew closer Hamish could see that they carried people and packages on their backs; closer still, and a wind caused by their massive wings began to whip the snow into fresh eddies. Along the tattered remains of the line a ragged cheer went up but at first, none of the birds landed – they circled around as if awaiting some order. Almost without thought Hamish grabbed his axe and wiped the blade, it glinted in the cold light. Angling the axe head to reflect the sun he began to signal, hoping that one of the people on the backs of the eagles could understand the flashing code – '*The Thane is here. Thane Huw is here.*' As he busied himself, a low groan came from Huw's throat indicating that there was still a spark of life there. '*Hurry,*' he signalled. '*Hurry. He is dying.*' A cramp shot up his arm as chilled muscles spasmed from the exertion and he dropped the axe with a cry and bent double over Huw's prostrate form in an effort to nurse the pain. Possibly he blanked out for a minute or so because the next thing he became aware of, was someone talking to him.

'Soldier . . . soldier? Was it you who signalled? Is this the Thane?' He looked up. All around the eagles were landing, almost soundlessly despite their massive size; some remained patiently waiting to be unloaded but others were already in their human form. Their cargo was precious indeed, warm animal pelts and blankets, one of which was being put around Hamish's shoulders even as he looked around.

'Soldier?' The man who addressed him had the sun at his back and Hamish squinted upwards, his eyes tender and reddened by exposure. It was Tristan. He could tell the man was a Thane because he wore a circlet crown similar to Huw's and light mail armour across his chest. There the similarity ended; the Thane of Soulis Mor was as twisted and crippled as he had heard, but he carried himself with such a bearing that he seemed every bit as noble as Huw or Lachlan – who was further down the line – and he was smiling encouragingly, waiting for Hamish's answer.

'Yes . . . Yessir.' Hamish's voice cracked and he knew he was in danger of losing his composure. 'I think he's dying, Sir,' he grated. Without knowing why, he cradled Huw's freezing body tighter against his, unwilling to let go. Tristan patted him reassuringly on the shoulder, ignoring the flood of tears which came as if from nowhere.

'How old are you, soldier? What's your name?'

'Eighteen, Sir. Name's Hamish, Sir.'

'Well, Hamish. You see that eagle over there? He is carrying broth in those skins which will soon be warmed through. Why don't you go and get some and leave Huw to us? I promise we'll look after him . . .'

Hamish shook his head. 'Can't, Sir . . . I can't walk. My legs . . .'

Thane Tristan looked shaken by this for a moment but then, without hesitation, he bent down and picked Hamish up – whose weight was almost equal to his own. He didn't carry him far but set him down on one of the large groundsheets the Sidhe had used to wrap their aid parcels. Then to Hamish's amazement, before he even spoke to those who had clustered around Huw, he went and retrieved his axe and brought it back to him.

'Can't lose that,' he muttered, seeming almost shy for an instant. 'It has done good service today . . . as have you.'

For a moment Hamish was speechless and a look of confused amazement must have been on his face because Tristan laughed slightly, puzzled by his reaction. 'Th-thank-you, Sir . . .' he said.

'Don't mention it, Hamish. We Thanes are nothing without our clansmen. I'm sure Huw would agree with me.' He turned and began to walk back towards the small gathering around Huw but as he did so, he motioned to a Sidhe standing nearby. 'Make sure this man gets a hot drink . . .'

On the same night that the southern army was dying of exposure, Talisker felt he might suffer a similar fate. He sat cross-legged atop one of the red stone columns around the wolf Sidhe campsite and stared up at the blazing stars, a mixture of resentment and frustration railing within him. A few yards behind him sat Eskarius, in human form – he was chanting quietly, almost under his breath so that the sound acquired a quality which was like static or white-noise.

Spirituality; it was something which Talisker had always been deeply suspicious of, although he respected others' right to be 'spiritual' he could never lose the feeling that it was all smoke and mirrors. Even in the face of the evidence of his life – his becoming part of a shared soul to defeat Corvus years before – he distrusted the idea that his spirit could achieve anything more special than anyone else's. And yet, the wolf Sidhe head shaman was insistent that the circle of shamans needed his help: Worldwalker, he who had walked between worlds. Personally, he thought Sandro would have been better, as a *Seanachaidh* he tapped into all this stuff . . . His thoughts became slightly unfocused, the head shaman had given him something herbal to drink and he hadn't been too surprised to feel pleasantly light-headed, but while his head felt one thing, his limbs felt another, they were cold and leaden already and he had only been up here an hour.

'Duncan Talisker. You must keep your thoughts still.'

He twisted back to look at Eskarius. 'How do you know what . . .'

'Just a guess,' Eskarius grinned wickedly, his teeth glinting white in the moonlight.

Talisker gave a quiet chuckle, 'I'm sorry, Eskarius, I'll try harder.'

'No. Don't try. Just do nothing. Be peaceful.'

'Peaceful . . .' he echoed, slightly despondently. He stared ahead once more as Eskarius returned to his chanting. On top of the other towers of rock, all around the plateau, other shamans were doing the same as he – a vision quest it was called – except that they had all been fasting for days, were better prepared . . .

Talisker would maintain afterwards that at best, the state he fell into could be called a 'daze' rather than a trance. It was peaceful on the top of the hill-tower, there was a sense of connection – as his senses became brighter, more attuned, he realised he could hear the other shamans chanting the same flat sound as Eskarius and that this sound had been what he had heard when he first came onto the plateau. It was like the wind and the fire, but deeper, beneath its surface, the sound was alive and . . . afraid.

Haltingly at first, Talisker joined in with the chant, amazed by the strange resonance which emerged from deep within his own chest, and as he chanted, rocking very slightly back and forward, time slipped away from him. Perhaps it was only minutes, perhaps hours later, that he saw something moving across the rough stones beside him. It was a small lizard, running with a fast scuttling motion towards Talisker's foot. Talisker disliked reptiles and reached his hand out to shoo it away. Strangely at odds with the speed of the creature, Talisker's hand moved in slow motion, leaving a silver trail of light behind it – it felt as though it was moving at a perfectly normal speed and Talisker, confused by this, shook it as if it were somehow defective. The lizard was perched on his shoe now, regarding him solemnly from jet black eyes.

'Go . . . away.' Talisker said. The words sounded unnaturally slow and deep, the sound reverberating out across the empty space in front of him, and Talisker – whose thoughts were running at normal speed – wondered just what the head shaman had put in his drink. After what seemed like a long time, his hand reached the lizard but instead of flicking it away, he touched its head, just between the intense black eyes.

The night exploded into colour. The stars fell down. Silver streamers unravelling into the plush blue of the sky. No rock beneath him, he was lost in a shifting, bedazzling array of colours and shapes which arrived from nowhere in defiance of the moonlight and centred on his consciousness. He thought he opened his mouth to gasp or groan but no sound issued forth. He imagined it was like drowning, panic and nausea gripped him like a physical presence but he fought them off – *Don't try . . . Be peaceful.* After long moments the shock wave subsided, the colours melting away again, trickling into blackness. And then . . . blackness was all there was. No stars, no sky. No suggestion that there might be anything other than pervasive black. Talisker groaned aloud and this time, he could hear himself. Other men would wonder at the nothingness of this place/time/state of being, but not Talisker. He knew what this was, but knowing brought no comfort. The time-between-times. Between worlds. Between life and death. He was in the void.

'Sandro . . . over here!' Above the babble of excited voices Sandro could hear Bea's voice although he couldn't see her at first. The Children were clustered around in a small, intensely shocked group. A couple of the women who had been the first out of the chamber had begun to talk quietly, to try and make some kind of sense of what had just happened to them, the others were still hugging, crying and praying. The park was eerily quiet considering almost a thousand people were camped within its borders; all eyes were fixed on the crags where the flickering light show continued. People were transfixed by it, their eyes shining with unconcealed, uncynical wonder; a few had lit candles or were holding up their lighters although there was no rational reason for this. Sandro had seen a couple of camcorders so it seemed likely discussion of what would no doubt be called 'natural phenomena' would rage for sometime – the Children of the Deluge were not the only people in the park praying . . .

'Sandro!' Bea pushed past one of the Children and

hugged him tightly. 'Did you find Regan? Where is she? What happened?' she asked breathlessly.

'No,' his throat tightened as he replied, 'She's still in there . . . Jahl . . .' he turned her away from the group and lowered his voice, 'Jahl is doing something to make himself more powerful – a spell like we said. I think he's trying to become a god. He may have succeeded already . . .'

'A god,' she echoed, still wrestling with the idea of incarnate gods. 'Is Regan dead?'

'No, I don't think so. She was kind of frozen – immobilised. But it doesn't look—'

'Sir?' One of the Children interrupted them. 'I'd like to thank you for your help in there. Without you and Daniel, we would never have survived.'

'Daniel?' Sandro frowned at the girl. Like Regan and LearnToFly, he had clearly seen Knox's face.

'Daniel is our spiritual leader. God took him up but he came back for us in our time of need.' Others of the Children clustered around, 'Yes, yes,' they nodded and murmured agreement.

'What about Knox?' Sandro asked innocently.

'Knox was deceived by a false prophet. We will pray for him . . .'

'I see. Excuse me,' Sandro smiled wanly and he and Beatrice walked slightly away from the group.

'What's wrong, sweetie?' Bea asked.

'It just doesn't seem right, Bea. It was definitely Knox – he's dead, Jahl killed him – he died saving them but they saw something else, someone else . . .'

'Maybe it's what he wanted,' she shrugged. 'After all, they have to make sense of it in their own way.

And who are we to say they're not right anyway?'

'I guess . . .' Sandro nodded. 'I suppose it could all be seen to confirm what they think.' He glanced back nervously at the light show on the crags. 'The end of the world,' he muttered. 'But Jahl doesn't belong here, in this world – magic and religion make strange bedfellows.'

'Maybe not. Maybe they're just two sides of one—' Bea's reasonable response was cut short as another aftershock began, but this one was different than the previous one. As the shaking began, a ripple of light flashed outwards from the hill in a low, scything circle which emanated outwards across the park. People began to scream as their tents were toppled and they were knocked from their feet, but when the front of the light-wave reached them, it did no harm, simply passed through the bodies of those still on their feet.

Bea and Sandro were knocked to the ground by the quake and Sandro scrabbled on his hands and knees towards Bea, who had rolled a few feet away. As he reached out and grabbed her hand, a narrow fissure opened in the ground. Bea screamed and pulled herself towards him, but the fissure didn't open wide, perhaps only ten inches or so; Sandro and Bea both happened to be looking down in the few seconds it took to open up beneath them – far below there was a movement which was not the earth. Red, moving fast, so fast that it took a mere instant for the widely spaced pattern to become apparent; scales, massive reptilian scales. The image was there one second and gone the next as the crack in the ground closed up again with a dull, booming thud. The earthquake ended moments later.

'Ohmigod.' Sandro remained sitting on the ground as though lacking the strength to stand up again, his face a white mask of shock. 'Did you . . .?'

Bea nodded, speechless. She shuffled over to where he sat and they clung together, no longer coping with the idea that the world might, in fact, be ending.

Without warning another ripple of light pulsed out from the hillside. Without a quake this time, a sound could be heard which accompanied the ripple – searing. It was stronger and brighter, flickering from green to blue and then to red, before it vanished.

'What do you think's happening in there?' Bea whispered.

'I don't know. I don't think I want to know.'

The park had fallen quiet again. The 'aftershock' had not been too severe and most people were uninjured. Still, the sound of people crying quietly and the distant sound of sirens in the city made an eerie backdrop.

'Listen to me. Do not be afraid. God is with us all but he has given us a sign that he will not wait for ever.' One of the Children, a young man – the one who had refused to come away from fighting the Scoor – was standing on the now horizontal trunk of a tree which had been uprooted in the first quake. He spoke with passion and authority, his eyes alight with a particular zeal – that of a man who has been vindicated. His voice carried quite far across the crowd. 'Then said Jesus unto him, except ye see signs and wonders, ye will not believe,' he continued. The Children of the Deluge made noises of encouragement and he smiled warmly at them. '*Brothers and sisters,*' he said, '*in every dominion of My kingdom men tremble and fear before the God of Daniel: for He is the living God, and steadfast for ever, and His kingdom that which shall not be destroyed, and His dominion shall be even unto the end. He delivereth and rescueth, and he worketh signs and wonders in heaven and in earth, who hath delivered Daniel . . .*'

'Here, here,' people called out. A steady trickle of people who would come to call themselves Daniel's Children began to make their way towards the young man, some stopping to light their lights and candles once more. Like rocks in a stream, Sandro and Bea remained where they sat, arms around one another, knowing that this night would get darker before dawn – perhaps because of this, they were the only ones in the park still looking towards the hillside when the trouble really began.

There were soft footsteps behind him, a kind of small scratching noise. Talisker stopped and turned around, behind him, as he had guessed, was Eskarius Vermesh travelling in his wolf form which was the form of his spirit.

'Eskarius, you didn't have to come.' Talisker's voice sounded flattened, dropping away into oblivion. 'The void can be . . . dangerous. Are you my guide?'

'How can I be, when I am walking behind you, Duncan Talisker? Keeping faith does not require that one must lead and the other follow. The shamans are looking through my eyes.'

Talisker stopped and waited for Eskarius to draw

level with him. The great wolf was as tall as the height of his chest and without thinking about it, Talisker reached out and touched the soft fur. *'You may climb onto my back if you wish. How far we might walk is unknown.'* Eskarius sat down patiently and Talisker climbed onto his broad back. They walked forward into a darkness which closed around them like liquid. There was no time here, no real distance to cover but it seemed reasonable to move on. Eventually, they heard a sound in the deep distance, it was difficult to identify at first but something about it gripped Talisker's stomach with unnamed anxiety. He realised he had no weapon at the same instant he recognised the sound – crying. It was a woman crying. The easy loping motion of Eskarius Vermesh's shoulders grew quicker but at the same time, Talisker's unease grew. He didn't want to see . . . he didn't want to see . . . why?

But then he saw. And he knew the reason for his fear. After a quarter of a century, seeing her was like a physical blow. Sweat rose on his brow, nausea in his tightened stomach and a cry of irrational denial to his lips. 'No . . .' the sound fell away as everything else did within this space but the woman stopped crying at least.

Something had happened to her; her spirit had lingered too long and the void was engulfing her. Where the long slender shape of her torso and legs should have been there was only blackness – it was defined blackness, suggestive of her form, but soon, even that would pass. Tendrils of the black encircled her breasts, reaching up to her shoulders where they met the raven darkness of her hair. She looked up as they approached, the cold, sourceless light glinting in eyes which had been damaged many years before; one a perfect bright blue and the other, the aerated white of an opal. A strange expression twisted across her stark features: confusion, fear and surprise. But no joy that she should be found by Duncan Talisker in such a state.

'Who is she?' Eskarius thought.

'It is the Lady Phyrr.' Pity stirred in Talisker's soul as he remembered her anger and pride. He slid off Eskarius's back and walked towards her, unsure of what to say.

'Can it be you, Talisker?' she frowned. 'You should be an old man by now.'

'Using the gateways can do strange things to a man,' he shrugs. 'What happened, Phyrr?'

'Our son happened. Come closer, Talisker, so I can tell you everything.' But he did not step closer, did not trust her even bound as she was.

'Do you know about the dragon?' he asked.

She looked mildly surprised at the question. 'Dragon? There are two dragons: Kivik and Hemmek – Hemmek, the ice dragon is threatening Sutra. His sibling is elsewhere . . .'

'There's another one—'

'He will be where my *beloved son* has gone.' She snarled, a ferocity on her face which was anything but maternal. 'He planned to go so he could conceal his magics from me in case I stopped him. It was almost unecessary in the end – except for the mess he has made in Soulis Mor. I didn't plan to stop him—'

'Why would you? You don't care about the Fine or the Sidhe – what does it matter to you?'

'You're very astute, Talisker. Always were . . . I had my own reasons for not getting involved, I wanted dissolution but he required my soul for the spell.'

'You wanted to die?'

'Does that surprise you? Eternity is not a prize, Talisker, it is a burden as Jahl will discover, if the unthinkable happens and he succeeds . . . but,' her expression changed suddenly, she appeared panic stricken, her blue eye lost focus and her jaw slackened. Saliva trickled from her mouth down towards her neck. Around her form the blackness shifted and moved with a constricting motion, thin thread-like tendrils curled around her throat, others reached out towards Talisker and he stepped back, repulsed by the hideous, almost sentient movement.

'Phyrr? Phyrr? What's happening to her, Eskarius?' The wolf padded forward, gazing intensely at Phyrr's face.

'I know not, Duncan Talisker. I suspect she is in some pain but she cannot die – part of her soul is missing . . .'

'You mean, she'll suffer for ever – never die – that's horrific.'

Eskarius continued to watch her face for long moments. *'Least we forget, Talisker, this is the Lady Phyrr, the Morrigan, despoiler of souls. Most would say that it is what she has earned. The dissolution she speaks of would be the peace she has denied others.'*

'Yes, but . . .' Unexpectedly, tears sprung to Talisker's eyes, 'she . . . she . . .'

'Perhaps we should move on, Duncan Talisker. Perhaps we can yet find the creature.'

'No. No, we've got to do something. Look, the void is placeless, timeless, it shows you what you need to see because everything else just . . . just falls away.'

'I do not understand. She is an enemy.'

'Yes, she is, but do the Sidhe not learn from their enemies?' Talisker did not wait for the wolf's answer but moved back towards Phyrr, his hands outstretched. As he touched the black vapour which surrounded her a cold gripped him, like some deadly vine, blackness encircling his wrists, drawing him forward. He began to pull at the bonds as if they were physical and real and in fact, he did seem to make some headway for a moment – gripping the freezing tendrils from around her throat and pulling them back. Phyrr drew a long breath and faint recognition entered her gaze once more.

'Why would you?' she whispered, 'Why would you help me?' Talisker ignored her question because he was unsure of the answer and continued ripping at the black threads. However, as he reached the level of her waist Phyrr let out a high scream: the threads had claimed her body and were inseparable from her flesh. Talisker started back in fright and revulsion but as he did so the black tendrils twined behind his waist pulling him back – he was in danger of being overwhelmed also. He yelled and cursed as he began to fight in earnest, tearing frantically, no longer differentiating between himself and Phyrr. Suddenly, something gripped his hair and reaching back to pull it from him, he discovered it was Phyrr's fingers. He had a brief glimpse of her face which was partly obscured by the tendrils which were now writhing in desperate motion – he thought she was saying something to him, her lips were moving – but then she pulled him forward also, into her treacherous embrace.

She kissed him. That was all really. Just a kiss. But he tried to fight, to pull back, her lips were like a chill flower, her dead flesh like poison, and the effect of the kiss was vampyric, sapping the warmth and life from his veins. Distantly he reminded himself that his body was truly still on the hilltop and she could not kill him this way – but his limbs were heavy and his soul-body refuted this idea. He felt himself go limp and leaden, closing his eyes to shut out the ghostly white of her face . . . he was drifting . . .

'Talisker?' He peered through his lashes – for an instant he thought he saw stars in the night sky, but then, felt a pulling sensation. It was like wakening from a dream in which he had been flying. Was it over? He expected to see Eskarius and he would know that they had failed. He opened his eyes.

Phyrr was standing over him. She was released from her bonds and she looked as she always had – beautiful but somehow, intensely frightening. She wore the light armoured vest that he remembered, even the black cloak. Perhaps she still carried the sword with which she had almost killed him . . .

'Thank-you,' she smiled; an unaccustomed warming of her features. 'Your soul was always special, "Worldwalker". I had to use your strength to escape the threads and also, I will need your ability if I am to manifest myself in the world of Edinburgh.

Perversely, it is easier for our son than I, as he is part mortal.'

'S'not a world . . .' Talisker muttered. 'Edinburgh . . .' He sat up, leaning back on his elbows. To his right Eskarius was sitting watching their exchange but he kept his thoughts silent.

'I must go,' Phyrr continued smoothly. 'I must destroy Jahl. He grows too powerful and too confident, like Corvus.' She nodded over to the wolf, 'It seems my first instincts were right. I was going to leave him to the wolves when he was born . . .'

'And perhaps he would have grown into a different man,' Eskarius thought. He growled slightly in the back of his throat, irritated by her implication, but Phyrr chose to ignore this. She turned as though to leave.

'Wait, Phyrr – please . . . You know where he is?'

'Indeed. He is in your home world, Talisker, and at this moment, the only opposition he faces is your daughter, Regan.'

'What?!' Talisker was horrified but as soon as Phyrr had spoken the words it made perfect sense; the Sluagh being in Edinburgh, looking for Tristan, only Jahl could have sent them through . . .'But how did Regan get mixed up in this?'

'The *Seanachaidh*, I presume. Talisker . . .' Phyrr's features softened slightly, 'I think there's something you should know. I may have to use Regan in order to defeat Jahl . . .'

'*Use?* What do you mean "use"?'

'Her body. I cannot have a physical presence in your world otherwise. My spirit is weakened by Jahl's interference, in your world I would be a mere shade . . .'

Her eyes narrowed and she watched Talisker's reaction closely, her right hand hidden in her cloak where, he had no doubt, she concealed a weapon. 'She may not survive this borrowing, Talisker. But if I fail, thousands of people in Sutra and your world will die. I believe many have already died in your land and in Sutra – the dragons' bonds are loosed by Jahl's inept magics . . .' she sighed. 'He was ever an impatient pupil.'

Talisker wasn't listening, his expression was of stark realisation. 'Wait, you're asking me to allow you to use – and kill – my daughter in order to kill your son.'

'No, I will use your daughter to kill *our* son,' she said quietly. 'And actually, I'm not asking your permission. I just thought you had the right to know. She will probably die anyway. Jahl has her trapped.'

'Oh,' his voice cracked, hot tears welled into his eyes, 'and that's supposed to make me feel better, is it?'

'The truth of it is, Talisker, few will mourn her. She and Jahl, our children, were tainted from the start. She by Corvus and Jahl . . . by me.' He knew it was true, but despite everything, his heart denied it. 'I will,' he said, 'I will mourn her. I thought she would be safe there. I . . .'

'I know,' her tone was not pitying because Phyrr disdained pity but she understood at least. 'I must go. Here.' She threw something to him and it landed in his palm, cold and heavy like a silver ingot. 'Give me five minutes,' she said firmly. 'You will find the dragons just ahead. Every creature held in limbo has a presence in the void. Throw this between them –

you'll know when . . . Goodbye, Duncan Talisker.'

Their gazes met for the space of a second, and it was there, like the first time – a frank understanding of the other's true being. And then it was over, Phyrr turned to go.

'No, wait.' He wasn't sure if he was weeping or not and he didn't care at this moment if he seemed weak. She was running ahead into the dark, the blackness of her cloak making her image appear to flicker between dark and light; dark and light. The sound of her light footfalls began to die away. Talisker ran after her. 'Wait!' he screamed. 'She'll die – she'll die in the next five minutes – is that what you're saying? Wait, Phyrr . . .'

He was running fast, his legs pumping hard. He could hear his own ragged breathing and the soft, strangled sound his constricted throat was making. Phyrr's running was effortless by comparison but he closed the gap. As he drew close, he reached out and grabbed for her cloak, jerking her to a halt. She turned. She had a dagger in her hand which she pointed towards his throat. 'Let go, Talisker,' she commanded. He was confused for a moment, didn't know what she meant.

'I – I can't,' he whispered. She sighed heavily but then, as he expected some response from her, she vanished. Eskarius found him kneeling on the ground, sobbing into the plush folds of a black cloak.

Things were bad. Things were very bad in the chamber. Regan could see the god now. Still Jahl, she supposed . . .

As the blood of Knox/Daniel flowed into the gully of the altar stone, Jahl threw the knife aside with a cry of triumph. Lifeblood had spattered onto his chin and chest but he made no attempt to wipe it away. The limp body of Knox/Daniel convulsed and then slid to the ground; Jahl stood before the shadow-god, his arms flung upwards in a shout of frenzied supplication. There was a deep low rumbling as the chamber began to shake violently; stalactites fell and shattered on the ground, the remaining two Scoor and the bodies of the slain were flung round as though riding a storm, only Regan – who was effectively frozen to the ground – and Jahl, remained unmoved. Regan knew she would be screaming if she were able but Jahl was too inattentive to care about the side-effects of his spell.

And it seemed the spell was working. The shadow-god reached down and took hold of Jahl by the shoulders. From where she was standing, Regan couldn't see Jahl's expression, but it seemed that some transference was happening. The god's face began to change: first, a blank mask, then, an echo of Jahl's glee and, just before it gained its own sentience, Jahl's tiny second of self-doubt. As the stalactites rained down around him, as the world shook and screamed, Jahl became a god. He screamed himself as he was pulled in towards the body he had created, then, there was a ripple of light – searing outwards from the intertwined bodies, passing out through the rock-face to be witnessed by the terrified people in the park. The tremor passed in moments but Jahl and the god were now indivisible, shrouded in a ball of bright light. Another ripple of light pulsed outward before the process was complete, and when it was past, Regan was the first to see the new Jahl; the god Jahl.

Inside the ball of light he had grown – he stood perhaps twenty feet tall – and he was still growing, expanding inexorably outwards and upwards. Regan could hear his insane laughter as his head and shoulders vanished from sight into the ceiling of the chamber. She knew instinctively that he would not be harmed by this, that he was truly invincible – for the moment his euphoria meant that he would give no thought to controlling his chaotic incarnation. The chamber fell silent as the bizarre image of the god's disappearing form continued by degrees to be less and less of a percentage of his shape. As Jahl reached such a size that all that was left planted in the chamber was his right leg and foot from the knee down, Regan first began to feel the return of sensation. She found she could move again and without any rational thought, reached straight for a weapon, pausing to consider the discarded gun and sword for a moment and then choosing the tin sword. The remaining Scoor did not attack; they remained immobile, waiting for instructions from their master who was far too preoccupied to concern himself with them.

Having crouched down to retrieve the sword, Regan's attention was caught and held by a different light than Jahl's. Just behind the altar stone, there was a branch, which threw delicate filigree patterns on the wall behind it. The branch was pulsing with an urgent pink light. Frowning, Regan reached towards it and, as she did so, the light reached out for her. This time she could scream. And she did.

Outside, the park is pandemonium. Jahl erupts forth from the hilltop, a massive figure composed of green light whose malicious expression is writ large on features already metres across. In time, perhaps only minutes, Jahl will calm down and when he does, he will allow himself to assume a less threatening form. For the moment though, he lifts his clenched fists in an expression of exuberant joy and laughs at the power surging through him. People in the park begin to flee, a wave of panic seizes them and they run with little regard for others; some trip and are trampled, tents are pulled over, people who have just found equilibrium moments before are swept up again in a tumult of fear. Less than a mile away, the details of Jahl's features are not to be seen – it appears as if a massive column of green light or gas has vented out through the hillside and anyone who is not there will never believe it afterwards. Sandro and Bea remain still, watching with awe and some sense of quiet resignation.

'Wait! Do not be afraid!' The young preacher calls out. But his voice is lost in a sea of pitched hysteria.

She feels it. It's like pain at first and she screams, helpless to fight it. But then, the pain changes. Regan can feel the spirit of the goddess and it's like warmth and heat inside her.

'Do not be afraid. We must defeat him.'

'Yes.' Regan knows. She understands the spirit is Jahl's mother. And she understands completely why he must die. She begins to grow, just as he has. Sharing his exaltation as power crashes through her body. As she reaches up to touch the encroaching ceiling of the chamber, she laughs in childish glee as her iridescent hands pass through the rock. She is dimly aware, that somewhere below, back on the floor of the chamber is her body; useless, discarded. But she doesn't care. She opens her mouth and a sound somewhere between a scream and a sigh issues forth.

'J-aaaa-hl.'

He turns and sees her. Shining, beautiful, vengeful.

Phyrr's spirit and Regan are inseparable now, one being, one mind. The idea that Jahl has simply been a wicked boy, strikes Regan as bizarre and she throws back her head and laughs; a sound which echoes across the parkland and some will say was thunder. She is going to kill him now and he doesn't even read her intention. To Jahl, the image is that of his mother. He begins to smile.

'But you must let him know it was me,' Regan thinks. Phyrr understands her need for retribution and it seems the least favour she can do for Talisker's doomed daughter. The image shifts and changes – and for the second time, Jahl is astounded to see Regan. His face is a picture of confusion. But not for long.

She looks down and sees the tin sword in her hand, it has grown with her, suffused with her power but for some reason its growth has stopped before her own; at this scale it assumes the proportions of a dagger, its legend scratched into the side, tiny and insignificant – she thinks distantly that she doesn't understand about what makes this world 'real'. She thrusts forward with the knife straight into his heart even as he reaches out to grab her by the throat.

'Regan?' Jahl vanishes – the green light dissipating like a cloud. The last she sees of him is the expression of bewilderment on his face as he looks at the wound she has inflicted. Vengeance, she decides, is something she could get used to . . .

. . . She turns and looks down at the twinkling lights and tiny fires in the park; most of the people have gone, but a few remain, looking up at her magnificence with awe and fear. In the background the lights and sirens of the night-clad city call to her like some inviting jewel. She reaches out towards it. They need gods in this land – they need something to worship. Regan will give them something she decides, she will make them understand that she is their saviour and she will be powerful and terrible. She will reign without Jahl but she will be more than he – she will be justice, law . . . she will be . . .

'No!' It is like a shout within her soul, flaring up inside of her as though her chest is on fire. 'No!' And then, as she casts around her in sudden fear, the voice comes again, more softly now. 'I am sorry, Regan.'

And then, everything is pain and fire.

He was unaware of having climbed onto Eskarius's back again, but they were running through the void as if pursued by a thousand demons. In the all pervasive darkness it was difficult to know how fast they were travelling but the sensation of speed was unmistakable. Talisker knew he was still weeping – still in early mourning for an inevitable moment perhaps yet to come – but his tears were silent and cold against his cheek. He looked down at the silver ingot Phyrr had given him; it was small, fitting into his palm as though it was made to be there. A plain silver shape, where he might have expected magical runes or carvings there were none . . . he was reminded of Morias complaining of men requiring bangs and flashes with their magic, and he managed a grim smile. He glanced ahead for an instant, sensing a change in the void and when he looked back down the ingot was changing, moving, liquid-like in his palm.

'Hurry, Eskarius,' he urged. 'Time is short . . .'

The wolf did not respond but Talisker could feel a renewed urgency in his pace, the heartbeat of the wolf Sidhe seemed to reverberate into Talisker's hearing and merged into his own. Up ahead . . . there was something there . . . it was hotter now.

'How will I know?' he agonised, 'How will I know when to throw it?'

'I do not know, Duncan Talisker.'

The ground becomes rougher suddenly, Eskarius blanches, almost stumbles and then regains his footing. But the terrain has changed, is shifting underfoot. It seems like minutes pass and Talisker and the wolf lurch and stagger around as if they are on the deck of a ship. The heat intensifies.

'Wh-what's happening?'

'It's moving . . . the ground, it's alive . . .'

'Wha—'

A light flares upwards; a long silver lance of light which is coming from the object Phyrr gave him. It seems bigger now, filling both of his hands. He stares at the orb, hypnotised for long moments by the pulsing metallic silver – it is like . . . it is like a silver heart.

'*Duncan Talisker.*' Eskarius's voice is low and urgent. Talisker looks up.

'Sweet Christ.'

CHAPTER NINETEEN

They stand in an endless space. And that space is filled with moving, entwined dragons. The silver light of the orb is thrown outwards enabling Talisker and Eskarius to see glimpses of what surrounds them. They have been climbing over the creatures without knowing and now stand on firmer ground. So vast are the dragons they form a landscape of shifting, changing landforms which slide across each other with slow, tectonic grandeur. A low – almost subliminal – grinding sound accompanies this process and the heat and cold of the two bodies produces gouts of steam which escape with a slow hiss. Outside the ring of light, Talisker can discern what he thinks is the end of the snout of the ice dragon, Hemmek; huge flared caverns of ice moving with glacial slowness over the red ground of the underlying scales of Kivik's tail plates.

'Where?' Talisker whispered. 'Where do I throw this thing?' The sound of his voice echoes as though carrying into a mountain range. The orb is growing larger still, some contact with the dragons has increased its rate of growth. The light becomes too dazzling to bear and Talisker has to hold it above his head so that he and Eskarius are beneath it.

'You must throw it soon, Duncan Talisker. I think they are coming for it.'

'What do you me— Oh no.'

It is true. The dragons are attracted to the light of the orb. The circle of clear ground becomes smaller, contracts, as the massive beasts turn inward. The heat of the flames and the blast of the ice is coming . . .

She knows she's dying. They both know. Pain wracks Regan's body, now all too human, vulnerable flesh. She's crying honest tears of pain and grief.

'I am sorry.' Phyrr appears beside her for a few seconds; the aspect of a goddess none have seen before – mercy. 'Your father would be so proud, Regan.' She reaches forward and touches Regan's cheek and in that moment she finds the dissolution she has sought. As a final farewell she takes Regan's pain with her.

'Thank-you,' Regan whispers.

. . . it's coming soon.

'Throw it now!'

'She said I'll know . . .'

'But they—'

A blast of lightning rents the air of the void earthing itself in the orb and then arcing outwards. Talisker is unharmed but he can smell something like charred ozone. The orb and the light it is making turn a deep crimson as if a lifeblood is inside it reincarnating to pure light. The sound and the light are violent and Talisker finds himself screaming as if the energy of his voice is captured, sucked up by the orb.

'Now! Now!' Eskarius yells.

He throws the orb towards the encroaching glinting dark which is Kivik's eye. Without waiting even to watch the arc of its flight, Eskarius begins to run. But there is nowhere to go. The circle is closing and they are held within it.

There is a huge explosion. Talisker finds himself thrust from Eskarius's back by the force of the blast. Flashes of crimson, lightning and fire burn onto his cornea like an afterimage. Finally, the sound, the sensation, everything . . . everything stops . . . fades to blissful, silent black.

Morning. The parkland looked like the debris in the wake of a hurricane – or possibly an extremely big rock concert. It was snowing lightly and people were wandering around in a subdued daze speaking of the night before in hushed tones. Emergency services had set up first aid stations at the edges of the park and the Salvation Army was passing around cups of hot tea. For the moment, no one was allowed back into the park to reclaim any belongings; it had been fenced off by the city council after reports of a massive gas plume venting from the hillside. Sandro and Bea sat perched on a fallen tree wrapped in the aluminium blankets someone was passing around and sipping tea, which both silently considered the best cup they'd ever tasted.

Bea stared back at Arthur's Seat from tired red-rimmed eyes. 'It'll be like Roswell,' she muttered.

'What?'

'Oh, nothing.' She nodded towards the remnants of the Children of the Deluge, a cluster of silver saints. 'They'll do pretty well out of it, I expect.'

'Yeah, well . . . can't say they haven't earned a break,' Sandro shrugged.

'I can't believe it! As I live and breathe! Alessandro Chaplin!' They looked up – DCI Stirling was standing there, an expression of joyful disbelief on his face which couldn't have been more remarkable if he'd been a witness to the happenings of the night before.

'Stirling,' Sandro nodded wearily. ''S'good to see you, man.' Stirling however, had more energy than that, he clapped Sandro on the back so hard, his tea slopped out of the cup.

'Alessandro Chaplin . . .' he kept repeating, 'I don't believe it . . .' After a minute or two, he calmed down and fixed Sandro with his intense gaze. 'Where the hell have you been, man? People were worried sick – after the fire and all – this wee girl here made herself ill . . .'

'Sir—'

'It's true, Beatrice.'

To Sandro, the fire, in a basement in Leith which had destroyed Finn Willis's body was over twenty-five years ago – a distant memory now. 'I'm sorry, Sir. I – I was confused, I had amnesia. When I recovered my memory, I was in Sicily . . . I've only just come back. I was going to come and see you Monday . . .' he broke off, too tired to discuss it.

'See that you do,' Stirling patted him on the back again, a slightly more conciliatory gesture this time. He chuckled slightly, 'S'pose you'll be wanting your job back . . . It won't be easy, Sandro . . .'

'No, Sir.'

'But come and talk to me eh?'

'I mean – I don't want my job back, Sir.'

'Oh.' Stirling looked momentarily disappointed but

then nodded sagely. 'Take your time, Sandro – but come and see me whatever . . .'

'Thanks.'

Stirling began to walk back to the group of uniformed officers who were dealing with the aftermath of the night's events, he turned back when he was a few feet away. 'Not got much of a tan . . .'

'Eh?' Sandro frowned.

'From Sicily.' Stirling gave an absent wave and carried on walking. Bea, who was snuggled up against Sandro's shoulder stifled a giggle.

Sandro grinned ruefully and rubbed at the stubble on his chin. 'Shit. That guy's never off duty. Let's go home, Bea.'

They stood up, still stiff from the cold, the sense of unreality of the morning difficult to shake. Sandro glanced back towards the crags, 'She's in there, Bea . . . her body . . .' he didn't think he'd ever feel the same way about his home town and, at the moment, the idea of going to Sicily seemed quite appealing. Bea squeezed his hand but said nothing.

They were just at the collapsed wall of Holyrood Palace when they saw LearnToFly. The tall youth was also wrapped in one of the foil blankets and he was walking away from the scene in an almost vague manner; he was hunched up against the cold, his glasses beginning to cloud over with snow, which was falling faster now.

'Are you all right?' Sandro called out. He hadn't spoken to him since they ran out of the hillside together.

LearnToFly removed his snow-covered glasses and blinked myopically towards Sandro for a moment before recognising him. 'Oh, hello,' he smiled and nodded slightly shyly.

'Aren't you going back with the others? It seems you have loads of new recruits since last night.'

Ignoring Sandro's question LearnToFly blurted out, 'You saw, didn't you?'

'Yes, I . . .'

'It was Knox wasn't it? They're saying it was D-Daniel . . . Daniel that came b-back from the dead – from Heaven – to save them. It's not true. It's not true . . .' He seemed distressed, blinking tears from his soft brown eyes, his chin trembled.

'Does it matter?' Sandro said softly. He moved closer to the boy and rubbed his shoulder, unconsciously mimicking the comfort Stirling had given to him only moments earlier. LearnToFly nodded stubbornly.

'I – I thought he w-was b-bad all the time – I don't think he really believed about The Rapture or any of it – he killed Daniel.'

'What?'

'Our original leader, you know, the one they think . . .'

'Yeah—'

'Knox k-killed him. I f-found his body in the basement of the meeting rooms. So it couldn't have b-been Daniel . . . God didn't take him up like Knox said . . . Thing is, despite that, I f-feel as if I m-misjudged him. It was him.'

Sandro nodded. 'Yes, I know. But you can't blame yourself . . . what's your name?'

'G-Gordon.'

'Knox made his own decisions, Gordon. And just because someone does bad things, it doesn't mean they are incapable of any goodness . . .' Sandro glanced back at the outline of the hillside again which was now softening in the falling snow. '. . . It doesn't mean they are lost to . . .'

'To God?' Gordon said.

Sandro shook himself, suddenly realising that he was close to tears, that he would mourn for Regan because no one else would ever know her. 'Yeah, whatever. Are you going back?' he jerked his head back towards where the Children of the Deluge were standing.

'N-no,' Gordon said softly. 'Let them keep their v-version. I'll keep mine – it's more . . . dunno . . . I'm s-still working it out.' He managed a tremulous smile.

'All the best then.' They shook hands and Gordon walked away in the direction of the new Parliament buildings clutching his silver cloak around him.

'Can we go home now, Sandro?'

'Yeah. Tell you what – let's hitch a lift.' Bea looked to where Sandro was pointing and laughed. The shire horse Regan had rescued was standing nonchalantly cropping grass at the edge of the park.

'You're joking right? I've never ridden a horse before.'

'Well then, madam, it's high time you learned.'

A world away, Talisker was unsure he was ready for the journey he was taking. The Sidhe shamans had worked hard on his physical wounds. The explosion in the void had caused burns so severe they had transferred to his entranced physical body; they covered the length of his back from the height of his knees up to his shoulders. Eskarius was also scorched and burned but both men would survive and neither were the type of people likely to inflict their suffering on others. The wolf clan were so proud of Eskarius . . .

'Do we have to come such a long way round?' Talisker grumbled. *'Can't we go straight to Soulis Mor?'*

'Thane Tristan asked me to bring you this way. He wanted you to see . . .' Tecumseh replied.

'See what?'

'There . . .' Tecumseh banked and circled lower, cutting through the fine cold mist of a cloud. *'What do you see?'*

'Why, Or Coille of course it's – oh.'

Or Coille was reborn – beneath them the expanse of blackened soil and snow was broken by the fresh, tender green of saplings breaking through the ground, the heat of the fire and the chill of the ice had served to cause miraculous re-growth, heart-stopping in its tenacity – the heart of Sutra which Jahl had ripped from it would return. 'But some are so tall . . . What happened?' Talisker breathed. 'It's not possible surely – I mean, I wasn't unconscious for a year or anything like that – it's only been a week right?'

'Indeed, Duncan Talisker,' Tecumseh agreed. *'The wise men think that Hemmek, the white dragon, was not wantonly destructive, he was in fact a creative force. It seems possible he somehow speeded the healing of the land as he died.'*

'It's fantastic.' Here and there the land rose sharply

into jagged low peaks – the topography was changed beneath its miraculous green – Hemmek had marked it for ever, but, looking at the impossibly tall saplings now swaying in a gentle breeze, Talisker felt that forgiveness should not be so difficult. For the first time since he had awoken from his vision quest, he forgot his pain and felt his spirit soar with the eagle. Tecumseh seemed to sense his elation and the call of the great bird echoed across the renewed forest – Talisker laughed and, letting go of the halter he was holding onto, lifted his hands high into the air letting out a whoop of joy.

It was late afternoon when they approached Soulis Mor. The changes to the landscape were more marked on the plains in front of the fortress city. Both Tecumseh's and Talisker's mood became sombre as they remembered the ice-quake and the sight of the legions of creatures Jahl had conjured from the void. About half a mile outside the city huge pyres were burning, disposing of the last of the bodies of the creatures, plumes of greasy smoke rising high into the air. There had been little attempt at defence by the time the army had arrived – the creatures were directionless without Jahl's command, a mere rabble of unintelligent beasts whose death was a release back to darkness. Only one had been found who had any power of speech; he had been sitting in Jahl's rooms in his high-backed chair. A strange looking beast by all accounts, quite unlike any of its comrades. As the doors of the chamber burst open, the beast spoke and then vanished before a sword could be brought to its flesh.

'Ree-gan lee-ving. Grell lee-ving.' It had said. The warriors searched the rooms but the demon was gone.

The southern army had been met by allies from Thane Ulla of Ruannoch Were and, by the time they had come to the battleground the forces were almost equal in number. There was no real battle, some said, it was more like extermination of the creatures who had been deserted by a leader who cared nothing for them but merely saw them as a means to an end.

Now, the city, battle-scarred, blackened by a hundred fires, rent asunder by the ice-quake, was in celebratory mood. As they landed on the escarpment before the plains, snatches of music and laughter could be heard, carried on the wind. Long colourful banners had been unfurled out of the many windows, covering the blackness of the stones with red, green and blue and gold which fluttered in the breeze in defiant pride.

'Are you sure you will not let me fly you into the city, Duncan Talisker?' Tecumseh asked. *'It will be my honour.'*

Talisker, who had dismounted, smiled and bowed slightly to the Sidhe Prince. 'My thanks, Tecumseh. But Soulis Mor and I . . . well, let's just say, I must enter the city on my own terms. Please tell Tristan I will be there shortly.'

'Very well. I hope the horse is to your satisfaction.' Talisker glanced over at the waiting stallion which had been sent for him. A young stable-hand was waiting, seated on a less grand pony holding the reins of the flighty looking creature. Talisker guessed correctly that Tristan had chosen the horse himself. He smiled

towards the stable lad who seemed rather nervous. 'I am sure it will be just fine.'

Tecumseh left without further comment and Talisker and the stable lad began to trot the mile or so across the plains. As they drew nearer, the sound of music grew louder. 'Sounds like the whole city is having a party lad,' Talisker remarked. 'Will you be having some ale tonight?'

'Yessir,' the boy replied enthusiastically. 'Thane Tristan has emptied the cellars, Sir.'

They approached the gates – Talisker had to admit to himself that he didn't feel as bad this time; his hands weren't trembling although his stomach was slightly queasy. The air of celebration certainly helped calm his nerves although he recognised that the city, party clothes or not, was still that place – always would be for him . . .

'Duncan Talisker,' he said to the sentry. He was mildly surprised when the young soldier stood to attention.

'Yessir. Thane Tristan asks that you go straight to the inner castle, Sir. Someone will show you to your quarters.'

Talisker frowned. 'I'm not staying, lad,' he muttered. He rode through the streets towards the inner castle noting as he passed the stable buildings that the colours of all of Sutra's Thanes were flying – Ulla's, Huw's, Lachlan's and Tristan's own. The streets were full of people, some of whom must have been those frozen by Jahl – released by the cessation of the spell and its creator – but they were making up for lost time. Musicians played on every corner and, although the party would not begin in earnest for a few hours, a happy air of frantic activity held sway. A cheer went up and, when Talisker looked towards its source, bonfires had been lit all along the northernmost tier of the battlements – not pyres this time, but simple celebratory fires.

When he finally reached the residential quarters he relinquished his horse to the stable-hand and walked in unchallenged; the corridors were decked out with colourful streamers and flowers which must have come from far south for the occasion. The smell of roasting meat wafted up from the kitchens and, as outside, people bustled about happily. For a moment Talisker stood there feeling slightly lost.

'Talisker . . . You came!' Eskarius had come out of the doorway of the Great Hall, a slightly preoccupied look on his face. The wolf Sidhe, in his human form, still showed signs of their shared destiny in the void; burns had scarred the side of his face, his right hand and shoulder – his hair, pinned back in its ceremonial style topped with feathers and beads, was slightly sparser on his right side also – but most of the damage would heal.

'Eskarius – I didn't know you were here.'

'I arrived yesterday. Tonight, after the Rededication of Tristan, he will honour the wolf clan Sidhe. The Thanes have agreed we will have the right to wander freely in all the land . . .'

'That's terrific. After everything Regan did, it's a clear message to both the Sidhe and the Fine.'

Eskarius nodded gravely, 'It is a beginning, Duncan Talisker . . . reconciliation takes time.'

'Indeed. Now, where is my son?'

'Ah well, there may be a slight problem there.' Eskarius glanced around anxiously and lowered his voice. 'None can find him. We are hoping he is somewhere meditating on his task to come. But there are only two hours to go. Some people are getting worried,' he confided.

'Who's looking?'

'Only a few – we don't want everyone to get alarmed. Morias is helping . . . the servants have been told to send word when they see Tristan under the pretext of some fitting of his robes . . .' he shrugged and smiled slightly ruefully. 'I'm sure he'll turn up. Anyway, let me take you to your rooms so you can wash and refresh yourself. I promise I will send word as soon as I know anything.'

An hour later – one hour to the Rededication – Talisker had heard nothing. He stood by the window of his chamber dressed in his finest green shirt and ceremonial plaid and stared out at the darkening city; the lights and the music seemed louder and brighter now, thrown into relief by the encroaching darkness. There would be snow later . . . An air of jubilant anticipation wafted upwards on the breeze. None of the revellers yet knew that their Thane was missing. Time was running short. Just as Talisker was considering going to search for Tristan himself, there was a quiet, timid knock on his door. He turned, expecting to see Eskarius or some servant come to tell him Tris had been found. It was Grace, Tristan's young maidservant whom they had rescued from the city. It seemed clear to Talisker that she was destined to be Tristan's consort

– whether or not he kept her a secret from the court. She was certainly dressed finely for the evening's events in a plush blue gown which shimmered with tiny silver beads – no maidservant could hope to own such a thing.

'Grace,' he smiled and bowed his head, uneasy with courtly formality. She beckoned him over at around the same moment he remembered she was unable to speak to him. 'What is . . .' She turned and began to walk down the stairwell, glancing back to check that he was following. Talisker grabbed his cloak from the chair and followed without further question.

He began to be suspicious as they left the main castle building and travelled towards the northern wall skirting around the cess pits and the back-kitchen staff quarters – why would Tristan ever come this way? He grabbed Grace's arm and frowned at her. 'What's going on, Grace?' She looked slightly frightened and pulled her arm away. 'I'm sorry,' he said. 'I didn't mean to frighten you. Do you know where he is?'

She nodded urgently and began to mouth 'come on'. Finally, they reached a small flight of four steps which led down to a brown door set into the castle wall. Grace stepped down without hesitation and pushed the door open. Then she stopped and beckoned Talisker onward. He thought she would walk in front of him but she motioned for him to go ahead. Bending low to fit through the door, he walked cautiously out.

It was a small woodland. In the gloom of dusk, blackbirds were singing a raucous evensong in the trees. Someone had lit paper lanterns and hung them in the trees on the lower branches. He followed the line of the lights noting that there was a path of sorts amongst the grass. Up ahead, he saw a figure sitting hunched up on a log-seat, his knees hugged up to his chest.

'Tris? Is that you?' The figure stood up and turned towards him. It was indeed his son; he wore the filigreed breastplate and plaid of a Thane, he carried a huge unwieldy battle-sword and a leather and silver tarn and he'd been crying. 'What's wrong, Tris? Why are you here? Everyone is frantic looking for you . . .'

Tris waved his hand dismissively. 'They can wait, can't they?' he muttered. Then he laughed shakily. 'Look at me, Father – have you ever seen a less Thane-like figure?'

'It's only for tonight, Tris – I know you probably feel uncomfortable, but after all the formalities you can rule in your own fashion. Is that what this is about . . . ?'

'No.' Tristan shook his head wearily and then sat down again on the seat. 'She used to come here you know. This was her place . . . when we first found it, I – I teased her a bit. I told her the trees grew so strongly where none would grow before because the soil was fertilized by the blood of the warriors who died here . . .' his voice trailed off as he remembered somewhat belatedly that his father was a veteran of the battle. 'I'm sorry, father . . .'

''S'okay, Tris.' Talisker sat beside him and stared distantly into the trees – now becoming moving shadows in the dark – 'You were possibly right. What did she say?'

'She didn't care. She liked coming here and so she

did. She wouldn't let me put her off. Look.' He pointed at the nearest tree trunk; Regan had carved her name there.

'She's dead, Tristan.' Talisker said the words as softly as he could but nothing could lessen their impact. Slowly, aware that they were running out of time, he told Tristan what the goddess Phyrr had said to him. Tristan said nothing for long moments, not trusting himself to speak.

Finally, he said, 'You know I said I would ensure no *Seanachaidh* tale would be told of her? I wish they wouldn't father. Sutra will not remember Regan with any love or kindness . . .'

'But that doesn't mean that we can't,' Talisker said. 'In the end, she came right—'

'Doesn't bring back the dead Sidhe though . . .'

'No. But it's got to count for something. We can remember her as,' Talisker swallowed, his voice cracking, 'my daughter . . .'

'. . . and my sister,' Tristan finished.

'Yeah.'

They sat in silence for a few minutes, looking at Regan's trees. Singing began, the Sidhe were celebrating the Rededication as much as the Fine, keen to put recent history behind them. It was a sound like no other, as pure and high as sunlight.

'We should go,' Talisker shook himself. 'People are frantic in there . . .' Tristan stood up somewhat reluctantly and began to walk back along the path.

'Tris,' Talisker called out.

'What?'

'I know you loved her, but you never *needed* her

you know. You will be a great Thane, son . . . always would have been . . . I – I'm very proud.'

'Thank you, Father.'

They walked back into the city together, the sound of singing cascading high into the night sky.

EPILOGUE

Nimah cries herself to sleep. She doesn't want to be a *Seanachaidh* any more she has decided. When Morias comes back to the valley she will tell him she's changed her mind . . .

In the darkness of the cottage Nimah awakes; she has keen senses and some movement has woken her. She sits upright in bed, holding her breath, listening for the sound again. After long moments she gets up and pads silently through to the living area. The fire has died away to embers, the room is warm and still, but, when Nimah sees the dark form of a figure seated in the big soft chair, she knows immediately who it is.

'Teacher. You came back.'

'Yes, child.' He sounds weary but content. 'You have something to tell me?'

'Yes.' She sits in the chair opposite without lighting the lantern and curls her knees up, tucking her feet into the hem of her nightgown. 'I don't think I can become a *Seanachaidh*, Morias,' she says solemnly.

'And why is that, Nimah? The land has chosen you.'

'I know . . . but . . . it's so sad. Stories . . . they're not just words are they? They happen to people.'

'Indeed. You have been watching the waters in my absence then? Don't you think Tristan deserves his happiness?'

'Oh, yes. But Regan . . . and that strange man . . .'

'Knox?'

'Yes. They did bad things, teacher . . . bad, cruel things . . .'

'But?'

'How do you know there is a "but"?'

'Well, isn't there?'

'Yes. But they were . . .' she shrugs, her youth and inexperience causing her mind to search for words to describe her feelings.

'Sad? Lonely? Unloved? None of these things are excuses, Nimah.'

'No,' she is crestfallen for a moment. 'But they did good things in the end, teacher – they did something good – when it counted. I can't *hate* them.'

'I am glad to hear it, little one. Perhaps what you mean to say is that they have earned something – redemption, a second chance.'

She smiles. The first light of dawn is creeping beneath the shutters and a bird begins its morning song in the elm outside the window. 'Yes, perhaps . . .'

Morias sighs, 'You are young, Nimah, you forgive easily. But perhaps we could all learn something . . . enlightening from your forgiveness. Look in my bag, I have brought something for you. Bring it here.'

She brings his bag over from the shelf by the door speculating briefly that it cannot be jewellery or anything very heavy because the bag is as light as if it contains nothing at all. She gives it to Morias and he pulls back the leather flap and undoes the draw-string. Nimah gasps.

The little room is flooded with shining white light

which spills out across Morias's face illuminating every line of his craggy old face.

'Here.' He reaches his hand in and gives her the source of the light: two shining orbs roll in the palm of her hand. There is something agitated about the lights, something alive.

'What are they, teacher?' she breathes.

'They are the spirits of Knox and Regan. I collected them for you. You must decide their fate. At sunrise I can let them go. Or, I may crush them beneath my foot,' he finishes sternly. 'What say you now the decision is really yours?'

Nimah can scarcely breathe. She stares down at the lights in her hand and thinks about the things she has witnessed. 'I – I cannot decide . . .' she stammers.

'You must,' Morias insists, 'soon. What does your heart tell you, Nimah?'

There is silence for long moments, and then the bird begins to sing again and Nimah's trance is broken. She walks to the window and pulls back the shutter. 'Do I just . . .?'

Morias nods and she puts her hand outside, still with the palm closed. Then she opens it slowly. They are like butterflies – they tremble in the faint morning breeze and then, they lift off her hand and float gently away, rising, rising, like the seeds of a flower dancing in the wind. And then, as if sensing something, they speed up and away to the east into the rising sun of the new day.

Nimah watches entranced until they are out of her sight and then she turns back to Morias smiling shyly. 'Was it a conjuring, Morias? Are you testing me?'

He laughs gently at her serious demeanour. 'Would I do that to you, Nimah . . . ? But if I were testing you, I should still know that, as ever, the land has chosen its new *Seanachaidh* well.'